THE SPARK WITHIN

THE SPARK WITHIN

SAMANTHA CHRISTOPHER

Spark Productions

THE SPARK WITHIN

Copyright © 2024 by Samantha Christopher.

All rights reserved. Printed in the United States of America. No part of this book may be used or reproduced in any manner whatsoever without written permission except in the case of brief quotations em- bodied in critical articles or reviews.

This book is a work of fiction. Names, characters, businesses, organizations, places, events and incidents either are the product of the author's imagination or are used fictitiously. Any resemblance to actual persons, living or dead, events, or locales is entirely coincidental.

For information contact:

samchristopherwrites.com

Book and Cover design by Maria Spada
Interior formatting and design by Samantha Christopher
Editing by Erin Young and Shannon Cave
ISBN: 979-8-9909365-0-8

First Edition: September 2024

For Alan,

who believed in me before I believed in myself.

1

Legionaries

"OUR FUTURE IS HERE!" I sing, collapsing onto the bench in front of the window, my eyes locked onto the trees I'm forbidden to enter. I imagine the lines on the frosted glass are bars in a jail cell as golden light creeps over the horizon, saturating the world in a faint glow. The dark cobalt of sky blends with shades of orange and pink as the grounds of LindonGale Manor awaken before my eyes. I blow out a ragged breath, grateful I made it in time.

"You see them?" Abby hollers as the shower turns off.

I look behind my shoulder at the light streaming through the opening of her bathroom door, illuminating her canopy bed covered in greenery. "Not yet, any moment!"

Six months have passed since the last group of legionaries arrived. More recruits to protect our secluded community in the mountains of Oregon from Commoners who see our abilities as a threat. New faces are always exciting, but this morning is different; my fate lies with one of them. I awoke in a panic, thinking I'd missed their arrival, and ran across the manor to Abby's room. She has the best view of the front grounds.

I wipe the condensation from the window to calm my racing heart. Breathing in, I twitch my fingertips, pulling the water into tiny droplets, and with a light exhale, they drift toward her wall of exotic flowers. The water collides with the thin petals of purple and pink beauties—a combination of amaryllis and rose.

My eyes latch onto motion beyond the garden, past the orchards, where the forest begins. Black shapes emerge from the trees, arriving as the first warm rays of a new day hit their faces. I wish I had a closer view, but I'm not allowed to be near them as an unmatched young woman, unless I want to be thrown out of the community, doomed to live alone among those who threaten to wipe out our people. Although, watching doesn't hurt.

The window squeaks in protest as I push it as high as it will go. The early spring air blows in, caressing my cheeks and raising goose bumps on my arms. I lean out a bit; being three stories up, I doubt they'll notice.

The figures are copies of each other, wearing all black, matching the darkness looming behind them. Dressed in high, laced-up boots, tight pants, long-sleeve shirts, and hooded vests that obscure their faces, they cover the front lawn of the manor, spreading through the beautifully crafted garden like roots from a tree. Their rhythmic footsteps draw closer to the structure next door: Legion Headquarters. The sharp-edged, cubed building veiled in windows reflecting the surrounding forest is nothing like the log manor I've been confined to for five years.

I lean out as far as I can, the window ledge digging into my stomach as I try to get a better look. At that moment, one of the dark legion soldiers tilts his head. The sun reflects off his startling bright blue eyes, a stark contrast against his sable face. Feeling his gaze, I smile timidly. My heart leaps. I've known I would be getting matched ever since the unpleasant medical intrusion we had to suffer to ensure our bodies were in prime development a year ago. Luckily for me, my reproductive system was given five stars. Before now, it hasn't felt real, but to be this close, knowing my mate is among those men, a shiver runs down my spine. Despite what I told my mom, I don't know if I'm ready to choose my forever companion.

"Why didn't you come get me?" Abby yells.

The noise makes me jump. I twist to see Abby coming out of her bathroom, draped in a robe and scrunching her wet auburn hair with a towel, her eyes throwing daggers at me. The movement upsets my balance, and my hands slip off the edge. I frantically grasp for something to hold onto, my arms flying out and seizing the ledge.

My fingers slip off the smooth windowsill, and I grapple with the rough texture of the logs beneath, digging my nails in, but there's nowhere to grip; gravity pulls me down. Abby's stunned expression, still frozen in the bathroom door frame, is the last thing I see as the air rushes past me.

I scream as the rose bushes below come to claim my demise. I squeeze my eyes shut, not wanting to die at eighteen without ever living a normal life or even experiencing my first kiss; yet I don't want to live through having every bone in my body broken. The only consolation would be my dad greeting me in whatever afterlife waits for us.

Wait, how am I still falling?

Opening my eyelids a fraction, I notice that I'm not on the ground, nor am I dead. My pulse is loud and clear in my ears. I'm suspended in midair with another two stories to drop. I flail my arms, letting out another shriek, and start my descent. Oh no. This could only mean one thing—the help of an Aura.

I crane my neck, trying to spot the Aura, who must be manipulating the air around me. To my horror, the whole legion is surrounding me. Faces become more distinct. Masculinity radiates from the group of chiseled jawlines and trimmed beards. My stomach drops as over thirty men take in my disheveled appearance: tattered gray sweats and my dad's old AC/DC shirt on full display.

I stretch out my legs, preparing to land as gracefully as possible, but instead, strong arms wrap around my torso and slide underneath my knees. I try, unsuccessfully, to slow my racing pulse as I look into the eyes of my savior.

Gold-flecked hazel eyes peer back from under the hood, a smile playing on his lips. I've seen those eyes before, I realize with a sudden certainty. As I try to place the tug on my memory, his eyebrows rise momentarily before his face hardens, and he sets me down. Was that a flicker of recognition?

"Thank you," I start, but as I turn, he's gone, lost in the hoard of legionaries.

"You're welcome," says a posh British voice.

Scanning the crowd to find the man attached to the dreamy accent, a guy steps forward, pulling back his hood to reveal a head of dirty-blond hair and light-gray eyes.

"You saved me? But what about—" I look around. The stranger whose arms I landed in is nowhere to be found, as if I imagined it. I shake my head in confusion.

"Yes, I slowed your descent." He smiles and looks at me in a way that makes heat rise in my cheeks.

I nervously pull on a loose curl from my top knot, but then cringe; my hair must be a mess. At least I have my bra on. I'm about to ask his name when a deep, threatening voice freezes the words in my mouth.

"Okay, that's enough. Get to Legion Headquarters," booms Commander Lawrence.

The Aura who saved me leaves with a wink, as I regrettably turn my attention to the tall man approaching me. His bald head glistens in the rising sun, and two thick caterpillar eyebrows raise in question. He's daunting to everyone else, but I've known him for as long as I can remember. I have memories of him and his family coming over for barbecue dinners while we lived in the suburbs of Portland. But that was before the violent chaos at the start of the war five years ago when the Coms attacked our kind. Most lost loved ones, and he lost his whole family: a mate and two daughters. Something like that can harden anyone's heart.

"Maya, you're very lucky. What were you thinking?" he grumbles, as if I purposely threw myself out of the window.

Holding myself back from rolling my eyes, I shrug. "I slipped."

He makes a noise in the back of his throat. "You are a matched young woman. Behaving in such a manner is inexcusable."

I open my mouth to argue, but he's right. With their arrival, I'm officially matched. I swallow, trying not to look at the line of men. One of my two matches is among them, and the other is who knows where. My mother, the geneticist and brains behind the matching system, didn't tell me that exact information when she revealed my upcoming future.

He holds back a smile at my struggle to find words, a small break in his hard exterior.

I say in a strangled voice, "I'll try not to, uh, fall out of a window again."

As I turn to flee, I use the chance to scan the departing legionaries casting looks in my direction. But I don't see the one with hazel eyes who caught me. I suppress a shudder, still feeling the warmth of his arms around my body. I couldn't have imagined that, could I?

"Five miles for whoever is still out here in ten seconds!"

He isn't talking to me, but just in case, I peel my eyes away and all but fly to the front doors. Throwing them open, Abby and I smack into each other, landing ungracefully on our backsides inside the foyer.

"Ow!"

"What are you doing?" I ask, rubbing my forehead.

"I came down as quickly as possible! I'm so sorry. I froze, Maya! You could have died, and it would have been all my fault."

I pull her in for a hug, smoothing her wet ringlets until she stops shaking. She wipes hastily at her big brown eyes and looks around. We're not supposed to display such emotions. Heightened emotions are dangerous. We can't control our elements properly in such a state.

We hurry up the grand staircase and through a mahogany door that matches the dozens of others lining the beige hallway. Only the sound of our feet against the winding metal stairs rings through the air as we pass the second floor filled with offices, labs, and the rec room and finish our ascent to the third floor, the level where all match-eligible young women live.

I close my bedroom door behind Abby, pass my tan leather couch, and fall onto my bed, unleashing a scream into my pillow. Frustrated, I replay the conversation with my mother two days ago, when she casually told me she had found my matches.

"Things are heating up on the war front, and the committee has decided to change the age of match eligibility. Anyone over

eighteen is eligible to get matched; we plan on making the announcement today," she said as I lounged on her bed, snacking on blueberries.

I choked on one as I sat up, accidentally squishing the rest in my palm. "What? I thought I had two more years?"

She shook her head. "I know, but you've known this was coming."

"In two years!"

"Do you not feel ready?"

I hesitated. This is what I wanted. To get matched, fall in love, and fulfill my duty in rearing a stronger generation to take out the Commoners. Or at least, it's what I'm supposed to want. "I'm ready."

She smiled, pride showing on her face. "I found your first match about a year ago."

I gasped. "You've known for that long?"

"Well, yes, dear, one match is fairly easy. But finding two that can completely enhance every trait of yours and, most importantly, the abilities you pass down to your children, can be challenging. I found your second match with the newest recruits coming in a couple days."

"Are you going to tell me what you're thinking, or am I going to have to get the vines to tie you up and force it out of you?" Abby asks, breaking me from the memory. Only a Terra would say such a thing.

"You wouldn't dare," I say, twisting my face toward her.

Abby is at the foot of my bed, twitching her fingers with a grin. I glance to my windows, where a thick green vine knocks. I throw my pillow at her, and she collapses in a fit of giggles.

I scoot against my headboard with a sigh. "I'm still reeling from the fact that we're getting matched so soon, and now they're here. And they all saw me fall out of a window, looking like this!" I point to myself, feeling the hysterics rising.

She sits up, placing a hand on my foot, her face serious. "I feel awful. I should have reacted. It's a good thing I won't be a legionary." She bites her lip, holding back a smile, as she releases me. "But, you know, if you had set your alarm like I did, none of this would have happened."

I glare at her perfect bouncy curls. She's always been the more beautiful one between us, even with bedhead. She is well-endowed, has hourglass curves, and gorgeous bronze skin. Guys have been drooling over her since puberty hit. We'd walk through the gardens near headquarters when we knew the legion was in training, and men would openly gawk at her like I wasn't even there. She shrugs me off whenever I mention it. On the other hand, puberty did nothing for me, and I have the body of a twelve-year-old boy.

"It's just a two-year jump." She shrugs. "I'm happy they made the change. Honestly, this is going to be so much fun! We'll finally get to talk to those smoking hot legionaries, Maya."

"Yeah, talk to, kiss, and then hope we choose the right one to bond ourselves to for an eternity." I won't admit it to Abby, but deep down, I'm terrified. I'm thrilled for a change after five years, excited for an opportunity to date, but so unbelievably scared. What if I don't fall in love? What if I choose wrong? What if I don't even like them? And under all that, I have no idea what I'm doing. Being prohibited from even talking to an unmatched male makes for very inexperienced females. I don't know how the other girls got through it. They were at least a little older. They didn't spend the entirety of their teen years in the remote wilderness. "You know we would just be graduating high school in the outside world?"

"That world doesn't exist anymore," she says, looking away from me, her face pained.

I wince, remembering the bombed, deserted streets of our old neighborhood that we drove through that last night, my little brother crying in the backseat, and the fire that almost devoured us on the only road out of the city.

I push down the memory where it belongs, locked away with the other painful experiences of my childhood. We escaped, and it's been five years since the night my family arrived on LyndonGale's doorstep and our new life of isolation began. Once I choose a match and am bonded, my abilities will strengthen, and I can join the war effort. I can't imagine ever doing anything worthy enough to be a commander like my mom, but I'll fulfill my duty, have children, and create a stronger generation to defeat the Coms. Then maybe we can ask to be transferred. Leaving these walls seems like a pipe dream. It could happen, though. I know there are other Elemental communities like ours out there. Freedom is only a match away.

I barely notice Abby drifting to my door, saying something about meeting me at breakfast. With a grunt goodbye, I force myself to get ready for the day. I throw on a pair of cotton shorts and a fresh tank. Braiding my hair down my back, I look at the few pictures I brought from home—my real home, which most likely isn't standing anymore—in the suburbs of Portland. Taped around my mirror are images of Abby and me as young children, easier days when all we had to worry about was getting home before the streetlights turned on. Boy talk back then wasn't as intense. Not like there were many cute boys to choose from among the Elemental kids. Those with abilities were few in number, since Elementals were often homeschooled. And I wouldn't have dared to have a crush on a Com boy, even back then, when they treated us semi-civilly. As unthinkable as it is to be with somebody of a different element, it's an act of terrorism to be with a Com, somebody without abilities.

At least I had Millie. I touch the picture of our old black Lab, feeling that prickle in my throat. She was the best dog. My parents got her when I was a toddler. She died right before the chaos started, a minor miracle. One picture of my baby brother, Cal, with cheeks you could nibble on for days is underneath, then one of my dad, holding me in his arms. My father's smile is forever frozen in time. It's how I remember him: his square-rimmed glasses hanging off his nose, his dark hair that looks just like Cal's, slightly mussed. I'm about four in the picture, my hair in pigtails and redder than the strawberry blonde it is now, peeking up at my dad. I was such a daddy's girl.

The pain creeps in, the burning sensation in my lungs crawling to take hold. Pushing it down, I shove away from my vanity and lace my tennis shoes. I head out my back glass doors toward the wild, unkempt grass behind the manor. Nothing will ever dim the pain of being responsible for his death.

2

Unlikely Pairing

T HE FRESH AIR CLEARS MY MIND, slowing my rising emotions as I step down the staircase from my balcony. Unlike Abby, whose room is on the front side of the manor, I get direct access to the outdoors.

The grounds have doubled in size since we added the legion a year ago, but from this view, it's the same as when we first arrived. The dark and foreboding forest surrounds and suffocates us, inching closer day by day. I stay on the trail so I don't have to fight against the weeds that will reach my height soon. The shimmering pond where I practice peeks through the brush, reflecting the brilliant, cloudless blue sky. The faint sounds of chirping birds reach me, further calming the sadness and self-loathing swirling under the surface, threatening to take me under.

After taking the long, unnecessary scenic route around the building, I open a side door, and the aroma of freshly baked bread and cinnamon guides me to the white light beaming from the opening of the dining hall on the main floor of the manor.

Families and young women fill the twelve long cafeteria tables in the extensive space. Light from the aurous crystal chandelier hanging from the wooden rafters above dances off the thick, dusty log walls. With her long, auburn locks cascading down her back, Abby sits at one end of a table. The other side holds three chatty girls around our age: Amanda, Liliana, and Presley. I pass them as I head toward the half-wall that opens into the brightly lit kitchen.

There is excitement in the air since the recruits arrived. Abby has bright eyes as she chats with the other girls.

"Hey," I say as I sit with my eggless French toast and greens. Sausage would be a better side, but unfortunately, meat is off-limits. Animals are not allowed in the community. Cows and chickens in the middle of the woods wouldn't help us lay low. Luckily, Terras are masters at creating various vegan meals and delights, shaping the land to grow anything they need.

Abby turns to me. Amanda, who's closest to us, angles away, letting her blonde hair fall as a curtain between us and their group.

"What's with her?" I mumble, scooting to the far end.

Abby joins me with a sly smile. "Everyone's heard of your mishap this morning. She's jealous you got to interact with the legionaries."

Blood drains from my face. "They have?" I peek around, noticing for the first time that others are glancing my way. My face falls into my hands as I let out a small moan. "They don't have anything better to talk about?"

Abby giggles. "Maya."

I peek at her, and she's giving me a knowing look. Of course, they don't have anything to talk about. We're a small community in the middle of nowhere; nothing ever happens.

"I think I'm going to go find my mom before my lessons. Catch ya later?" I stand with my tray.

"Embrace it, Maya!" Abby calls.

I shoot her a withering look as I hurry away and up the stairs, my food threatening to spill over the tray.

"Mom! Mom!" I call after racing up to the old living quarters I called home until a few weeks ago, before I was moved to the level with the rest of the match-eligible girls.

My little brother stumbles out of his room as I walk through the tidy living room. It's the same layout as everyone else's on the family level: a small living room with a couch and a short hallway with three doors. Cal is currently at the end of it, rubbing his eyes, his dark hair askew. The place is immaculate, Mom must have been on Cal about picking up his stuff since I left. A lone stuffed dinosaur sits on a folded blanket in the middle of the gray, frayed couch, the only sign a child lives here.

I lean on the arm of the couch, biting into an apple. I don't have much of an appetite right now, but I'll regret it during lessons if I don't eat something. "Sorry, Cal, I didn't mean to wake you. Brought you some food," I say, gesturing to the tray on the coffee table.

His eyes brighten mid-yawn. He settles onto the sofa, hugging the stuffy and plunging into my food.

"Has Mom left yet? I need to talk to her."

"I dunno, probably," he replies unhelpfully.

I tussle his hair as I pass, opening the door across from Cal's room. She's not in bed, but the shower is running. "Mom!" I yell, barging into the bathroom.

She lets out a startled scream behind the navy blue shower curtain. "Maya! What on earth are you doing here?"

"I need to talk to you."

"Now?"

"I want to know more about my matches."

She laughs, shutting off the water. "So impatient, just like your father. Hand me a towel."

I grab a large white one off the metal rail and shove it at her flailing hand. She steps out with it wrapped around her body. Her face is devoid of makeup, looking young and impassive. Her strawberry blonde hair, which I inherited, slicks down her slender neck and pointy shoulders as she shoots me a curious look.

"Did you see them this morning?"

I keep my face neutral, not wanting to reveal my incident. I'm sure she'll learn soon enough, and I hope to be nowhere near when she does.

"Take that as a yes." With a flip of her wrist, water droplets pull from her hair strands and gather into a ball above her head before falling back into the shower. Her dry hair falls lightly around her thin face and blue eyes. She shakes it out as she says, "You know I can't talk to you about it."

"You're my mom. What's the point of having a mom who's an awe-inspiring commander and a wicked smart geneticist if I can't be in on all the secrets?" I brag, trying to draw the truth from her. It stings though, knowing I'll never have the same sway as her. *Maybe, once I'm matched and have children,* I remind myself. Then, the commanders will see me as more than just a girl with a working reproductive system. But I'll never have the same scientific mind as my mother. I may look just like her, but I'm more like Dad on the inside.

Her eyes flash, and she smiles. "Let me get dressed."

I sit on the edge of her bed to wait, not so patiently. Catching a glimpse of myself in her gold-framed, floor-length mirror, my vibrant green eyes stare back. The color has always brought comments, since most Elementals don't have them. My mom doesn't have green eyes and neither did my dad. I look away from the reminder of my abnormality.

My thoughts return to the guy who caught me. Well, at least I *think* there was a guy whose arms I landed in. Could I have imagined it? Maybe I landed on the ground after that Aura boy slowed my descent. But I remember hazel eyes. There was something about his eyes; I've looked into them before. I know it.

A distant memory tugs on me, but when I reach for it, it slips through the cracks. He could have been somebody I went to school with before the war. No. With that jawline, he has to be older, probably in his early twenties. Besides, I knew all the other Elemental kids back then. But some could have been hiding their abilities like me. I remember how Coms regarded our kind and talked about them behind their backs. With my mom's position at Oregon Health and Science University, she heard rumors from Coms she was close with. When I started public school, she told me never to talk about my abilities or show them to anyone, no matter the friendship, even when other Elementals were openly using theirs. I followed that rule; I followed all the rules. I was friends with Coms and Elementals. But it sure didn't help once things took a turn for the worse.

Images of red flash in my mind, the wall of flames coming at us, faster and faster, Mom not slowing the car, screaming at me to help her, even though I had barely used my abilities yet, the huge wave from the lake smashing into us. I blink away the images before they drag me down.

She walks out with her hair half pinned up, wearing business pants and a fluffy white blouse.

"Can I get names? Pictures?" I ask with little hope. We're not supposed to know who they are before we meet, to remain unbiased, but she owes me.

"Maya, you know the rules," she says with a hint of indecisiveness as she avoids my gaze and grabs her communicator, pocketing it.

"C'mon, Mom, a name isn't going to hurt. It's not like I'm ever among them. I won't tell anyone, not even Abby."

She looks back reluctantly. "I'm not going to give you their names."

My shoulders cave in, defeated.

"But I'll tell you their abilities."

I stiffen. Wouldn't they control water like me—a Lympha? Like Mom and Dad and every generation before me?

"One is an Igna, and the other an Aura." She bites her lip, studying my reaction.

My stomach twists. I'm matched to a fire-wielder. All those stories of Ignas losing control and burning someone unintentionally. What if that happens to me? My heart pounds in my ears. This has to be a mistake. Then there is the Aura. Air and light wouldn't be too bad, and their ability to communicate through air links would be handy. But still—

I work to slow my rising blood pressure. "Not Lymphas? Are you sure?"

Her blue eyes sharpen, and I know she's about to use medical jargon. "Through my research with genomes, I found that selective mating can strengthen the gene that gives us our specific abilities. My program matches people from different groups so perfectly that when their DNA combines to form an offspring, the child can have multiple abilities."

My jaw drops.

"I know it's a lot to take in, but I need to get going now." She pushes me toward the door.

I look back, but her expression makes me press my lips together. She's already thinking about other things—more important things. Not that she just told me life-altering news. Nope, it's just another Wednesday.

I barely register the opening and closing of doors throughout the hall and the rising voices as I contemplate the flood of information. It's always been taboo to bond with somebody from a different Elemental group. Although, it's better than choosing to be with a Com. Those children may not be born with abilities at all. This opens up so many possibilities if it works. But how can fire and water cohabitate? One will undoubtedly hurt the other.

3

Remember your Sage

"HEY, SETH!" I CALL as I reach the end of the outside path leading to our Terra-made lake.

My trainer stands with his back to me on the edge, looking across the blue water, taking in the beautiful sight. Before us, the lake stretches like a mirror, its calm surface reflecting the expanse of clouds above. Embracing the glass and angled structure of Legion Headquarters, the lake winds like a serpent, with the enormous wooden hydropower wheel serving as its head, churning and supplying power to our buildings. The opposite side narrows until the water disappears into the dense green forest surrounding the community. The breeze blows the hair out of my face, bringing with it the scent of pine and freshwater.

He turns at the sound of my voice. His white-blond, slicked-back hair pops in contrast with his tan skin. "Today, we're going to work on generating water transports."

Just like Seth to skip the small talk, though I'm incredibly grateful for it this time. At least he's not gawking at me.

"Sweet!" I respond as I pull up next to him. I've been begging him for months to teach me.

He smiles. "I thought you'd be excited. There have been several cases of bonded pairs losing control because of the influx of power after the ceremony. Now that you're matched, I'm kicking up your lessons a notch."

My heart leaps at the reminder. I'll have to choose between an Igna and an Aura, fire and air. The last thing I need is an Aura blowing me to a different planet—or worse, an Igna turning me into bacon.

"Let's start with manipulation."

With his palms down, he hovers his hands over the water. The water rises above the surface at the incremental turning of his hands. It's second nature for me to do this part, having been practicing it since I turned twelve and gained my abilities. I copy his movements, and the water before me ascends.

"Just enough to cover your head," he cautions.

I relax my right hand until some water drips down. I twist my hand back once the water hovering before me is about my head's worth. I smile in triumph as Seth nods.

"Good. Now, the hard part. Bring the water towards you and submerge your head inside. The mass will dull your senses, but focus. The goal is to create an air pocket and have your head safely inside."

"Easy enough." I shrug.

"We'll see," he mumbles. "Watch me first."

His sphere of water approaches his face until it masks it completely. I bite my cheek to keep from laughing. He looks like a bobblehead. His fingers weave a dance, causing the bubble to grow larger. Once the bubble is twice the size of his head—the air chamber clear to see—he lowers his hands. Through the haze, I see a slanted version of his face; his light blue eyes are open, and a smile hovers on his lips. The bubble bursts, the water splashing against my feet.

My turn.

With my nerves buzzing, I bring my sphere closer to my face until it grazes my nose. I take a deep breath and force it around my head. Submerging my head in water, while keeping my body dry, is extraordinary. Seth is right. Once the water slips over my ears, my senses dull. Sound dampens, my vision blurs, and the area around me becomes distorted. There's a tightening in my chest as the seconds tick by without a breath. I empty my mind from the water suffocating my mouth and nose and push outward. Nothing happens. I'm not used to channeling that area of my body. I feel the water droplets around my mouth and exert my energy into pulling them away.

Finally, there's movement. The water separates, and my mouth is almost free. The burning in my chest distracts me, and the water's edge slips back. I force it outward and breathe. Water shoots down my throat. Whoops. Coughing spasms rack my body as the water unceremoniously drips down my face. I hunch over as Seth pounds on my back.

Seth laughs. "It's okay. Nobody gets it on the first try, but for a second there, I thought you might."

I glare at him, straightening my spine and filling my chest with fresh air. He's laughing at me, when I tried so hard not to laugh at his water-bobblehead. I won't try so hard next time.

"Again," I insist.

Seth's face relaxes, but his eyes fill with anticipation.

I get in position with my hands outstretched and ready myself.

It takes me two more attempts to push the water off my face, but it comes crashing down at the last moment. I grumble as I wring out the bottom of my gray tank, not bothering to wick the water away, saving my mental power for the task.

"Here you go," Seth comments, watching me. With a twist of his fingers, water flings from my body, and I'm dry again.

"Thanks," I mumble. I have to give it to him. That was much faster and more graceful than I could have done.

"Ready to try again?"

I sigh. "Yeah." Seth made it look so easy earlier. He could lower his hands and shift his weight. The water around his head remained the same size. Maybe he wasn't breathing. "Seth?"

"Remember your Sage. You've got this, Maya."

I nod, closing my eyes to focus on my senses and connect myself to the earth and, most importantly, my element, where our Sage resides. We're taught about the Sage at a young age. It's the part of our mind that connects us with our elements. We practice finding it through meditation, so once our abilities manifest, they become second nature to wield. I imagine my father next to me, talking me through the exercises he so often did, always preparing me for the day my abilities would emerge, even though he never got to see it. I easily fall into the motions, focusing on touch first.

There is a slight breeze in the air, caressing my skin, almost cold enough to make me shiver. I take a deep breath and let the smell of sweet, musky spring flowers fill me. It combines with the faint scent of vanilla from the shampoo I used this morning. The wind rustles the long grass surrounding the lake, and I hear Seth taking deep, steady breaths. I reach further and listen to the subtle voices from the balconies behind me, the faint tapping of a bird's beak against a tree trunk. The sounds of the lake come alive. Its calmness and stillness envelop my mind. I sway to the ripples and bubbles popping on its surface as the water moves with me, becoming one with it.

Without raising my hands, I breathe in, and slowly, the water rises and extends as the air expands in my lungs. Twitching my fingertips, I form a ball of water, the weight of it in my mind. My hands rise, my fingers grazing the water a few inches from my face. I inhale and exhale, focusing on the weight of the water and how it feels as it molds around my nose, cheeks, ears, and the back of my neck. I pull at it in my mind. The water expands until the air pocket is large enough to pucker my lips and imagine blowing it up. It grows in size until the water is off my head. I blink away water droplets stuck to my eyelashes and release my breath. The air bounces off the inside walls as I keep it steady. I carefully suck in a breath and adjust the water to the air I breathe.

"I did it!" I shout as the water falls from my hold.

Seth is beaming. He strides over and clasps me on the shoulder. "Well done!"

Pride radiates from him, and I can't help but wonder if my dad would have had the same reaction if he had been teaching me. Seth has been my instructor for two years now. After bonding with his match, he was eligible to teach if he wished. He has a cute little girl with another on the way. Those little girls are so lucky to have him.

"That was good for today. See you tomorrow," Seth says.

"But I just figured it out. There's still so much—"

"I know, and you can work on expanding it in your free time. My next session is coming up."

I glance at my watch. The hour went by quickly. I look up to ask him for more tips, but his eyes focus on a spot behind me. I follow his stare, and my breath catches. Two men are coming our way. A tall redhead with freckled cheeks that I don't recognize, and the other has hazel eyes and chestnut curls that brush the bottom of his chin. My heart rate quickens. Those dark eyes. It's the man from this morning. He's real.

4

Unraveled

"TREVOR, YOU'RE EARLY. I was just finishing my nine o'clock," Seth tells the redhead.

They're both staring at me, but as soon as Seth speaks, their attention focuses on him. The unnamed man's eyes flash briefly back to mine before settling firmly on Seth's.

"I'm sorry, I didn't mean to interrupt. I thought I would get an early start. I've heard you're the best Lympha trainer on the base, sir," Trevor says

"Thank you, but I wouldn't call myself the best. All the trainers are at the very top of their element." Seth turns to the other man.

"James, are you interested in learning about a new element?"

James smiles. His teeth are straight and white, but it doesn't reach his eyes. Those remain clouded. The hazel color has flecks of blue, green, and gold, with a complete set of long thick eyelashes surrounding them. He has stubble along his strong jaw and rounded chin. I have an odd sensation of wanting to reach out and touch it to see if it prickles my fingertips. Being this close and with his full attention on Seth, it's the only socially acceptable time to observe him.

While studying his face, I feel another tug on my memory.

"Well, of course, water must be so interesting, but sadly, I'm here only on duty to my new comrade. I'm on my way to my training, sir." James gestures toward Trevor. His husky voice echoes in my head, doing weird things to my insides, because that, too, is familiar.

Seth nods and then turns to me. "Maya, make sure to practice, and you'll get a full water transport in no time, maybe even by our next training session."

I regrettably pull my eyes from examining James. "Will do! I'll see you tomorrow."

I turn on my heel and stride towards the manor. I avoid the gazes of the two men as I walk past them, keeping my eyes straight ahead. But instead of my normally brisk pace, I slow down, straining my ears for any more information spoken between the men before I'm too far away.

"Thank you, James, for your help. Trevor, let's get started."

I don't hear any other conversation, but I do hear footsteps. Oh no. I lengthen my stride, but it's too late.

"Hello," comes his deep voice directly behind me.

I whip around, too startled to remember I'm not supposed to talk to him.

"Uh, hi," is all my intelligent brain can come up with.

James's hazel eyes are locked on mine, lips quirked into a smirk. He casually walks up next to me with hands in his pockets, still keeping a respectful distance. I could reach out and touch him if I wanted to, though.

I can't remember the last time I was this close to an unmatched man. He's taller than me, and I notice a dimple on his left cheek.

I suddenly remember where we are and glance at our surroundings. We've rounded a maple tree, obscured by its branches and the bushes beneath, the lake out of view.

"Don't worry, nobody can see us," he says, watching me.

I regard him warily. Does he want me alone for some reason? I should keep walking, but my feet remain planted. Maybe he recognizes me, too. There is more I want to know, and a gravitational pull about him keeps me from leaving.

"My name is James," he says as he puts his hand out. Sadly, the name doesn't spark anything in my memory.

I hesitate but place my hand in his. "I'm Maya."

His hand is rough but warm. He gives mine a slight shake.

"I know." He grins. This smile *does* reach his eyes as the corners crinkle.

"Oh, so you were there this morning?" I ask, pretending that he wasn't the one that caught me.

He chuckles. "You could say that."

"I promise I'm not usually such a damsel in distress."

His laugh is even more familiar than his eyes. Listening to that laugh, I feel like a little kid.

"I wouldn't mind if you were."

Heat crawls up my cheeks, and I have to clear my throat as my breath quickens. "We shouldn't be talking. Has nobody told you the rules? You're one of the new recruits, right?"

He shrugs. "Then don't talk to me." But he doesn't make a move to leave, and I don't either. He quirks an eyebrow at me.

"You haven't answered my question."

His grin returns. "Yes."

"Yes, they haven't told you the rules, or yes, you're one of the new recruits?"

He rubs his chin, and I can't help but notice the way his sleeve stretches over his bicep.

"They did tell me all your eighteenth-century rules."

"We have them for a reason," I retort. I'm taking too big a risk by still talking to him. What am I doing? "I should probably get going." I take two steps, and he joins me, keeping pace. I glance at him. "What are you doing?"

"Walking you to the door."

My stomach flutters at his words.

"So, tell me about these rules."

I peer at him. He's looking ahead of us with a smile on his lips. "What? Is there one you don't understand?" Probably the one stating that we're not allowed to be alone with the opposite sex.

He shakes his head. "Do you always follow all the rules?"

I don't hesitate. "Of course." Well, that's not entirely true. Abby and I have broken the nine o'clock curfew. Not like it's enforced.

"Hmm, so you're a sheep?" he insinuates, eyeing me.

That stops me short. "No!" I say a little too loudly and look around. We're still the only ones between the lake and this side of the manor.

"Hit a nerve?"

"Ugh, I don't blindly follow. The rules keep us safe and are what's best for us. You know, like the one where I'm not to be around you, an unmatched man. Matches are made for a reason. If we run around with whomever, making attachments, then we might not have children with strong enough abilities, and if that happens, our kind might eventually die out. Were you under a rock before you got recruited? We're at war here, trying not to be killed off!" I say, waving my hands about. Great, I'm snowballing.

James is regarding me with great interest, waiting for me to end my tangent. I close my mouth and start walking. Again, he keeps up with me.

"If you don't want me talking to you, just say the word."

I haven't actually told him to leave. I open my mouth to tell him so, but the words choke me. Instead, I try to ignore him, which isn't too hard since he stopped talking. Maybe something I said helped him come to his senses, or maybe not, since he's still walking next to me. Our footsteps crunch softly in the grass and twigs. Why haven't I told him to leave?

We're almost to the side door when he speaks up. "Maya?"

Against my better judgement, I stop.

He opens his mouth but closes it again. He pushes a hand through his curls before saying, "It was nice to meet you."

My heart warms at his sincerity, but I have a feeling that's not what he was going to say.

He starts off, but my hand has a mind of its own and reaches out to touch his arm. His skin is surprisingly soft under my fingertips. "Wait."

His eyebrows rise, and he looks at where I'm touching him. My hand falls.

"I just—" Not knowing why I stopped him, before I can think about what I'm saying, words tumble out. "Do I know you? Like, have we met before, before this morning?" I might not see him again, and he could help give me the piece that must be missing in my head.

There is a tightening in his eyes, but other than that, his expression remains controlled. "I don't think so. But, as I said, it was nice to meet you. I hope to run into you again, and maybe you can persuade me why the rules here are so important. Because I'm still not convinced." His lips pull up at the corners. "Better yet, maybe I can convince you why they're not." Then he's gone.

I stand there, gaping at where he disappeared into the brush, unraveled by his bold statement, letting the breeze whip my hair in front of my face. The rules *are* important. Aren't they? There is still a possibility I know him. Maybe he doesn't remember either. I really shouldn't talk to him again, though. Unless I can figure it out by getting to know him.

I shake off the thoughts. Maybe I hit my head when I fell out of the window this morning. This is not me. It'll be best if I don't run into him again, I decide, and turn to enter the building. But the gnawing sensation at the back of my mind doesn't let up as I return to my room, and even after lunch, when I'm on my way to the education hall to fulfill my teacher-aide duties. Those dark eyes continue to consume my thoughts.

A familiar dark-haired boy runs past, breaking me free. "Cal!"

His face brightens when he notices me and waves enthusiastically but keeps running into his classroom. I've never known a nine-year-old to be so punctual.

Two boys ahead playfully push each other back and forth until one shoves a little too hard, and the boy falls into a dark-haired girl, who shrieks.

"Umm, sorry," he mumbles, running back to his pal.

I jog up to the little girl. "Hey, are you okay?"

"Yeah," she says, glaring at their backs before looking up at me. "You're Miss Mayfield, right? You were in my class last month."

I nod.

"When will you be back? I like you better than Miss Sienfer, who we have now. You actually help us," she says, scrunching up her nose.

I smile. It's good to know little kids like me, at least. "Thanks. I believe I'll be back in your class. Oh—"

"What is it?" She eyes me curiously.

"It's nothing." Now that I'm matched, I'm not sure if I'll be in the classroom anymore. Our duties lessen when we match, so we can focus all our time and energy on courting and training. "I'm matched, is all."

"You're matched!" Her face lights up with enthusiasm.

I can't help but grin back. "Yes, just recently."

"Oh, you are so lucky. I can't wait to be matched." She takes on this dreamy expression. "Are they so handsome?"

I chuckle. "I haven't met them yet, but I'm hopeful."

We arrive outside her classroom, but then she peers up at me. With all the wisdom of somebody much older, she says, "Good luck, Miss Mayfield. Choose who you love, not who other people want you to love." And then she walks into her class with a pep in her step.

I stare after her, shaking my head. Kids these days have to grow up way too fast.

As I'm almost to my class, the ground begins moving beneath my feet, and the walls quake. Siren's blare throughout the hallways. The kids cover their ears and look around frantically.

My heart pounds in my chest as I freeze. Is this an earthquake? No, we don't have earthquakes. What else could be causing this? Unless— my heart drops— we've been found.

5

Bunker

THE FEAR IN THE KIDS' EYES snaps me out of my terror. I wave at them to follow and grab the two that are crying. I push them into the classroom and run to the head teacher.

The building shudders again, but this time harder. Books crash to the floor. I try to keep my footing and hold onto the chalkboard for balance. Mrs. Martinez gawks at me with terror-stricken eyes. Isn't she supposed to remain calm for the children?

Adrenaline kicks in, and I gather kids, placing them under tables. At least I remember that much from elementary school drills.

Something is happening outside these walls. I scramble to the windows. A giant tree trunk obscures my view, and with a muttered curse, I turn to Mrs. Martinez and grip her shoulders.

I yell over the sirens, slightly shaking her, "Make sure the kids stay under the desks, okay?"

Her wide eyes stare at me, frozen, but a heartbeat later, she nods.

I run into the hall, half expecting an army of Coms to be charging at me, but it's deserted. I dash into the classroom on the opposite side; they have a better view of the grounds.

The teacher has all the kids huddled in the corner, away from the windows. At least Professor Roberts knows what he's doing. Cal lunges out of the group and wraps his arms around me.

I bend down, slowly peeling him off. "Stay with your class, okay? You're in good hands. I just need to check things out." There's panic in his eyes, and I look at him hard. "You're brave, right?"

He nods.

"Can you show me how brave you are?"

He nods again, and I lead him back to the group. Professor Roberts takes his hand.

"You should stay in here. I'm sure it's a drill," he grunts, but his amber eyes say otherwise.

I rush to the window. Dark smoke obscures the land. This can't be just a drill. I imagine Coms flooding in, killing us all, and push the image away. They wouldn't be able to get in with legionaries surrounding the place. I should stay right here with the kids and wait it out.

I mean to step towards them, but my feet lead me to the door instead. I look at Cal. "I'll be right back." I wink.

Once around the corner, I sprint, an unknown force pulling me in a different direction. I'm either brave or stupid, but I'm going to help, and if I live through this, I'll ask Seth to teach me water combat skills.

I turn the corner, and I'm greeted by the commanders and generals in the main entrance, just chatting. My mother in her dark lab coat and strawberry blonde hair falling out of her clip stands among them. How can they even hear above these sirens? None of them appear scared, although it's their job not to be afraid.

I reach my mom and tap her on her shoulder.

For a moment I see a flicker of fear in her expression before her face hardens. "Maya! What are you doing here?"

I don't answer her question. Telling her I'm ready to dive into the fight isn't the best thing to tell my overprotective mother. "Mom, what is going on? Is this a drill?"

She hesitates. "We'll explain later, but you need to find somewhere safe in the meantime."

I shake my head. "I'm not going anywhere, Mom. Not until I know what's happening."

She levels me with her gaze. "Maya, go to the rec now. We'll speak later." She turns and walks away from me.

My shoulders tense at the authoritative voice. She never speaks to me like that. I let out an irritated sigh and rush up the grand staircase.

The rec room is the first opening on the right. When I push open the double doors, I'm greeted by a handful of people huddled against the dark brown walls. There are shelves lining the room to the ceiling, holding hundreds of old books that nobody reads, bindings torn from half of them. I'm sure it was quite the library back in the day, but an old pool table now fills the middle of the space, a lumpy couch in one corner, and a tall silver lamp in the other. Abby is in the corner under the lamp, waving at me, her face lined with worry.

I jog over, and everyone looks at me expectantly, like I have some information to explain what's happening. I sit next to Abby.

"Do you know what's going on?" she asks. "It felt like a bomb went off."

"I know! I don't know anything, though." When I say that, the sirens finally stop, and I'm talking so loudly that everyone hears me. At least nobody else will ask.

"Where were you?" she whispers.

I'm momentarily distracted by the ringing in my ears. "I was in the education wing. The kids were terrified."

"Why are you here then? Shouldn't you be with them?"

I look at her diffidently. "Well, I thought I could help."

"Maya! Were you going to just run into a war if that's what was happening?"

I shrug.

Abby shakes her head.

Luckily, one of the sergeants walks through the door, saving me from having to explain myself further.

"I know everybody must be wondering what is going on. Get to the commons, and everything will be explained."

Everybody glances back and forth at each other. Confusion is evident on their faces, but we all dutifully rise to leave the room.

When we reach the dining hall, tables are pushed against the far wall, and families are gathered in the center. Adults are talking over one another, and children are huddled together or being held, still shaken. I find Cal with his class, and he wraps his arms around me tightly.

I rub his back. "It's okay, we're okay."

He looks up at me, chin quivering with emotion. I can tell he's trying to be strong. "I'm not scared, but I'm glad you're okay." His voice falters a bit. He's always trying to take care of Mom and me, the little man of the house.

I kiss his forehead. "I'm happy you are safe, too. You did good, listening to your teacher." I peer over to his skilled Igna teacher. He would protect his class, no matter what.

Cal lets me go but stays close as I search for Mom. I finally give up and lead Cal over to Abby and her mom. Mrs. Stevens enfolds us in a hug. I've always seen her as our second mom. We were practically neighbors when I was little. Cal visibly relaxes once we're with her. Luckily, he still gets to be a kid, since his abilities haven't manifested. He spends a lot of time with either her or our mom. Mrs. Stevens tends to spoil him as her certified chocolate taster. She's the best chocolate maker out of all the Terras. My mom told me once that Cal reminds Mrs. Stevens of her late son—Abby's older brother—and helps soothe the part of her that is broken. One's heart can never truly heal from losing a child or the person you're bonded to. Mrs. Stevens lost both. Part of her will always be gone. My heart aches for her and Abby. I know what it's like to lose a parent, but a sibling? I hope I never have to go through that pain.

Abby ruffles his hair. "Hey, squirt."

"How are you, sweetheart?" Mrs. Stevens coos at him.

Cal stands a little taller. "I'm great! I wasn't scared at all." He's looking more like Dad every day. With his dark hair and blue eyes, he has the same oval face shape, but with Mom's pointy nose. It's comforting, like he's still with us somehow. I feel bad Cal never got to meet him. Then again, you can't miss what you never knew.

My parents tried to have another child after me for a long time, but it wasn't happening. Once they made peace with it, Mom discovered she was pregnant with Cal. They were their happiest for those few short months before his death. Afterward, I didn't think Mom would ever be joyful again. But two months later, Cal was born. He was the light that drove out the darkness and hasn't dimmed since.

My mom calling our names breaks me out of my memories. She comes straight for us, pulling Cal into her arms and planting a kiss on his head. She whispers in his ear, and he smiles wide. She rubs my shoulder and briefly looks at me as she passes. I question her with my eyes. She mouths, *listen,* and nods toward the front of the room.

She joins the other commanders between two large pillars. All six commanders gather in a loose semi-circle. Kirt Lawrence is commandeering the middle, eyes sharp. A breeze ripples among the people, a dominant presence brushing our faces towards him. Everyone immediately quiets down. Flanked to his left are my mom and Don, an elderly man with graying hair and fragile-looking limbs, the oldest and wisest of them all. I only see him during the ceremonies when he performs the bonding matches. His shoulders are hunched, and his eyes are cast down, but it's only a shell for the power he holds as the high Aura.

Flanked to his right are the other three commanders of the legion. Zhang—a fairly young man with jet-black hair and squinty eyes—is a Terra. Next to him stands a massive man with a face that appears to be in constant pain, probably from the stick up his rear end. I try to avoid the Igna Commander Barlowe whenever possible.

And that leaves Wixx, a middle-aged, dark-skinned woman with all-knowing eyes…a Lympha. She notices me and gives me a wink. I've always liked her. In order to get to such positions, they have to be the most intelligent, the strongest in their element, and to have proven their loyalty in the war. Wixx is the only one who hasn't let the rank go to her head.

They are all dressed in dark legion uniforms—except my mom in her lab coat—with only the power exuding from them to tell them apart from a regular legionary.

Their eyes travel to Commander Lawrence as he addresses us. "I know you all must be worried, but let me put your fears to rest: this was a drill. We didn't warn you, because we needed to know how everyone would respond. Now that we know, we can better prepare you if the real thing were to happen."

An uneasiness spreads over me, and by the hushed words of those around me, many more feel the same.

"It's time to show you all the bunker."

The quiet conversations intensify at the announcement. Is he talking about the dingy storage rooms in the basement? I strongly doubt we could fit everyone in those.

"Quiet, please! If everyone can follow me, I will show you where to go the next time we have a drill."

Or not a drill. Something about this feels off. The details don't add up. Why would they need to blow things up? Wouldn't sirens suffice for a drill? And I swear I saw fear in my mom's eyes earlier.

We're led down the metal staircase, passing the medical level and continuing to the basement. We walk past the storage rooms deeper down the hall. I don't remember the hallway extending this far.

Around a corner, we are greeted by a massive metal door taking up the whole width and height of the hallway. I can tell by the gasping, most people didn't know about it.

Commander Lawrence raises his voice to be heard over all the sudden chatter. "Nothing can get past this door or around it. Metal walls surround the entire bunker. The only way in is with this scanning device." His hand gestures to a silver square object embedded in the wall. "But that can be shut off from the inside. This will scan your face and your voice and unlock the door. Everyone is already in its system. The legion quarters on the other side of the base have the same setup, so there are only two access points."

He turns toward the scanner, and it beeps before the sound of metal scraping fills the hallway as the colossal door slides open. We all slowly file in, taking in the room before us. The air is stale, with no outside light, but rows of incandescent beams on the low ceiling light the huge space. Everyone wears the same expressions of wonder as they look around.

"This is so cool," Cal says, speaking for the first time as he holds tight to my hand.

Some people spread out toward the rows of metal bunk beds to our left, while others stay near the door, pointing at the shelves filled with clear bins of food and supplies, covering every square inch of the wall as far as I can see. Wary voices echo off the walls. There is no décor. It feels and looks like a dungeon, but I guess a dark, somber dungeon that can keep you alive for months is better than nothing.

"There are bathrooms down there." Commander Lawrence points toward dark openings in the middle of the concrete wall. "And there are enough supplies for us to survive for about three months if needed."

A question is finally voiced. "Is that something that's going to happen then?"

Another woman speaks up. "Have they found us? Are they coming?"

The group turns inward as nervous chatter intensifies and fills the empty corners of the dungeon.

With a raised hand and a hard gust of wind, Commander Lawrence silences them. "I know you all must be worried, but this is a worst-case scenario. It's not a bad thing to be prepared, and no, we're not expecting ever to need it. We are safe here." He says it so full of authority that I almost believe him.

6

Un-Rules

WHERE ARE YOU? *We need to talk about this!!!*

The words flash on my communicator. I pick up the thin, silver device—our only communication inside the walls that can't be tracked. No part of me wants to relive the awkward events of this morning, the drill from yesterday already forgotten as people have something new to chatter about, but I know she won't stop pestering me until I respond.

In my room…avoiding everyone.

When she doesn't reply, I know she's on her way, so I sprawl on my sofa, staring at the wooden planks of the ceiling. I've found a tsunami wave in the swirling lines in the wood and a set of eyes that remind me of a certain person, when Abby barges in.

"I hope you didn't mean *me*," she says with a huge smile plastered on her face.

"Thanks for knocking."

She rolls her eyes before joining me on the couch, curls bouncing against her pink blouse. I quickly pull my feet up before she sits on them.

"I'm dying to know what you think of all this. I would have come sooner, but I had lunch duty." When I don't respond, she shakes my shoulder. "Maya!"

"They seem to want us to choose our match as soon as possible," I say. My mom didn't come right out and say it at the meeting this morning, but it was implied.

"No kidding." She leans closer. "We'll have so much privacy now." She wiggles her eyebrows, but her fair cheeks burn pink, ruining the effect.

Abby, I, and the three other eighteen and nineteen-year-olds, met with our families and my mother to discuss the specifics of the upcoming matches. Everything was fine until she announced the new rules.

"Change number one," I mimic my mom's voice as I focus on my desk along the far wall, the one with pictures around the silver mirror. It reflects the expanse of my new living quarters, which are made up of one bed, one nightstand, one couch, one coffee table, and one desk. All for a party of one. "You no longer have to meet with your matches in the public eye."

Abby squeals, and I roll my eyes.

Then she says, "You're forgetting the best part." She clears her throat and uses the same voice I did. "The biggest change in the regular quartering procedure will be first meeting your matches in your rooms instead of the foyer." She kicks her feet with giddiness. "My mom wasn't too happy about that change…but the *next* one. Did you see her face? I can't believe the commanders got the parents to okay that one."

I tilt my head. How *did* the commanders get the parents on board with such a big change? Were they given a choice?

"Which brings us to the next change." Abby bites her lip. "The restriction of sexual relations is lifted," Abby murmurs with the first hint of nerves in her voice. When it comes down to it, Abby is all talk. She's never done anything with a boy, and she is as scared as I am.

I grab her hand. "You know you don't have to do anything you don't want to do."

"I know, I know. And I won't, but, Maya, what if they don't like me?" she asks, biting her lip.

"Abby, you are beautiful, smart, the best Terra I know. They are going to fall madly in love with you, and you're definitely going to break somebody's heart."

"Thank you." She squeezes my hand. "You always know just what to say."

"I'm so happy we're matched at the same time." And I mean it. I can't imagine going through this alone. I swallow the building emotion.

She smiles. "Me too. Oh! And those weren't even the biggest changes." She shakes her head, and I realize I never told her I knew about the last one. "Getting matched with somebody from a different group." She sighs, leaning back. "I'm not sure about that new un-rule."

"Un-rule?"

"Because she reversed the rules. Un-rule." She smiles proudly.

I nod. I guess that makes sense. "I'm matched to an Igna," I blurt.

Her back straightens, eyes on me. "What! You know?"

I suck in my bottom lip and nod. "I begged it from her yesterday."

Her mouth gapes open. "And you didn't tell me?"

I look at her guiltily, and she brushes it off. "It's okay, a lot happened yesterday. That's crazy. Are you worried?"

Everyone knows Ignas can have tempers. I chew on my finger. "I'm sure it'll be fine."

"And the other?"

"Aura."

She wrinkles her nose. "Not a Terra? I'm going to have to talk with your mother."

I giggle, and she begins rambling about the possibilities of her matches and soon enters her own world. Now, all I have to do is nod as she takes over the conversation, not letting me get a word in.

I can't imagine being bonded to an Igna. Fire has always scared me. How it can destroy everything it touches. How it almost killed us when we escaped. I swallow. Maybe I should give it a chance.

As a Lympha, I could easily put a fire out, just like I did with my mom that night five years ago. I can still feel the heat of the fire barrier that blocked the road, hear the sizzle of the flames as our water smashed into it a split second before we would have been burnt to a crisp. If I can do that, I can do anything. My abilities will strengthen when I become one with my match, but I'll also be expected to do other things that I have no experience with. That's what all this is for. To create a stronger generation. I know the semantics of intimacy, but I thought I would still have months to prepare. Imagining being vulnerable with a man so soon—maybe in weeks instead of months...or even *days*. My stomach twists at the thought.

"You've got all this insider knowledge. Were there any that stood out to you? Anybody super cute?" Abby says, interrupting my thoughts.

I glance at her, with no idea what she's talking about. The wheels turn in my mind. Oh…my whole two seconds with them when I fell. "Um yeah, I guess so," I respond a second too late, and she eyes me curiously.

She narrows her dark eyes and pinches her plump pink lips. "What are you not telling me?"

I'm not ready to tell her about my insecurities. "Nothing. I was just trying to think back at who I saw. There was this British guy. Yeah, he was super cute." I throw at her, hoping her curiosity takes over.

She asks me more questions about him and others. By the time I'm done talking, I've made up four guys, because the only face I can recall is James's. The feeling that I know him is like an itch I can't scratch. Those memories must be just out of reach. Maybe it's the mental block I created to shield myself from memories that makes it hard to breathe. Or, most likely, it's all in my head, and we really *don't* know each other. I don't even know what his element is. With his hazel eyes, he could be a Terra or possibly an Igna. I recall seeing flecks of amber in them. Could he be my match?

Our conversation from yesterday springs to mind and how he talked about our eighteenth-century guidelines. Ugh. I could never be with a man who doesn't respect the rules. But, at the same time, his point of view is so new to me. Am I a sheep? I've never doubted what the leaders tell us until recently, with all the changes and the inconsistencies with the so-called drill. I do make decisions for myself, don't I? Maybe I should start. I could try to talk to James again and learn what I can about him. But is it worth breaking the rules over?

It's now or never. Once I meet my matches, all my time will be spent with them, and I doubt I'll even have the desire to be around another man.

I take the small break in chitchat to give her an excuse. "Abby, I need to get some practice in before dinner. I'll meet you there, okay?"

Abby blinks at me, then shrugs her shoulders. "Sure."

I head for my balcony door, but before I open it, Abby asks, "You want me to come with you? I don't have anything to do right now. We can practice together again."

I hesitate. "No, I need to practice alone. Seth has been teaching me about water transports. They're pretty difficult, so I need to focus. Next time, okay?"

"I'll see ya at dinner," she chirps. She must be excited about our matches coming up not to be let down.

"See ya," I say, closing the door behind me. A part of me wants to turn back and tell her the truth. I hope to practice, but that's not the main reason I want to head out.

Shaking off the guilt, I watch the sun peek over the treetops. The grass ripples like golden waves, reaching toward the shimmering pond where I practice.

I stride down the stairs, but instead of taking the path to my little pond, I take a left and head to the lake. If I want to run into James again, I might as well go where I saw him last.

The lake is as close as I'm allowed to get to Legion Headquarters. The building shines like a kaleidoscope in the sun. It supposedly blends in from above, but I swear the thing is more of a beacon. There's an imaginary line between our two buildings, stretching down the middle of the lake, legionaries on one side and families on the other.

I reach the lake in record time with a good hour to "practice" before I need to head for dinner. I raise my hand to shield from the lowering sun. There's a family at the training spot I was at earlier today. The two parents are playing with their toddler in the sand, and there's a young boy in the water, about Cal's age, with a mischievous expression on his face. A small ball of water hovers near his side as he closes in on his dad. His dad looks over to him as the boy hurls water at his face, drenching him.

I chuckle as the dad lunges at his son, taking him under the water. They both come up laughing, the mom smiles, and the toddler jumps up, wanting to join in on the fun. Watching them makes life seem almost normal, and I feel a sharp sting in my heart thinking about my adventures with my family before my dad passed. But there's also a sense of longing for my soon-to-be family. Hopefully, this will be me in a few years, with my own children and the man I'm matched with, tickling our kids.

I stop walking. What am I doing here? I should actually be practicing, not seeking out some random guy because I might know him. It seems insignificant now after watching this family.

Striding past the family and down the lake, I see a spot cleared from the thick vegetation. Just enough room for me to find my footing and reach the rocks. I take off my shoes and place them on an algae-coated rock, jutting out of the water.

I wade into the cool water until it's up to my shins. The lake has been warmed by the sun all day, so it's a little more comfortable than this morning. Small twigs and dead leaves float on its surface as water striders scurry around my legs. My body and soul crave the water. I want to dive in and let it consume me, wash away all negative thoughts and insecurities in the pure joy of feeling complete and one with my element.

Breathing deeply, I take in the fresh mountain air. It smells like rain. The water parts before me as I stretch my hands forward, taking it and shaping it into an arc. The sunlight hits it from an angle, turning it shades of red, blue, yellow, and green. Who needs rain when you can make your own rainbow?

I summon more water into it and let it grow. A world of color surrounds me as I shape the water around my body. I skim my hands and spin in a circle, touching it at all angles. The light dances on my skin. The water slides off my feet as I wiggle my toes between the mud and pebbles. I release the water, letting it wash back onto my legs. Maybe I will go for a swim after all.

I peer behind me and am taken aback when my eyes fall on a figure observing me.

He's leaning against a broad tree with his arms crossed, watching me unashamedly. I shade my eyes from the sun now touching the horizon to get a better look. James grins and raises his hand in a slight wave. Well, there goes my late afternoon swim and my new resolution to focus on practicing.

I pull my feet out of the mud, making quiet sloshing sounds as I let the water guide my feet to soft spots on the lake floor.

His eyes brighten. "Fancy seeing you here."

"Oh, and I ought to believe you came here for the view of the lake?"

"Not of the lake."

I can't fight the heat that rises in my cheeks as my heart skips a beat. No, he can't be flirting. He knows I'm matched. He was there when Commander Lawrence took it upon himself to announce it to the world.

"That was dazzling," he says, pointing to the water.

"And why are you watching me?"

"Why are you practicing right in front of where I'm standing?"

I shake my head as I reach the shore, trying not to smile and failing. "I practice here all the time, and I know you're not a Lympha. What is your element, anyway?"

He slides a hand through his thick hair. "Any guesses?"

Do I really want to get into a conversation with him? It'll be impossible to continue practicing with him staring at me. I'll have to go to a different spot.

I slip my shoes on and make my way back through the brush, careful not to catch my bare legs on a twig jutting out. "Terra?"

"You got it," he says, as he snaps his fingers.

The bushes before me clear a perfect path to him.

I falter. Not where I was heading, but I'd rather not brave those prickly weeds again. I sigh and start up the pathway he made.

"How'd you know?"

I shrug. "Your eyes." But it was more of an educated guess. Many people have an eye color that matches their element, but it's not always the case, like me. Brown for Terra, blue for Lympha, gray for Aura, and amber for Igna. I'm happy to have gotten his element right. Maybe I'm right about other things.

I reach him, and he's standing right where I need to pass, just a foot away. "Thanks for the help. Excuse me," I mutter, stepping to his side, expecting him to move.

But he doesn't, and I end up stepping too close. I glance at him, irritated, but he's a mere few inches away from me. The look in his eyes takes my breath away, stunning me for a moment. The intensity of his stare holds mine, and I can't break away. It's like he can read my every thought. My senses come alive as if, before this moment, they were dulled. Everything is more vibrant: lush emerald ivy crawling up the dark mahogany tree trunk, which isn't just brown anymore. There are hues of burgundy in the bark, and white cobwebs encase small openings. The tree bark matches his eyes, the colors of blue-green, gold, and russet swirling around his dark pupils. An electric current sparks between us, drawing me closer.

"Maya," his voice comes out, my name a whisper on his lips. His breath is on my face, smelling of mint and a subtle sweetness.

I bite my lip, and he notices, lowering his piercing gaze to them. The loss of eye contact breaks the unsettling spell, and I come to my senses and step back.

I should put him in his place, but when I open my mouth, all that comes out is, "Uh."

Great, I can't even form words. So, I charge straight for the bushes, not caring I'm about to get cut up. But as I reach them, they clear out of my way.

I keep running, and I don't look back.

THE REST OF THE EVENING is a blur. I briefly remember getting dinner, but I didn't say much to Abby. Hopefully, she thought it was nerves about getting matched.

I'm lying in bed, now, begging for sleep to come. I should have never gone to the lake, never let him get close to me. No way I would have kissed him, but if somebody were to have caught us so close to each other, I'd probably be packing my bags. No, I'd most likely get a warning, but James… I can hear my mom now.

All it takes is one kiss, Maya. A kiss is an intimate connection to the mind of another and should only be shared between matches.

According to her, you can fall in love the moment you kiss somebody. That's what it was like with her and Dad anyway. I've never been in love, but once it happens, I doubt it can be undone. Then I would be stuck with the guy instead of my perfect match.

Rolling over and pulling the feather pillow over my face, I groan. I'm not going to get any sleep.

I slip out of bed, change into my one-piece black bathing suit, and blanket myself with my white robe for the chilly night. Nothing a midnight swim can't fix.

The pond is closer than the lake, about the size of a large swimming pool, with a creek running from it. Unlike the lake, this is a natural part of the landscape, untouched by my people. I wonder where the other end of the creek goes. Maybe it can take me out of this place if I follow it. Once, I tried, but only got far enough to find a decaying tree that had crashed to the forest floor long ago, covered in green moss, making the perfect bench. Going further into the forest made me feel unprotected, far from the manor. It's not like anything is out there. Walls surround us to protect us from the wildlife and camouflage us, in case the unthinkable were to happen and the Coms locate us. I once heard you can't tell the walls apart from the surrounding forest, but I've never seen them for myself.

The stars splatter the night sky and the gibbous moon peers down at me as I envision the world outside the manor at peace. But the smoke in the air says otherwise. Something is always burning—Ignas getting carried away, which infuriates the Auras, who have to clean up their mess so the smoke doesn't make it outside the base.

When the legionaries first showed up a year ago, it was exciting, finally a change from the past four years, but it soon became otherwise. Before, we could at least pretend the world wasn't at war—out here in our little bubble, fifty miles away from the nearest Oregon town. But they brought with them the painful reminder that it is at war. We are at war with the Coms, who fear our abilities are too powerful. The legion is here to protect us, Elementals who have chosen to fight. Similar bases are set up worldwide, with Elementals in hiding. We were sitting ducks a year ago, but if they found us now, we'd have a fighting chance.

Thinking about it too much brings a sense of doom, so I hang my robe on a branch nearby and dive into the cold glassy surface. As soon as the crisp water touches my skin, tranquility washes over me. Nothing else matters. If I had physical wounds, they would heal. I wish it could heal the wounds in my heart. The water mutes them, at least, making them more bearable. Only in the water can I think of my dad and my life before the war.

My home on the cul-de-sac, with white shutters and a bright blue door. I had a treehouse in my backyard. One of my earliest memories was when Abby fell out of it. I can remember that day clearly. My dad caught her with the water from the stream in the backyard. The way she froze mid-fall, with the water encircling her. That's when I started to beg him for lessons, even though I was years from when my abilities would emerge. Day after day, he would show me his tricks. Up until that fateful afternoon, my ninth birthday.

My lungs burn thinking about it. Even the water can't swallow the pain.

I let the water push me back to the surface and float on my back. Floating, drifting, unattached from my issues, I connect with my body and the earth. In a world of turmoil, you need something to ground you and keep you sane. I breathe in the cool air for a while, keeping my mind clear. Drowsiness tugs me down eventually, so I pull myself out of the pond to head back to bed.

As I stand, I hear a noise among the trees and stiffen. My heart picks up speed, and I suck in a breath. Waiting.

Straining my ears, I slowly move my fingertips. I have little training in water combat, but I could protect myself if needed. A twig snaps, and there's more rustling. I move the water into the air, preparing myself. I can't get emotional and let fear take control. If I have to fight, I need only to think, not feel.

Breathing in and out slowly, I harness my Sage, my connection to the earth, and let it calm my racing heart. The sounds get closer. Water from the pond rises. I wait, holding my breath as a little gray-and-white rabbit hops into the opening.

My body relaxes as I drop the water and smile. It's just a bunny, unaware of the dangers of the world. Taking a step forward, leaves crunch underfoot, and it turns and flees back into the bushes. In a way, I'm like that bunny, fleeing at the first sign of danger. Maybe I should stop running.

7

Secrets

TRAINING IS DIFFICULT TODAY. I don't get much further with my water transport. I'm too in my head, distracted by what—or more like *who*—might come when the training is over. I can't help feeling a little ruffled after what happened yesterday.

Waving goodbye to Seth, I head up the path back to the manor. As I round the corner, there he is, in the same spot as yesterday, leaning against the giant maple tree. Does he have nothing better to do?

I keep my eyes trained on the manor and I'm almost past him when he speaks up.

"Hey, wait, Maya. Can I talk to you?"

I shake my head and lengthen my stride.

"I'm sorry about yesterday. I won't get close to you again, even though, technically, you came to me."

That stops me, and I slowly level his gaze.

He reads my face and thinks better of it. "Okay, okay, I was in the way, but really, I just want to be friends, Scout's honor," he says, holding up three fingers.

I furrow my eyebrows. The hand gesture seems familiar.

"You don't know what that means?" he asks. "Hmm, it means, I promise, okay? Just friends."

I hesitate, wanting to keep walking. Can I just be friends with a guy? Abby's been my only true friend for as long as I can remember. "Why do you want to be friends with me?"

He rubs the back of his neck and lets it drop. Finally, he shrugs. "I like you."

I raise my eyebrows, surprised by his candor.

"Not like that, okay? I like you as a person. I want to get to know you. Outside of this place, men and women can be friends. You haven't been here your whole life. You must remember how it was. You've got to admit, it's pretty strict here. And if you feel uncomfortable around me, say the words, and I'll be gone." He smiles wide, completely changing his face to soften the hard lines and angles.

But, still, I would be choosing to go against a significant rule. I couldn't have been the only one who felt something between us yesterday. Although he is the first single guy I have talked to in five years, it might feel like that with any attractive man.

My resolve wavers as he stares at me with hope-filled eyes. Do I really want to be like that bunny I saw last night, always running? He's right. Men and women used to be friends all the time. I've followed the rules my whole life. It's about time I take risks and live a little. At least until I've met my matches. Which could only be for a few more days. A couple of days of friendship won't hurt.

"Okay," I sigh. "Just friends?" I point at him.

"Just friends." He nods.

"And you promise not to take advantage of me?"

He puts a hand over his heart. "Who do you think I am?" But then he reconfigures his face into a smolder and puts a hand through his dark hair. "A womanizer coming here to steal the innocence of all the young ladies I come across?" He smiles devilishly.

I know he's joking, but his facial expressions cause my heart to skip a beat, and I swallow. "I don't know you," I fire back.

His face relaxes. "Good point. Well, only if you ask, then."

My eyes bug out, and he laughs.

"I'm kidding! First lesson, you need to learn how to not be so serious all the time."

"Oh, you're giving me life lessons now, are you?"

"That's what friends are for. You need them. You've been trapped in this hellhole for how long?"

"Since I was thirteen, and it's not terrible here," I snap, defending the manor I call a prison.

"And how old are you now?"

"Eighteen."

He smiles wryly and rubs his chin. Just like before, his bicep makes an appearance, and I can't help but scan his muscular arm before returning to his face.

"You definitely need my advice then. You have little to no experience of the real world, and you're about to start dating two men, correct?"

I press my lips into a thin line and nod.

"Yeah, you need some practice."

"Oh, and I'm guessing you're volunteering to help me *practice*."

"Sure, if that's what you want." He grins.

"I do not." I scowl, even though my stomach flips.

"Then I'm here for any questions about the male population. Have you ever had the talk?" he asks, wiggling his eyebrows. He looks weirdly like Abby when he does that.

My cheeks burn. "Of course, I'm not a five-year-old."

He smirks, probably liking how he's disarmed me.

I try to change the subject. "Okay, you've convinced me you would be a valuable friend to have around. But we can't walk around together. It's still a rule."

As if to prove my point, a figure rounds the corner, coming straight toward us. I immediately bend down and sift through the packed dirt and wood chips.

"What are you—"

"Shh! Somebody is coming," I mumble, keeping my head down.

He catches on quickly. "Oh, let me help you, miss!"

"No, no, I'm fine," I declare loudly, keeping up the charade.

James bends down anyway and pretends to look through the weeds.

It's Mr. Fox, one of the few elderly men who live here. He peers at us but keeps walking.

Once he's long gone. I stand, pretending to find something. "That was too close."

James's smile grows mischievous. "We need a secret meetup spot then."

"I do know of one," I say slowly, still unsure if I can trust him enough to be alone with him.

Better yet, do I trust myself?

MOMENTS LATER, I FIND MYSELF at the bench-shaped trunk inside the tree line. The silhouette of these trees is visible from my back door, and I have never seen anybody coming and going from them. James should be here soon. He took a long way around.

There are fallen tree branches on the untouched moss-covered floor. This is one of the few areas of vegetation surrounding the manor that hasn't been repurposed. After clearing some leaves and blowing off tiny bugs, I sit.

My nerves catch up with me. This is probably the stupidest thing I've ever done. Yeah, Maya, let's meet an unmatched man alone in the woods. I laugh at myself nervously.

"What's so funny?" James asks as he sits next to me.

I jump, not expecting to hear his voice so close. Terras and their silent footfalls.

"Nothing, just thinking how crazy I am for doing this."

He shakes his head. "The only thing that's crazy is having to isolate ourselves to have a conversation with a person."

I try to think about it from his perspective. This *would* be weird for an outsider.

"You've never been to a base like this? I assumed they were similar all over the country."

He places a hand in his pocket. "Well, to tell you the truth, I've just been drafted."

"You really *are* a new recruit. I didn't realize there were still Elementals not helping in the war effort." I realize too late how patronizing I sound. "Sorry, I didn't mean—"

He cranes his neck toward the treetops, seemingly lost in thought. His curls fall off his tan face as he tilts his head up. "No, you're right. I was away at college when everything went down. I had decided to go to a Com school. My parents weren't happy with me, but I wanted a normal life." His face grows somber as he looks at his callus-covered hands. "They didn't bomb the school like they did the Elemental ones. My dad was a professor at Elementum Academy. He didn't make it. I'll spare you those details," he says, shaking his head. "Of course, I had to go to a school as far away from my family as possible."

He glances at me sideways. "I had a complex back then, wanted to prove I could make it on my own. Well, I got my wish. By the time I was able to get back home, nobody was there, the house ransacked. I don't know what I was thinking. I guess if I had found bodies, it would give me closure at least, but I didn't, and I never found them. That's the worst part, not knowing if they're still alive or not."

I'm surprised again by his honesty. I inch closer to him and put my hand over his. I don't know how to give comfort, but this feels right. People rarely share intimate details about their life with me. "I'm so sorry, James."

He peers at me, his lips curving up. "There you go, trying to get close to me again."

I smile but drop my hand.

"Fast forward to last week, I came across Captain Vargas. He was searching for recruits and told me about this place, about maybe getting matched to a 'pretty lady'—his words. So, I get to officially fight in the war and possibly get a mate. Life isn't easy out there on your own. I said, why not? It's time I do something with my life."

I nod, fascinated with his story. A million questions buzz around in my head. "How old are you?"

"Twenty-one." That would have put him at sixteen or seventeen when he started college.

"Did you graduate early?" I ask, perplexed.

He grins. "You could say that. What's your story?"

I think about his question, not knowing if I trust him, but he has been honest with me. "You already know I've been here for the last five years. My mom, little brother, and I came straight here when everything went haywire. We barely made it out. My mom knew about it from a friend. Their great-grandpa, who was a Terra, built it long ago. Lucky for us, he made it so big. You should see the basement. My best friend and I used to explore down there when we were bored growing up. There's a bunch of old stuff," I say, smiling at the memories.

"What about your dad?"

My lungs spasm. "He died," I murmur.

"In the war?"

I shake my head and wipe my sweaty palms. I don't want to discuss this. "No, a couple of years prior. There was an accident." I won't explain further, and he doesn't push it. "Anyway, more and more Elementals started showing up, through word of mouth mostly, until Commander Lawrence took over. He expanded it to house legionaries passing through and soon realized we would need a whole new building."

I gaze through the trees at Legion Headquarters, spotting the sun reflecting off the top of its glassy surface. "My mom is Commander Mayfield. She's actually the one who develops the matches."

"I met her once. You two look a lot alike."

"It's just the hair. My mom says I look more like my grandma. That's where the green eyes come from."

"They're beautiful," he says, the intensity of his gaze pinning me to my seat.

I cast my eyes away. "Thanks."

"How do you feel about the legion taking over the place?"

I shrug. "It was exciting at first, but you guys just keep coming." I smirk. "No offense."

"I'd feel the same way, all these people taking over my home."

I guess this *is* my home. I've never wanted to think of it as home, but it's become that over the years. It's where my family is. I can't imagine being like James, with no family and nowhere to call home.

"Have you been matched yet?" I ask nonchalantly.

"Why do you want to know?" He looks sideways at me, raising an eyebrow. "Wondering if I could possibly be your match?"

I shake my head. "Don't flatter yourself. I'm not matched to a Terra."

He laughs, a deep raspy sound. "Too bad. Yet you're wondering if I'm still available."

My cheeks burn. "Forget I said anything."

"Nah, I haven't been matched yet."

The relief I feel surprises me. It shouldn't matter if he's matched.

"My mom told me one of my matches is among the newest recruits."

"Really? Those guys?" He rubs his chin.

I perk up. He could know who it is. I don't know what they tell the men when they're matched, but maybe they've given them my name.

"Do you know who one of my matches is?" I urge, trying not to sound desperate.

"No, but there's not much to choose from; they're a bunch of schmucks."

I deflate a little, and he notices.

"There's a couple of 'em that are all right, I guess. I don't know them very well."

I straighten. "So how about you get to know them then? You could give me good intel."

James moves one of his hands gracefully through the air, and wide, brown leaves start dancing, rising higher, surrounding us in a whirlwind. My hair pulls into the updraft. I use both hands to keep it down as a giggle escapes.

He smiles at me, then moves his hand out and grabs a giant maple leaf. He lets the rest fall all around us. He studies it, tracing the veins.

"You should laugh more often. It's nice."

I duck my head at the compliment.

"Why do you think I'm out here with you, instead of in there getting to know them?"

I stare at him, not having the faintest of ideas.

"I'm not like them. I'm not into following orders. Plain and simple."

Well, that's obvious.

"The commanders don't trust me, and it's rubbed off on these other guys. They know I don't belong. Also, nobody is fun around here. Even after training, all these guys just go to bed. Honestly, I think I'd rather be alone than deal with any more robots. When you fell out of the sky in that rock 'n' roll T-shirt…" He chuckles. "You're the only real person I've met here."

"Well, I'm glad you enjoyed it," I grumble.

I've never met anyone like him. To be able to talk so openly. I've been taught to bottle up any emotion for years. Emotions are dangerous. We can't control our element when our feelings get in the way. But looking at James, his face still holding a bit of humor, I can see the pain in his eyes of feeling out of place.

"You called us robots."

"I called *them* robots."

"I am one of *them*," I argue, but it comes out flat.

He stares at me, squinting. I want to wriggle out of his sight, but I stay put and stare back into those hazel depths, waiting for him to see what I don't see in myself.

"You pretend to be…or you wouldn't be here with me."

I don't know how to respond, so I peer down at my watch. "Oh! I'm late. I'm on lunch duty today." I jump up. "I'll see you later?"

He's still sitting on the log, playing with the leaf. "I'm sure we'll run into each other again."

"Oh, I don't doubt it," I mumble as I rush off in a different direction than the one I came. I end up having to double back because of it, giving me enough time to think of a good excuse for being late.

Great, breaking two rules in one morning. James is rubbing off on me. I shouldn't see him again, but he's intriguing and oddly carefree. I've been stuck inside these walls for too long as a prisoner, physically and mentally, never able to express myself freely. Maybe James is the key to my freedom from at least one of those things.

8

The Note

I SLIDE MY SLIPPERS ON to make my way over to Abby's, and my thoughts wander to James. It's been two days since I last saw him. I thought he would pop up somewhere. He'd been a nice change to my normal daily schedule. A knock startles me out of my thoughts.

"Abby, you're so impatient," I grumble.

"Hi, honey," my mom says, leaning in to hug me as soon as I open the door.

I step back, surprised.

She walks to my mirror, palming the photograph of me and Dad. "I always loved this picture."

"Mom, what's going on?" I ask, tilting my head.

She turns on her heel with a closed-lip smile and a gleam in her eyes. "Can't I drop in to see my daughter? I miss you."

"Yeah," I say hesitantly, not believing she's just dropping in.

"But, yes, I did come to tell you that the men will come to your room tomorrow at six."

I forget how to breathe as my heart goes into overdrive. Tomorrow?

She sees my expression and places a hand on my cheek. "Do you have any questions?"

About a million, but I say, "Mom, why did the rules change?"

"More privacy will best speed up the process."

I raise my eyebrows at the confirmation of my suspicions.

"Of course, I want you to go at your own pace. There's no rush."

Does she not hear how contradictory she sounds?

"Which one is it, Mom? Speed it up, jump in bed with them, or take it slow?" My cheeks fill with heat at the words.

Her eyebrows pull down. "Come here." She sighs, moving to the couch.

I hesitate for a moment, then sit next to her.

She puts an arm around me as her familiar soap-and-lilac scent soothes my nerves. "I don't want you to do anything you're uncomfortable with."

"But what about Claire?" The reason for the rules in the first place. Her arm feels too heavy. I want to wriggle out from under her touch.

"That was a complicated scenario, but we now know intimacy is the sure way to know who your match is. But neither I, nor anyone else, would pressure you either way. Between you and me, I'd be delighted if you decided to wait. There have been lots of lovely matches without relations involved. But as I said, it is up to you. I want you to keep in mind that both of these men are very respectable, and they will have your best interests at heart. And if you tell me otherwise, I will have them thrown out in a heartbeat, no matter if they are your perfect matches. I will have to keep looking."

I smile at that. I need no reassurance that my mom loves me, but the situation is still unusual. Why are they rushing us in the first place?

She gives me a quick kiss on the head before heading to the door. "Bye, honey," she calls without another glance.

They are speeding up the process, no matter the ramifications. My heart pounds in my chest. If my mom isn't going to tell me why, there has to be another way to find out. Would James know? They might tell him different things as a legionary.

I smile. Luckily, we're friends now.

There is a flash of white at the corner of my vision. I stride to my back door, where a piece of paper has slipped through the opening at the bottom, onto the wooden floor.

Grabbing it carefully, I open the door to poke my head out. It's late afternoon. The sun is shining on the bare wooden balcony. A breeze ruffles my hair as I look past the railing. The grass stretches out, no shadowed figures to be seen.

I close the door and turn the thick golden lock. I cautiously unfold the paper.

Maya,

If you feel like breaking the rules again, meet me at our spot 10 pm

James

My heart leaps into my throat. One short sentence is all that is scribbled onto the otherwise blank piece of white paper. I reread it. I did want to talk to him, but not like this, sneaking out after curfew with a guy. Prior to meeting James, I had never felt the urge to break the rules. I'm crazy for even considering it.

Then again, I need answers before meeting my matches, and it is my last night of freedom. One night. I need to tell him I'm meeting my matches anyway.

Once again, I read the note, *our spot*. My stomach twists. I fold the piece of paper until it's a small square and head for the trash, but instead, I place it into my side drawer and head for the door. Something in me wants to hold on to it.

A few moments later, I find myself curled up in Abby's pink-and-brown canopy bed, giggling over another of her crazy ideas.

"Just hear me out. A double ceremony can take place in the gardens. We'll be back-to-back, holding our guys' hands." She stands to show me the position we would be in. Her hair is in a high ponytail, and she's wearing a cheetah-print shirt with hot-pink shorts, not a ceremonial white dress.

"You know this isn't a Com wedding. The ceremonies are quick and simple."

"Oh no, not *my* ceremony. I will have music and flowers. Lots of flowers!" As she talks, she moves her fingers toward her dark ivy-covered walls, and beautiful pink roses and white orchids bloom before me. "I'll take care of everything for the both of us." She smiles sweetly.

She picks flowers from her wall, makes a small bouquet, and tosses it to me. I catch it, the sweet scent wafting into my face as I breathe into them.

"These smell heavenly, Abby."

"Thank you!" she sings, jumping onto the bed next to me. "Just tell me the colors you want, and I'll make it happen."

Tears catch in my throat. "Abby, I'm going to miss this."

She jerks her head toward me. "Maya, you're acting like you're marching to your doom tomorrow. Is it just nerves?"

She wasn't as surprised as I thought she would be learning that I'm meeting my matches tomorrow. She has a couple more days before meeting hers, something about one of them being off base at the moment.

"Yeah, probably, or maybe cold feet?" As I say it, I realize that might be why I'm in this weird mood.

"Cold feet? I'm sure that's normal. But you are ready to get matched, aren't you?" she asks warily.

My thoughts go to James. No, he can't be the reason for my cold feet. It has to be something else. "Yeah, I'm ready. That's not it. It's just—" I hesitate, unsure if I want to tell her about my other reservations. I go a different direction. "They're not Lymphas, Abby. I didn't think I would care, but now that I'm meeting them tomorrow, I don't know. I guess I'm just worried…one is an Igna, remember?"

"Maya, would your mom give you anyone unsuitable? You have such an advantage with your matching, because not only will they be impeccable on paper, but your mom *knows* you, your personality, and your men will be no less than perfect, trust me."

I smile. "You're right. I shouldn't be complaining."

She shrugs. "Well, you wouldn't be human if you weren't anxious right now." Her face lights up. "Do you know what you're wearing tomorrow? Or better yet, what you're wearing underneath?"

"Nothing!" I gasp.

"Oh, Maya, you are daring." She laughs.

I hit her arm and groan. "Not like that. I guess I haven't told you, but I don't want to be with them like that until I've made the bond."

She purses her lips but doesn't say anything.

"If I were to do that with both of them, I would feel so, so…"

Abby nods. "I kind of feel like that, too."

My eyebrows shoot up to my hairline. "You do?"

"I said, kind of. If a moment were to come and it felt right, though, why not?"

"But what about Claire?" I stammer.

We both shiver at the name.

"Well, that's like one in a million."

I can tell she's trying to convince herself that wouldn't happen to her.

Most of our matching rules are because of Claire, one of the first girls to get matched four years ago. She was beautiful, with striking bright red hair. Her matches were both Ignas, like her. Some people blame what happened on the fact that they were fire Elementals, known to have tempers, letting emotion drive them. The details have changed a bit over the years, but the lessons still hold, nonetheless.

Claire made a mistake when choosing a match. She slept with both of them and fell pregnant. Of course, she didn't know who the father was. Both matches had strong feelings for her, but she ultimately had to choose. They had their ceremony, the bond was made, and all was well. She had the baby eight months later—a beautiful little girl with the same striking red hair. But the baby had green eyes like the man Claire *hadn't* chosen to be her match.

The rarity of the color made him suspect, and he demanded a test to see if the child was his. The man was right, and then her bonded partner suspiciously fell ill a week later and passed away.

Since the bond between two matches is so absolute—a piece of their power going into the other and amplifying their abilities— if one dies, that power gets taken from them forever. A literal piece is gone. Claire ended up dutifully bonding with the father of her child, losing yet another piece of her power. Some believe she was too broken at that point, and that's why she ran away, leaving her daughter behind.

It is such a tragic story. The guy, shortly thereafter, fled with his daughter, probably to find Claire, and nobody knows what happened to them. Rumors went wild, and many believed he murdered her first match and she ran away from him.

I never understood why she hadn't taken her daughter with her, if that was the case. Why leave a child with a murderer? We might never know the truth, but we all learned valuable lessons from it. Matching became more public, with no solo dates, and there was one important rule: no sexual relations.

I break the silence first. "Why do you think they changed the rules?"

Abby shrugs. I can tell she's thinking about Claire's story, too.

"It doesn't make sense, after what happened to Claire, and with the rules, that obviously hasn't happened again."

"Well, to our knowledge."

I cock my head. "Have you heard about any murders in the last couple of years?"

"I don't believe he murdered him. But, it still could have happened. Maybe half the babies and toddlers here don't know their real fathers."

That stops me short. It never occurred to me that people could still be having relations with both their matches. "Okay, that's it. I'm definitely waiting."

Abby laughs under her breath. "I'm pulling your leg, girl. Haven't you ever heard of protection?"

"Of course, but it's not like they're giving condoms out. Where would you even get them?" I throw back, my cheeks heating.

"You can get them in the infirmary," Abby says nonchalantly.

I forget how to breathe for a second. "What? You can?"

She flashes an impish grin. "Yeah. But they're for those who are matched. Ever since they changed the rules, they have a bunch of condoms down there. The council probably gave up thinking people were actually going to follow that rule, so they would rather us be safe."

"Do you have any?" I whisper. I have no idea why I'm using a hushed tone. We're alone in Abby's room, but I can't help it.

She shakes her head. "I don't have the courage," she says, giggling slightly. "You wanna come with me?"

"No," I gasp.

"Okay, well, I won't try to sway you if that's what you want." But then her bottom lip juts out. "Maybe just in case?"

"No, Abby, I'm not even going to be tempted."

"Fine," she says, leaning back and folding her arms. "You're probably right; it's best to wait until after the ceremony."

I keep myself from smiling, knowing I've won the argument. If "sheltered, inexperienced girl" had a picture next to it in the dictionary, it would be of our faces. Even though I blame this stupid place, I don't know how different we would be if this war hadn't begun. Sure, we would have dated, or at least Abby would have, while I'd have been the third wheel. We're not sisters by blood, but she's the closest thing I have to one. We've gone through all this craziness together, and we're usually both on the same page. It's nice to have similar feelings on something this important. But I won't judge her for anything she does with her matches either. We've got our own stories to tell, and it's her choice at the end of the day. I'll support her no matter what, and I know she'll do the same for me.

We end up chatting until it's time for dinner.

We eat another vegan meal—butternut squash spaghetti—and don't mention our upcoming matches again until we're about to go our separate ways.

She leans in and hugs me. "Maya, I'm so excited for you. I want to know all the details ASAP, got it?" She leans back to look me in the face, her dark brown eyes serious. "Like, as soon as you're alone again, let me know. I don't care what time it is. I'll be there."

I smile, not wanting to give anything away. Abby is too good.

"You're going to be fine. Don't be anxious, really. I know they're going to fall head over heels for you."

My smile wavers. She has no idea about the true reason I'm anxious.

"Try to get some sleep," she calls as she walks away. "Night!"

I wonder what she would think about me sneaking out after curfew with a boy.

"Goodnight, Abby," I murmur, as guilt washes over me.

9

Escapade

IT'S ALREADY CURFEW, and I have an hour to spare before I meet James. The nerves kick in as I think about sneaking out. Needing to distract myself, I dig through my desk for my worn copy of *Pride and Prejudice*.

Not too long after—having barely glanced through a couple of pages—I put it on the cushion, the spine caving in on itself. Not even Mr. Darcy can distract me tonight. I feel like I've swallowed a bowling ball.

I head for my dresser. My bright orange sweater will not cut it for sneaking out undetected. I pull on a black turtleneck and dark jeans. It's a chilly night. Layering it with my gray raincoat, I check myself in the mirror hanging off my bathroom door. I braid my hair down my back so it's out of my way and think about putting makeup on. I immediately push the idea out of my mind. That's not why I'm going tonight. I'll ask my questions, tell James about meeting my matches tomorrow, and wish him luck in his future endeavors.

I check my communicator…ten more minutes.

Shoving my feet into black boots, similar to those legionaries wear, I lace them slowly, ensuring they're nice and tight. It's been raining on and off today. I need to be prepared for slick mud.

I peer out of my window, thinking I may see him waiting, but there is only the dark obscurity of nightfall. It is reassuring nobody will be able to see me either.

Slowly, I open my door and tiptoe onto the terrace. Avoiding the creaky steps, I make my way down the staircase, squinting into the darkness and waiting for my eyes to adjust. It's a full moon tonight. The clouds drift across it, making the night feel ominous. The wind's icy fingers slide down my neck. I wrap my jacket tightly around me and head towards the trees before I change my mind.

My anxiety eases when I make it to the tree line. The scent of fresh pine and rain fills the air. I start carefully, making my way through the bushes, entangled vines, and roots jutting out.

I'm focusing on my feet, trying not to faceplant into a thorn bush, when I run into a warm body. A soft groan escapes me as I fall, but two strong hands catch me. I gasp, looking into hazel eyes.

"Oh, sorry!"

James stifles a laugh. "No worries. I was watching you as you made it through, and I assumed you would have seen me. Guess not."

"Wait, you were watching me and did nothing to help?"

He shrugs, smirking. "You were doing so well on your own."

I push past him in a huff to sit on the bench. I'm proud of myself for finding the spot in the dark. And I certainly don't need the help of a man to walk through a forest. I shouldn't even be upset.

He clears his throat. "So, you got my note." His voice is deep, husky, and smooth.

I can see his barely there silhouette under the trees, shaded from the moon. With nothing but his voice to focus on, I realize how nice it sounds, reminding me of home. The crunch of his footsteps comes closer until I feel the trunk shift underneath me.

"Yup, I guess I felt like breaking the rules again. Happy I've come to the dark side?"

He lets out a soft laugh. "I'm glad you're in a rule-breaking mood, because I've got an idea."

I have a feeling nothing good can come from his ideas. I should tell him now and get it over with. It'll help that I can't see him.

I open my mouth to break the news that I'm meeting my matches tomorrow, but he says, "Have you ever been outside the base?"

"Of course, I have," I respond indignantly.

He leans on his knees, studying me. "When was the last time?"

I avoid his gaze. I might not be able to see his eyes, but I can feel them. I don't want him to know how sheltered I've been, if he hasn't already guessed. "Four years ago, I guess. I went out a couple of times with my mom for supplies the first year, but never to any towns. We're too far from them."

"You don't know what's going on out there, huh?" His tone is bleak.

"I wouldn't say that. They tell us everything that's happening."

As the words leave my mouth, I realize I don't believe them. When my mom was first telling me about the age-limit change, she said things were heating up on the war front, but she never told me what that meant.

"But from whose viewpoint?"

That takes me by surprise. "Ours, of course."

What a weird thing to say. Even if the commanders aren't telling us *everything*, should we see the war from somebody else's perspective? The Coms, perhaps? They're the ones murdering Elementals, trying to destroy our kind.

Anger rises, so I take a deep breath to steady myself before I go off on him. "Whose else would I want it from?" I say calmly, proud of myself.

"Your own."

I nod, not knowing if I *want* to experience it firsthand. The other day, I was ready to jump in and fight, but that was the adrenaline. I'd probably just get in the way now. But I could help with proper training. Even then, though, I would never be allowed to fight. I'm not meant for that life, since learning I'm match-eligible. I am to choose a companion, procreate, and raise the next generation of stronger Elementals. It's my duty. My mom instilled in me from a young age the importance of continuing our line, but a year after we went into hiding, with so many of our own slaughtered, it became the forefront of all Elementals' minds. And now, with what my mom is trying to do, having stronger Elementals could secure our future and turn the tide of the war.

I've been quiet for a while, and I can tell James is letting me think it over. I like that he doesn't push for answers from me.

Finally, he speaks up. "Maya, do you want to go outside the wall?"

"I will eventually." I shrug.

"How about tonight?" James murmurs.

"Tonight?" I say a little too loudly and glance around in the dark.

"Yeah, I know a spot."

"Wait. Have you left since getting here? Didn't they tell you you're not allowed to?"

"Another rule," he spits, shaking his head and avoiding my question.

I keep staring at him. "Have you?" I repeat.

He waves me off. "Doesn't matter. Do you want to come or not?"

I decide not to push it. "Is it safe? Aren't the legionaries patrolling? What about the Coms?"

"Maya, do you know why this place has been undetected for so long?"

"They do know about us; that's why the legion is here," I retort, not understanding where he's going with this.

"They do, and they don't. They know we're somewhere out here but don't know the precise location. We're concealed well. And no, there aren't guards patrolling. There are cameras about a mile out, surrounding the place, that detect motion. We rotate shifts watching those." He hesitates and then adds, "Well, there've been a couple of them patrolling since the incident, but they're looking in the sky, not on the ground."

"Wait, back up, incident? You mean the drill?"

"Ha! That wasn't a drill, Maya. They don't know our precise location, but they're trying to figure it out. Every now and then, they shoot small missiles into our region, trying to draw us out. Last Thursday, they hit about ten miles out, the closest yet."

I knew it! It wasn't a drill. "Why would they lie to us?"

"It's understandable. They don't want everyone freaking out. But there's no reason to worry. They can't touch us."

"That's hard to believe. If they hit that close, you're saying, all of a sudden, they could blow us to smithereens." I straighten my spine and take a deep breath, trying to shake off the tightening in my chest.

James puts his hand on mine. The warmth of his palm calms me. "Maya, it's okay. That's exactly why they told you it was a drill…you're already starting to panic. That's why the legion is here. If anything comes at us, we've got quite a few Auras who could fling a missile halfway across the ocean. The Coms have nothing against us."

The panic dissipates. "You're right. I know you're right. Of course, Auras can do stuff like that. I'm guessing they didn't do that to the missile that hit because it would reveal our location?"

"You got it."

If they lied to us about the drill, then there must be more. "James?" I hesitate, his hand still on mine. "Do you know anything about why they're pushing us to get matched so soon?"

There's a beat of silence between us before he says slowly, "I may have overheard something."

My heart leaps.

"I don't want you to panic more though."

I try to calm my racing heart with little success. "I can take it."

He sighs. "Well, I believe they brought in new recruits because of the two Elemental communities that fell. I can only assume that's why they're speeding up the matching process as well. We could be running out of time."

Two communities fell? All those people—our people—murdered. That's why they showed us the Bunker. It's not just a precaution but a real possibility. I swallow the rising panic and stand, wanting to change the conversation, maybe even go on his escapade. His hand falls off mine, and a part of me misses the warmth.

"Let's do it," I almost beg.

He eyes me for a moment. "You can tell me what you're feeling, you know."

"No, I'm okay, I want to go." I squeeze my hands together to keep them from shaking and put on a brave front. I can handle knowing stuff like this. If I freak out, I just prove that the commanders are right for keeping it from us.

He continues to stare at me before rising to his feet. "Okay." He starts in the opposite direction from where we came, going deeper into the forest.

If we really are running out of time, I want to know what's out there. I take a few steps to follow him and quickly realize I should have brought a flashlight.

"Um, James?"

He looks over his shoulder, "Yeah?"

"You know the branches and bushes don't part for me, right?"

He chuckles and returns to my side. "Is it okay if I hold your hand? It'll be much easier and quicker for the both of us."

I waver. Hand-holding is pretty intimate, but he's guiding me through the woods, not trying to woo me. "I guess so. I'd rather not walk into a tree."

He grabs my hand and starts again, pulling me along. My hand is tiny in his grasp. An electric current pulses between us as warmth travels up my arm. I've never held a boy's hand before. It's more than pleasant.

I try not to think about it as we make our way through the trees.

The trees stretch on, becoming denser and more hazardous, but as long as I follow James, the path we walk is as simple as walking down the hall.

My feet ache, and I'm about to ask how much farther when he stops. I'm expecting a massive metal gate with barbed wire at the top, but standing before us is a wall of dark green vines that blends in with the trees and surrounding forest. I can't tell where it begins or ends.

"Lucky for us, this strip of forest in your backyard goes right up to the wall." With a wave of his hand, the vines crawl off an invisible barrier like slithering snakes, and the rest of the forest opens up before our eyes. The sound of crickets intensifies, obscuring all other noises. A dark abyss lies ahead. Anything could be out there.

"Impressive," I declare, trying to sound confident. I don't want James to think I'm scared. Though he may already know because of my sweaty palm in his hand. I'm protected as long as I stay on the base, but out there, it's just me and the unknown.

I take a deep breath, trying to calm my nerves, but it doesn't help. I bite my lip. I've walked all the way here, but I'm too chicken to take one more step. Oh man, what is James going to think of me?

He's waiting for me to make the first move and walk through, but I can't. I'm not ready.

"James, I–I'm sorry," I stammer, feeling defeated. I let go of his hand.

He studies me for a moment before saying, "That's okay, I can show you another time. It would be better in the light anyway."

Relief flows through me. He's not making fun of me.

Wait, did he say another time? Then I remember the thing I need to tell him. I can't believe I forgot, swallowed up by the moment.

"Actually, there's something I need to—"

Before I can finish my sentence, a hand covers my mouth, and my back slams into James's chest.

His lips are at my ear. "Shh, don't freak out, but somebody is coming."

His breath on my neck creates goosebumps on my skin that have nothing to do with the cold, and then I hear it. The quiet crunching of footsteps approaching from our left, right along the wall. I'm whisked off my feet, and before I can even blink, I'm on the other side of the wall, and the vines are slithering closed behind us.

He releases my mouth and grabs my hand again. I look at him frantically.

Barely visible in the dim moonlight, I see him mouth, *Sorry,* as he guides me deeper into the woods, where he pulls us behind a tree. I'm back up against his chest, but this time, we're face to face, or more like, my face to his neck. A branch cuts into my thigh. I bite my tongue hard, trying not to move or make a noise, and I taste blood. Straining my ears, I focus on what I can hear instead of the pain.

There is muffled talking on the other side of the wall. Definitely a male voice. "I thought I heard somebody," he says.

"Should we check the other side?" Two male voices.

James presses me harder into his chest. The branch cuts my skin as it comes free. I try to breathe in short bursts through the sudden pain. His heartbeat pounds through my body. Or maybe it's mine, our hearts beating as one. Every part of me is touching every part of him. With the heat of our bodies and this stupid turtleneck, sweat trickles down my neck.

Bushes and branches from the tree encircle us, camouflaging our bodies. All I smell is James, my face is buried in the soft fabric at his shoulder. He has an earthy sweet scent, as if I'm lounging in a field after a light rain. Being in his arms makes me feel almost as safe as being in my bedroom within the walls of the manor.

I don't know what to do with that revelation.

My initial fright of nearly being found out slowly wears off. Yet, the men are still out there. Any second, we could be caught. James would be worse off than me. He would immediately be kicked out, having zero connections here. He'd go back to fending for himself on the streets, Coms trying to kill him. I can't let that happen. I don't know what this relationship is—can I even call it friendship?—but I don't want him hurt.

The minutes tick by. I don't know how long we've been standing in this position. It could have been ten minutes or an hour.

James finally loosens his hold, and I slowly lean back. To my surprise, he's smiling.

"Well, that was close," he whispers.

I let out the shaky breath I've been holding for too long. "How do you know they're gone?"

He reaches out and pats the tree like it's a good friend. "The trees tell me."

That's new. "You can hear the trees talk?"

"No, not like you're thinking. It's more of a feeling. Trees are living things and communicate, like sending messages to their roots to absorb water or telling the leaves when it's time to fall."

He runs a hand through his messy hair. Leaves are sticking out of it, and I bite my lip, trying not to laugh, but it doesn't stop my smile. He looks like a real mountain man out here.

"It's hard to explain," he says, turning back to me. "What?"

I shake my head. "Nothing, you just seem…in your element out here."

Being in nature must feel to him as it does when I'm swimming, like it's where I'm meant to be. Still, the water doesn't talk to me.

"And you've got…some leaves in your hair." I take them out myself, since I'm still so close.

"Hey, I like that look." He gives me a goofy smile. "I think I like the look on you even better, though."

I cringe as my hands fly to my hair. Great. My hair is an actual bird's nest. I try to pull them out but give up. The twigs are knotted in there. It's hopeless.

"Here, let me." He expertly combs his fingers through my hair and a shiver runs up my spine. I'm twig-free in no time.

"Thanks," I say.

His stunning smile lights up the space, momentarily dazing me. The same sensation I felt a few days ago of wanting to draw closer to him creeps in. Like our bodies smashed together for who knows how long wasn't enough. But it's different now. There's no danger, and I *still* want to be near him.

My eyes travel to his lips, pink and perfect. Oh no, not again.

I take two steps back and almost trip over a log. He reaches out to help.

"No! No, I'm good," I say as I regain my footing. The last thing I need is for him to touch me again.

My legs are wobbly, and my arms stiff from being in the same position for so long…at least that's what I'm blaming it on. Not that my heart is beating too fast for no apparent reason. I stretch a little, trying to shake off the curious feelings stirring inside.

"Whelp, you got me out here. Are you going to tie me up and cart me off somewhere?" I chuckle.

He raises an eyebrow. "Is that what you want?"

I gulp. "We should probably get back."

He steps closer, looking at me with a mischievous smile on his lips. I know he's seeking a response, and even though my instincts tell me to run, I stand my ground, not wanting to give him the reaction he wants. I even tilt my chin up. *Bring it.*

He tackles me to the ground so quickly I don't see him move. One moment, he's standing a few feet in front of me with his head angled and a sly smile on his lips and the next his arms are delicately wrapped around my waist.

As I fall, I blast water from my fingertips, absorbing the moisture from the air and trees around me, directing it all to him. I land gracefully in a pile of leaves.

His landing is less graceful on the hard ground next to me. I can't help but think that's what he initially planned, never allowing me to get hurt.

James is in shock when he sits up, completely soaked.

I burst out laughing at his expression, and then quickly cover my mouth, looking around.

He shakes his head like a wet dog, water droplets from his hair splattering me on the face. "Don't worry, those guys are long gone."

He rises in one fluid movement and offers me a hand. I take it and stand, still giggling at him.

"We should be getting back before I freeze to death," he grumbles.

I point at him. "You deserved that."

"Got it. Tackling a Lympha is like tackling a sponge."

I smile. "Give me a sec." Closing my eyes, I let my mind attune to my surroundings. I breathe in and out slowly, searching for the closest water source. Once I feel it, I hear it, a stream about a hundred yards in front of us. My eyes open to James, eyeing me. "I was looking for water. I can't walk all the way back without a drink now."

He rolls up the bottom of his sweater and wrings it out. "You can have some of mine, if you want."

I walk past him, and he flicks more water on me like a five-year-old. Most people would hate it, but with how parched my body is after that hike, I'll take anything that lands on my skin. It soaks it right up.

I start walking, knowing exactly where to go, but I pause after a few steps. "Are there bears out here?"

He nods. "And mountain lions," he whispers, delighted.

Of course, a *Terra* would love it if we came upon an animal, a new friend.

I trudge forward, deciding not to ask for his help to part the way. I can do this on my own. I slow as we get into the thicker brush, my leg throbbing where I cut it. The pain increases as my adrenaline decreases. If I can just hold out until we get to the water, I can heal myself.

It's not as scary outside the walls as I thought. It's just more trees. I don't know what I was afraid of. The increased sounds of wildlife are a bit disconcerting, but they're also kind of soothing. This is home for many, not some scary unknown place where Coms are waiting to attack at every turn. James had said there were cameras a mile out anyway. We're safe.

The bubbling sounds of a creek get closer, and I hop over bushes instead of going around them. When I reach the water's edge, I fall to my knees, ignoring the pain of the tiny rocks digging into them. I take a handful of water and scoop it into my mouth, repeating the process until I've had my fill.

Sitting back on my heels, I wipe the water off my chin with my sleeve, then shift my weight so I can sit and roll up my pant leg. There's blood, dark brown, caked onto my calf. A lot of blood. I keep rolling, but I can't get high enough to uncover the wound.

I search for James, who's sitting on a rock looking downstream. I can really see him for the first time since entering the woods, encased in the moonlight. His wet hair glistens as it falls around his face in beautiful dark ringlets. His face is the perfect profile, with a nicely curved nose and plump lips. He's taken off his coat, and his biceps are stretching his shirt sleeve.

My gaze travels the length of his arm and comes to rest on his interlaced hands. I know the feel of those hands now. Rough and strong but delicate.

I look back up at his face, and he's staring back. I drop my eyes, grateful he can't see me blushing in the dark.

I'm momentarily dazed. What was I doing?

"Maya, are you alright?" James calls.

Right, my wound.

"Yeah! I just need you to turn around for a moment. I need some privacy."

He scrunches his nose.

Ugh, I'm going to have to explain myself. "I need to take off my pants to heal myself."

He immediately rises to join me, which is the opposite of giving me privacy.

"You're hurt? Why didn't you say anything?" His eyes travel over my body, resting on my blood-encrusted leg. "Whoa, Maya, when did that happen?" He bends down, his hands hovering over my leg, clearly wanting to help but unsure what to do.

"I'm fine. It happened when we were hiding. There was a branch. I'm going to heal myself real quick, and I'll be good to go." I gesture toward the water.

His eyes flash to the stream, back at me, and then at my leg. He purses his lips, but nods, eyeing me. "I'll be over here if you need anything." He walks back to his rock.

I watch him for a minute until he's settled onto it, his back to me.

I wait another moment to ensure he's not trying to sneak a peek, then I kick off my boots and quickly strip off my pants. I wince. The cut is more extensive than I expected. It's a couple inches across, and still pulsing out blood. My vision clouds.

Scooping water into my palms, I pour it onto my thigh. The cut sizzles, pain shooting down my leg. "Ow!" The bleeding at least stops.

"Are you okay? You sure you don't need my help?" He starts twisting in his seat.

"No! Don't turn around. Almost done."

It will take forever scooping the water on. I'll have to get in.

I wade into the stream, but it's not deep enough. I kneel until my thigh is in the water. I choke back a cry from the pain, shoving a fist in my mouth. But the pain recedes after a few moments.

When the cut is just a small scratch, I climb out of the water and try to pull my pants on. My wet legs stick to the insides. James is still facing the trees, so I close my eyes, focusing on the water droplets around my legs. I push them away, and the water wicks off.

I quickly pull my pants and boots back on and join him. "Thanks, all better!"

He regards me for a moment. "You sure you're okay?"

"Yup, after you."

As I follow him back to the wall, exhaustion hits me. I know healing takes quite a bit of energy, but I've never felt this drained before. I don't know if it's from the blood loss, all the cardio, the adrenaline wearing off, or staying up so late—or maybe a mixture of everything—but by the time we make it to the wall, I'm ready to collapse.

I look at my watch for the first time; it's almost one in the morning. I can't believe so much time has passed. I remember Abby telling me to get a good night's sleep and grimace. She would not believe I did something like this.

James glances my way a few times before finally saying, "You look pale, Maya."

"Just tired." I yawn to help the effect of my statement.

"I can carry you back if you want."

That sends me out of my stupor. "I can walk!" I retort, becoming more alert. I push myself forward, past the vines, not even remembering him parting them. Jeez, I *must* be out of it.

I let him retake my hand to guide us back through the caliginous woods before us. I trip about ten times before agreeing to let him slide his arm behind my back to take some of my weight.

My eyelids get heavier, though, and soon, I lose my balance completely.

He scoops me into his arms. I weakly try arguing, but since I can't keep my eyes open, I finally concede to him. He's warm, even though his T-shirt is still damp. I should tell him I can pull the moisture out of it, but I don't have the energy to speak up.

So, instead, I focus on lifting the water particles as I go in and out of consciousness. After a while, it seems dryer. My face isn't as wet lying against his chest. It's hard to fight against his rhythmic footsteps rocking me to sleep, and the last thing I remember is his woodsy scent before drifting off.

10

Mister tall, dark, and Handsome

I WAKE IN THE MORNING, keeping my eyes closed to dwell upon my dream. It was so vivid, and James was there. It can't be a good sign I'm dreaming about him.

I shift in my bed, and my thigh aches. Wait, didn't I cut my leg in the dream?

Ripping the blanket off, I sit straight up, the grogginess gone. I'm still in my dark clothes, my pant leg ripped to mid-thigh, but my shoes are off, at least. I gasp. It wasn't a dream.

I fall against my pillow, pushing my palms into my eyes. I don't remember getting home. He must have carried me all the way back and tucked me in.

I jump out of bed, half expecting to find him sleeping on the couch at the end of my bed. But there's no sign of him.

I pace in front of my couch. I didn't even tell him I'm getting matched tomorrow…well, today. This cannot be happening. I pretty much broke all the rules last night. I can't believe he carried me to my bed! What if he was seen? No, somebody would be here already. Still, I crack my door to peer down my hallway. It's clear.

I chew on my finger. Worrying isn't going to help. What's done is done. The best thing I can do is push James out of my mind for right now.

I'm getting matched today. Today, I'm meeting the man I'll be bonded to for the rest of my life.

Butterflies dive-bomb my stomach as I check the time. How is it already ten o'clock? I never sleep in. I have my usual training session, but other than that, my day is wide open to prepare for meeting my matches. I rub my face, and my hand comes away with brown smears on it. I cringe, feeling the caked-on sweat and dirt on my body from my trek through the woods. A shower would be an excellent place to start.

Shortly after, I'm on my way to meet Seth, feeling like a new person. I asked Seth after the "drill" if he could teach me water combat skills, and even though he agreed, there was one condition: I had to master the water transfer first. Saturday, I'd successfully completed one with me *and* Seth inside. It had been surreal to walk on the lake's bed in a giant bubble, with the fish swimming around us.

I arrive at my training spot, but Seth isn't here yet. There's no sign of him up or down the rocky area. Strange, I'd never been earlier than Seth before.

I double-check the time on my watch. It's precisely eleven o'clock. I circle, expecting him to appear out of thin air. We all have those days. I'll give him a few minutes before trying my communicator.

Setting my sandals on a rock, I head for the water to dip my feet in. My eyes slide closed as I tune into my Sage. If I'm going to practice combat skills today, I'll need all the energy I can get from the earth. Just feel, don't think. I count my breaths, focusing on the sounds of the water: the gentle lapping on the rocks, the tiny bubbles bursting on the surface from the fish and amphibians beneath. I listen more intently, trying to find the furthest thing I can hear. The wind ripples the water, and then there are footsteps coming my way, but not just one pair, two.

I open my eyes and swing around. Seth is coming down the slope to the lake with another man.

Not any normal man, but a dark-skinned *model*, looking like he just completed a photo shoot for one of those romance novels my mom used to read. He's wearing a black, short-sleeved, tight shirt with dark pants. Mister Tall, Dark, and Handsome reeks of confidence as he strolls down with a hand in one pocket, looking like he belongs on a runway.

He notices me admiring him and flashes a dazzling smile, two rows of perfect, pearly white teeth. My mind blanks, and I can't remove my eyes from studying his flawless face as he closes the distance between us.

"I'm sorry I'm late. I was looking for a volunteer to help us out this morning. Maya, this is Sebastian." Seth introduces the stunning man by his side with a simple hand gesture.

Sebastian holds out a hand, and I stare at it in a daze. It's connected to a very muscular arm. Much more of this, and I might start to drool.

"Yes," I squeak, before clearing my throat and trying again. "Hi! I'm Maya."

Ugh, Seth already told him that.

I finally take his hand and shake it. His hand is hot to the touch, but not in a painful way, like when you drink hot tea, and it burns slightly as it goes down, warming your body to your toes. I let go and regret it.

"I'm Sebastian." His voice is husky and deep.

His eyes are a piercing deep blue—the color of the ocean on a sunny day. I could swim in them. His face is clean-shaven, and his dark hair is short, but tiny ringlets are trying to break out of the uniform shape.

It takes every ounce of strength to break eye contact and look at Seth. "So why did you need a volunteer?" I say, surprised I didn't stutter.

"You still want to learn water combat?" Seth asks.

I nod eagerly but still wonder why that requires a volunteer.

"Sebastian here is a fire Elemental."

That piques my interest. One of my matches is an Igna. Could I be so lucky? No way, I would never be matched with a man as gorgeous as him. My eyes flick back to his. I've never seen an Igna with blue eyes.

Seth continues. "The best way to teach water combat is to show you. Since you won't ever be fighting, you need to learn basic self-defense moves. Ignas can copy Coms' weapons pretty closely."

I nod, trying not to let my disappointment show. It sucks I can't learn legitimate combat skills, but self-defense is better than nothing.

Seth looks over to Sebastian. "Ready?"

Sebastian nods and clasps his hands together, making a ball with them. I have a flashback of making snowballs as a kid, shaping them the same way with my hands. But once he opens his hands, it's not snow inside, but tiny little fireballs. About five of them are floating above his palm.

I gasp as he shoots them one by one at Seth, who had moved to stand farther away, ready. He'd created a wall of water a couple of inches thick, levitating in front of him, as a shield. The red fireballs sizzle as they hit the wall.

Sebastian throws each consecutive fireball harder. They sink into the water before completely extinguishing.

Seth drops the shield and turns to face me. "That one, you can probably tell, was a water shield." He waves his hand, beckoning me forward.

I join him, steadying myself on the rocks.

"This is simple water manipulation. Bring the water in front of you so it covers your whole body. The water will stop any size fireball without a problem, so it doesn't need to be very thick. But bullets will go further into the water. I want you to create a shield about three feet thick, which should be plenty to slow any bullet."

I feel Sebastian's eyes on me, but I try not to let my self-consciousness distract me. This should be easy.

I reach out with my mind and grab the water, forcing it into the air, and bring more and more water to join it until I have what I think is enough. I guide it with my hands in front of me and shape it in my mind into a thick wall. The water obeys.

"Good, now hold it there. Sebastian! Go ahead," Seth yells.

The wall ripples in front of me, and only a faint outline of Sebastian is visible. My nerves spike, thinking about a bunch of fireballs hurtling my way, and my water shield quivers.

"Hold it," Seth instructs.

Something strikes me, but without pain. It hits again and still no pain. By the third time, I realize the fire balls are hitting the shield.

"It's working!"

It hits twice more before Seth declares, "You can release the shield now."

I do what he says, but instead of releasing it where it was—doing so would soak me—I toss it towards the lake with a huge splash. The ensuing waves run over my feet. Sebastian claps for me. A huge stupid grin spreads on my face.

"Okay, now you need to practice doing it faster. If you were facing an enemy in real life, they wouldn't stand there and wait for you to put up your shield. This time, I want you to do it instantly. It's okay if it's not as big, but at least aim for it to protect your major organs."

I do what he instructs, but it takes multiple attempts before I get it into the correct position. On the first try, I slam myself with the water and fall onto the rocks, scraping my elbow. The pain is short-lived, because Sebastian runs over to help me up valiantly. His touch instantly dulls the pain.

On the second try, I accidentally smash it into Seth standing next to me, but he keeps his footing better than I did. The expression on his face is comical as he dries himself.

Third try, I manage to get it in front of me. From the corner of my eye, I notice Sebastian flinch, a chip in his perfect armor. Ignas don't like water. This is another reason I can't believe I could be compatible with one.

"A shield is a wonderful tool, but it's not always the best one," Seth tells me, "especially if the enemy is close. You might have noticed you can't see very well through it. In that case, you could do a couple of things: one is a water hold. You know the feeling when you try to run in the water?"

I nod, understanding where he's going with this.

"You're going to immerse whatever you need to slow inside the water, whether that's their feet, to keep them from running toward you, or a weapon in their hands that you don't want them to use." Seth finishes and turns to Sebastian, who's been patiently waiting for further instruction with his hands behind his back. "Sebastian, come at me."

Sebastian barrels toward Seth, face set in determination. He gets two long strides in before slowing down. His feet are still moving but are now encapsulated in water. The rest of his body strains against the pressure. He gets half a step when his hands start glowing red, but before he can do anything, water surrounds them too.

A crease forms on Sebastian's brow before Seth releases him. Sebastian wipes his hands off on the bottom of his shirt as Seth says, "Thanks for being a good sport, Sebastian. I know that must have been uncomfortable for you. You can go now."

"It was nothing. I'm glad I can help." He bows his head to me. "It was so nice to meet you, Maya." Then he flashes me another dazzling smile that makes my heart skip a beat, and my legs turn into Jell-O.

How can there be this many good-looking men in the legion? First James, and now this man. I can't compare the two, though. They are completely different when it comes to looks. I try to remind myself I'm getting matched today and shouldn't be thinking about other men in this way, but it doesn't stop me from studying his broad shoulders and muscled back as he walks away.

"It was nice meeting you too," I say, lamely now that he's out of earshot.

Seth clears his throat, and I immediately turn back, remembering I'm in the middle of a training session. Embarrassment heats my cheeks, but Seth doesn't mention it.

"Okay, now I want you to try it on me."

The rest of the training continues in the same fashion, but it's not nearly as exciting with Sebastian missing. At the end of the hour, I master water shields, water holds, and even water slings—

using the water to chuck big rocks or tree limbs at a person. The only one I didn't complete successfully was a water grab. Tiny stones hit me repeatedly, only entrapping one with my water sphere by the end of it.

AFTER LUNCH, I RETURN to my room with one thing to do: prepare myself for the most significant moment in my eighteen years of life. The pressure closes in as I fling clothes out of my drawers. I don't have many choices. I have two dresses I wear to the ceremonies held every few months. My heart flutters. *My* ceremony may very well be next. One dress is a pink-and-white floral day dress with ruffle sleeves, and the other is baby blue with spaghetti straps. Neither says, *Hey there, I'm your future mate, fall in love with me*. I want to be beautiful. I want them to see me and feel like the luckiest guys in the world. I sigh. A pair of blue jeans it is.

As I survey my folded shirts, an idea hits me. I could raid my mom's closet. I've never had much desire to wear her clothes, or reason to, until now.

I open my door, determined to find date-appropriate attire and see a stack of boxes with legs and familiar hair.

"Mom!" I shout as I jump back. Only the top of her forehead is visible, with her bangs bobbing on the boxes stacked in her arms. "What are you doing?"

"Oh, thank goodness, Maya, I was trying to figure out how to open your door."

I take half of the boxes and lead her back to my room. She continues past me and places her stack on my coffee table. I follow her lead.

"What are these?" I scan the boxes teetering dangerously close to the edge of the small table in front of my couch.

"These are some new clothes."

"Wait, really?"

Her eyes light up as she nods.

"How?" Did the scouts risk going into Portland? Everything else had been destroyed, unless the Coms had rebuilt.

Flashes of our torn-up town fill my mind. It was dark when we left, but I was able to make out the shops and homes of Elementals, all in pieces. My mom didn't want me to look, but it's where I grew up. How could I *not* look?

I shake my head, expelling the memories. I haven't heard about the town being rebuilt, but then again, I'm not told much.

"There are towns," is all she says. She moves to open the top box.

"Towns? But isn't that dangerous?"

"It's nothing you need to worry about. Come on, try these on."

I want to ask more questions, but something colorful catches my eye. I'm so tired of hand-me-downs and homemade clothes.

I step closer as she pulls out a pink silk dress. I touch the fabric in awe. It slides between my fingers effortlessly.

"Right?" My mom smiles wide.

"I was about to raid your closet, you know."

"You wouldn't want any of my old women's clothes. Those will not win over any men."

I roll my eyes. "You're not old. Hey, you should wear some of these. Get back out there. You're only forty-five, Mom."

She snorts. "Maya, my childbearing years are long over. No need for that."

"You know there are more reasons to be with a man than to have children, like companionship, for example?"

She rolls her eyes and pulls out more garments. There are dresses, crop tops, skinny jeans, shorts, midi skirts, and even lingerie. My excitement turns into dread.

Mom notices me examining the lingerie and takes my hands in hers. "Pick out what you would feel confident in, and remember most of this will be worn in private. Have fun with it. I need to go now, but this—" she reaches into the pile and pulls out a solid, light green, long-sleeve dress with a slit that would hit me mid-thigh, "—would really bring out your eyes. And invite Abby over. She can pick out some things, too, then pass them on to the other girls." She stands and kisses my head. "I can't wait to hear all about it. I love you."

As I peer into her eyes, James's words return to me: *we're running out of time*. I want to ask her about it, but there's no way I could voice it without giving myself away. She doesn't seem frightened or worried, so maybe he was just being dramatic. I push it to the back of my mind. All I can do is give it my all to choose a match and fulfill my duty.

"I love you, too, and thanks. I'll definitely share. Some of this stuff is more their style anyway." I think about Amanda, who chooses to wear clothes much too small for her, leaving very little to the imagination.

Mom leaves, and I turn back to the boxes. *Well, this was unexpected.* I inspect the clothes and set some aside that I like. Trying to have an open mind, I grab some more scanty clothing articles. I'm sure there will come a time when I'll want to wear these.

A black dress catches my eye, so I take it to the mirror. It's sleeveless, tight in the bodice and waist, and flares out, coming to rest above the knee. I try it on, and it fits perfectly. This is the one. Don't want to show too much skin for a first meeting, but I do want them to think I'm beautiful and sexy.

In the bathroom, I take a brush to my hair, trying to tame the frizz. Remembering some product my mom gave me a while back, I let the spray bring out my natural curls. I don't have tight curls like Abby's, but more of a wave. I braid my grown-out bangs behind my ear, then coat my eyelashes with mascara.

I flutter them flirtatiously. "Hello, boys," I say seductively in the mirror. Or maybe "Hi, how's it going?" I shake my head. I have no idea what I'm doing.

The knot in my stomach grows. Too nervous to grab dinner, I force down some stale crackers from my drawer and chug some water.

I clean my room again. Once it's practically sparkling, I sit on my couch to stare at my door, glancing at my communicator for the hundredth time. Twenty more minutes and they'll be knocking.

I fidget with my hair. Should I have it draped forward or maybe behind my ears? I need to pee again.

After going to the bathroom for the third time and brushing my teeth twice, I go outside for air. I'm suddenly very grateful for my own space. How awkward would this meeting be with my little brother and mom in our tiny living room? I smile, imagining what Cal would do. Probably talk their ears off. I wouldn't even get a word in. It's quieter these days without him, but it won't be for long once I choose my match and start having my own children. My breath catches in my throat. Am I really ready for that?

I stand on my balcony in the fading sun. Twilight is my favorite part of the day, watching as the sky turns a beautiful violet-blue, the sun's rays piercing the brilliant pink clouds dotting the horizon. Nature is still, as if even the birds are watching the sun descend over the mountains. Then the breeze picks up, and I breathe in the smell of pine trees and blooming flowers. Birds start up their final songs. The shadows reach me as the light fades, and a chill runs up my legs, driving me back inside.

As I close my back door, a faint knock echoes through my room. My heart speeds off.

They're here.

11

Suitors

I SLOWLY WALK TO THE DOOR, counting my breaths, and fixing my hair. I open it to find a handsome man standing before me, with gray eyes and tousled dirty-blond hair that makes just getting out of bed look sexy. High cheekbones outline his face and there's a dimple at the bottom of his chin. His eyes rake over my body as I fight my blush.

Wait a minute, isn't he the one—

He flashes me a huge smile. "It's you!" he says, in that unforgettable British accent.

My stomach drops, just like it did when I fell out of the window and he used his abilities to gently lower me into James's arms. He's not in uniform as before but a tight white V-neck, which shows off his lean, muscular body.

"Um." This cannot be happening.

"Hi, Maya," comes a deep voice next to him.

His companion has dark skin, muscles rippling down his arms, and hands relaxed at his side. He's wearing a light blue collared shirt and dark jeans. My eyes travel to his face and heat flows in my veins. Sebastian. Recognition shows in his blazing blue eyes, and his face lights up.

My heart takes off. I'm matched with *him*? That can't be. He's too…beautiful for me.

But the Aura can, indeed, hold his own.

If anything, they're polar opposites when it comes to looks. The only thing similar about them is their height. My eyes bob back and forth between them, taking it all in, but realizing I should say something more coherent.

"Hi."

The blue-eyed model holds out his hand. "I'm Sebastian." He must not want to let the other man know he's already met me. Little does he know, I've met them both.

I stare at them for a second longer before a wave of confidence washes over me. "Oh, let's not be so formal. Come in already." I grab his hand and pull him through the entrance.

The other man follows. "Well, this is quite the surprise."

I spin quickly and stare at him. He stops with his mouth ajar and eyes trained on me. I don't think I'll ever get over that accent.

Sebastian elbows him in the ribs when he doesn't continue speaking. "What's a surprise?"

"Oh…oh, yes," he stammers out. "The fact that the adorable woman I saved from falling to her death is my match."

I suck in a breath as Sebastian looks at him oddly and then turns to me with a smile. "I remember."

"You were there too?" Heat fills my cheeks.

"How could anyone have missed it?" The British guy chuckles.

"Lovely," I grumble to myself. "What's your name?" I ask, trying to redirect the conversation.

"Oh, I'm sorry. I'm William. I transferred here from London."

"Thank you, William, for saving me."

He nods. "My pleasure."

Sebastian shifts on his feet. "Well, you're not the only one to have met her. I got the chance to train with Maya this morning."

William raises his eyebrows at Sebastian. They share a look before turning back to me.

"Yeah." I bite my lip and rock back on my heels. "Definitely didn't know you were my match. Obviously, Seth didn't either."

Sebastian shrugs and smiles as William says, "Bloody hell. We are quite the lucky pair."

I giggle. "I love your accent by the way."

He smiles wide.

"Well, this is my place," I say, waving my hand around the room. Tired of standing, I sit on the couch and wave for them to do the same.

There is a sudden heaviness in the air, and I come to the horrible realization that they may have been told to speed up the matching process. Which means they could be expecting more from me. My heart beats irregularly.

Sebastian clears his throat. "It's nice."

They are still looking at me awkwardly. What are they waiting for? A giggle escapes. Oh no. I keep giggling and feel like an idiot. *Stop laughing, stop laughing,* I tell myself, but the giggling gets louder. The men smile, probably thinking they're matched to a lunatic.

William strides over and sits next to me.

I clamp my mouth shut. "Sorry, I don't know what came over me. This is all just too weird."

They both exhale like they've been holding it in since they entered the room.

William says, "I know, right?"

Sebastian steps towards us. "We can take things slow. Let's start with getting to know each other. William is right. Lucky for us, we got the initial meeting out of the way."

The tension breaks in the room. Maybe they don't know, or they really are good guys, like my mom said.

"Sounds like a plan." I sigh.

The rest of the night is spent talking. Sebastian makes himself comfortable at the end of my bed. I tell them parts of my story. I learn they're both nineteen. Sebastian's fire abilities still concern me, but his calm demeanor is comforting. And I'm ecstatic William is nothing like Commander Lawrence, the only other Aura I know. The men are best friends, which shocks me; usually, the two matches don't know each other. I doubt my mom knew.

Sebastian met William in Europe while stationed there but transferred here a year ago. It's hard for the guys in this not to get jealous, and I hope their friendship will help, but what if it has the opposite effect? Especially when I have to choose.

I'm listening to William's voice, not understanding a single word, but nodding in agreement when he says, "You have! Did you like it?"

"Sorry, what?"

He smiles. "You weren't listening, were you?"

"I'm sorry, I could listen to you talk all day. I guess you put me in some sort of trance." I grin.

Sebastian rolls his eyes. "Oh, you really must not have been listening, or you would be asleep instead."

William throws a pillow at him and snorts. "You're just jealous. I've heard you in the bathroom practicing a British accent."

Sebastian chucks the pillow back, hitting him hard in the side of the head. "Liar!"

I think things are about to get heated, but they both start laughing instead.

"Okay, settle down, boys. I have an idea. Would it be okay if I talked to each of you individually?"

William promptly stands. "I'm down! Umm…" He looks around.

"Let's go out on my balcony," I suggest, joining him.

I smile an apology at Sebastian.

He nods and raises a hand in understanding. "Don't worry about me. I'll just—" he glances around until he notices the copy of *Pride and Prejudice* I was reading last night on my nightstand, "—do some light reading. Oh, a classic."

I eye him. "You like historical romance?"

He considers the book, opening to the first page. "I'm up for anything." He grins, making my heart skip a beat.

William follows my lead and closes the door behind us, leaving Sebastian to his light reading. I don't know if this is the best idea. It's not like I have an instruction manual on how to date my matches, but the more time I get with each of them, the better I can develop individual relationships.

I stride to the railing to gaze over the trees. The smooth wood is cool beneath my palms. Everything is swallowed up by the night, but I must pretend to do something. The air is filled with unseen crickets chirping and frogs croaking. The moon is obscured by clouds tonight.

William comes from behind and touches my arm. "So, what do you *really* want to know about me?"

It's hard not to flinch away from his touch. I've been told for the last five years to stay far away from boys, to push down any feelings towards them, and to definitely never act on any. So, it's understandably weird to be able to let a guy touch me and lean into it instead of away.

I turn around, and my breath catches. He's closer than I expected him to be, and in the dark, with the filtered light from the windows basking us, he looks dark and mysterious. I take a step back.

His hand slides to my wrist before dropping. "Sorry, that was a bit cheeky of me."

"No, it's not you. I'm new to this. I'll warm up quickly, I promise. So, why did you transfer here?"

William moves to lean against the railing next to me. "Once the war started in the US, it didn't take long to reach the UK. My family stayed close to London, waiting for the chance to return to our flat, but after all these years, my parents wanted me to move forward with my life instead of dwelling on the past. I remembered my good mate Sebastian, who told me about this place, and the rest is history."

"I understand that feeling of hope we'll return home one day. It's a day's drive to the town where I grew up, but you know, I think I'd rather keep the memories of how it was than see what it's become."

"You're bloody correct with that assumption. You know, I snuck back into the city once, and there's so much hate for our kind, it's unbelievable…all of our homes and buildings destroyed or vandalized." He shakes his head, perhaps trying to shake off the memory.

I didn't mean our conversation to turn melancholy. I must be a terrible flirt. "I'm sorry you saw that. I would be crushed to see my childhood home in ruin."

He nods in response. His eyes aren't sad, though.

"What about your family? You said your parents pushed you to come here?"

"More like kicked," he says with a boyish grin. "I have two older sisters that have gotten themselves bonded. I wanted to stay and help with my little sister. She has spina bifida, paralyzed from the waist down, but boy, is she a firecracker, doesn't let anything slow her. My parents wouldn't let me, though. They said it was my turn to fly the nest."

"You truly love your family."

He nods, smiling. "I do."

"Three sisters, huh?"

One side of his mouth twists up. "They used to doll me up. It was rather embarrassing."

I laugh. "I always wanted sisters. I have a little brother."

"Hmm, and I always wanted a brother. Wanna trade?" he says with a wink.

I laugh. "It's nice to hear about a family still intact."

"I know it's rare not to have lost somebody at this point. For some one-off reason, it makes me feel guilty."

"I'm happy for you. I understand how you feel, though. Survivor's guilt is real." I glance up, and he's watching me. I cast my eyes down and wiggle my toes. They're starting to numb.

"You're very beautiful, and I'm working hard to be a gentleman right now and not touch you."

I smile timidly. Maybe I should give this flirting thing a shot. "I am cold."

"Bollocks, this would be the perfect moment to take off my jacket and offer it to you, but I was a twat and didn't wear one today. Do you mind?" he asks, reaching out his arms.

I shake my head and carefully step into them. He wraps his arms around me and rubs my arm in soothing circular motions. At first, it's a little uncomfortable, but he's warm, and I lean against him. He smells of honey and tea.

"Why did you decide to be matched, if you don't mind me asking?" Unlike women, who have to undergo testing for match eligibility, men get a choice to be tested. It's not a sure thing for them. The woman might not choose them.

He arches a brow. "The truth?"

I scan his eyes. "Always."

"I didn't originally want to be matched. I thought the idea was a bit loony. Dating can be awkward enough, and then throw in another mate." He laughs.

"So, you've dated before?" I bite my lip. I am so out of my element here.

"Oh, sure. But nothing serious, of course. My parents had always been insistent on this path for me."

My heart drops a little. Is this even his choice?

He continues. "Sebastian talked me into it, but in no way did either of us expect to be matched to the same woman. A gorgeous one, I might add."

I smile at the compliment. He slowly slides his hand down my arm and interlaces his fingers in mine, giving me every opportunity to pull back, but I don't. Then he turns me to face him. He places his left hand on the other side of mine, gently holding it in both hands.

"After meeting you tonight, my doubts have been squandered. I'm all in, Maya Mayfield." His gray eyes hold mine, and I know he means it. My heart warms at the declaration. He likes me.

"Can I show you something?" he asks.

"Only if you answer one more question."

He pretends to think it over, squinting his eyes. "Okay."

"Are there real towns out there?" I can't stop imagining the bombed streets and shops.

"Certainly. It's not as depressing as you might think."

So, they *have* rebuilt. I wonder if my mom would let me go out if I asked. Would my town look whole again? What if it's less hostile out there? But then I remember what James told me about the Coms bombing us and shudder. Definitely not less hostile.

I open my mouth to ask another question, when he puts up a finger.

"My turn. Give me your other hand."

I sigh and do what he asks. He takes both in his soft hands and closes his eyes. A light shines through our fingertips. I suck in a breath. He opens my palms, and the brightness changes color. Slowly, it forms into a ball that begins to peel back, like an orange, revealing a beautiful blooming flower made of light in my hands. It holds all the colors on the spectrum. The outer edges are violet, then indigo and blue. As the light travels over the petals, I see shades of green and orange. Then, as it nears the center, hues of pink and a brilliant red in the middle.

I can't take my eyes off it. It's the most exquisite thing I've ever seen. "It's breathtaking."

His eyes are curious, watching me. "I'm glad you like it." He gently taps the red center with his pointer finger. The colors disperse into the air, swirling higher and higher.

"Wow." I watch until they fade into the night sky. "Show me more."

He laughs. "In due time, I'll show you even more amazing things." Then he winks, making me think he isn't just talking about his abilities. "I want to know more about you. You came here five years ago?"

I nod. I'm not sure I'm ready to be too open with him. I'd much rather learn more about him and his element. But I know I need to give him something. "Yeah, that's right."

He looks at me expectantly.

"I love to dance." I blurt out, not knowing why I said that. I haven't danced in years, but I go with it. "Do you dance?"

"A little. Remember there's a lot of women in my family."

"Wanna try?"

"We don't have music."

"I guess that does pose a problem." I grin.

"You know, another mate of mine has a music player. I can ask to borrow it, and you can teach me, maybe tomorrow?"

I nod. "It's a date."

His eyes light up at the word. "Meet me in the foyer at three?"

"Okay," I say, excited by the idea of my first actual date.

"Great, well, I should let you have some time with Sebastian before we go," he says ruefully.

"Yeah." I sigh. It's a good sign I don't want my time with William to end. I'm just scratching the surface. I want to know everything.

He guides me back to the door, with my hand still in his. His hands are soft and warm, and I don't want to let go.

As I open the door, he says, "I think I'll stay out here, the fresh air feels splendid, if you don't mind."

"Of course, I'll come get you when we're done."

"Don't take too long." He brings up the right side of his mouth in a lopsided grin.

I close the door behind me and turn to Sebastian. He's spread out on my bed, reading my book, but he quickly puts it down and rises when he hears me.

"William wants to wait outside," I say as I walk towards him. Unlike my shyness at William's touch, I'm more comfortable around Sebastian. It could be because I met him earlier today or something else entirely.

Looking at his chiseled jaw and perfect face, I realize he's way out of my league. My heart drops. I might not have a choice if my match doesn't even find me attractive.

"Would you like to sit?" he asks, stepping toward the couch.

I nod and walk around the coffee table to sit on the loveseat. He hesitates as his eyes dart between the couch and the bed as if he doesn't know if he should sit so close to me.

"It's okay. I don't bite," I say, a little bothered. My fear with this process could be coming true, one of them not liking me.

"Of course not." He laughs nervously. "I just don't want to be too forward. Whatever you're comfortable with. Is it okay if I sit next to you?"

I nod, wondering where his confidence from earlier went. I underestimate his size, because I automatically fall against him as he sits—practically in his lap.

He jumps up. "Oh, I'm sorry."

I face plant into the couch, heat filling my face. I pick myself up, trying to right my dress. Hopefully, I didn't show off anything mistakenly.

"I'm fine. Let's try this again." I gently touch his arm, and we sit slowly. "There. Let's pretend that didn't happen." I laugh awkwardly.

"Agreed," he says gruffly. Once settled, he says, "You were amazing today, Maya. I'm impressed with what you can do."

"Thank you, and what you did with the fireballs was incredible."

"That was nothing. I can show you more if you want."

"I would love that." Even though I'm more hesitant in seeing his abilities than William's. William can't accidentally catch me on fire. Maybe if we were next to a body of water, just in case. "What about tomorrow? I arranged a date with William and would love to have time with you. Want to meet me tomorrow evening near my training spot?"

His lips turn up. "Yes, that would be great." Then his smile falters, and he rubs his hands together. "I need to tell you something."

I raise my eyebrows.

"I wish I'd been the one to catch you."

My heart flutters, and I bite my lip, glancing away. "I can't believe you guys saw me fall out of a window." Looking disheveled. I can't imagine what they must think of me.

He presses a finger under my chin and turns me back to him. Heat flows from the touch.

He smiles and pulls his hand away. "It was a grand entrance. Just wish I'd been closer and been the one to hold you in my arms. I haven't been able to stop thinking about that girl since, so I think it did more good than anything."

Despite my best efforts, I can't stop the heat from flowing to my cheeks and my heart from racing.

"You're not worried about being matched with a Lympha?" As soon as the question is out, I regret it.

A smile plays on his lips as he assesses me. As if he has a wonderful secret to share and doesn't know if he should tell it. "My parents are from two different groups: water and fire."

My mouth drops open. It's almost unheard of to find people from our parents' generation who bonded with a person of a different element group. "Your blue eyes!"

He nods.

That explains so much. "Wow, so you didn't know whose abilities you would have."

He shakes his head. "My father was a bit disappointed I didn't take after him, but my mom was ecstatic."

I nod, smiling. I would likely feel the same way. "Did you have a preference?"

"No, not really. Both my parents were wonderful in their element. I would have been happy either way, and that is why I have no worries about being with a Lympha. My parents did it so well." His blue eyes brighten. "Opposites attract."

My breath escapes me, and my heart goes into overdrive. "Are you saying you're attracted to me?" I laugh half-heartedly. Why did I say that?

He raises a hand to touch my cheek, but then drops it. "Maya, I think you're gorgeous. Just looking into your eyes takes my breath away."

Butterflies swirl in my stomach.

"But I believe you are also beautiful on the inside. That's what I care most about."

He doesn't hesitate to touch me this time. He grazes my cheek with his fingertips, leaving fire in their path. I breathe through the sudden desire he creates in my body. I reach up and grasp his hand, holding it there for a moment before pulling it down and holding it in my lap.

"You barely know me," I whisper, fearing any loud noises might ruin the moment.

He smiles devilishly. "You're right, but I like what I see thus far."

We stare into each other's eyes for a minute, neither wanting to move. I feel a pull towards him, wanting to get closer, but lose my nerve.

I break eye contact and admire his hand in mine, feeling the heat beat off him.

"You're so hot," I say without thinking. "I mean, uh, not physically… Well yeah, you're attractive, um, just that your skin is incredibly warm to the touch." I kick myself internally.

"I know what you mean." His lips pinch as if he's holding in a laugh. "Just part of being an Igna." His brows pull down. "Does that bother you?"

"No, not at all! I like it. You're so warm. It's like having my own personal heater next to me. I don't think I'll be cold again. Do you get cold?"

"Rarely. The temperature has to really drop to make me cold. It's quite uncomfortable, too. It feels like I always have this flame burning inside, and if I get cold or wet, the fire diminishes. The lower my body temperature is, the more difficult it is to create fire."

It's fascinating hearing about his element. "Have you ever not been able to create fire?"

"No, I've gotten cold, but not that chilled, thankfully."

"The snow must suck for you."

He laughs, a deep musical sound that makes me smile. "I wear a lot of layers."

"Where did you grow up?"

"Florida. Stayed nice and warm." He chuckles. "I'm talking too much. Tell me about yourself."

I know this is part of the whole get-to-know-you process, but my life is incredibly dull compared to theirs.

Before I can say anything, his communicator beeps loudly. William comes in a moment later, communicator in hand too.

"That's our cue!" Sebastian stands, his mouth twisting down. "Sorry to cut our night short, but we're needed."

"Is there something wrong?"

Sebastian shares a look with William, who's running a hand through his hair. "Uh."

My eyes narrow. "Would you tell me if something was happening?"

Sebastian speaks up, "I'm sorry, Maya, we can't talk about it."

I nod, feeling a little hurt, but understanding.

Sebastian holds out a hand. Not sure what he's doing, I hesitantly place my hand in his. He bows his head and kisses the back of it with a feather-like touch. That one kiss sends a lick of fire through my body. I can't imagine what an *actual* kiss would feel like.

He peers at me through his thick eyelashes. "Goodbye for now."

William strides over once Sebastian approaches the door. "Could I give you a hug?"

I smile. "Sure."

He helps me stand then wraps both arms around me and nuzzles his face into my hair. My mind returns to the woods, the last—and only—time I've been this close to a guy. A peculiar feeling spreads over me.

He releases me and says goodbye, but the words don't reach my ears. It's not quite how I felt in James's arms, but not bad. I did just meet the guy a few hours ago.

The door starts to close, and I shake off the strange sensation and rush to it. William looks over his shoulder at his sudden inability to close it, and smiles. Sebastian must feel him stop because he turns, too.

I admire the two beautiful men. I'm the luckiest girl in the world. I'll have to thank my mom for this.

William raises an eyebrow.

"Oh, I just wanted to tell you two to be safe."

Sebastian smiles. "Thank you."

William rolls his eyes.

"Goodbye, I'll see you tomorrow." I close the door, smiling ear to ear.

I LAY IN BED, not tired at all. If anything, I still have all this nervous energy pent up inside. Is it okay to go out? I gaze out the dark window. Nothing seems to be happening. If we were in danger, there would be sirens.

After contemplating for half a second, I jump out of bed, thinking about the last few hours—the way their eyes followed my every movement, the tingles in my body when they were close. Sebastian was the perfect gentleman, and William was so funny. I could listen to their banter all day.

I reach the soft grass at the end of the stairs and wiggle my toes in it. The landscape is in shadows, but soon my eyes adjust, and the moonlight, making its appearance just in time, is enough to guide me to the pond a few yards away. I come so often, there is a perfect trodden-down path. Everywhere else, the grass is tall and overgrown. The silhouettes of the trees dance in the moonlight.

My feet reach the cold water, and I graze it with my fingertips. Standing tall, bringing my hands out wide, the water in the pond rises to float midair. It continues to ascend higher until I bring my palms together and press tightly. The water explodes into a million little drops. I let go, and it falls.

Just as it's about to drench me, I raise a palm, and it stops. I twitch my fingers, guiding it back to the pond, and set it gracefully back inside without dropping a single teaspoon. I haven't done it that perfectly before. I do a little happy dance, and then it dawns on me. Could it be? Could meeting my matches today have made a difference? I know once I make the bond, my abilities will strengthen, but maybe it begins when you make the first connection. I inspect my hand, not believing it. No way. I'm in a good mood is all.

The sound of quiet clapping disturbs my thoughts. I whip my head around toward the trees. A black silhouette steps out, and my heart quickens. I twitch my fingertips, trying to remember the self-defense moves I learned, but the profile has awfully familiar curly hair.

The shadow takes another step into the moonlight.

"James!" I whisper loudly.

He's hovering on the rim of the woods, probably unsure if he should risk being out in the open with me again. I run towards him, making the decision for him.

As I get closer, he's smiling, but his eyes are guarded. I grab his hand and take him into the cover of darkness. I surprise myself with how casually I can touch him.

When we're hidden under the trees, I drop his hand. I can't forget I am a matched woman now.

"That was beautiful. I've never seen anything like it."

My ears feel hot. I didn't mean for anyone to see. "Thanks," I mutter, looking away. Only for a moment, though, before remembering. My eyes catch his. "James, what happened last night?"

"I brought you to bed." He shrugs, letting his eyes drift toward the trees.

I survey him quizzically. Something is off. "Well, yeah, that much I understand. Is something wrong?"

He shakes his head as he sits on our tree. "I tried waking you when we got to the edge, but you were completely out of it. I decided to risk it and take you to your room. Would you rather I'd left you alone in the woods to sleep?" He's uncharacteristically sharp.

"No, of course not." I join him on the bench. "James, something is wrong. What happened?"

"Nothing's wrong," he snaps and heaves himself up to stand. He paces the small clearing in front of us. Obviously, he doesn't want to talk about it.

I can't make him talk, so I change the subject. "Do I have my very own personal stalker now? This is, what, the third time you were spying on me while I was practicing? Makes one think you have a hidden agenda." I tease.

He stops his pacing to study me. His eyes soften, and the look in them makes my heart beat irregularly. He takes a step closer, eyes scanning my face. He takes another step and crouches down, cupping my face gently.

I am completely frozen, a deer caught in the headlights before its tragic death.

His face inches closer, painfully slowly, giving me every opportunity to pull away, but I can't. I'm lost in the depths of his dark eyes. They're waiting for me to react to him, but I can't move, breathe, or do anything at all.

Our lips are mere centimeters apart when he releases his hold on me and pulls away.

He slumps on the ground before me and rests his head against my knee. I stare at the same spot as if he hadn't moved, not knowing how to feel or think. Was he going to kiss me? Did he want me to kiss him?

"You look beautiful tonight," he says softly.

I don't respond, and after a minute, he touches the top of my thigh with a feather-like caress. "How's your leg?"

His touch breaks me. "It's—"

Suddenly, the sky fills with light. I incline my head, dazzled, but quickly realize what it is. That must be why the boys ran off, an alert that there might be another attack.

I glance at James. His eyes are on the sky. I'm laser-focused on his hand still on my leg, the lights only a momentary distraction from the electricity I feel from his touch.

"We need to get back now," he urges. His hand moves to my arm as he pulls me out of focus.

We race back and stop at the edge of the woods.

"You're in the clear."

I'm about to run out but stop. "Thank you for taking me back home last night. Will I see you again?" I half expect him to say no. He *should* say no. And I really shouldn't be asking him. I don't know what happened between us just now, but there's been a shift. Thinking about never seeing him again…I don't think I could do that.

He smiles, and this time, it does reach his eyes. "Of course, whenever you feel daring again, I'll be here, or even if you want to escape for a moment—" he hesitates and then adds "—or for longer. You know where to find me."

"Actually, I don't," I say with a humorless laugh, trying not to react to him subtly asking me to escape with him.

His eyes plead for me to understand something. Then he looks past my shoulder, and I follow his line of sight to my balcony. Nothing's there. I peer back at him, wondering what he's thinking.

I'm about to ask when he says, "Good luck," and then he's gone, swallowed up by the darkness.

I race across the grass and up the steps, taking them two at a time, reach my door, and slam it shut. *Good luck?* Was he talking about returning to my room safely, or…?

A chill runs up my spine…he could see my balcony. He must have seen me with William, and that's why he was acting so strange. We're getting too close if we're both feeling something we shouldn't.

My heart leaps, but I quickly squash it. It's against the rules. I have William and Sebastian now.

A light shines through my windows, lighting my room up— more air strikes. I think about William and Sebastian. I remind myself they are both skilled legionaries or they wouldn't be here. And what about James?

I fall into my bed, pulling a pillow over my face, and try to chase the worrisome thoughts away. If it were severe, they would have set off the alarms, and we'd be heading to the bunker. Who knew I would have so many guys to worry about? A week ago, I didn't even know I could be matched. A week ago, I hadn't even touched an unmatched guy.

I laugh at the craziness of it all and focus on the faces of my new suitors, the only men I should be thinking about. I think about my upcoming dates with them, maybe of being in their arms again. Peace replaces the anxiety, wrapping around me like strong, warm arms.

As I drift off to sleep, it's not Sebastian's or William's arms wrapped around my thoughts, though, but James's.

12

First Date

MY COMMUNICATOR BEEPS REPEATEDLY. I groan and ignore it. It stops, and I try to return to my dream, but it starts beeping again.

I grab the annoying device to see who's contacting me. Of course, it's Abby. She'll want to know all the details. The voice calls aren't outstanding on the thing, but they're doable.

I pick it up. "Hello," I croak.

"Maya!" comes a crackling, high-pitched voice.

"Abby, it's seven in the morning."

"I know, but you're awake, right?"

"Well, now I am."

"Okay, I'll be over in five minutes!"

"Huh?"

The line goes dead, and I roll back over. Sleep begins overtaking me when Abby barges in and jumps onto my bed. I open one of my eyes halfway and glare at her. She sits cross-legged in her zebra pajama shorts and black tank top. Her hair is in a high bun, sticking out every which way, and she's looking at me with way too much animation for the time of day.

I'm about to throw my pillow at her when she reaches from behind her back and hands me a large chocolate muffin.

My stomach growls. "Okay," I groan and sit up. Leaning against my headboard, I snatch the muffin from her. It smells heavenly.

"You didn't message me," she accuses.

I pick off a chunk and plop it in my mouth; it tastes even better than it looks. The chocolate melts on my tongue. "Abby, I'm sorry. We stayed up late talking, and I was so tired." I give her my best puppy-dog eyes.

She shakes her head and waves her hands. "Already forgiven. Just spill already."

I spend the next half hour going over every detail about my conversation with the two men. Telling her about Sebastian's bright blue eyes and William's dreamy voice.

"Maya! I cannot believe it's the same guy that saved you. It's totally meant to be. And he's British. Ah!"

"Not only that, he's funny, too." I practically swoon. "And Sebastian was the perfect gentleman. Abby, these two are really something. How will I choose?"

She squints at me until I lock eyes with her. "Maya," she says thoughtfully. "I think you'll know once you're knocking boots with them."

"Abby!" I squeal and push her back, almost shoving her off the bed. "You know I want to wait."

"Umm, after seeing the drool coming out of your mouth while talking about them…no way you can wait."

"I was not drooling! And, of course, I can." I check my mouth with my finger, just in case.

Abby rolls her eyes. "Okay, keep telling yourself that."

I doubt I will ever convince her, so I change the subject. "Just three more days for you, right?"

That works. She starts on about the new details she's learned since the last time we talked twenty-four hours ago, which isn't much.

"Don't you need to go?" Abby asks suddenly.

"Oh! My lessons start in twenty minutes!" They're earlier than usual today.

I shoot out of bed and jump in the shower without a backward glance at Abby.

"Have fun!" she shouts. I barely hear her over the running water.

I quickly wash. Moments like these are when I'm glad I'm a Lympha. Before jumping out, I start at my toes and focus on the water droplets clinging to my body and move up through my legs, up my torso, to my shoulders, and my face, expelling the water. I reach my hair and close my eyes, clearing my mind and feeling the water in each strand of hair. I breathe in and then push the water away from my body on the exhale.

I grab my shorts off the floor, stick each leg in, and hobble to my dresser. Once I'm decent, I run out into the hallway.

Not surprisingly, Seth found somebody else to stand in to help me learn defensive skills. Her name is Rachel, a Terra. She's shorter than me, but intimidating nonetheless. She has muscles rippling down her arms like I've never seen on a woman and wears her dark hair in a pixie cut. Her face is pretty, with dark brown eyes.

I bet it's hard being a woman in the legion; everyone knows that means you can't have children. I've only known a handful of girls not to be match-eligible. I wonder if she wants a family, but

I'd never dare ask such a personal question. She's happy enough helping me and definitely not taking it easy.

Another boulder hurls in my direction. I focus on grabbing and throwing it into the lake. It makes it about a foot in front of me before I encase it in water and whisk it away. That was too close.

"You're getting better," Rachel says encouragingly.

"Again." My voice is thick with determination.

This time, she picks up a small log off the ground to my left. I can feel where it's at, and I focus on sending the water to intercede its path. I miss.

I scream as it hits me squarely in the chest, flinging me backward into the water. I try to breathe in, but I can't fill my lungs. I barely register Seth and Rachel running for me.

"Are you okay?" Seth asks, helping me up.

My breathing comes in short bursts, and I hold up a finger. Finally, I'm able to draw in a breath. "Yeah, I think so." That's going to leave a bruise. I rub the spot where it hit me, wincing a little. If I want to fight, I need to be able to take some blows. "Let's do it again."

Seth eyes me. "Are you sure?"

"I'm fine."

"Rachel, lessen the speed." He grunts.

"No, I got this."

Rachel looks to Seth, and he nods. She raises her eyebrows.

Seth helps me up and I take a deep breath, removing all doubt from my mind. This time, the log comes from behind me. I can hear it before I can sense it. I make my water sphere bigger than usual, placing my foot behind me and twisting as I throw it toward the incoming log, perfectly encapsulating it, hovering about three feet away.

"Yes!" I yell and let it drop to the ground.

Rachel's smiling at me, and Seth claps once. "Good job! That's it for today." He turns towards Rachel. "Thank you for your help."

"It was nice meeting you," I call.

"Anytime," she says to Seth, smiling warmly at me before walking off.

I rush back to my room after practice, anticipation growing for my first date with William.

After much deliberation in front of the mirror, I find myself in high-rise shorts and a blue crop top. I leave my hair down and natural.

I wait for William in the large foyer of the manor. This space must have been charming once, but it's been cleared of all furniture except one lone high-backed wooden bench in the corner with a picture of a beautiful mountainous landscape above it, very similar to the one surrounding us. Somebody must have painted it looking out these very windows. Before I can give it much thought, the door opens behind me.

William's face lights up when he sees me, eyes warm and inviting. He's wearing his legionary uniform. I've always secretly wanted one. All black form-fitting pants, short-sleeve shirt, and vest with silver buckles down the middle. His golden locks are in the same disheveled style as last night.

He sees me studying his outfit. "Sorry, I didn't have time to change." He chuckles. "You look lovely. Is that normal dancing attire?"

I smile timidly and shrug. "It could be, I guess. I love the uniform."

"Thank you. Oh!" He digs into one of his pockets. "I brought this." He holds up a white rectangular MP3 player.

"That's perfect." I grab it. "I haven't seen one of these in a decade." I study the tiny silver screen and round circle for choosing a song. All markings have been rubbed off.

"And I'll be dead if I lose it."

I giggle but realize he's serious. "Maybe we should do something else then."

He shakes his head. "No way, I want to see your moves." He smiles boyishly.

"C'mon then." I nod toward the grand staircase in the middle of the foyer. As I make my way up, he joins me by my side. I lead him to the commons room. "It's not the end of the day yet, so hopefully—" I open the doors, "—it's empty."

William admires the tall bookcases that line the room. "Whoa, this is smashing, much more inviting than ours."

"Really?" That gets me thinking. "Do you think I could ever see it? I've never been to Legion Headquarters. I'm not allowed, but with you..."

"There's not much to see, but sure, how about on our next date?"

The chance of seeing anything other than these walls is too good an opportunity to pass up. I wonder if he'd take me now. But how to convince him?

I bite my lip, walk up slowly to him, and stop a few inches from his face. I peer through my eyelashes and flutter them, hopefully not resembling somebody having a stroke. "Could we go now?"

I seem to have some effect on him, because his light eyes glaze over, and his mouth opens, but nothing comes out.

I inch closer and try to put on my best innocent smile.

"Uh, um…" he stammers out. He leans into me as if I have a gravitational pull. "Yeah, sure, whatever you want." His honey-scented breath is on my face.

A tiny part of me wants to close the distance, but it's not strong enough.

"Great!" I say, casually stepping back and clasping my hands together. I start toward the doors, dance lessons forgotten, William following in haste. I have a feeling I could get him to follow me anywhere.

When we arrive, I take in the vast expanse of the legionary building. The manor, which looks like a log cabin next to the massive cube-shaped glass building, seems comical. I can see why Terras chose glass. From afar, you can hardly tell it's here, as it reflects the greenery surrounding it.

William pushes open the door, "After you, my lady." He winks.

"Thank you." I smile and walk past him.

I take in my surroundings. Where the manor is rustic and beautiful, this place is dark and brooding. Cement walls surround us. Ironically, even though the building appears to be made of windows, there isn't a single window in sight. This place could probably withstand an explosion.

"Homey."

William chuckles. "Wait until you see the rest of it."

We walk deeper inside. It's well-lit by golden sconces lining the walls. Other men walk about, not paying us any attention. But then a thought occurs to me.

"Is Sebastian around here somewhere?"

"Don't worry, we won't run into him. He's out patrolling today."

I nod, feeling a little relieved and also bummed.

We continue to wander the halls, everything looking exactly the same. "Do you ever get lost in here?"

He chuckles. "For the first couple of days, I did. It's a maze. Every door I opened was a bathroom. Met lots of people that way."

I giggle, then he grabs my hand and pulls me through a charcoal door.

"Here we go, our glamorous commons room."

It seems more like a gym, with weights surrounding the walls, and pads in one corner. There's even a boxing dummy. They do have a pool table, though. I wonder who thought a pool table would suffice for "fun"?

"Don't you have a gym?"

"Oh yeah, on every floor. That's what these guys do for fun, so the leftover equipment gets put in here."

"What about the women who live here? There are zero feminine touches."

He shrugs. "They have their own floor. I've never been up there." He rubs his hands together. "So how about a game of pool?"

I did insist on us coming here, and now I have to live with my choice. At least they have all the balls.

I try to sound excited. "Yeah, pool is fun. But I have to be honest, I'm not very good."

"Me neither. I'm more into billiards. But this suffices."

It must be a British thing.

He starts placing the balls into a triangle when I hear the creak of the door behind us. I ignore it and help William finish setting up.

As I find the cue sticks on the wall, I hear a familiar voice.

"Care to play teams?"

I whip my head around to see James, who just entered the room with Rachel, the girl from my training session earlier. I have about two seconds to erase the shock off my face and replace it with casual interest before William's eyes sweep to mine.

"I don't mind, do you?"

I smile tightly. "Sure, let's do it."

James looks smoothly between us, hands in his pockets, with no hint of surprise. He either has a great poker face, or as I suspected, he saw us together last night. He's in the same uniform as William, looking more dashing than usual. Rachel seems pleased to see me. I can't help but notice how the same clothes make her curves stand out, especially in the chest region. She's a lot bustier than I remember.

I grind my teeth together when she places her hand on James's arm and fight the unusual desire to push her from the room. I stop myself, confused by where my thoughts are taking me.

"Hi, Maya. It's good to see you again. This is James," Rachel says, nudging him in the side.

James nods in my direction, making eye contact. I can't get a read on him or draw my eyes away. He wears a bored expression.

"Hey," I say lamely.

William says, "James, you're a Terra, right?"

"Yup, and you're an Aura," he recalls matter-of-factly, his eyes never leaving my face.

William faces me and gestures toward James. "We came in together with the latest recruits, but we haven't had much time to get to know each other." He turns back to James. "So, this is great!"

James releases me from his gaze to briefly look at William. He strides confidently to the pool table and picks up a cue stick.

"I would love to get to know you, William." One side of his mouth rises in mock humor. "And it's good to meet you, Maya."

Rachel puts her hand gracefully on his back, leaning into him. "And I'm Rachel, also a Terra. Maya, a Lympha. Alright then, now that we've gotten introductions out of the way, girls vs. boys or couples?"

I do *not* like the way she says "couples." That atypical feeling washes over me again to react violently. I control myself and pick up a cue.

"Couples," William and I say at the same time. I glance at him. "Jinx."

He chortles and glides over to me, wrapping a hand around my waist. I hold in my gasp at his sudden touch, reminding myself to embrace it. Which would be a lot easier without James in the room.

I risk a peek at him. His eyes are hooded, his hand in a tight fist around his cue.

"Couples, it is. But I have to warn you, I'm pretty good. No funny business, Aura," Rachel says, pointing at William with her cue.

William raises his hands in mock horror. "Hey, I don't cheat!" But then he angles his face away from them and winks at me.

Rachel and James are tough competitors, and we lose when I accidentally hit the eight ball in. William isn't upset and seems rather happy that the game is finally over. I tried not to let Rachel's flirtatious touching get to me, but by the end, I had to physically control myself from "accidentally" hitting her with my cue or outright throwing a ball at her.

"Does anybody want to play again?" Rachel asks, studying the three of us. One look at James's bewildered expression,

William's slow shake of his head as he eyes me, and me trying to look anywhere but at her, she sighs. "Well, *I* had fun."

"No, it was great. I just need to get back." I smile, hoping she believes me.

I gather the cue sticks to return them to the wall when James speaks up.

"Here, let me help you." He holds onto his, grabs the triangle, and saunters in my direction.

I peer at William, who's putting the rest of the balls in the pockets, and jump on my chance to tell James something.

As we insert the sticks into the holders, I whisper, "Five o'clock, our spot." I don't risk peering at him to see if he understands, but stride back towards William, who looks too happy for somebody who just lost. I'm starting to sense he can find the good in anything.

He places a hand on the small of my back. "Ready to go?"

We walk silently for a bit, and it's not awkward. Neither of us feels the need to fill in every break in conversation with meaningless chatter.

He chuckles suddenly. I give him a once-over, and he looks at me, his hair covering one of his eyes.

"You know, I did try to cheat, and we still lost." He lets out a breath of air that twirls his hair back onto the top of his head.

I laugh. "We didn't stand a chance."

"I would have stopped that eight ball from going in, but it would have been too obvious. It's like you were *trying* to get it in."

I laugh even harder, and soon, we're both reduced to tears, unable to stop the hysteria.

Once I can breathe again, I say, "I told you I wasn't good."

"Yeah, you did. Hey, do you want to sit on the bench over there?"

We're almost to the front doors of the manor, and I'm not quite ready for our date to end either. I nod, and we walk to a metal bench shaded by a bare tree about to bloom, covered in white buds. The pink bushes underneath have already started to. A fragrant floral scent wafts through the air as we near.

"You never did get to show me your dance moves," he comments.

"Do you still have that MP3 player?"

"I better," he says, raising his eyebrows at me and digging through his pocket.

I grab it from his outstretched hand and scroll through the songs, trying to find the perfect one. I turn on an upbeat love song and press the volume until it's on as loud as it will go. I hold out my hand, prompting him to dance with me. He eyes me warily but stands.

"Okay, so just feel the rhythm." I grab his hands and start moving my hips and shoulders. "Like this, see?"

He gives me a goofy grin and starts to do it, but in a more robotic way.

"Loosen up." I grab his muscular shoulders and move them in tune with mine, but he's so much bigger than me that it makes him look silly. I let go. "Let's try this. Close your eyes, feel the beat, and move how you want."

"This is fun. I think I can do that."

I close my eyes to show him. I open one of them to see if he's doing it. His eyes are indeed closed, and he's shaking his whole body and waving his hands, looking like a drunk monkey. I quickly shut mine again so I don't accidentally laugh at him; that would be one way to make him never want to do this again. Then I just let go.

It's been so long since I've danced in such a carefree way. I put my arms in the air and sway to the rhythm, shaking my hips, spinning, putting my face to the sun, becoming one with the music.

When the song ends, I open my eyes. I'm smiling so much that my cheeks hurt. I catch William staring at me with an awestruck expression. I instantly feel self-conscious. A flicker of light catches me, and I notice the water dancing around me in the air, the light refracting from it. I'm in a liquid disco ball.

Amazed, I touch it with my fingertips, and it falls. I didn't even realize I was doing that.

William scoops me into his arms and twirls me around. "Blimey, Maya! I've never seen anything like it. Absolutely stunning! You were so in your element, no pun intended." He laughs at his joke. "I opened my eyes, and you were dancing in a lit-up water sphere. Did you mean to do that?"

I giggle as he sets me back on my feet, keeping his arms around my waist. "No, I had no idea. I'm just as stunned as you are."

He releases my waist but holds onto my hand. He walks me back over to the bench, where the MP3 player is balancing between two rods. "Let's do it again, but can we do it my way this time?"

"Sure," I agree, wondering what his way of dancing is. "Is this another British thing?"

He chuckles. "No, no. Well, I don't think it is." He shrugs and selects a slow song. "May I have this dance, my lady?" He holds out an arm.

I smile, feeling like I'm in my very own historical romance novel. I interlock my arm with his, and he guides me two steps before placing his arms around my waist again. I shyly put mine around his neck, and we start swaying and twirling together.

"This is just about where I saved your life."

I glance up. He's right. Abby's window is just above us.

I smirk. "You're never going to let me live that down, are you?"

Letting go of my waist, he traces his fingers down my arms until he reaches my hands. I shiver at the touch. He grabs my hands and steps back, one hand in the air, gently pushing me into a spin under it with the other. He then pulls me back into his arms and dips me.

He looks into my eyes, smiling devilishly. "Never."

He pulls me back up and continues to spin me around him. Even though I have never danced this way with somebody, he makes me feel graceful.

Once the song ends, I'm so dizzy from all the twirling and dipping that I hold onto him, giggling and trying to catch my breath. I pull back, and we stare into each other's eyes, smiling. I can see it. I can see why we're matched. We fit well together. Everything with William comes with ease. I could see myself looking into his light gray eyes forever. It would be a future full of laughter, and maybe even love one day.

He leans down, and I let him kiss my forehead. It's sweet and tender. We pull apart.

"I should be returning now, but thank you for this. I had fun," I say.

"It was fun. When will I see you again?"

"Tomorrow? Maybe the three of us can have lunch together."

His smile falters, but if he's upset by the idea of seeing me with Sebastian, it's not in his voice. "I'll plan for it. See ya later."

I make my way back home, grateful for my building's arched doorways and natural light-filled hallways.

AT PRECISELY FIVE O'CLOCK, I take a casual stroll along the tree line. People are milling about, in training sessions or in couples enjoying the sunshine, but nobody is paying me attention as I slip into the shadows.

James is already sitting on our tree, waiting for me. The light filters through its branches, casting strange shadows on his face. I notice a perfect seat carved out of the trunk beside him. Usually, I wouldn't have seen that, but meeting during light hours has perks, along with the risks.

"Did you do that?" I say, pointing at the log.

"Thought I would make it more comfortable. I'm out here more than my bunk."

I lift my eyebrows. "You are?"

"It's cozy out here."

I wouldn't say cozy is the right word, but it is a rather perfect spot. The trees are clustered around us, shielding us from prying eyes. It's bare, not a flower or twig within a few yards of the bench. I wonder if it's always been like that.

"Might as well bring your bed out here."

He smirks but keeps his eyes down. "I thought about it. There's nowhere else I'd rather be than under the trees. I bet you feel the same about your element."

"Oh yes, I would live in the water if I could," I say, sitting down.

His eyes meet mine. "That doesn't sound comfortable."

"Oh, and being in the dirt does," I retort.

He smiles but is strangely quiet. There's a heaviness between us. I don't like it. A minute of silence stretches before I can't take it any longer.

"I thought you didn't have any friends?"

He purses his lips. "First you want me to make friends, and now you don't? Or is this because my friend is not a man?"

He hits the nail on the head.

I fight the heat wanting to fill my cheeks. "Is that what she is, just a friend?"

He shrugs his shoulders. "Whatever you want to call it."

He continues to eye me, waiting for me to show a sign of weakness. I should just let it go. Of course, he can be friends with a woman. Why do I even care? I think about how she touched his hands, helping him line up his shots, and then how he placed his hands on her waist for that fleeting moment. This time, I can't fight the blush burning in my cheeks. I look away, trying to hide it.

James voices my thoughts. "Are you jealous, Maya?"

I refuse to turn to him, knowing my face will give me away. He gently touches my chin, nudging my face towards him. His face softens, his mouth opening to a silent *Oh*. Although he can see it plainly on my face, I still refuse it.

"Of course not. You can be friends, or more than friends, with whomever you want."

His hazel eyes boring into mine fills my body with heat, so I stand, needing space between us.

"That's not fair. Have you forgotten that you're dating two men at the moment?"

I remember how he acted after seeing me with William. I study his face. Hurt flashes in his eyes. He's jealous too.

"We're just friends," I say helplessly.

He slides a hand through his dark curls and stands. "Yeah," he scoffs.

"I'm sorry I didn't tell you I had started dating my matches. I wanted to, but…" I let my voice drift off.

"I'm not upset you didn't tell me. Not my business."

"Something was off with you last night. You saw me with William, didn't you?"

His eyes hold mine, daring me to look away. "Yeah, I did, but that's not why I was upset."

"Then what was wrong?"

"Do you want me to say it, Maya? Do you honestly want to know?"

I hesitate, then shake my head like a coward. As he said, it's utterly unfair to him. I am matched to two amazing guys, and there is no reason I should feel this way. But I do. I can't deny the effect James has on me. I had a marvelous date today, and another yet to go, but I'm out here with him. He shouldn't even be a thought in my mind. But he is. If he tells me he has similar feelings, I can do nothing about it. My future is set. I'm matched, and he would get hurt.

No, I decide, I don't want to know why he was upset last night.

But as my brain tells me to say one thing, my treacherous heart has different plans. My heart needs to know.

"Yes, I want to know."

He steps closer and grabs a wisp of my strawberry blonde hair. He tucks it behind my ear. His touch causes flutters in my stomach, and desire floods my veins.

"I lied when I told you I just wanted to be friends."

My heart beats faster.

"When I held you in my arms that morning you fell, time stood still. You captivate me with your smile, your words, and your eyes. I've never seen such beautiful green eyes. They are the exact color of when the light catches the treetops." He tenderly touches my cheek. "And the more time I spend with you…it's never enough. I want more. I want to know who you are to the very core. So, yes, when I saw you with another man on your balcony, I was overcome with emotions I couldn't control. I've never felt such rage, Maya. I completely wiped this place out." He chuckles darkly.

That's why the space is so clean. I now notice that even the lower tree limbs are bare.

I return to his eyes. The colors in them are more vibrant as everything else fades.

"And then I saw you with the water, such beauty…it calmed me. But, obviously, I got worked up again. Sorry about that." He steps closer to grab my hand and put it to his heart. It is beating as fast as mine. "I promised I wouldn't touch you without you asking me, remember?"

I nod, focusing on his hand around mine, remembering that moment we almost kissed. He was waiting for me.

"That's not what I mean, and you know it," he whispers.

I scan his face.

"All you need to do is ask, Maya. I'm yours."

I open my mouth, overcome with emotion I can't decipher yet, but I know one thing for certain. I want him, even though every bone in my body shouts at me to walk away. I envision how it would feel to have his lips on mine. My strength falters, forgetting about being matched and all the rules. I'm just a girl, and he's just a boy, professing his true feelings for me. I want him to kiss me.

I lean closer, looking at the perfect shape of his lips. "James, will you—"

My request is left unfinished as somebody gasps loudly nearby. My eyes lock on Abby, over James's shoulder and I freeze. James stiffens at the sound, staring at me wide-eyed.

"Oh, sorry, I noticed you coming out here and wanted to talk, but I can see you're busy," she says with a wink. "Pretend I didn't intrude. We can talk later." She backs away slowly, eyes still on James's back.

I glance at him, feeling relieved. She hasn't seen my matches yet, or James's face. I can let her go, and she won't be any the wiser.

Just as I feel not all is lost, James does the unthinkable. He turns to face her.

"Abigail! Is—Is that you?" he stutters.

My hands fall to my sides as the air thickens in my throat.

She stares dumbstruck at James, but the recognition clicks a second later, and her eyes fill with tears, spilling over freely as she runs at us. She jumps over tree limbs and bushes, forgetting she's a Terra who could effortlessly move them aside.

James closes the gap, and they embrace.

"Avery!" She sobs as James holds her tightly against him.

Without the faintest clue of what's happening, I stand there with one thing on my mind: did she call him Avery?

13

Together Again

I'M NOT PROUD OF THE THOUGHTS that race through my mind as I watch my best friend and my only guy friend—who might be more than a friend—embrace and cry in each other's arms. One thing I painfully realize is that I would rather be found out than lose James to my best friend.

How could she possibly know him?

I rack my brain, trying to figure it out, but come up empty. The name Avery does sound familiar. I keep hearing "You're alive?" and "How is this possible?" mumbled between them.

I stand back, wondering if they'll remember my existence, when they finally pull apart. Abby locks eyes with me. She wipes tears away, with a million questions in her eyes. James glances in my direction, and it hits me, looking at their faces side by side. The familiarity I felt when I first met him, his eyes, his laughter, even the way he moves his eyebrows. How could I not have realized? Sure, I had only met him a handful of times. He's a lot older now, and his hair is longer. A boy transformed into a man. But still, I should have remembered him.

Abby clears her throat enough to speak. "Avery, how are you here? And…" Her hand flies to her mouth as her eyes bounce between us. "Maya, are you matched to my brother?"

She forgot about the tidbit I'm not matched with a Terra, but now is not the time to remind her. I don't know how to talk my way out of this, so I look to James…or *Avery*. I don't even know what to call him now.

Red, hot anger bubbles up inside. "You lied to me," I hiss.

"Okay, let's sit down, and I'll explain everything." His eyes plead with me. Then he gazes at his sister with nothing but tenderness.

Abby collapses onto the bench, the tears still flowing after five years of bottled emotion. She has never spoken of Avery, and I never asked. Anger, confusion, and betrayal are swirling, threatening to break the surface.

I close my eyes, trying to control my emotions. "I'm not sitting," I choke out. "Just talk."

He exhales, probably thinking of more lies. I keep my eyes closed. Maybe I should give him the benefit of the doubt.

"Abigail, is Mom alive?"

I can hear the despair mixed with hope in his voice, breaking the tension and calming me.

She smiles and nods. "Yes, Mom is fine. But where have you been? We thought you were dead. It's been *five years*, Avery."

Even though I want answers, I know this is more important for Abby. Her long-lost brother back from the dead takes priority.

"I thought the same about you. When the attacks started, I went straight to Dad's." His lips turn down. "You knew about Dad, at least?"

She nods.

"Well, after that, I came to find you and Mom, but the house was destroyed. After seeing Dad, I thought the worst. But I didn't give up. I searched for you guys. I went by my middle name to fit in with the Coms, since I wasn't recognized in the area. I stayed around for a while, hoping you'd come back." He looks at me. "I didn't mean to lie about my name. I've been going by James for so long." He shrugs, like that also explains him lying about knowing me. Why didn't he ask me about them if he genuinely sought his family?

His eyes return to Abby. "Obviously, I never found you, and people were getting suspicious, so I eventually left. I've been traveling around. Sometimes pretending to be a Com or hiding out with the Elementals. I was in California when Captain Vargas found me. He mentioned the base in Oregon, so I jumped on it. I had no idea you guys would be here. Hiding in plain sight this whole time." He lets out a shaky laugh.

Abby jumps back up and throws her arms around him again. "I still can't believe you're alive. I can't call you James, though; that's weird." She pulls back to admire him. "Let's go get Mom!"

He gives her a watery smile, eyes glistening, but hesitantly looks at me.

I nod, holding my emotions at bay for the moment. Abby deserves this. I can't imagine finding out my dad is still alive.

The thought brings pain to my chest, and I wrap my arms around my torso, trying to control the burning. The ache in my lungs feels like an old memory. It's too familiar, the feeling of absolute despair and fear that would override my senses, causing my heart to race and air to become a precious commodity. The panic attacks were frequent in the years after the accident.

I inhale slowly, filling my lungs with cool air. *The pain isn't real, it's not real, I can breathe. I. can. breathe.*

They turn to walk away when Abby, having forgotten about me again, abruptly stops and whips around.

I manage to straighten myself.

"Maya, you didn't recognize him?" I shake my head tightly, exhaling through the pain.

She turns to her brother. "And you didn't recognize her?"

He wavers for a split second. "No." His response brings me back to reality, and the pain in my lungs subsides. He can't be telling the truth.

"Wow, and now you guys are matched? That's incredible!" She breaks away from James to embrace me, but I can't manage to return the hug. "We're going to be sisters now! Wait, sorry, that's if she chooses you," she says, clenching her teeth together.

The blood drains from my face. How am I to tell her that, not only have I had this secret life, but I'm also not matched to her brother?

I swallow, prepping myself. James doesn't look much better, his jaw tense and eyes wide.

He rubs the back of his neck. "Um, Abigail?"

She wrinkles up her face. "Avery, I know I haven't talked to you in five years, but please don't call me that." She then sees his troubled expression. "What is it?"

I brace myself.

"Maya and I aren't matched."

Her mouth drops open. Her face goes from shocked to accusatory. "Then what are you guys doing?" Color fills her cheeks as she looks back and forth at us.

I find my voice. "It's not what you think." Even though, if she had shown up a moment later, it would have been precisely what she's thinking.

I can see the wheels circling in her mind as her eyes widen and then narrow. "You guys can explain later, and you better have a good explanation. Do you know how many rules you're breaking? But, right now, we need to get to Mom."

She grabs my hand, pulling me along with her, wrapping her free arm around her brother's, and dragging him, too. I feel like a little kid in trouble, being towed along by her mom.

I risk a glance at James. He's staring at me. I can tell he wants to say something, so I drop my head. I can't believe I was about to compromise my whole future for one heated moment. A couple of nice words, and I was ready to throw myself into his arms. I need to be more careful with my heart. I can only give it to one man. Unfortunately, James isn't one of them.

Their family reunion is too emotional to watch. It's uncomfortable seeing them cry openly, when keeping our emotions in check is often shoved down our throats. Although, it's not every day you find out your dead son is alive.

Once word got out, practically everyone in the building wanted to see for themselves, and I'm able to slip out of Mrs. Stevens's overcrowded living room quietly.

I'm so foolish. I didn't even know his real name. My brain unlocks my faded memories of him. I was so young that I only remember briefly seeing him in his room or at their family gatherings. When I was around seven or eight, Abby's parents split, and he went with his dad. I didn't see him after that. I do remember he would practice his abilities in the backyard. Abby and I were still too young, so seeing others use their element was always fascinating. One time, he caught me spying on him from

Abby's bedroom window. He waved at me and, embarrassed, I avoided him from then on. His curly hair was short then, face round with baby fat, but his eyes were the same.

How could I have forgotten those eyes?

It's nice not to feel crazy anymore. From the first moment I saw James, I did recognize him, and he recognized me. I can't figure out why he lied, though.

And I almost kissed him! Abby's big brother.

I chuckle darkly to myself, even though it's not funny. At least it'll be easier to stay away from him now. No more secret meetups. I'll have to tell Abby the truth eventually, and once everything is out in the open, it would destroy our friendship to blatantly lie to her again. I can only hope she'll forgive me for keeping it a secret as long as I did. All I can do is focus on my matches and try to forget about him.

On my way to my room, I remember I still have another date today. Maybe I should cancel, but it could be a welcome distraction.

I'll go to dinner. Food always helps in decision-making.

14

Beautiful Flames

THE SUN IS SETTING over the trees, creating swirling, cotton candy clouds above me, as the air cools. I'm grateful I replaced my clothes with leggings and a long-sleeve shirt. The sky changes colors and fades as I walk to the lake, where I meet Sebastian. He's waiting under the big maple tree near my training spot.

He flashes me his dazzling smile. My stomach flutters, and just like that, my worries drift away, and my mind fills with the handsome man before me.

He's standing casually, with one finger hooked through his belt loop. When I'm close enough, he brings his arms around my back. The hug is warm, and his touch is feather-light. But it's over too quickly. He must be done for the day, out of his uniform and in a black short-sleeve polo and dark jeans.

"It's nice to see you. How was your day? I want to know everything," he says politely, but eagerly, as if genuinely interested.

I smile. "That might take a while. It was an eventful day, to say the least."

We make our way around the lake towards the legion side. I tell him about my lessons this morning and briefly mention my date with William, strongly doubting he wants those details, but he nods graciously, not the least uncomfortable.

"I'm glad you had fun with him. He's a great guy."

How can he be so kind about his competition? Not like I'm a prize, but still.

"Aren't you supposed to talk *yourself* up and not your competition?"

He wrinkles his brow. "I don't see him as competition. I'd be very happy for him if he won your heart. I'm not saying I wouldn't be sad for myself, but at the end of the day, the heart wants what the heart wants." He shrugs.

I ponder that. "Do you believe in soulmates or love at first sight?"

He stares off in thought. "Yes and no. I believe love grows and deepens over time. Do I doubt those who fall in love quickly? No. I think everyone experiences love differently. And soulmates? Possibly. It's nice to think there is that one person out there who's your other half. But there are so many people. How would you even begin to find them? That's why I like this process so much. Sure does narrow it down." He glances down at me, his eyes gleaming.

I smile, liking his thoughts on love.

He nudges me. "You didn't finish telling me about your day."

"I haven't told you about Abby yet. She's my best friend. We've been friends since we were toddlers. She lost her brother and dad, and it's obviously taken a toll on her. Well, today, we found out her brother is alive and here! Can you believe it? You may know him…James? He came in at the same time as William. His real name is Avery, though, long story."

"Wow, you did have an eventful day. I know him. He keeps to himself, but he seems nice enough. You must be thrilled for her. Did you know him then? Since you grew up together?"

"No, not really. He's older than me and lived with his dad, so we didn't cross paths that much." I twist and untwist my hands. James probably wasn't the best choice of topic.

"Where are we going?" We are on the other side of the lake now, and the sun has entirely set, with only a pink glow on the horizon.

"You'll see, we're almost there. You wanted to observe me more in my element, right?"

"Yeah, but it's getting dark," I say uneasily.

"It'll be worth it, I promise. I know you might think my abilities only cause pain and destruction." He eyes me, waiting for me to contradict him. I don't, so he continues. "I'm not offended. Most people do, and it's true for Ignas with little experience, but I want to show you fire can be beautiful, too. It's about who wields it."

He snaps his fingers, and a tiny flame hovers above his fingertips. It dances momentarily, and then he throws it like a baseball. I watch as it hits and lights up a tiki torch I hadn't noticed. He forms more tiny dancing flames and lights nine torches ahead of us.

He offers me his arm, and I take it eagerly. "Follow me."

The lake is to our right, the moon reflecting on its glassy surface. It's comforting to have access to water. And ahead of us, lining the path, are the flickering flames. So far, not scary at all.

As we near the trail's end, stone steps descend into a crater about the size of my old bedroom. It's lined with smooth, flat stones with boulders surrounding the space as seats. In the center is a colossal fire pit. Sebastian leads me to one of the boulders.

"This is where I practice the more…*tame* side of my element."

In a clockwise motion, he swirls his hands in the air. Sparks fly out. As his arms move faster, the sparks catch and start blazing. The blaze grows, forming a tornado of flames. Unexpectedly, I'm not afraid. Nor do I want to flinch away. Instead, I'm drawn to it, having to will myself to not reach out and touch it.

He moves the fire tornado into the pit, fueling it even more. The flames reach up like fingers grasping at the sky. I can't take my eyes off it. The fingers beckon me, inviting me to its warmth. A hand grasps my shoulder. I cringe, thinking the fingers got their hold on me, but the hand belongs to Sebastian. He's regarding me curiously, and I realize I've walked up to the fire pit. I don't even recall moving.

I smile, trying to shake off the haze.

"I know, it's almost hypnotizing, isn't it?" he says, his eyes reflecting the red-orange flickering flames.

"It's beautiful."

"This is just the fire. Wait until you see what I can make with it."

The flames dance off his face, casting shadows, making his cheekbones sharper and his chin more angled. His eyes are wide, excited, his blue irises being the only bright spot on his face, the color of the ocean before a storm.

He raises his hands, and there's something in his palm…a gnarled piece of dark metal.

"Watch," he whispers, his hushed tone full of anticipation.

I draw in a sharp breath as he places his hand in the fire, exposing the chunk of metal. The flame licks his hand but does no harm. You couldn't say the same about the metal. It glows red hot, growing brighter, yet retaining its chunky shape.

He pulls it out when I think it's about to melt from the heat. His eyebrows crease as he molds the metal like clay. As it dims, he places it back in the flames and continues to work. The only sound is the crackle from the fire.

I observe in wonder as his hands move in rhythmic motions in and out of the fire, changing this ugly piece of metal, elongating it, and transforming it into something thin and smooth. He twists it onto itself until it's a spiral shape.

"That's amazing," I say, breaking the silence.

"For you," he says, handing it to me.

I waver.

"It's not hot. Here, give me your hand."

Trusting him, I place my hand in his. He weaves what is now a bracelet onto my wrist. It's warm, a sweet reminder of my favorite fire-wielder.

I run my finger along the sleek black surface and smile at him. "Thank you."

He beams, and I want to lean into him like a moth to a light…my personal flame. And then I realize I can…and should. So, I do.

I watch him carefully, looking for any sign of him not wanting to touch me as I lean in, place my face on his chest, and wrap my arms around his waist. He returns my embrace, setting his cheek on my head. He's solid, entirely made of muscle. I can feel the hard muscles of his chest, stomach, and back.

We stand like that for a minute, just holding each other. I breathe him in. He smells like smoke and spice. He starts idly playing with my hair. I peer up at him, and his features are smooth, eyes heavy.

"Ever thought you'd be embracing an Igna?"

I grin. "Can't say it's crossed my mind. But it's okay. I can put you out if you catch fire."

He chuckles at my attempt to flirt, and it reverberates against my body. I could get used to this.

I release him and sit on one of the boulders.

We chat, and I ask him more questions about his parents, fascinated by their relationship. Luckily, he loves talking about his family. I also learn that he has two brothers, both younger than him.

"One's an Igna like me, and the other takes after my dad."

"Whoa, that's so cool. I can only imagine the trouble you three caused. Your poor parents."

He laughs. "They were relieved when Henry developed water abilities…somebody else to help put out the fires."

"That's terrifying!"

He shrugs. "Could be in your future."

I haven't thought about that, but it's true. If I choose Sebastian, I could have little Igna babies running around soon. I don't have a response, so I stare off toward the lake. I'd barely be able to tell it's there in the dark, if it weren't for my sensitivity to all things water.

"Tell me more about your family," he insists.

"I've already told you about my mom and little brother."

"What about your dad?"

I stiffen.

"It's okay if you don't want to talk about him."

"No, it's not that. I loved my dad. He passed away when I was nine. I just still have a hard time with it."

"Do you want to talk about it?" His eyes are sincere and sweet.

I have never wanted to talk about it, but the way he's looking at me, I want to be vulnerable.

I bite my lip. I can't fall in love if I'm unwilling to open up. But I've never recounted the story to anyone. My lungs hurt as they did earlier, opening up old wounds. My hand flutters to my chest as I try to breathe through it.

Sebastian grabs my other hand, his eyes darting between mine. "Honestly, you don't need to tell me if you're not ready."

I press my lips into a thin line. His hand is a lifeline that brings me back to the surface. The pain subsides. I can do this with him.

I smile. "I want to."

He squeezes my hand encouragingly. I stare into the flames as they crackle and sway, letting them take me into the memories I have always pushed down.

I look back to the ocean in Sebastian's eyes, remembering. "It was my ninth birthday. My parents had surprised me with a trip to the coast," I begin.

It was a beautiful sunny day in Bandon, a rarity, since it rains eighty-five percent of the year. My dad said it was the sky telling me happy birthday. We were set up on the beach near the pier. Because of the riptides, my parents told me never to swim near the dock. So, I always kept a safe distance away. They gifted me a pink boogie board with little blue flowers on it for my birthday, and my dad was teaching me how to surf.

"Here comes the wave, Maya. Get ready!" he shouted as I jumped on the board, lying on my stomach, and surfed the wave to the beach, giggling the whole way.

I would get back on, and he'd manipulate the water to push me back to him. Eventually, I told him I wanted to try on my own, and he joined Mom on the sand. She was heavily pregnant with

Cal at the time. The waves were bigger near the pier, and since I was now nine and pretty confident in my swimming abilities, I decided it would be fine to get a little close. It was fun riding the bigger waves, and I got distracted, drifting near the dock.

One moment, I was riding a wave, and the next, my parents were distant specks. They realized it, too, because they ran towards me right before I felt a tug from beneath the water. I tried to hold onto my board and stay afloat, but it ripped from my hands, and I went under.

The ocean doesn't care how good of a swimmer you are. I didn't know which way to turn. I felt myself getting sucked deeper and deeper into the depths. I didn't have abilities at the time…no way to help myself.

As I felt myself slipping away, my dad grabbed me. He was able to place me in a water transport, and I took my first breath inside the air pocket.

Somehow, though, his foot got wedged between something, and I watched in horror as he struggled for his life. I couldn't understand why he wasn't trying to do something to save himself. He stopped fighting against the current and rocks and looked up at me with his dark blue eyes. They were so clear, like he knew exactly what he needed to do and wasn't scared at all.

"Daddy!" I screamed as I banged against the translucent bubble that separated me from him.

Terror constrained my heart when I realized he had given up. I reached for him, and he reached back, mouthing, *I love you.*

Instead of grabbing my hand, though, he used the last of his energy to push me to the surface.

I screamed at him all the way up as I choked back tears. "No! Please, Daddy, I can help. Let me out! No!"

I remember feeling petrified and helpless. He watched me, his face peaceful, as I got farther and farther from him, until I couldn't see him anymore and broke the surface.

My mother quickly snatched me up…I never saw my dad again. They found his body soon after. His foot had indeed been caught between some rocks, and he had suffered a blow to the head, which is probably why he didn't use his ability to free himself, instead focusing on making sure I made it to the surface.

I'm surprised by the tears that escape. "It's my fault he died."

Sebastian pulls me into him. "It's not, Maya. He saved your life."

I shake my head but don't bother arguing. My mom, and everyone else, tells me the same thing. They don't understand. He would have lived if it wasn't for me trying to get close to that pier. I killed him.

Sebastian wipes my tears with his thumb. "I'm honored you shared such deep pain with me. I'm so sorry." His eyes are full of sincerity.

I wipe the rest of my tears, feeling raw inside. "It's getting late," I sigh.

"Can I walk you back?" He rises with me still in his arms.

I step away, and he releases me. "Actually, I think I'm going to swim back. It'll help clear my head from all the emotion."

He scrutinizes the lake. "Really? That's pretty far."

"I've done it dozens of times." I take his arm and let him lead me to the sandy bank. I squeeze his hand. "Thanks for a great evening. Sorry I ruined it with my blubbering."

"Don't apologize. You didn't ruin a thing."

My hand is still on his arm, and the heat seeps into my skin. We stare into each other's eyes, something playing behind his. As

I'm about to try and decipher it, he blinks, and it's gone. He looks over the lake again, a crease forming between his eyebrows.

"I'll be fine, trust me."

I slip off my sandals and shove them into my waistband, grateful I didn't wear a jacket to slow me down. I wave at him before diving in. I can tell he wants to stop me, but I'm grateful he doesn't.

I come out of the water myself again, leaving my anguish on the other side of the lake. I'm glad I told him. A weight has been lifted from my chest that I didn't know I was carrying.

I peer at my watch. That was my quickest lap yet, seven minutes and twenty-two seconds, and in clothes!

I work on drying myself off as I walk to my terrace. I admire the sleek onyx bracelet Sebastian made for me, still in awe. Nobody has ever made me anything.

The lights should have been my first clue that something wasn't right, but I'm too busy daydreaming about Sebastian to notice.

Inside, my senses should have alerted me to the second obvious clue that somebody was in my room. Once again, I'm too distracted.

I kick my shoes off and head towards my dresser to change while humming a tune. I never hum. I put *Sebastian makes me hum* on my mental lists of my two men. I grab my clothes, deciding not to change right there. As I turn, there's movement.

Before my mind registers who is sitting leisurely on my couch in the middle of my room, an ear-shattering scream escapes, and I drop my clothes.

James scowls and rubs his ears, faking pain. "I was wondering when you were going to notice me," he says slyly.

"What in the world! Why are you in my room? How did you get in here?" I look around, uneasy. "Were you just waiting for the show?" I yell, placing a hand on my hip.

"If you want to put one on, I won't protest," he says, lifting one side of his mouth.

Anger swells inside me, as I reach for something to throw at him.

"I wouldn't do that if I were you," he warns, reading my mind.

My hand lands on something sturdy, and I chuck it at his head. He dodges it smoothly, and I glare at him.

"Out!" I say, pointing at the door, not thinking of how that would look if someone was in the hall to notice. I don't care at the moment.

He stands up and raises his hands innocently. "Calm down, I'm just joking. Look, I want to talk. We didn't get a chance earlier." He pushes his hair out of his eyes. I recognize it as one of his nervous gestures. "I thought you'd see me once you walked in. Not my fault you came in your back door. What were you doing anyways? It's late." He scowls.

"None of your business," I snap. I breathe through the adrenaline coursing through my veins. I don't want to flood my room.

It might be worth it, though. My fingers twitch towards my sink.

"That's new," he says, examining my bracelet.

I cross my arms over my chest to hide it. "Again, none of your business."

I should yell at him to leave, but I want answers. Sitting on the edge of the coffee table, I keep my arms crossed and my spine stiff.

I glare at him, eyes hostile. "Go ahead."

He sits back down but doesn't bring his eyes to meet mine. He leans on his knees with his elbows and stares at his hands as he talks, his curly bronze hair obscuring his face. "Everything I said earlier is the truth, I did change my name to fit in with the Coms, but I should have told you my real name. I didn't think it mattered anymore. You have no idea what it's like to lose your whole family. I had nobody, Maya. After I started going by James, it eased the pain a bit. Instead of being Avery, the guy that lost everything, I was just James. Abby and my mom see me as who I was, but I'm not Avery anymore."

A little bubble of empathy threatens to surface but I push it down, keeping the scowl on my face.

He focuses on me. "Maya, I'm sorry." He says it with such emotion behind those hazel eyes, I almost believe him.

"You lied to me," I hiss.

"I know, and I'm trying to apologize. Didn't you—"

I cut him off. "I'm not talking about your name. When we first met, I asked you if I knew you. I could tell you recognized me when we first saw each other. You knew me! And you made me feel so dumb. You lied to me and have been lying ever since. I can't trust anything you ever told me." I stand, having enough. "Out."

"You're right," he says, surprising me. "I did recognize you, but I didn't know from where. Maya, you were a little kid the last time I saw you. I didn't know who you were, and I told you that. It clicked once I saw Abby, as it did for you."

It makes sense. Why would he remember me from when I was that young? I didn't remember either. It still doesn't take away the feelings of betrayal though. He never even mentioned Abby.

"I need to think. Please go."

"Okay, I'll leave you alone. But I want to warn you that you might see more of me."

My eyes narrow.

"My mom doesn't want to let me out of her sight, so I'm staying with her for now. I could only come to your room because I told her I needed to get some of my things, which I still need to do." He glances at his watch. "And there's Abby. Wow, she's grown up to be quite the woman. I'm a little jealous that you know her more than I do." His eyes are sad.

My resolve falters, and I want to wrap my arms around him.

But before I can take a step, he says, "And make sure to lock the door. Who knows what other creeps will end up on your couch." He grins wryly and turns toward my back door. Of course, he didn't stride in through the front.

I let him leave without another word, not trusting myself to even say goodbye.

15

Picnic

THE NEXT FIVE DAYS are spent avoiding James. I finally told Abby about my secret friendship with him, and she hasn't talked to me since. I know she needs space, but she met her matches this week, and I have yet to speak with her. We're supposed to go through this together, and I ruined it. I betrayed our friendship. She probably would have forgiven me quicker if it was some random guy. But her brother? I've known about him this whole time, and if I had just been honest, their reunion would have been much sooner. When she asked me why I didn't tell her about him, I couldn't even give her a straight answer. I don't *know* why I didn't tell her. I was being completely selfish.

William and Sebastian have been a welcome distraction. They know something is up with me, but they haven't pried. I've gone on another date with them, but they weren't quite as exciting as the first ones. There's only so much to do for fun around here. I look forward to our meals with one another. We try to plan at least one daily.

I slide my legs into cut-off pants and throw a black V-neck on. William chose today—breakfast, his favorite meal—and Sebastian suggested taking it outside. It's a perfect spring day.

I peer out the window. Not a cloud in the sky, like William predicted. Auras are amazing weather forecasters.

I close my patio door behind me with a blanket tucked underneath my arm, remembering what James said about locking it. I don't listen, since he's the only creep who would be trying to sneak in. And maybe there's a small part of me that wants him to.

I squash the thought, hating that I still think about him.

Neither of the boys are at the spot we agreed to meet. I unroll the blanket. The smell of fresh water and sweet clover wafts in the air. I'm near my pond and choose an area of grass and weeds, where the soil is dry. We'll have much more privacy here than near the lake, where everyone practices and the families visit.

I can't help but glance over to the woods, hoping to see a familiar face watching me and waving me over to join him in our secret location. But the only movements are the tree branches swaying in the light breeze.

I shake my head. It's been almost a week since our near kiss, and still, my thoughts betray me.

The sun is warm on my skin, making me glad I chose a short-sleeve shirt. I sit on the blanket to wait. They both insisted on getting breakfast for me. It's a sweet gesture, but I'm curious about what they'll choose. I could make this a test to see how well they each know me.

It's been a week, and I already feel the pressure from my mom to make a choice.

"First impressions are crucial," she'd said during a conversation yesterday. *"Which one do you gravitate towards?*

Who gives you butterflies? Some girls only need a few days because of an obvious connection. Anything like that for you?"

It's frustrating having her breathing down my neck and not knowing how to answer her questions. All it does is freak me out that we really are running out of time.

They are both exceptional men, and I can see how each of them would make a great partner, in different ways, but feelings take time to grow. I don't think I can make a decision anytime soon. And what if they don't develop? What if I'm incapable of love?

Before I can worry anymore, my stomach rumbles, bringing me back to reality. I've got to take this one day at a time. Love can't be rushed.

Where are those boys? Just when I decide to go find them, I hear their familiar voices drawing closer. I turn and wave enthusiastically.

Their faces light up when they see me. They're carrying trays stacked with food, enough to feed half a dozen people. As they draw closer, I notice Sebastian gracefully carrying a tray in each hand, not even breaking a sweat. William isn't touching his trays—they're floating slightly ahead of him.

I tilt my head, intrigued.

"Cool, huh? Perks of being an Aura," he proudly states.

"Pft, I'm surprised you even need to use your ability. These things are so light. Perks of having big arms," Sebastian retorts, smiling devilishly at me.

My eyes travel the length of his smooth brown arms as he flexes them.

A giggle escapes my lips. Sebastian has opened up much more since I told him about my dad. It's nice seeing his true personality come out the more comfortable he gets around me.

He's still a high-quality gentleman, but also funny, sweet, and charismatic.

Not in the same way as William, though. William is down to earth, goofy, and impossible not to like, and he's always been an open book, while Sebastian can be hard to read sometimes.

"Yeah, they go great with your big head," William throws back as he sets the food down on the blanket.

Sebastian, right behind him, smiles wider. "So, you admit it, my arms are bigger than yours."

"What did you get?" I say eagerly, interrupting their banter before they start comparing biceps. It would be a little better than two days ago, when they measured their calf muscles and tried to get me to feel them.

Sebastian sets down his plates. "A little bit of everything. We thought you'd like lots of choices."

There are two plates full of only fruit: sliced apples, whole peaches, strawberries, blueberries, and a creamy pink fruit dip. The other plates have bagels, French toast, croissants, and Danishes. The heavenly scents waft into my face, making me almost drool.

"Thanks, guys, this is kind of you."

They passed this test with flying colors. Although, I can't imagine them failing anything food-related.

Sebastian folds himself onto the blanket, and I realize I should have brought an oversized quilt. How could I forget their size compared to mine? I move to the edge, but once William sits, I end up between them with my knee pressed up against William's thigh and my shoulder grazing Sebastian's. Even though I'm used to their touches now, there's an electric current between the contact of our bodies. I try not to think about it and dig in.

Minutes pass before anyone speaks.

"You have lessons today, right?" William breaks the silence first.

I glance at Sebastian and quickly realize that the question is for me. I had just taken a bite of a croissant and still have a mouth full.

After I get most of it down, I put a hand in front of my mouth and choke out, "Yeah, Seth is teaching me offensive moves now."

I still haven't asked him why my training has transitioned from defensive to offensive, too scared he'll change his mind.

William asks, "Do you want some help today? I notice sometimes your trainer seeks out assistance."

Usually, Rachel helps when Seth wants to simulate an attack. I've been getting used to her being at my lessons. The jealousy I felt the last time I saw her has dissipated. It helps that James hasn't been around. Everything is twisted when I think about him, a giant knot of feelings that I don't care to unravel. I'm not angry anymore, just a circumstance of miscommunication. But he's still Abby's brother. And I have my matches.

William is looking at me, waiting for an answer. Rachel is great, but William would be a lot more interesting. I haven't seen an Aura's attack skills before.

"Sure, I'll talk to Seth. That would be fun." *And I've already done it with Sebastian.*

Sebastian clears his throat. "What's your favorite food, Maya?"

"Cheeseburgers," I say instantly.

Sebastian chuckles in response. "We certainly don't have any of those around."

"I know." I sigh.

"Not unless you count the veggie burgers," William chimes in.

I blanch and vigorously shake my head. "Those don't deserve to have the same name."

Both the men laugh.

"Yeah, they do taste pretty rotten." William chuckles.

"Did you have a favorite place for a good burger, you know, back in the day?" Sebastian asks.

I wait for my anxiety to peak, thinking about the past, but it doesn't. Since I was vulnerable with Sebastian, it's become easier to talk about my life before the war. Nothing can be worse than the memory of my dad's death.

"Jasper's Café."

"I haven't heard of that one."

"It was one of those hole-in-the-wall places in the town I grew up in. They had the most delicious burger—uh, the name escapes me—but it had bacon, onion rings, raspberry sauce, jalapeño cream cheese. Guys, it was amazing…" My voice trails off when I notice three figures walking toward us.

"That sounds delicious. Great, now I'm craving a cheeseburger," William scoffs.

"Me too…"

Their voices drift off as I focus on the figures. I know right away who one of them is by how she moves her hips when she walks and how her dark, auburn hair radiates in the sunlight. But the other two…

"What are you looking at?" Both men follow my line of sight and then stand to greet the trio. They reach out to help me up. I study each hand, feeling like it's some sort of test. Which one *do* I gravitate towards? I sigh inwardly and take both. I'm up in a flash.

"Abby?"

Walking in her shadow are two men. One was the redhead I met when he and James came to the end of my lesson, a Lympha like me. I can't think of his name. The other is really tall, towering over all five of us. He's handsome, though, with dark hair, light eyes, and a nice, trimmed beard. He could be in his mid-twenties.

"Hey, sorry to intrude. I saw you guys and thought we should all meet," Abby says merrily. Her men hang on her every word. I knew any guy Abby matched with would swoon over her. She turns to them. "This is Maya. We've been friends since we were little."

"*Best* friends," I add, but Abby doesn't notice. I can't tell if she's still mad or not. If she was, she wouldn't have come over here. Although, she has to be in the loop about everything, so maybe it's just curiosity.

She introduces her matches. "Trevor and Peter."

I try to gauge her feelings. Hostile or friendly? Her eyes are calm, and her smile seems genuine, but there's an edge to it.

I give the same introductions.

They both nod to the other guys, probably already knowing each other.

"It's nice to finally meet you, Abby. Maya has told us so much about you." Of course, Sebastian would say something like that. He's too polite.

She checks him out for a split second and then faces me. "I'm sorry, but I must steal Maya for a minute. We'll be right back."

Her matches deflate at the announcement. She grabs my hand and gently pulls me towards the tree line.

I peer back at Sebastian and William who are already in a conversation with the other men. They'll be fine.

Once we're far enough away from their ears, at the base of an oak tree, she turns on me.

I speak first. I might not get another chance. "Abby, I know I've already said this, but I'll keep repeating it and do whatever I can to deserve your trust again: I'm *so* sorry. I shouldn't have kept a secret like that from you. I was so selfish. Is there any way you can forgive me?" I stare at her, pleading, hoping, and praying that I can get my best friend back.

She stays silent for half a minute, eyes slitted, calculating. "I'm not mad at you. I actually forgave you on day two, but I thought you deserved silence for the same number of days you did it to me," she says brazenly, staring me down, daring me to get upset.

I don't flinch, but smile wide instead, and wrap my arms around her. It was actually six days, but I won't be the one to correct her.

She returns the hug without wavering, and I know I'm undoubtedly forgiven.

"You are, beyond question, the best. I was ready to grovel," I say.

"That would have been nice to see. You still can if you want."

I roll my eyes. "I missed you."

Her face grows serious. "Me too. I've been dying to tell you about my matches."

I peek over her shoulder. "They're pretty cute, Abby."

Her cheeks turn rosy.

"You really like them, don't you? Tell me everything," I insist.

"I want to." She leans in and speaks from the side of her mouth. "You forgot to mention how smoking hot your matches are, by the way." She leans back, pretending to fan herself.

I grin.

"But first, I want to talk about my brother. He told me some things."

My thoughts jump to the moments of closeness with him. That first time I found myself near him, that unmistakable gravitational pull I had, or when he held my face in his palms, or even that last time in the woods when I decided to make the choice that could have ruined me.

A pit forms in my stomach, and I want to look away from her eyes that will see through mine. Instead, I wipe my face of emotion, pushing the memories down, readying myself for whatever she might say next. Maybe she wants to chastise me? Or worse, ask if I have feelings for him.

She bites her lip and lowers her voice. "I want to go outside the walls."

I stare at her, uncomprehending. It's not what I was expecting at all. I was ready to deny anything she asked me, but *this*? I study her a moment longer before remembering our little adventure. "He told you about that?"

"I asked him to take me, but he won't. He said you guys almost got caught. But I really want to go, Maya. We've been stuck inside this place too long. I need to breathe. You know what I mean?"

"Even if I wanted to go out there again, I wouldn't know where to go. It was dark, and we walked for what seemed like forever. He's the one who opened up the wall, and there *were* guards. It's idiotic and dangerous to do that again."

She's still staring at me with those pleading eyes. "C'mon. You owe me. You had all this fun without me, leaving me in the dark. I'm your best friend! And with my *brother*," she says accusingly.

I have no desire to return to the forest outside the walls, but she's right. "Okay, okay, but we can't go by ourselves."

"Can you talk to Avery for me? I'm sure you could convince him to go again. I'm still just his baby sister, but you…" She looks at me like she knows more than she's letting on, making the pit return.

I'm tempted to take her right now and aimlessly trip through the forest rather than talk to James about this, but we would either get caught or lost. "Okay, I can try, but no—" she jumps up excitedly, "—promises," I finish.

At the same time, Abby says, "Thank you! This is going to be so much fun!" She clearly didn't hear me at all.

16

Persuasion

I'M BACK TO SITTING on our log, the last place I thought I'd be after Abby found out. It's windy today, but you wouldn't know it in the protection of the trees, where there is only soft whistling in the air. The sunshine from this morning is still hanging around, creating beams of light that drift down from the canopy. Little specks dance inside the angled columns. The earthy smell is almost comforting now, not as much as the smell of fresh water, but close. James had started to convince me of the beauty of being among the trees: the large brown trunks of hundred-year-old giants, the green moss that seems to attach itself to anything bare, the clovers and pine cones covering the rough ground, the vibrant wildflowers springing from odd places like decaying logs or blackened tree bark, and the quiet stillness of only hearing the birds chirp.

Abby would make good on her promise to tell James to meet me after lunch, since this was her idea. I wonder if she'll come with him. It would be better if we weren't alone again. But it's also possible he told her no.

I'll wait five more minutes before I leave.

My mind drifts back to my lesson with William and Seth. Definitely the most entertaining training I've had. A combination of defensive and offensive skills, and the first time I had an Aura in my head. It wasn't entirely unpleasant. He used his air link to whisper jokes in my ear as a distraction and got me almost every time I went to block an attack from Seth. I foolishly kept turning my head and getting soaked, thinking he was right there.

Seth told me it's essential to be able to fight among distractions and thought William was perfect for the job. Auras can put thoughts into your mind, but they can only establish a connection if you permit them. Once the link is there, you can talk to each other without speaking and even show one another memories. I can see how it can help in combat, but it certainly didn't help me during the lesson.

The soft padding of footsteps, that only a Terra could make in a forest this dense, interrupts my thoughts.

I whirl around, waiting for James to appear, but the footsteps stop.

An eerie feeling washes over me. Goosebumps run down my arms as I inspect my surroundings. Nothing has changed. Not like the trees would get up and walk away.

"James, is that you?"

No answer.

It's unusually silent—even the birds have quieted—and it feels like somebody is watching me. I strain my ears, trying to pick up any sound of movement or breathing.

"C'mon, this isn't funny." I stand, biting my cheek, trying to not let myself get scared.

My eyes scan the trees, so I overlook the vines crawling slowly toward my feet until it's too late.

"Oh!" I gasp as they wrap tightly around my ankles. "What the…?"

There's a burst of laughter from my left. I flinch away from it and lose balance, toppling over my bound feet. I brace for a hard impact, but it's soft, instead, as something catches me.

"Sorry, I didn't mean to scare you," says a young feminine voice. "Well, I did, but not like that, just with the vines. How was my camouflage? You didn't see me at all!" She squeals. More vines have caught my arms and are now righting me. They slither off me like snakes back into the shadows of the trees.

I finally see her. She's standing a few feet away, in front of a pine tree, wearing an oversized dark brown sweatshirt and green pants that are rolled up a few times. The sweatshirt's color is the same as her long, straight, brunette hair and big brown eyes, bringing out the color of her olive skin. Her face is round. She can't be more than eleven. She fits in with the trees quite well, but not enough to be completely invisible.

"Yup, you got me. How did I not see you?"

She smiles wide, obviously pleased with herself, and then she vanishes.

What in the world? I look around, bewildered. "Um."

Then, just as quickly as she disappeared, she reappears in the same spot, still with the biggest smile plastered to her face.

My eyes widen, "How did you do that?"

She giggles, a high-pitched bell sound. "I'm a Terra, of course." As if that explained everything.

I've never seen a Terra do that before.

"I just got my abilities this morning!" She jumps up and down, unable to contain her excitement.

"Wow, the first day on the job, and you can do that?"

"I know, isn't it wonderful? I could feel something changing in my body and have been coming out here the last couple of days, practicing, then today, it finally worked. Sorry, you had to be my first victim. When I saw you, I just had to try." She giggles.

Her joy is contagious, and I smile with her. "You've got real talent, kid. You must be new. What's your name?"

"Annabelle, but call me Ann."

"It's nice to meet you, Ann. I'm Maya. You should get back. I'm sure your parents are worried about you."

She shakes her head, and her smile disappears. "I don't have parents, and Jodi doesn't care what I do." Her small shoulders slump.

My heart softens. "Who's Jodi?"

"My aunt, but she's got her hands full with the twins."

Her story seems like a long one, and since James could arrive at any moment, I'll keep my questions for later. I have a feeling this isn't the last time I'll see her. She's a curious one.

"Well then, I'm sure she can use your help." I step forward to physically nudge her to leave.

"Oh, you're meeting your boyfriend out here, huh? Is that who James is?"

Luckily, she's so short, and I'm so close that she can't see my face pale. "Come now, you shouldn't be out here alone. It's not safe."

She folds her arms and plants her feet. "You're out here alone."

"No, I'm not," I say too soon, cursing myself.

Her lips curve up. "I want to meet your boyfriend. You're probably not matched to him since you're meeting out here. He must be really cute."

My mouth falls open in shock, and I'm not quick enough to snap it back closed.

"It's okay, I won't tell. I find this whole matching thing really gross anyway," she whispers.

"He's not my boyfriend," I grumble. The little girl is getting on my nerves. Any positive feelings I had toward her are gone now. I grab her arm and head out the way I came, none too gently.

"Is that what *he'll* say?" she says, looking past me.

I turn around to catch James making his grand entry. He sees me and smiles but then notices Ann and stops.

"Hello, ladies. Didn't know anybody would be out here," he says without hesitation.

I peer down at Ann with little hope she'll believe him, and find her holding in her laughter. I let go of her with a loud sigh, throwing my hands in the air.

James studies us, probably trying to decide whether he should keep up the charade.

"Don't bother," I say weakly.

"He's cute," she snickers.

I glare at her.

James makes his way to us, "And you are?"

"I'm Annabelle, but call me Ann," she chirps. "And you must be James."

His eyes flash to mine. I press my lips into a thin line and lift my shoulders.

"Do you want to see something cool?" Ann exclaims.

Before he can respond, just like before, she vanishes, but I can make out her outline this time. It's the angle or my proximity, but it almost looks like the greenery is bending in places.

James stiffens, eyes widening. I was right. It must not be a common ability in Terras.

She giggles and reappears. "Maya had the same expression."

"You can't camouflage like that?" I ask James.

"No, I've never seen a Terra with that ability."

I give her a once-over. Could this be a unique ability manifesting itself? "My mom would know. She's studied every ability out there."

Ann's face falls, and I see the first hint of nervousness. "Who's your mom?"

"Commander Mayfield."

Her eyes widen as she chews on her lip. "Oh, you know I should be going. Aunt Jodi is probably looking for me."

"What about the twins?" I ask, raising my eyebrows.

She shrugs, taking a few steps back. "They're looking for me, too."

"Right."

"Gotta go, bye!" She dashes away.

"That was weird. Should we stop her?" James takes a step towards her.

I shake my head. "Nah, she's sneaky. She won't want people to know she was out here. You know she tried to scare me? Crept up on me and wrapped vines around my legs. I almost fell. Glad to be rid of her."

"But she knows about us."

"We can only hope that whatever I said to spook her off will keep her mouth closed, too."

James's eyes relax, but one side of his mouth twitches to smile. "So, you wanted to see me again? I knew you couldn't resist me forever."

I roll my eyes. "Get over yourself. This is for Abby."

His eyes become slits. "This isn't about her crazy idea to go beyond the wall, is it?"

I grimace.

"*No.* No way I'm taking her out there. She could get hurt," he fumes.

"Oh, so you don't worry about my safety, but you worry about hers?"

He purses his lips. "The risk wasn't that high."

"And it is now?"

"There would be three of us. I'm guessing you would be coming too?"

I hesitate, remembering my promise to Abby, then nod.

He smirks but continues. "They've upped the patrol. The attacks are getting more frequent. Yes, the risk is higher."

"You're in the legion. I'm sure you could figure out a way around the patrol, and you know your sister can take care of herself quite well. She's not a little girl anymore." I can't believe I'm the one trying to talk him into something dangerous now.

My thoughts go to Abby. I told her I would try, and if I give up at his first denial, that wouldn't be trying. I could try to sway him as I did William on our first date, when I convinced him to take me to Legion Headquarters. All I had to do was get a little too close and blink a lot. I stop myself. Nope, not going there.

"I know." I'm surprised by the bitterness in his voice, but when he speaks again, it's playful. "What do I get out of it?"

"Mine and your sister's sincere gratitude."

He pretends to think that over. "Next."

"I don't have anything you want."

"Maybe you do," he whispers, observing me from underneath the hair that's falling into his face.

I can barely make out his words. But when I do, a shiver runs down my spine, and heat threatens to fill my cheeks.

He cocks his head, taking a step towards me. I feel the gravitational pull again and plant my feet. He watches me for a moment, his eyes softening. Heat swirls inside of me.

"A kiss?" I blurt out.

His eyes widen and flash to my lips. I slowly close the gap between us, unable to breathe or think, showing him I'm serious. I've never kissed anyone before, but I want to. I want to feel his lips against mine just once.

His hand grazes my arm, his eyes holding me captive with such tenderness.

"A kiss?" he asks so faintly I almost don't hear him. He leans in, and I freeze. His lips are mere millimeters from mine when he pulls back. "You know what? Never mind. I'll take you guys, no strings attached. Meet me here. Well, on second thought, we need a new spot. This one is obviously too—"

Hurt slashes my insides, making me ache. "You don't want to kiss me?"

He sighs, "Of course, I want to kiss you, Maya, but not like this. Not because you want something. You're off the hook."

I narrow my eyes. "Why are you going to take us then?"

"What can I say? You got through to me."

I want to argue with him but think of Abby and shut my mouth. I don't need to know his reasons.

"First, we need to figure out a new meetup spot." He paces the area. "Walking along the forest's perimeter will take you to the lake. Let's meet where the trees intersect the waterline."

I try to process his words but can't. I can still feel the way our breaths intermingled and how his lips were so achingly close. When I don't respond, he looks at me. His words finally register and I ask, "Can we get through the wall over there?"

"Sure. We can go through anywhere. It's just about doing it at the right time." He looks at me pointedly.

"What?" I say, suddenly defensive.

"I don't know if you're up for it. You did fall asleep on me last time. I didn't mind, but it would be a lot easier if you could stay awake. We'd need to leave at two in the morning."

"That wasn't because I was tired. Well, yeah, I *was* tired, but healing took a lot out of me."

"Sure, sure," he says, holding back a smile.

"You don't need to worry about me. I got this." Deciding I've had enough of our little chat, I push past him.

He chuckles as I walk away. He says something else, but I'm too far away. I may not be a trained legionary, but I have endurance. I can stay awake all night if I need to.

But just in case, maybe I should stop by the kitchen and grab some guarana before bed. I'm not too fond of the taste of it, but if I'm going to prove myself, I'll need the energy boost.

17

Better in the Daylight

I CAN STILL TASTE THE TARTNESS on my lips as I wait for Abby at the bottom steps of my balcony. Guarana has a subtle sweetness, like kiwi. But unlike kiwi, I can feel it coursing through my veins, making me dance on my toes with enough energy to swim across the lake and back fifteen times. Fatigue shouldn't hit me for hours.

"Hey!" A whisper comes from the shadows under the wooden beam.

I swing around to face Abby. Her hair, dark brown in the black night, is pulled up tight into a braided ponytail.

She raises a brow. "Did you drink it or eat it raw?"

I stop bouncing. Of course, she knows. "I ate the berries. Is that bad?"

She shakes her head and walks towards me, the moonlight shining on her pinched face. "Why didn't you ask me? Based on the hours you needed the boost, I could have whipped you up a drink. Eating the berries by themselves will keep you up all night."

I shrug. She always gets like this with plants. "That's the plan."

"You're going to crash. Hard. And probably unexpectedly."

I dismiss her worries with my hand. "I'll be fine. Let's go!"

I review our surroundings one last time. There's nobody to be seen. Keeping my head low, my body crouched, I race across the plain into the trees. Once in the safety of the forest, I straighten and peer over my shoulder to ensure Abby keeps up. She's right on my heels, face lit up with excitement, eyes focused.

"That was fun." She breathes out.

I smile, feeling more confident having her by my side. I start towards the general area where James said he would meet us.

After walking in silence for a couple of minutes, Abby chuckles softly at my side. I can barely make out her face in the shadows.

She shakes her head. "My brother must have been a terrible influence on you."

"What?"

"Look at you. The girl who doesn't break a single rule out here sneaking around after curfew. And you're not even scared. My heart is pounding."

I remember James's words when we first met, calling me a sheep and telling me he'd try to convince me that we didn't need to follow all the rules. He did, in a way, but not as a bad influence. He just opened my eyes a little wider.

"I'm usually terrified, but having you with me is easier. Your brother made me realize we're in this bubble, completely shielded from the rest of the world. We don't know what's happening outside those walls. I'm more curious, is all."

She doesn't respond straight off, so I glance over, worried I said too much.

She's studying her feet. "I've been thinking the same things for a long time, but you never seemed to think anything was off, so I kept it to myself. You have no idea how it feels for me to hear you say that. Maya, what if what they're telling us isn't the truth? All these strict rules, the matching ceremonies being sped up. I mean, I'm totally down for getting hitched, but I don't know. Is our only value in popping out babies?" Her voice trails off, and I realize the gravity of what she's saying.

My feet feeling like they're filled with lead, I stop walking. Abby advances a few paces before realizing I'm not with her and turns around. She plays with her hair nervously.

"Abby, what you're saying—" I lower my voice even more. "You're flirting with treason."

"Don't things ever feel off to you? Like the drill. Was that even a drill?"

I hesitate, not knowing how much I should share with her, but I regret it. I've kept enough secrets from her—she's my best friend, and she should know the truth.

I start walking again, a little faster this time. The only sound is the soft crunching of our footsteps as I swing around trees and hop over roots that have broken the surface. Unlike James, Abby doesn't make a path for me, but I also don't need it anymore. My feet are getting used to walking on uneven ground, and I can easily find the openings. The half-crescent moon peeks through the trees every so often. The light is welcoming in the shadow-filled foliage.

"It wasn't a drill," I say, breaking the silence.

She trips over her feet but rights herself quickly. "It wasn't?"

I tell her everything I know, everything James told me about the strategic bombings and the other communities being wiped out. It feels so good to let her in.

"Whoa…It makes sense that they don't want to cause unnecessary chaos, but they're seriously underestimating us. Like, we know we're in a war. They need to tell everyone so we can all be better prepared. You should talk to your mom."

That's the last thing I should do. If I go to my mom, she'll ask where I heard it from. Nope, can't do that.

I'm about to tell Abby this when there's movement ahead of us. I come to a halt, putting my hand out to stop her. Her eyes follow mine, but she doesn't have to squint. Terras have better night vision than any other Elemental. There's a black shadow against a tree ahead of us with a human shape.

"It's Avery," Abby says confidently.

"Are you sure?" We're still several yards from the water, and I can barely make out the lake's outline.

"Yup, I can see him." She steps forward, and the shadow starts towards us.

I back away. "I don't know, Abby."

But as it closes in, I recognize the familiar shape of shoulders and slender build, then the curls. James is smiling at us as he jogs to where we stand. I can't help but notice his eyes linger on me, making my pulse quicken as I remember how close his lips were to mine earlier.

"Took ya long enough. We have about a thirty-minute window. Come on. Unless you want me thrown to the wolves," he orders.

Abby and I share a look before following.

"You wouldn't really get thrown out of here, right?" Abby says.

James shakes his head as he starts to walk away. "Oh, my naive little sister."

She looks at me again, and I nod.

"Wanna go back?" I ask.

She sets her shoulders and follows after her brother. I sigh, trailing after her.

"Of course not. It's not her neck on the line," James murmurs.

Abby whacks him on the back of his head. He rubs it, shooting a glare at her. I stifle my giggle.

Even though I'm getting better at finding a path through the woods, the deeper we go, the denser it becomes, and the less moonlight there is to guide us. I can make out James ahead of me and try to walk where he does, but I still find myself wincing whenever a branch breaks underfoot or I crash into a bush.

Finally, James turns and offers me his hand. "Jeez, you'd think a giant was making its way through here." A smile plays on his lips.

"I'm sorry, I don't have the agility of a squirrel," I scoff, accepting his hand.

Abby looks at us curiously but moves around us, taking the lead.

"Just keep heading north," James tells her.

I have no idea how she knows where north is, but after about twenty minutes, the wall of vines appears, catching me off guard again.

James slows, grabs the back of Abby's jacket, and pulls us behind a fallen tree. He puts a finger to his lips and whispers so quietly I have to lean in until his breath is on my ear. It sends butterflies to my stomach.

"Everyone is more lax on Sundays about patrolling since it's our off-day."

"Technically, it's Monday," I mumble.

His lips twitch, but he continues. "On *Sunday* nights, half the normal guards make rounds, giving us a larger window to get out and back in. If my timing is correct—" he checks his watch, "—they should be here in exactly three minutes."

We stoop low, obscuring ourselves behind the massive trunk and foliage. My heart races, but I try to keep my breathing even. With James's intoxicating aroma so close, it's hard to concentrate.

Abby's breathing hitches. They must be near. As Terras, she and James sense them before I can.

A moment later, I hear footfall. I hold my breath, hoping they pass quickly. Light sweeps the trees, and I impulsively lean into James. His warmth radiates off his chest into my shoulder. His arm rises automatically, protectively wrapping around me. My heart decelerates at the touch.

As the footsteps get closer, I squeeze my eyes shut. It feels like he's right on top of us. I wish I had Ann's invisibility right now.

Then the sounds of the guard fade until I can no longer hear him. I finally inhale.

James stands, bringing Abby and me with him. I teeter on my legs, but James releases Abby and steadies me, studying me anxiously.

"Probably should have breathed more," I let out.

Abby's eyes are wide. "That was insane."

I laugh, but only an exhale of breath comes out. That was nothing compared to the last time we hid in the trees. I don't mention it, since I would rather not have her know how much time I've spent in her brother's arms.

I step forward, shaking James's warm hands off. "Shall we?"

We walk up to the wall of vines. They're various hues of green and brown, overlapping each other, making it well camouflaged among the thick trees from a distance. Only up close can I tell it's out of place.

My eyes travel up to the highest point, just below the treetops that blot out the stars.

"How do you get past it?" Abby asks. Her hand is pressed against the wall. The vines shudder at her touch but don't part as they did for James.

"That's a trade secret, Abigail," James says from directly behind me.

I resist the urge to twist around and try to decipher his thoughts. If he's thinking about the last time, how I was a coward and wanted to turn back.

"Are you sure about this?" I don't know if he's talking to Abby or me, but she nods for the both of us.

Like before, he makes a sweeping motion with his hands, and the vines crawl back one by one, opening up a doorway.

"C'mon, you gotta tell me how to do that," Abby whines.

"Darling sister of mine, when you're a legionary like myself, there are things—"

"Oh, shut up," she snaps, stepping through the opening.

I follow after her, without indecision this time.

"Nice to know the loving effects of my reincarnation are wearing off," he retorts.

"I forgot how annoying you could be," she mutters.

"What was that?"

"Nothing, my darling brother."

"I swear I heard you call me annoying. My ears must be clogged."

As they banter behind me, I let their voices drift off. I absorb the forest, unlike before when my mind was clouded by fear, pain, and drowsiness. It's the same as our side but louder and more alive.

I listen to the wind whistling around the trunks, crickets chirping wildly, the soft sounds of owls hooting, and the flapping of unseen wings overhead. Pines stretch up like arrows into the sky, casting long shadows, blacker than the night, hiding creatures of all sizes. But I can see patches of sky overhead, a few stars winking at me.

"Maya?"

I break out of my reverie and notice Abby and James walking ahead, Abby looking at me with an eyebrow raised. I obviously missed something she said.

"Yeah, coming," I call.

We wander for a bit, keeping close to the river. My lack of sight sharpens my other senses, and my body attunes to the moisture shift in the air. My dad taught me how to tell when it would rain. How the air feels heavier, and the smell of wet earth intensifies.

I glance up as a big, fat raindrop splashes onto my cheek. I smile, soaking it in. More fall, and I raise my arms, palms out, welcoming the water. The trees shield most of it, but I walk into the openings, trying to get as much as possible to soak into my skin.

"If I'm a squirrel, you're a fish," James says.

I look ahead, not realizing I was being watched. "Thank you."

"I know how much you enjoy the rain, Maya, but it's not mutual. Maybe we should head back. I thought this would be more exciting. But it's just more of the same," Abby says, referencing past the wall of vines we can no longer see behind us. She pulls up her hood and wraps her arms around herself.

I tilt my head at her. "Are you giving up?"

"No, there's just nothing to see."

James is watching our exchange with a bored expression.

"Is she right? Is there nothing?" But he'd tried convincing me the first time. "Wait a minute. Last time we came out here, you wanted to show me something or some *place*."

It'll be better in the light, he had said.

He purses his lips, and there's a glint in his eye. His lips curve up. "This way."

We follow the stream until it curves off to the left. The rain holds steady. We're damp but not soaked, as we would be without tree cover. I miss the soft crunch of our footsteps as the terrain becomes rockier and more slippery. I hit my shins on unseen obstacles.

"Okay, I take it back. I don't want to see it." I collapse onto a boulder jutting out of the ground at perfect sitting height. I still have the energy from the guarana, but I thought we would be walking, not climbing. The muscles in my legs are protesting.

I barely feel the tension in my feet and legs relax when I'm hoisted up by the crook of my elbow.

"Oh no, you don't. We're almost there."

It's almost scary how he can hurl me around like I weigh nothing.

"Place your feet where I do, okay?"

I watch James's torso and legs, but his feet disappear into the darkness, even with my night-adjusted eyes.

"It would be nice if I could actually see your feet," I murmur.

He sighs and grabs my waist. His touch sends a shock through me, and he lifts me onto a high boulder in front of him. Abby's just ahead, leaping gracefully from one rock to the next, ignoring us.

The rocks grow in size. The surrounding trees create a canopy above our heads, their trunks out of sight below us. All around us are boulders larger than my body, and I stiffen at a sound I would have registered earlier if I hadn't been so focused on not twisting my ankle. There's a roar of water up ahead, like hundreds of cymbals crashing together. It's muffled for now, but we're getting close.

I study Abby's ballerina-like movements and try to copy them, jumping from one boulder to another. I probably look less like a dancer and more like a billy goat, but at least I'm moving forward.

The roaring intensifies and propels me, as if an imaginary string attaches me to the water. I faintly hear James behind me, presumably just as graceful as Abby, but I don't risk glancing backward.

Abby slows to a stop, staring down beyond the boulders. I finally catch up, but the rocks are slippery. I put my hands down in a crouch to keep from falling. Feeling more stable, I slowly straighten and peer down. I can see just enough to know there is an edge. Frothy white water disappears into the abyss below. The rain subsides, and the sky is beginning to clear. Thousands of stars blink above us.

"What do you think?" James's voice is barely audible over the roar of the water.

Abby and I respond at the same time. "It's beautiful!"

"This *would* be better in the daylight," I call.

"Yeah, at least you can see the waterfall with the sky semi-clear. There's a plunge pool down there, and then the valley stretches out to the mountains. It's quite the view on a normal sunny day."

I want to sit on the edge to reach out and touch the water with my feet, but that's probably a bad idea. Instead, I walk upriver, where I can't fall to my death.

Abby stays to take in the view that I can't see, settling herself in the crease of a rock. James follows closely behind me. I try to ignore him as I take off my shoes and socks, rolling up my pant cuffs. I step into the water, and its icy tendrils shoot up my foot into my leg.

"I'm glad you convinced me to take you here. It's one of my favorite spots." His voice almost sounds reverent, but it's clearer now that we are further from the cliff.

"You come out here often, then?"

"No, just once."

"What were you doing?"

His hands are in his pockets, and he's taking in the valley, seemingly lost in thought.

"James?"

He looks at me with a smile.

"What were you doing out here?"

"Oh. Nothing." He looks away and bends down to grab something. He hurls what looks like a rock over the cliff. "Have you ever wanted to leave this place?"

All the time. But, instead, I say, "Where would I go?"

He flings his arms out toward the black expanse. "Anywhere. It's beautiful out there."

"Is it?" I scoff, imagining war-torn streets, Coms trying to kill us everywhere we go.

He turns to me. He looks like he's about to say something but then faces the cliff's edge once again.

"What was it like?" I ask.

"Lonely," he says without looking at me.

"Were you scared?"

"Nah, not with—I stayed away from extremists. Kept moving."

Extremists? Doesn't he mean Coms?

I'm about to ask when he says, "I'm going to check on Abby," and walks off.

I study the water sloshing around my feet, undisturbed by me, and continuing towards the waterfall. The current is strong, pulling me, wanting to sweep me away. It surely would if I stepped in any deeper. Pins and needles attack my feet, as my toes start to numb. I sigh and step back out of the water. Slipping my shoes on, I join James on the rocks.

Cold seeps through my thin rain jacket, causing me to hug my arms to my chest. And now my feet are freezing. The one time my desire to be in the water does me harm. Night vision would be a lot handier right now. All *my* element wants to do is get me killed at the moment.

"Are you cold?" James places a hand on my arm. It sends a jolt through me, and I shiver. I pretend it's from the cold.

"A little. I shouldn't have put my feet in. The water is freezing."

"Well, we are higher up. That's ice melt from the snow on the mountains."

"That would have been good to know. I didn't grow up in the woods."

"Well, actually you did."

I roll my eyes, and he chuckles, rubbing my arm in rhythmic motions, trying to warm me. His touch makes me shudder harder.

"Here, take my vest. I'm not that cold." He's not in uniform but wearing a long-sleeved black shirt and a dark gray puffer vest that he's now unzipping.

"No, I'm fine. I just need to get moving."

He holds the vest to me. "Take it, Maya."

His hazel eyes capture me, and I give in. It's big on me, but I'm already warming up, his body heat transferring to me. His delightful rain-and-earth scent wafts off it, and I fight the urge to bring the vest to my nose and breathe in.

"Thank you. Let me know if you start getting cold, and I'll give it right back." My eyes slide over his body, over the outline of his pecs and ab muscles underneath his tight shirt. I glance away before he catches me checking him out.

We're quiet for a while, and then he says, "I'm sorry about your dad."

I suck in a breath, looking at him.

His eyes hold deep emotion. "Ever since I realized it was you, I've been thinking about your family. Your dad was a good guy. Did you know our dads were friends?"

I shake my head slowly. Abby never mentioned that, but it makes sense. We lived pretty close to each other.

"Yeah, he would come over and play this ball game with my dad. I don't quite remember the rules, but there was an exchange of earth and water spheres. They'd hit them. I'm not sure what happened from there. Anyway, I was up late once, and they let me join. Your dad was so patient with me as I learned how to hit one. I didn't have my abilities yet, and he just kept throwing his water balls, never getting frustrated, which was the opposite of my dad. I think he threw two ground balls and was done with me."

I'm awestruck. It's lovely to hear a story about my dad I haven't heard before. James notices my expression and grins. Then reaches out and grabs a strand of hair off my shoulder, twirling it between his fingers. I stiffen.

"My dad eventually told me the details of your father's accident."

"Yeah, a Lympha who drowns. That's quite the story." I chuckle darkly.

He tenderly places his hand on my cheek, forcing me to meet his gaze, his eyes full of sympathy and understanding. "I understand why you don't like talking about it. I can only imagine how you feel, him dying to save your life. But making a sacrifice like that for your child…I don't think a parent would want to go any other way. He must have loved you so much. But I'm so sorry you have to bear that burden."

Tears well up in my eyes, threatening to escape.

"We gotta come back in the daylight, Maya. The view is breathtaking," Abby announces, walking up to us.

James quickly drops his hand, and I step back, not realizing how close we are, and dry my eyes with the back of my hand.

She catches sight of us and hesitates. "Is everything okay?"

"Yup," I try to say cheerfully, but it sounds like a croak.

She looks at my jacket, noticing her brother's vest, but says nothing. "We should probably head back now if we want to beat the sunrise," she suggests, still eyeing me suspiciously.

We start towards the rocks, but I say, "Can we go a different way down by chance?"

I look for another opening in the trees, but something catches my attention—a flash of movement near the tree line across the river. The clouds clear for a moment, and in the moonlight, a bundle of fur moves…but I notice a man's face as it stands. He has a long beard, the same color as the dark brown fur he's wearing. He smiles at me and something flashes on his side.

I scream and involuntarily step back, bumping into Abby.

James and Abby whip around just as the man turns to flee. Oh good, he's not trying to attack. But my stomach drops at a different realization. He's got to have come from somewhere. He'll tell his people our location.

"We can't let him get away," James yells. "I'll go after him. You two need to get back. Abby, follow your instincts. You'll be able to open the wall."

Abby and I don't move. We just stare at him like he's grown another arm.

Panic and fear billow inside of me. "James, no. There…There could be more of them," I stammer.

Seemingly out of nowhere, he pulls weapons, a knife and a gun, from behind him. I thought we didn't fight with guns.

He hands me the sheathed knife and curls my fingers around the hilt. "Just in case." He breathes, staring into my eyes. His eyes are bright and full of determination, with no trace of fear. "I'm trained for this. I'll be fine. Just go!" he shouts to both of us.

"Avery," Abby whimpers, reaching toward him, but he's already racing off to the river's edge.

I watch him getting closer to the water, and at the last second, I fling my hands out to separate it for him, but he launches into the air, clearing the water altogether and landing on the other side.

Before we can take another breath, he's lost in the trees.

18

Trek

SHOVING THE KNIFE through the loop in my pants, I grab Abby's hand, and run. She's resistant at first but follows, tears streaming silently down her face.

"He'll be okay," I say, trying to believe it myself.

But then a terrifying thought enters my mind: there could be more of them.

I take in our surroundings as we run, jump, and slide downhill, looking for movement. It's too dark to see much. Tree branches catch on my clothes, sometimes slashing at my face. My palms are bloodied from falling on the rocks, but I push myself forward.

We reach flat ground, but a tree comes out of nowhere, and I smack right into it, falling into the dirt. Abby's by my side instantly. I grab her outreached hand, ready to launch back into a full sprint when she holds me back.

"Maya, stop. You're running like a maniac. Are you even paying attention to where we are?"

I use the opportunity to catch my breath. My throat burns. I need water. Water. We were supposed to be following the river.

"No, not at all." I glance around, feeling jumpy, adrenaline and guarana still coursing through my veins.

"Okay, let's take a minute to calm down. We need to find the river," she says.

"I thought you're supposed to be a walking compass."

Her eyebrows pull down. "I'm out of practice, Maya. I haven't been in the open forest since I was eleven."

I deflate a little, knowing I'm taking out my distress on her. "I know, sorry. Hold on."

Closing my eyes, I focus on my Sage. I hear the wind whistling through the trees, the quiet rustling of small animals, then the shuffling of something bigger.

I stiffen. "There's something out there, Abby."

"It could be an animal," Abby says hopefully.

"I don't know, but let's get moving. I believe the river is this way. I can feel it." I point east, or well, I hope it's east.

Our footsteps crunch quietly for a while and not as quickly, not wanting to bring attention to ourselves. Once we come up to the sounds of rushing water, we pick up speed. I'm about to launch into the river for a drink when Abby holds me back.

She has a finger up to her lips, eyes wide. My gaze follows hers to two tiny heaps of fur, baby black bears on the river's edge. She backs away slowly, bringing me with her. I don't understand why she looks frightened—they're just babies—but after a moment, I do. Our footsteps bring the attention of something much more significant that I'd overlooked…the mama bear.

The bear is large, with jet-black fur, pointed white teeth poking out of its top lip, a glistening snout, and narrowed dark eyes. She is not pleased to see us, but the babies are none the wiser, still playing in the water happily. We interrupted the little family getting a drink.

A growl escapes the beast and I stifle a gasp as my heart beats out of my chest. I continue stepping backward and fight the urge to run. I have little experience with bear encounters, but I do remember my dog loving to chase me when I ran.

"It's okay. She's just nervous," Abby whispers.

The cubs' ears perk up, noticing us as the mom huffs, forcefully blowing air out of her flared nostrils.

"Can you tell her we come in peace?" I whisper, keeping my voice barely above a breath.

The bear bows its head, keeping an eye on us, and nudges one of her cubs. It nips at her ear, then runs off, the other cub following suit. They leap onto a black cottonwood tree and climb up and out of sight. Great, she's getting rid of her babies so she can eat us in peace.

She rises on her hind legs and comes down hard with her two front paws, thankfully not getting closer. I jump, and Abby elbows me in the ribs. One of her arms is raised, palm facing the bear, their eyes locked into a staring match. The seconds tick by without a breath.

I have to do something. What if it decides to charge us? Abby will be no help.

I focus, instead, on the water, pulling it into the air. A good-sized amount hovers above its head. I'm about to release it onto the bear, hoping it doesn't make it angrier, when Abby whispers "Stop," out of the side of her mouth.

I hold it, waiting.

The bear holds her gaze and huffs again before finally backing away. When it gets close enough to the tree her babies had scaled, she turns and climbs it.

Abby exhales and I release the water.

"Let's get away from here," she says.

"Don't have to tell me twice." My thirst is long forgotten.

THE SKY IS LIGHTENING. We'd already given up trying to get back before the sun rose, and now we hope to get back before breakfast. The adrenaline I felt is long gone, and now only guarana and the pure desire to never see a tree again keeps me going. Every once in a while, the knot in my stomach returns as I think about James. Is he okay? Did he catch up with that Com? Where is he now? But I have to push the questions out of my mind. Worrying about him won't help us right now. Abby doesn't say anything, but I know she's worried, too. She just got him back.

We stay far from the river, not wanting to risk another wildlife encounter. Abby and I both have doubts as we wander through the forest, me thinking we're on the wrong side of the mountain and Abby thinking we're following the incorrect river. After what seems like hours, we finally reach the wall of vines.

"Oh, thank you!" Abby shouts and falls against it.

"Are you hugging it?" I was beginning to think being out here didn't worry her at all. Maybe all Terras are perfectly at home in the forest like James, but she looks as relieved as I feel.

"I could kiss it, too." She smiles lazily.

I giggle, feeling loopy from staying up all night and being lost in the forest for half of it. "Okay, do your magic. Get us inside."

She pulls back to study the wall. Closing her eyes, her chest rises and falls slowly, deep in concentration. She reaches her hand out and waves it as James did.

Nothing happens.

She opens her eyes. A flicker of frustration crosses her face before she slumps to the ground. "Whelp, that's all I got." Her head falls back against the white tree trunk and her eyes flutter sleepily.

"No! That can't be it. Come on. James said something about instincts. You should be able to," I beg.

Her eyes are closed, and all she says is, "His name is Avery."

I huff and sit beside her. "We could climb it." Rows of dark round branches circle the thick tree above us. We'd have to climb at least a hundred feet to get over, and even then, it's not close enough.

My eyes travel down the tree bark that is peeled off the trunk, leaving a white smooth surface.

I shake Abby, and she peers at me. "Try to move the tree, I have an idea."

She sighs and heaves herself up.

After two failed attempts, I catch her as she passes out on the third attempt. I lower her to the ground, check her breathing, and settle next to her. Hopefully, another wild animal doesn't try to kill us while she's out.

Trying not to give up hope, I pull out my communicator. There are two people I can call. I twist the bracelet Sebastian gave me as the line connects.

William answers quickly. "Hello?" He sounds confused but not groggy. Good, he's already awake.

"William, it's me, Maya."

"Maya!" he says excitedly. "It's six in the morning. I didn't peg you as an early riser, but hey, I'm definitely not complaining about getting a call from my girl. What's up?"

"Okay, this is going to sound crazy, but you'll just have to trust me." I take a deep breath, already cringing. "I'm stuck outside the wall and need help getting back in."

He's silent for a beat and then, "Oh boy, I can't wait to hear this story. I'll be there. Wait, where are you exactly?"

I laugh nervously. "I don't know. We got lost."

"We?"

"Abby and I. Oh! Another thing. Peter, Abby's match. He's a Terra. Hopefully, he can open the wall. Do you think you can bring him?"

"Brilliant. Your knight in shining armor is on his way. I also want to clarify that I know you're fully capable, but since you called me and need help…"

"No, I'm not above being saved. Call me a damsel in distress, why don't you."

He chuckles. "We'll come as quickly as we can. I should be able to ping your communicator. You caught me at a good time. An alert went off, and only after I got up and dressed were we told it was a false alarm. I'll see you soon."

"Thank you."

"You can count on me, Maya. As I told you before, I'm here for you."

The call ends, and I'm wrapped in the quiet sounds of the forest once more. Abby doesn't fidget once. She must be drained. I wonder when it'll hit me.

I lean against the trunk to wait a while, grateful to not be walking anymore. And remember my physical state. My clothes are dirt-stained and bloody from all the times I fell or got attacked by branches. I pull my fingers through my hair but give up. Unfortunately, the only thing that will help is a shower. Then the hunger pains hit me. At least it rained earlier, letting me siphon water from the trees, or I would be in worse shape.

I shift my weight on the uncomfortable ground of pine needles and pieces of bark, and something pokes my leg. James's knife! I completely forgot about it. I pull it out carefully and turn it over in my hand. It comes to a sharp silver point, and the hilt is hand-carved out of wood. I move my fingers over the design. There are letters at the base, spelling out AJS. This is his, Avery James Stevens.

Now that I'm alone, I lower my face to his vest and breathe in. It smells like him. His sweet, earthy aroma—like being caught in the rain shortly after a fresh shower. I can almost imagine him here. My throat thickens, but I will myself not to be overcome by emotion. I can't let my guys find me a weeping mess. If the tears come now, they won't stop.

After only about fifteen minutes of waiting, I see the wall shimmer and move. I shake my friend. "Abby, wake up!"

"No, stahp, leave meh ah-lone." She pushes me weakly away from her.

I shake her harder, but she won't open her eyes. "You asked for it." I reach my hands out, and the water droplets fly off the trees around us, gathering into a ball above her head. Then I let it drop.

"Agh!" Abby screams and jumps up, toppling me over. She shoots me an accusatory look. "Why'd you do that?" Her wet hair is plastered to her face.

I rise to my feet, trying to dust the dirt off my pants, but it's useless, "You wouldn't wake up, look." I point to the wall. The hole widens as the dark vines slither from the center.

"Oh!" Abby exclaims. She sweeps her wet hair back from her face, forgetting her anger. "Did James make it back?"

She takes one look at my expression and her face crumples.

I grab her hand as we walk up to the hole, giving it a slight squeeze before facing the widening space. "You're much faster than—" I begin, but stop dead when I realize the figures in front of us aren't our matches but our mothers.

19

Consequence

I T'S A PAINFULLY LONG WALK of shame back to the manor, not only with our mothers, but with Commander Lawrence and three other legionaries. I'm surprised they don't handcuff us with the backup they brought. Thankfully, none of them are our matches, and I silently hope we don't run into them. No need to get our guys in trouble too.

I have never seen Mrs. Stevens so enraged. My mom has yet to say anything. Her quiet intensity is plenty loud though. Abby's face is pinched, but she doesn't talk about her brother. I take that as my cue to stay silent about him as well.

We're escorted to my mom's office, which doubles as her lab. The legionaries stand outside the doors like we're a couple of escaped prisoners, not teenage girls. At least it's a comforting space, with walls painted a soft blue.

Abby and I take our seats on the small, plush, brown couch in the corner, holding back our sighs of contentment. The couch is luxurious compared to the hard forest floor. No wonder my mom has spent more nights sleeping on this than her own bed.

She takes a seat behind her messy desk, papers scattered across it, one overlapping a picture with Dad in it. The old brown, dingy frame encases our only family picture. Cal is inside my mom's stomach, but it still counts.

Mrs. Stevens trades her look of disdain for one of worry as she moves to the other side of the room.

Commander Lawrence towers over us. "What were you two thinking?" his deep voice belts through the room.

I flinch as a gust of wind hits me and throws my hair behind my shoulders.

Abby is casually checking her dirt-filled nails. "What? We just wanted to go on an early morning hike. It gets boring around here. It's not like we're prisoners." I know, under her easygoing facade, she's freaking out.

The commander carefully folds his arms. I swear I can see the air ripple around him. "No, you're not prisoners, but you know the rules. They are for your safety."

"Fine, we won't do it again. Can we go now?" Abby says indifferently.

This time it's Mrs. Stevens's shrill voice. "No, you cannot go, young lady. We just barely got your brother back. You could have been taken or killed by a Com. Why would you do something so stupid?" She sniffles and chokes out, "I can't lose you, too."

Abby's composure crumples. "I'm sorry, Mom. We just wanted to explore a little. Maya and I have grown up in this place. Never having the chance to leave. You don't know what it's like." She looks at all three of them. "You have lived a whole life and experienced things outside these walls. We haven't. We didn't go far. We just wanted to see what was out there." She raises her eyebrows at me, silently asking if I plan on chiming in.

"Yeah, we were just curious, that's all," I murmur.

"Well, you did go pretty far, or you wouldn't have triggered the barrier alarms," Commander Lawrence growls.

In trying to stay far from the river on our way back, we must have crossed that invisible barrier.

He lowers his gaze to me. "Curiosity kills people out there."

My thoughts go to James. No, he's still alive. He has to be.

"Who helped you get beyond the wall?"

Abby has yet to bring up James, probably for a good reason. But if he's hurt somewhere, shouldn't we tell them what happened? He could also be fine. Maybe he's already back, and confessing would just get him kicked out. I let Abby answer this one.

"Nobody. I opened it," Abby finally responds.

He looks at her hard, unblinking, and she doesn't break his gaze. She's good.

"How do you open it then?" He sneers, his lips curving up.

She places her hands delicately on her crossed leg, shrugs her shoulders, and says, "Instinct."

His face turns an awful shade of red as he shifts on his feet. "A legionary was with you, or one showed you how to do it. You wouldn't have been stuck out there, unable to get back otherwise. You *will* tell me."

Abby slumps back on the couch, half closing her eyes—the picture of exhaustion. "Nobody was with us. I couldn't open it back up because I was too tired. I used up all my energy." She appears to have a hard time tilting her chin back up, her face sorrowful. I will have to applaud her acting skills when we're alone.

My mom speaks up for the first time. "Kirt, I believe her. Let them go. They need to get some sleep, obviously."

"Oh no, they don't. They have duties to fulfill. These girls made their beds, and now they must lie in them. Also, you're not allowed to see each other until I say otherwise." He shoves out his hand. "Give me your communicators."

"No!" we both whine in protest.

"We need them. You can't do that. How do we contact anyone about anything?" I ask.

"Is that really necessary?" Mrs. Stevens questions. "I know these two. Not seeing each other will be punishment enough. They do need to be in contact with their matches."

"Fine, but delete each other's information. No contact at all."

We reluctantly do as he demands, showing him when we've done so, and he releases us.

Outside his door, Abby pulls me in for a quick hug. After one last crestfallen glance, we leave in opposite directions.

ONCE I GET TO MY BEDROOM DOOR, I expect my mom to leave, but she follows me in.

"Are you going to tell me the real reason you went out there? Don't give me this exploring crap."

I look at her dumbfoundedly. "Why else would we go out there?"

"I don't know. You have never once asked to leave. You've always followed all the rules without complaining. Honestly, I'm a little relieved."

Okay, she's losing it. "What are you talking about, Mom?"

"You, never testing boundaries or questioning things. Maya, I used to be your age, and I definitely wasn't as complacent. I'm glad to know you have your own mind. I hope you found answers for whatever reasons you went out there, because now you're on Kirt's radar. He'll be watching you."

"Wait, back up. You're *glad* I broke a rule?"

"No, going beyond the walls is dangerous. I wish you'd come to me first. But if you must break a rule, that's not the worst. I hope you got it all out of your system. I bet you don't want to go back out there, huh?"

I shake my head at her, squinting into her light blue eyes. "I think I'm hallucinating from sleep deprivation."

"Sorry, honey, but no sleep for you. You've got to go help prepare breakfast. But, please, shower first. You look like you got into a fight with a bear."

I turn before she can see me smirk and walk into my bathroom, closing and locking the door behind me. If she only knew.

Finally alone, I let myself think about James as I take off his vest, and feel the burning sensation in my eyes. I throw myself in the shower and twist the knob as far as it will go. Everything that I've pushed down—the fear, sadness, and guilt—all come bubbling up and break the surface, and I'm not sure I can stop it.

A sob escapes my throat, and I slump down, still in my clothes, letting the fresh, hot water wash away the caked-on blood, dirt, and tears.

AFTER BREAKFAST, THE EFFECTS of the guarana begin wearing off. My head is foggy, my feet heavy, and I have a strange ringing in my ears. My movements become sluggish as I make my way to my room.

I'm so out of it I don't see the two figures waiting at my door.

"Maya, are you okay? What happened?" William asks.

I stop short, William's and Sebastian's worried faces swim into view, and I immediately forget what he just said.

"Huh?" I stagger towards my door and reach for the knob but miss. I bring my hand up in front of my face, study it, and slowly grab the knob, successfully this time. I smile triumphantly.

"Maya?"

I jump back, startled. I study William's long eyelashes and then linger on his lips. They're moving, I realize, a moment too late. I wonder what it would be like to kiss them. I sway forward a little. No, not here.

He looks over to Sebastian, whose lips are also moving. Those perfect plump lips…I wonder if they can breathe fire. I laugh. He's not a dragon.

My eyes slowly travel up to his baby blues. A thousand unsaid words are swimming in their depths. Maybe I'll hear them one day. His eyebrows are pulled down. Their words finally make it to my ears.

"Do you think she took something?"

"She sounded fine on the communicator."

"We should get someone."

"Nah, we've got this, mate. Don't want to get her in more trouble than she surely is already in. How else do you think she got through the barrier?"

Their faces mold into one: dark skin, brown eyes, blond hair…now he has light skin.

I try to shake my head out of the fog but trip over my own feet into my room. Huh. I did get my door open. I steady myself as multiple arms reach out. I brush them off.

"I'm fine, just tired," I mumble, but something incoherent comes out instead.

William grabs me lightly around the waist and steers me to the couch. He's never had a problem touching me. I wish Sebastian would do that. I stare at him as I sit, none too gracefully.

He purses his lips but then turns his back on me, reappearing a moment later with a glass of water.

I shake my head and try to focus on my words. "It's just the guarana. I need sleep."

Sebastian peers at William, who is studying my face, "Did you get that?"

"Sleep?" William guesses.

I nod and lay down on the couch. My eyes close instantly. A pillow slides under my head, and my shoes slip off as a blanket wraps around me. I want to open my eyes and thank them, but I can't move. I try to lift my arm, hand, finger, *anything*, but I can't. Weights are wrapped around every ligament in my body, and I don't have the strength to push them off.

"Are you sure we shouldn't get somebody?" Sebastian asks.

There's a hand on my forehead and then cold fingers on my neck. "Her pulse is strong. She doesn't have a fever. She must just be exhausted. She was out all night," William reassures.

"Well, I don't want to leave her alone," Sebastian rumbles.

"I agree," William responds. "She's out. I'll take the first watch."

"I've still got time. I'll hang out, too."

My mind drifts: flashes of color, blurred faces, snippets of trees, swimming through the water, and then words break through.

"Are you spending time with her that I don't know about?"

"No. What's with you?"

The silence that follows almost pulls me under again.

"She called you."

"So?"

"It means something."

"You're overthinking it."

"Whatever. Time to go. I'll switch you out when I'm done."

"Hey, Sebastian, wait!"

I hear the click of a door before being dragged back under once again. No more colors or images this time, just a dark void.

20

Unwanted Answers

MY BRAIN RATTLES against the inside of my head.

"Maya, Maya, come on. You gotta wake up."

I open my eyes, wondering where I am, and why my room is blurred. I quickly sit up, knocking my forehead into something hard, and fall back down onto the pillow.

"Ouch!" a masculine voice grunts.

I rub my head and look around as my mind clears. "Sebastian?" He's standing over me, also rubbing his head. "Sorry," I mumble.

"I'm okay, just relieved to see you're alright."

"Why wouldn't I be? And what are you doing here?" The memories from before I fell asleep come rushing back, and the blood drains from my face. "Oh no." I slap my hands over my eyes, feeling more embarrassed than ever. "I can't believe you guys saw me like that. Stupid guarana," I hiss into my palms.

He chuckles. "That explains it. I notice you're still wearing my bracelet."

I drop my hands and touch the metal. It's become a part of me. "I love it."

He smiles in a way that takes my breath away. His eyes brighten, and my heart beats irregularly. Wow, he's so beautiful.

"You're trying to distract me. You must be completely unattracted to me now."

He moves to sit on the couch. "May I?"

"Yeah, of course." I move my legs and sit up straighter, pulling my fingers through my hair.

"If anything, I find you more adorable."

"I don't believe you. I completely embarrassed myself."

"Vulnerability is attractive."

I look at him sideways, and his intense stare catches me off guard. He's sitting so close, those beautiful blue eyes inviting me in. I want to reach out and touch him, but I hold still because he starts to lean in.

His face inches closer to mine, those eyes trained on me, making my mind go blank. He's inches from my lips when I turn my face, and he presses them to my cheek as softly as a butterfly's wing.

He pulls back abruptly. It sends a lick of fire through my body, almost like he burned me—a fire I *want* to consume me whole.

"I'm sorry. I don't know what came over me. For…forgive me," he stammers, looking at his feet.

My fingers come up to where his lips touched me. The spot is warmer than the rest of my face. Why in the world did I turn my face? That could have been my first kiss.

He stands up, his cheeks darkening. He still isn't looking at me. "William must have plugged your communicator in. It went off. You have lessons starting soon."

Then he rushes out the door, leaving me still as a statue.

Once I find the ability to move, I scramble to my lesson. No defensive or offensive training today. I'm back to water agility. Not too complicated, which is a relief, because my mind isn't present. I can't stop thinking about Sebastian, trying to figure out how he makes me feel. Why didn't I let him kiss me? He's not only good-looking, but he has an energy that draws me in. I love being around him, but— An image of James jumping over the river surges to my mind like a punch to the gut. I accidentally drop the water on myself. Where is he? Is he back? I survey the land, as if he'd be lingering next to a tree someplace.

"What is with you today? You seem distracted. Is it those boys?" Seth chuckles. "We can be done early if you want."

"Yeah, that'd be great!" I say, a little too enthusiastically, and start up the path.

"I expect your head to be here tomorrow!" he shouts.

I wave my hand at him without a backward glance and hear him muttering. "Who am I kidding? I won't get her back until after her ceremony…and probably not even then."

I barely register what he says. There's only one thing on my mind now, finding Mrs. Stevens.

"MRS. STEVENS!" I CALL OUT, locating her in the gardens. I was worried Abby might be here, too, since I'm not supposed to talk to her. Luck is on my side, though, because Mrs. Stevens is by herself, bringing pears through their entire plant cycle. They're currently in the blossoming stage. I can smell the potent floral scent as the white flower-filled trees sway in the wind.

She looks at me pointedly. "Abby's not here, and you're not to be talking to her."

"I'm not looking for her. I know we made a huge mistake, and I'm not complaining about our punishment."

She eyes me in the same manner a second longer before her face returns to her usual cheerful demeanor. "What can I do for you, sweetheart?"

"I just have a question. Are there any long-lasting effects from taking guarana?"

She doesn't skip a beat at my random question. "You mean after it has worn off?" she asks as the flowers wilt and fall to the ground.

"Yes."

"Well, depending on how much is taken and whether it was in its pure form or mixed."

"Pure," I respond.

"Long-lasting? No. There are many short-term side effects. They include drowsiness, memory loss, trouble thinking, mood changes, poor balance, high blood pressure, dizziness, and slurred speech. Once you get adequate rest, those issues resolve." She continues to caress one of the tree's branches, and leaves start growing from the limbs. Soon I'm surrounded by rows of full, leafy green trees.

"That's good to know." I sigh and think about how to broach the actual reason for my intrusion.

She studies me with her brown eyes. "I'm guessing you took some last night? How are you feeling?"

"You caught me," I say sheepishly. "I got some sleep, so much better now. I just wanted to make sure I wouldn't randomly pass out again."

She nods as tiny pears grow from the branches, getting greener and plumper.

It's now or never. "You know we haven't spoken much since Ja— *Avery* returned. I'm sure it's wonderful having your son back. I know Abby's been thrilled."

She smiles politely, but her eyebrows turn down. "Yes, it has been, but I haven't seen him today, strangely enough."

I gulp. "He's staying with you, right?"

She nods again, her eyebrows furrowing even more. "He was gone when I woke. I thought he must have had some duties earlier than usual, but I'm getting a little worried now." Her eyes cloud over, and the pears stop growing.

My heart picks up speed. He still isn't back. The knot in my stomach returns, and my legs weaken.

Her smile recovers as she says, "I'm sure he's fine. He must be having a busy day. I bet I'll see him at dinner." The pears grow again, and she plucks one, turning to me. "Hungry?"

I don't know if I rearranged my facial expression back to casual interest in time. "No thanks." I missed lunch because of my nap, but I have no appetite now. "It was nice chatting with you. I need to get back."

I turn, but Mrs. Stevens calls, "Let me know if you see him?" Her face is hopeful.

I nod and try to smile, then hurry away.

Don't panic. Don't panic. They will realize he's missing soon, when nobody has seen him. I can't talk to Abby about it either. Maybe I should tell my mom the truth. James getting in trouble here is better than being tortured by Coms. What else could keep him away for so long? He must have been captured. My heart pounds in my ears. We need to save him.

I reach the end of the vineyard and head towards the building, feeling more resolute. I need to get help out there to search for James. Inside, I start for the stairs, but a familiar face comes down the grand staircase.

"Maya, I was just looking for you," says William.

"Oh hey." I know I can't ignore him and keep walking. He'll expect answers. The last time I coherently talked to him, I asked him to save me outside the wall. I try to push down my worry. "I'm glad I ran into you. I wanted to apologize," I say, biting my lip.

"No need, I'm glad you're okay. You had me worried this morning, but Sebastian told me you woke up and were yourself again. I've been trying to find you since. I hoped to catch you after lessons, but Seth said you left early. You're a hard girl to track down," he babbles, letting out a short laugh.

"Well, you found me. I probably should have my communicator on me. Sorry, I left it in my room."

He waves away my apology.

"I hope I didn't get you in trouble earlier."

"You didn't. Got the news about you being found right before I left. But I am curious why you were out there." His hands are in his pockets, and he's missing his cheerful demeanor.

"It was dumb of Abby and me to do it. I can tell you about it another time, but I was just on my way to see my mom. I do want to thank you, though. You were so willing to come to my rescue." I reach out and grab his hand. "That means a lot to me."

He grins, then pulls me in unexpectedly for a hug. "I'm really glad you're okay," he murmurs in my ear before pulling back. "I can't wait to hear that story. Dinner? It's nice today. We can eat outside if you want."

"Yeah, sure, that'll be great," I reply, even though I doubt I'll be able to eat.

"Okay, it's a date." His smile is big, making his dimple show.

I can't help but grin back. He's so cute, with his mussy hair and that dreamy smile.

As soon as he's gone, though, guilt claws at me. How can I be gushing over a boy while James could be stuck in some Com confinement somewhere…or worse?

When I reach my mom's lab, she's not alone. Another deeper voice floats into the hall. Commander Lawrence.

"Evelynn, somebody had to have helped them. I'm going to find him, and I'm going to kill him." His angry voice booms out of her office.

I slink to the wall and listen at the crack of the door.

"You don't mean that," my mom responds.

"When I'm done with him, he'll wish he were dead. For some scoundrel to take two young women—*matched* young women—out of my base! I don't know. I might kill him, Evy."

"Why do you think it's a boy?"

"Seriously? You were a teenager once. Who did you sneak around with when you were her age? And not only that, ninety-five percent of our legion are men. They're the only ones who know how to get in and out," he growls.

"Let's say you're right. Where was he when we found them? We only saw the girls on the cameras," she asks.

"He left them out there to die!" A loud bang sounds, making me jump.

"Don't hit my desk. Calm down, Kirt. None of our legionaries would leave a woman by themselves. Maybe he's still out there. Something could have happened."

His voice is softer when he responds. "That's a possibility. Anyone missing today?"

I hold my breath.

"No, everyone is here and accounted for."

Head counts are done every morning. How could they have missed James? Footsteps approach the door, so I flee down the corridor, open the first door I come to, and throw myself in. It's a small broom closet, dark, damp, and smells strongly of chemicals.

I put my ear to the door, waiting for more footsteps or voices. Nothing. I wait a few more minutes before opening the door. When I peer out, the hall is empty, and I leave in the opposite direction of my mom's lab.

I need to get a message to Abby somehow. We must give James more time to return. They can't know it was him. I have no idea how he got counted today, but I'll take it. The miscount likely won't happen again, though. I can only hope he's back by then.

I get to my room and grab my communicator off my nightstand. There are missed messages from William, probably when he was searching for me. As I stare at my dented wooden nightstand, I see a corner of a piece of paper jutting out of the one crooked drawer, and it hits me.

I yank it open and grab James's letter to me, then dig under the other miscellaneous items in the drawer until my hand touches a plastic spiral. I grab my notebook, rip out a piece of paper and jot down a few sentences. I slip it into my pocket. It'll be easy enough to slide it under her door on the way to dinner.

In the bathroom, my clothes are in a wet pile in the corner. The knife is still hidden in my coat pocket. I stride over to the mound and gingerly pull it out, rubbing my finger over the initials again. I think about holding onto it, but hide it in my bathroom drawer instead.

James's vest is on the counter where I put it before sinking into the shower fully clothed this morning. I press it against my face. It still smells like him. I consider putting it on but think better of it, placing it on a shelf in my closet instead. Such an ordinary article of clothing, but it's a piece of him.

He'll be back for it.

WILLIAM IS ALREADY WAITING for me in the same spot we had breakfast yesterday. He's transformed it, my simple blanket replaced by a wire table and chairs, set up with a single unlit candle in the middle. The sky is dimming, casting beautiful yellow, orange, and pink rays into the clouds above. The lake behind him reflects the sky like a mirror. The whole scene is so serene. He has a tray of food in front of him. We both brought potato soup, his being a larger portion than mine, with a stack of rolls teetering dangerously beside his silver bowl.

"William, this is beautiful," I say as I near the table.

He promptly stands and pulls out my chair. He's out of his usual black uniform, wearing dark jeans with a beige button-up shirt. The top three buttons are open, showing his smooth chest. My eyes linger there for a moment before returning to his smiling face. I am underdressed in my black leggings and maroon shirt. I didn't even think of wearing one of my dresses. At least I changed out of my training clothes.

"It's nothing. The sky is doing most of the work," he replies as I sit in one of the chairs.

I chuckle. "Where did you even find these?"

"Near the gardens. Hopefully, nobody misses them." He grimaces.

"And the candle?"

"That was more difficult. I may or may not have nicked it. Sorry, it's not lit. I didn't want to ask Sebastian to do it." He winks, taking his seat.

I was expecting to see Sebastian, since we usually all eat together. I didn't realize this would be a romantic date between us. I don't feel uncomfortable, at least. William would be a wonderful companion. He cares for me and is funny. No doubt my life with him would be full of laughter. And his voice…I'd never tire of hearing that accent.

As I'm staring at him, admiring his model-like hair and perfectly shaped nose, another face floats into my imagination. One with hazel eyes and curly dark hair. Their jawlines are similar.

I stop myself. I'm only thinking about him because I'm worried, no other reason.

"Penny, for your thoughts?" William asks.

"What? Oh." I laugh and try to fight the blush. "I was thinking about you, actually." *And somebody else.*

"You were? Now I'm very intrigued." William chuckles, sitting up taller and bringing the spoon to his mouth.

I dig in too. Eating will give me time to think of a response. Part of the truth can't hurt. "I was thinking how I feel comfortable around you," I say finally. "And that I like your humor. You care for me…well, at least, I think you do."

"I do." William places his spoon down, his face growing serious, though he avoids my gaze. "I've been wanting to tell you something." He pauses, and I can't help but lean in. Then he glances up with a smile hovering on his lips. "I fancy you." He chuckles nervously and reaches a hand out towards me.

I let him take my hand. It's warm, but I don't know if it's the hand I want around mine right now.

"I know our time together has been short, but I truly care for you. I don't expect a response. I just wanted you to know that my feelings are growing."

"Oh," is all that comes out, since I have no idea how to respond to somebody's declaration of feelings. I nervously twist the bracelet on my arm, a new habit I've adopted since Sebastian gave it to me.

"Really, you don't need to say anything. Now you know." He visibly relaxes, and his eyes flick to my wrist. "And I couldn't help but notice the bracelet you've been wearing. Am I right in assuming that it's a gift from Sebastian?"

I stop twisting it and bite my cheek. "Yeah, it is."

He reaches into his jacket pocket and pulls out something enclosed in his fist. "I was wondering if you would also accept a gift from me?"

I smile, and his eyes shine. He rises from his chair and walks around the table. I see a flash of gold before his hands wrap gingerly around my neck.

My fingers come up, touching a thin chain. "William, you don't need to do this."

He sits back down. "I want to. It was my mother's."

"I can't take this." I move my fingers to unclasp the chain, but he grabs my hand.

"Maya, it's a gift. I won't take it back. She gave me a couple of things when I came to the States, hoping I would find somebody. This necklace was made for you. It suits you perfectly," he says, flashing me a genuine smile.

I sigh, giving in. "Okay, if you insist. Thank you."

He smiles and happily digs into his mountain of rolls. *I fancy you*. It's a statement that should have me kicking my heels and squealing, but it's too much right now. I'm overwhelmed with my own thoughts and emotions and can't handle anyone else's.

"So, what's the story?" he asks.

I furrow my eyebrows.

"Your early morning hike?"

"Right. It was Abby's crazy idea. We found this beautiful waterfall, but something spooked us, and we got lost in our hurry to get back."

"Was that your first time outside the wall?"

I pick at my roll and nod, feeling a bit guilty about lying to him.

"Wow, I don't blame you then. Being stuck in one place for five years, I'd want to go, too. I would have taken you, if you asked." His face grows mischievous.

"Next time, though there probably won't be one. I'm in enough trouble as it is."

"I wouldn't get caught." He smiles boyishly.

I try to laugh, but it falls flat. "Thank you for putting this together, but I'm feeling drained still. Mind if I turn in early?"

"Of course," he says, but his face falls a little.

He gives me a farewell kiss on the forehead, similar to our first date, but this time, it makes me squirm.

21

Dream

A S I LAY IN BED, relieved to be alone finally, I try to decipher my feelings. James missing, Sebastian trying to kiss me, William announcing his feelings, and being unable to talk to Abby is all too overwhelming. I squeeze my eyes shut, waiting to be overcome by sleep.

After about five minutes, I sit up in defeat. Now that I'm alone and want to disappear into my dreams for a little while, sleep evades me. I grab my robe and step outside for some fresh air. The sun shines brightly, warming my skin.

Wait a minute.

I peer down at myself. I'm wearing a pink sundress and not standing on my terrace but in the backyard of my childhood home, my feet in the grass.

I look around, and Millie comes bounding down the steps, barking happily. She jumps up, knocking me down. I giggle as she covers my face in slobbery kisses.

"Oh, I've missed you, girl!" I say, shoving the black Labrador aside and sitting up.

She darts under the steps and comes back with a ball in her mouth, excitedly wagging her tail. Her ears perk up, and her tongue lolls out from behind her teeth.

"Millie, come!" a deep voice shouts from inside the house.

After a second, a face appears from behind the screen door. He has short, dark, wavy hair and concerned blue eyes behind rectangular glasses.

"Maya, are you okay? Millie, bad dog!" He runs down the steps and scoops me up.

Millie's tail goes between her legs.

"Dad?" I say in disbelief.

I touch his face. I can feel his warmth. He's *actually* here.

I throw my arms around him. I can even smell the cologne he used to wear, a musky, familiar scent. Hundreds of forgotten memories wrap around me.

"Are you hurt?" he says, grabbing my arms and inspecting them.

"No, I'm fine." I find my legs and stand back up.

Millie drops the ball and wags her tail again.

"She's just excited to see me."

He snorts. "You've only been out here for three minutes, hon."

"Dad, how am I here?"

"I don't know what you mean." He tilts his head.

"Never mind, Dad, I love you," I say, choking back emotion and throwing my arms around him again.

"I love you, too," he says, puzzled. "What's with you?" He feels my head. "Did you hit your head on something?"

I laugh. "No, I'm just happy to see you."

He smiles but then his face falls as he pulls back his hand, eyes widening. Blood glistens on his fingertips. "Maya, you did hit your head!"

I touch the same spot he had, but nothing is there. He grabs my hand and leads me to the creek behind the house, where our lawn stops and the woods begin.

"This is a pretty bad cut. It may need stitches, but I'm going to try something first. Hold still. You're going to be okay."

His eyes focus, and he raises his hand, channeling the water from the stream. The droplets connect in midair and move toward my head.

"Dad, I'm scared," a small voice says.

"It's just water, honey. It won't hurt."

I look at who he's talking to and see my eight-year-old self in a grass-stained pink dress looking worriedly up at my father. I watch in fascination as the water encases the left side of her head, and then the memory comes to me. This is when he healed me with water for the first time.

I reach back behind my left ear and still can't feel anything. I know this happened, though, because that was the day I found out I'd become a Lympha.

"Maya, it worked. You're healed. This means you're going to come into your element soon." My dad cheers.

My eight-year-old self jumps up and down and bends over to touch the water from the stream. My dad faces the house. I turn around and see my mom. She has her hand up to her mouth, shaking her head, eyes sorrowful. Why would this make her upset?

I glance at my dad, and he mouths, "I told you," at her, before turning back towards me. "My little Lympha."

"Dad, of course, I'm a Lympha. I remember everything you taught me."

After that day, he takes me to the stream daily to try to draw my abilities out. It doesn't work, but I love watching him do it…until, "*No!*"

I yell and reach out towards him. He's fading away, along with the scene in front of me, until all that is left is darkness.

"Dad, come back! I need to tell you something! Dad!" My voice is swallowed up in the darkness. Tears prick my eyes. He can't be gone. A light turns on in the distance, and I run toward it. I trip and get back up, but my feet slow, and taking a step becomes challenging, like running through water. Voices drift from the light.

"Can I see her?" comes a deep voice that is not my dad's.

"Absolutely not. You knew the deal, no interaction whatsoever," my mom's high-pitched voice rings out.

"Come on, what would it hurt?" the man says.

"No." My dad's voice. There's a finality in his tone.

"What? You're never going to tell her? She should know."

It feels like I'm running in wet cement. I push harder and inch closer. Familiar gray furniture materializes. It's my old living room. My parents' backs are turned, and there is a small shape on the steps, hidden from view. I'm not surprised when I realize it's me, at the age of four or five, wearing a blue floral pajama set.

"We will if that's warranted, but we still don't know what—" my mom hesitates, "—will happen," she finishes softly.

"Don't ever show up at our front door again," my dad snarls.

I'm almost to the light. Just two more steps, and I'll be able to see who my parents are talking to. I hear what must be the front door creaking and closing, and just as I'm about to step into the light, my four-year-old self peers around the corner.

Suddenly, I don't have to take that last step. An image of a man's face with short dark hair and startling familiar green eyes flashes before me. The man smiles at me before the door closes, obscuring him from view.

22

Sisters

I STARTLE AWAKE, my body wrapped tightly in the sheets. Relief floods me. What a strange dream. I still vividly remember my dad in front of me, his warm embrace, his smell. It's been years since I've dreamt of him.

I hurriedly grab my notebook and jot down the details before they're gone forever. The clock reads 4:30 a.m., and I'm wide awake. There's no way I'll be able to sleep after that, even though part of me wants to try to see my dad again. No, I'll go for a swim. Nobody should be out there this early. I'll have the whole lake to myself.

I make it to the lake, the morning air crisp. I know dawn isn't far off, but a thick blanket of night still covers the area. I walk down the rockier side until I find the bigger rocks I can dive off of. The boulders remind me of the ones Abby, James, and I scaled, and my chest tightens.

I stop momentarily, waiting for him to appear from the trees as he often did. But there's nothing but the gentle breeze.

I shake off my fear for him and jump, letting the air hold me for a moment before my hands break through the glassy surface. The dream brought up more memories of my dad. We'd swim together often after he taught me when I was a toddler. He always said I was a natural swimmer and gravitated to the water, even as an infant, like that did me any good that fateful day in the ocean. It didn't scare me from swimming, but I have yet to return to the ocean.

As I propel myself forward, skimming across the cool water, I flip for a backstroke. A crescent moon shines in the sky, thousands of stars surrounding it, a perk of living in the middle of nowhere. The sky was so different in the town I grew up in, right outside Portland, where we were only able to see the big and little dippers every now and then. Now I can see Orion, Taurus, and Gemini, along with hundreds of other constellations I don't know. I imagine I'm up there, swimming through the Milky Way, the stars guiding my future.

All of a sudden, a brighter light shines to my left, casting the stars away. *That's weird.* It shouldn't be sunrise for another hour.

I stop to look for the source. A floating orb of light on the shore grows in size and then splits in two. It's not flickering, but more luminescent. It must be an Aura.

Discreetly, I wade closer to the land. Somebody is basked in a white glow, the light from the orbs, now four in number. A girl with long white hair, almost to her waist, is focused on the objects in the air, paying me no attention.

I continue my swim and ignore her, but she must have excellent hearing because she calls out, "Who's out there?"

"Hi! I'm just out for a swim."

"Oh. In the dark?" Her voice is lovely, soothing even.

"Yup, I thought I would get out here before anyone else."

She laughs like a Disney princess — as if she's calling small talking animals to her. "I guess we were both thinking the same thing. I tend to get up pretty early to practice light casting."

"Well, don't mind me." Chatting while treading water isn't my favorite thing to do.

"Carry on!" she replies.

I continue to swim, letting the water guide me, occasionally submerging myself and practicing my water transports. I take in the obscurity around me. My thoughts clear until it feels like I'm the only one in the universe…until I see it brightening around me.

I break the surface and watch the sky come to life, filling with color, giving me renewed hope for the day ahead. Today will be significant, I feel it in my soul.

Time to get out. I don't want to run into anyone else. I make my way out of the water and notice the white-haired girl again, still practicing, but now she's moved on to manipulating the wind, her hair flying upward.

I walk past her, not wanting to interrupt, but her voice stops me, "Hi! You're Maya Mayfield, right?"

I'm tired, and the last thing I want to do is socialize, but I turn politely, wishing I didn't have manners. "Yeah, sorry, I don't know your name."

"That's okay, I'm Juliet. My little sister, mom, and I arrived here a couple of days ago. I've heard about Commander Mayfield's daughter. You're matched, right?" she babbles excitedly.

I wonder what she's heard. Thinking about the past few weeks, maybe not good things. "I am. Are you?"

"No, not yet, but I just got my results from the testing, so hopefully soon!"

I cringe, remembering the eligibility testing, which includes ensuring our reproduction system is intact and working. "Oof, you okay after all that?"

She nods. "Wasn't the most pleasant thing."

I wince again.

"Your mom talks a lot about you. You're lucky to have her. I bet your matches are perfect."

"She makes sure they are perfect for everyone who gets matched. You have nothing to worry about," I say, shivering as the breeze hits my wet body.

"I'm not. My little sister is, though. She can be annoying about it."

"Oh," I say, ready to get back indoors. She's cozy in a beige sweater dress that reaches her shins. I start to turn away, but she keeps talking, not getting the hint.

"Her name is Annabelle, but she's not an Aura. Terra, actually. We're technically half-sisters, but I'm her only family."

My eyes widen, and I wonder if she's talking about the same little girl who snuck up on me in the forest. "That's nice you have a sister. I have a little brother. I should get going though. We can get breakfast and keep chatting if you want. Have your little sister join."

She smiles wide. I can see her face better now that the sun has broken over the horizon. Sunlight falls on her fair skin, a light dusting of freckles across her cheeks, and blue-gray eyes. Under her long, straight, flowing hair, she has a thin, petite figure, totally matching her sing-songy voice and bubbly personality.

"That would be wonderful. I'll just finish here and meet you in the dining hall," she says spritely.

After a quick morning nap—swimming had exhausted my body—I make it to breakfast before eight. Juliet and Ann are already at a table. I must be caught up in my own world to have missed them before. They are night and day when it comes to appearance. Juliet with her creamy pale skin and white-blonde locks. Ann with her tan, olive skin tone, dark eyes and hair. I wouldn't think they were sisters.

I walk over to them, looking directly at Ann. The little girl notices me right before I sit, and the shock on her face is comical.

Juliet brightens up. "Maya! This is Annabelle."

"Ann," she retorts, pushing her thick, curly hair out of her eyes.

"And this is Maya, Commander Mayfield's daughter. She's matched!" Juliet says, as excitedly as she had earlier, her eyes shining more blue than gray.

Ann sits up straight and grins at me knowingly. "Oh, really."

I ignore her. "Their names are William and Sebastian. They're sweet."

"Are they cute?" Juliet giggles.

I smile. "They are."

Ann rolls her eyes. She's more impassive than she was in the forest.

"That's a beautiful necklace," Juliet says, eyeing my neck.

My hand flies up to my throat. I haven't taken it off since William put it on me. It's so delicate I forgot it was there.

"The topaz stones look lovely against your skin tone."

"Thank you. It was a gift from one of my matches," I say, making a mental note to check the mirror.

"Awww! Tell me more. What do you do together?"

"We have to get creative. There's not a whole lot around here," I say, wishing I had more.

She lowers her voice and covers her sister's ears. "Have you kissed them?" she whispers. Her cheeks color as she says it, making her look modelesque.

I smirk. "I don't kiss and tell."

"Oh, come on," Juliet says as Ann looks quizzically at her sister and slaps her hands away.

"I'd like to eat now. You're making me sick," Ann says, picking at her scrambled tofu and berries with her fork.

"It's probably just the food," I say, eyeing the tofu.

She scoffs. "Yeah, where's the sausage?"

Juliet stares at her sister like a foreign specimen.

"What?"

"You're a *Terra*," Juliet scolds.

"Barely." Ann shrugs. "No pigs have talked to me yet."

I hold back a laugh.

"Oh, you should tell Maya about gaining your abilities," Juliet insists. Ann perks up, but Juliet starts before she can get a word in. "She got them just two days ago!"

"Is that so? Any more victims?" I tease, throwing a pointed look at Ann.

Ann chokes on her food, coughs out a blueberry, and laughs nervously, her already tan skin getting darker. Juliet looks lost, but seems happy to see her sister cheerful, and giggles along.

"Where are you from?"

Ann shares a look with Juliet, who's finally gained control of herself and is chewing again. "New Mexico," Ann says as Juliet says, "We moved around a lot."

I look between them as Juliet nudges Ann with her elbow, and she returns with a glare. That was weird.

"Okay… Well, I better get some food. It was nice *meeting you*, Ann," I say, rising to my feet and meeting her dark eyes with a wink once I'm facing away from Juliet. Hopefully, this solidifies that our secrets are safe.

"I'm sure we'll run into each other again," Juliet says positively.

I nod and move towards the food table, grateful the little girl didn't out me. As I approach the serving area, I catch Abby heading in the same direction. I glance around—no commanders yet—and dart forward until she sees me. We end up on opposite sides of the table.

Keeping my head down, I murmur, "You got my letter?"

"Yeah, but I'm worried, Maya."

"Me, too. But like I said, let's give him to the end of the day, then we'll come clean. Try to stay positive. Maybe he just got lost."

"That doesn't make me feel better," Abby whispers.

"He'll find his way back." I finish dishing up my food and risk glancing at her briefly to give her an encouraging smile.

She wears a deep frown and dark circles under her eyes. I'm about to grab her hand, tell her it will be okay, but I hear a grunt from behind me.

I whip around. Of course, it's Commander Lawrence.

"Girls," he grunts, scowling.

"I'm just getting my food, Commander," I say, turning back toward the tables. I sit as far away as possible from the serving area and inhale my food, tofu and all.

THE REST OF THE DAY moves slowly. With each passing minute, it becomes more painful not to see James anywhere. It worsens when Sebastian and William find me after my late afternoon lesson. Sebastian doesn't bring up the innocent kiss, and neither do I. William doesn't bring up his expression of feelings, and neither do I. With me strung up with worry for James and dreading having to go to the commanders in the morning, it's the first time since meeting them that it's awkward. Conversation is impossible. I say one thing, one of them says something else, and then it sizzles out. I end up making up an excuse and escaping to my room. I'm disappointed in myself for not trying harder.

After dinner, I take a long shower, debating whether to go for another swim, since it's not nearly late enough to try to sleep. I take off William's necklace beforehand, not wanting to ruin it. It's certainly beautiful. The gold chain is dainty with small topaz stones set along the length of it. I place it on my counter to put back on later.

Ultimately, I don't have the energy to swim and snuggle up on my couch with *Pride and Prejudice* and my favorite blanket. I'd like to lose myself in a book this evening and escape my life for a time.

I'm a couple of chapters in when a noise catches my attention. The knob on my back door turns, and I only have enough time to jump to my feet—the book in my hands my only weapon—before a familiar face walks in.

"James?" I gasp.

"Didn't I tell you to lock that door? I'm disappointed in you, Maya," he grumbles, shaking his head and noticing my stance. "Are you really going to try to get the upper hand on me with a romance novel?"

As he chuckles, I surprise myself by jumping over the couch and throwing myself at him. I bury my face in his shoulder when he catches me. He smells like sweat and dirt, but I don't care. I note briefly that he's still in the same dark long-sleeve shirt but has added a leather jacket.

I inspect his face. He's smiling, eyes bright and unharmed. He raises a hand and wipes something wet off my cheek.

"Sorry, I've been doing that a lot lately," I say, sniffling.

"Don't apologize for crying. It's a normal human reaction."

"I thought you were dead." A sob breaks through, and he pulls me tight to his chest. I wrap my arms around his waist. His clothes are stiff from the cold. I hope he soaks up some of my body heat.

He rubs my back soothingly. "It's okay, I'm fine."

"But how? You've been gone for two days!"

"What, you don't believe me? My living and breathing body isn't enough for you?" He chuckles. His chest pulses against me. He really is okay.

"Where have you been?" I mumble, tears still streaming down my face.

"It's a long story, and I don't have long. I came to see you first. I still need to tell Abby I'm okay."

I suck in a ragged breath and pull back. His face is streaked with dirt, but his hazel eyes are clear. Looking at me, through me.

He pulls a hand free and brings it to my face, pushing the hair that fell out of my top knot out of my eyes. He leaves his hand on my cheek and wipes the rest of my tears with his thumb.

"You came to see me first?" I say slowly.

He nods, a smile hovering on his lips. As we stand there, embracing, only a few inches from each other's faces, his smile melts into something else, a deep longing. I glance at his lips. The pull is back, stronger than it has ever been. An electric current flows between us. This time, I don't want to fight it.

I reach up on my tippy toes towards him. His eyes widen for a fraction of a second before I close mine. I pause, knowing I'm a mere inch from his mouth, waiting, feeling his breath on my face. I exhale shakily, and his arms tighten around me. He caresses my cheek, my face now between his palms.

"Are you sure?" he breathes.

"Just kiss me already."

There is no hesitation this time. His lips press against mine. My lips part, breathing him in. He tastes like salt, probably my own tears. He's not gentle. I trip back from his intensity and find myself pressed against the wall. I use it as leverage to mold myself to his body, and the kiss deepens.

My hands go to his hair, winding my fingers through his curls. I've never kissed anyone before, but my body has a mind of its own.

His tongue caresses my bottom lip, and I gasp. His body responds to the sound, strong hands travel up my back hungrily. I can't get close enough. His lips release mine, but only to travel down to my neck, my body melting against him.

I work on trying to catch my breath and clear my mind, but it's almost impossible with his lips touching me. A tiny voice tells me to stop, but before I can register it, our lips meet again, gentler this time. We kiss once, twice, three times.

His hands drift to my hair, and mine travel down his back. Before I realize what I'm doing, I shuck his jacket off so I can feel the ridges of his muscles. His kisses travel to my jawline, and the tiny voice intensifies, but my body craves his touch. I want to pull him closer, but I know I must push him away.

"James, st—"

He returns to my mouth, silencing me.

"Stop," I try again, but it comes out mumbled with his lips on mine. I weakly bring my hands to his chest to push.

As soon as he realizes what I'm doing, he freezes and releases his hold on me.

"Is something wrong?" he asks tenderly. He leans an arm on the wall and reaches with the other to touch my flushed cheek. He smiles lazily, his lips slightly swollen.

I bring my finger to his bottom lip, and he shivers. I drop my hand. "We shouldn't be doing this," I mutter, longing to throw myself at him, to let go of all control. But I can't. I won't.

He plays with my hair, a dreamy look in his eyes and that lazy smile on his lips. "And?"

"I'm having my ceremony soon."

That hits a nerve. He drops his hand and pulls it through his own hair as he straightens, closing his eyes. "Maya, do you love one of them?"

"I, uh, well, not yet. I haven't even kissed them." I wrap my hair around my finger nervously, not believing I just admitted that.

His eyes open. "Really? I'm your first kiss?" He flashes me a crooked smile.

"I already told you I hadn't, remember?"

"Yes, I remember, but I've been gone. That could have easily changed with two men wrapped around your finger like that hair there."

Dropping my hand, I sigh. "I was too worried about you to focus on them." And now he's here, perfectly fine. Why didn't he return sooner?

My anger rises, so I step around him rather than staying trapped between his warm body and the wall. My temper boils over, and I cross my arms, turning to him. "Where were you anyway?"

He clicks his tongue, leaning a shoulder against the wall I'd just left. "Remember me telling you about the alert system around the barrier? I'm guessing you don't, since you and Abby set it off. After the two of you got caught, I had to wait until just the right time to slip through unnoticed. It took a while."

That's how they discovered where we were. But that doesn't explain— "How did you manage to get counted for two days?"

"I can't reveal all my secrets," he says slyly. "Can we stop talking and kiss some more now?" He stalks towards me, traveling a hand up my arm.

The electricity flows once again and my breathing hitches. It takes everything in me not to give in.

I shake my head. "I shouldn't have done that. It won't happen again," I declare, doing my best to keep my voice even.

I brush past him, fighting the urge to turn. He grabs my hand and whips me around. I'm in his arms again, and his mouth is at my ear.

"Run away with me," he whispers. "You don't have to choose either of those idiots. You don't love them and never will. I'll keep you safe, I promise."

I can't help it. My mind flashes images of us together, free to touch and kiss however we want. Life outside the walls, not having to follow any rules, and being free to settle down whenever I please. We could keep each other safe, even pretend to be Coms, and make a life for ourselves.

At my hesitation, he kisses me softly again. Once in my hair, then on my temple, lower on my cheek, slowly making his way to my lips. If I don't stop it now, I know I never will.

I gather my strength and push him away, harder this time.

He gawks at me as if I slapped him.

"You can't do that, say those things to me, kiss me. I'm matched! And you don't know my heart, James. I could fall in love with one of them. They're supposed to be perfect for me, why wouldn't I?" I inhale, trying to calm my racing pulse. "Anyways, I couldn't do that to my family. What about *your* family? Do they not matter to you?"

He doesn't respond, just continues to stare at me with a hardening expression.

"I want you out of my room," I say softly.

His eyes darken, and his jaw tenses.

"Out!" I shout, turning away, my face hot.

Without a word, he goes, his footsteps clicking sharply towards my back door, withdrawing and disappearing altogether.

I stand breathing hard for a minute before gaining the willpower to close the door behind him. I fall against it in a puddle of tears. Might as well let it all out now. Tomorrow, I'll only think of my matches. I'm sure I can gain these same feelings for one of them.

Once my anger diminishes, I regret yelling at him. I drag myself off the floor, noticing his jacket lying across my sofa. I wrap it around me like a blanket and lay down on my bed, breathing him in. This is as close as I can get to having him with me. I snuggle into the soft leather, thinking about how his lips fit perfectly against mine. But then my hand comes across something solid.

I feel around the jacket, looking for the source. I check the pockets and pull out a shiny, gray metal object. I turn my lamp on.

At first, it reminds me of a calculator…I used one in grade school. There are lots of buttons and a tiny rectangular screen at the top. But instead of numbers, there are letters.

I press one, and the screen lights up, forming a single sentence: *You have one week.*

23

Stuck in the Middle

THE FOLLOWING DAY I'm determined to make it up to William and Sebastian. Now that I know that James is safe, I lock up my feelings for him and bury them deep inside. My matches deserve a chance.

I message them that I have a date planned and ask them to meet me after lunch. I have no idea what to do. Abby's sidelined, so, hopefully, my new friend Juliet will have some ideas.

My mom has her face to a microscope lens as I enter her office to ask her where Juliet's room is. She sits in front of the wide window, sunlight filling the room. It's never enough, though, because the gold lamp over her head is always on, beaming onto her studies. She's wearing a black lab coat with her hair pulled up with a clip on the back of her head.

"Hey, Mom."

"Hi, honey, what do you need?"

"I was wondering if you knew which room Juliet is in?"

She continues to survey her sample, writes something down, and then glances my way with a smile. "The Myler family?"

I shrug. I don't know her last name.

"Juliet Myler has requested to stay on the family level because of her family's…unique circumstances."

"What do you mean?" I ask.

"That's up to them to divulge. But I've heard the youngest Myler girl has come into her element, another Terra. How exciting. I can't wait until your brother does. It'll be in the next year, if he's anything like you."

"Yeah, me, too. I'd like to show him everything Dad taught me. He would want him to know."

"He'll learn all those things in class," she replies, diminishing Dad's importance in our lives in a single sentence as she stands to shuffle through papers.

I don't respond, and she notices my silence. "Oh, not like that, honey. I'm sorry. Yes, he'll want to know everything Dad taught you."

"Have you completely forgotten about Dad? You never bring him up anymore."

She finds whatever she is looking for and returns to her microscope. "A day doesn't go by that I don't think about your father. We were bonded, and a piece of him will forever live inside of me. And I see him in you and your brother, so it feels like he's still with us, in a way. But he's gone, and I received my closure long ago. That doesn't mean I don't miss him," she says with genuine emotion. "Your brother never met him, and I carry that with me. I'm so glad he has you to remind him of your father's legacy. I didn't mean for that to come out like I don't want you talking about Dad. I meant that you have a lot on your plate right now. You don't have to worry about training your brother."

My voice wavers. "I had a dream about him the other night."

"Really? Tell me about it." She turns away from her work and looks at me encouragingly, trying to make up for her comment.

"It was unusual, less like a dream and more like a memory."

She nods, giving me her full attention.

"Millie was there too."

Her lower lip juts out. "I miss that dog," she says, her eyes glistening.

Oh, so she shows more emotion for the dog than Dad? I try hard not to roll my eyes at her.

"We were in the backyard of our house. Millie knocked me down in the grass, and Dad rushed down the stairs, worried I was hurt. It felt like he was really there. I could touch and even smell him, Mom. It was surreal." I remember how it felt being safe in his arms again. I push down the burning sensation at the back of my throat and continue. "I ended up having a cut on my head…right here," I say, pointing behind my ear.

Her hands still as she gives me a mystified expression.

I'm too lost in the story to stop. "I wasn't actually bleeding, but somehow, the blood got on Dad. He took me to the stream, the one behind our house, and he healed me. Then my point of view changed. One moment he was talking to me, and the next, I was seeing myself as a little girl going through it. It was bizarre, but then I remembered it actually happening, because it was the day I realized—"

"The first time we knew you'd have Lympha abilities," she finishes for me.

"Yeah, wait, so it *was* a memory?"

"Yes, I remember that day," she says quietly.

"And there was something else. If it was my memory, then I would've only seen what I experienced, right?"

She nods.

"But while my younger self had her back turned, you and Dad exchanged glances, and he mouthed something like 'I told you so.' Why would he say that?"

She blanches for a second but regains her composure. "It was a dream mixed with your memories. I don't remember him doing that, just that we were both excited."

"But that's the thing. You didn't seem excited; you looked almost disappointed."

She smiles at me. "You know I had a dream once that I was a dancing kangaroo, so I wouldn't read too much into it."

I nod, accepting that, since it's more plausible than the alternative. That somehow, Dad visited me in my dreams to give me the memory, which sounds absurd.

"Well, I have a lot of work to do. Let me know if you have any more dreams about Dad. I really do miss him."

She begins writing, and I know my window has closed. I want to tell her about the second part of my dream, but something makes me keep that to myself for now.

I CLIMB THE METAL STAIRS two at a time and jog down the hall of my old living quarters. The sounds of laughter and bickering children come from the large oak doors that blend in with the slightly lighter brown shade of walls stretching down the long corridor. I make it to Juliet's room, and Annabelle answers the door. She's wearing all green today, bright emerald pants, and a dark green top with brown polka dots on it. Her dark hair is in braided pigtails, which is probably Juliet's doing. Juliet seems like the braiding-hair-while-giggling type.

"Maya?"

"Hi, Ann. Is your sister here?"

"Yeah, I can get her." She responds but doesn't leave. Instead, she leans out the door and whispers, "Thanks for not saying anything yesterday to Juliet. I wasn't supposed to be out there."

"And I'm guessing there are no twins?" I murmur.

She shakes her head slowly.

"And Aunt Jodi?"

"She's real! I was telling the truth that she doesn't care what I do." She smiles. But it doesn't reach her eyes.

"But *Juliet* very much does," I guess.

She nods. "You don't have to worry about me saying anything about you know who. I'm good at keeping secrets." She reassures me with a sly smile.

I shrug my shoulders. "He's just a friend, but I must admit it looks bad. Thanks."

She raises her voice. "Yeah, come on in, Maya." She opens the door wide as Juliet walks towards us from their living room.

"Hi, Maya!" she says, her eyes gleaming. She's wearing another dress—does the girl not own pants? This one is light blue with short sleeves and delicate embroidered flowers.

"Hey, sorry for the intrusion. I need some advice and thought you might be able to help me."

"Of course, come on in. My room is down here."

I follow her. Their living space is sparser than Mom and Cal's, with only a chair in the living room. Hopefully, they will get more furniture soon. Ann is following behind me as we turn down the hall.

Once we get to Juliet's room, she shakes her head at her little sister. Ann deflates.

"It wouldn't interest you anyway. It's boy stuff," I offer, hoping that helps.

"I guess I'll just go stare at the wall," she mutters, turning on her heel.

"You know what? Go ahead and practice, but stay where I can see you from the window, okay?" Juliet cautions.

"Sweet!" she sings, dancing on her toes. She races down the hall, disappearing out of sight.

The room is small, just big enough for two beds, one on each wall, and a small table in the middle. Juliet sits on one of the beds, which is nicely made with a taut comforter. The other, I'm guessing, is Ann's. It has blankets strewn across it, and the pillow is about to fall off one side.

I sit on that bed, our knees almost knocking. "You're protective of her," I say.

"I'm all she has. I promised our dad I would take care of her. He and her mom died during the first raid."

"I'm sorry. I've also lost my dad. What about your mom?" I say carefully, curious about her story but not wanting to pry.

"She's here, but..." She pauses. "There's just some old family drama she holds onto, and she sadly takes it out on Annabelle."

"That's not good," I say, intrigued now. "It's okay. You don't have to tell me about it."

"It's nice having another girl my age to talk to, honestly. My mom tries, but my dad did leave her for Annabelle's mom, so there are some things people can never get over."

"Whoa, that's intense. I'm so sorry." As Elementals, our blood bonding ceremony seals two together for life. For one to break that bond in such a way causes insufferable heartache and a possible loss in one's abilities. Some say it's worse than death.

"It happened a long time ago," she says, shrugging. "And he's gone now. My mom took Annabelle in, but that's where her good graces stop."

"But that's not fair to Ann. She's just a child," I say, getting defensive over the little girl.

"I know, but she has me, at least."

I wait for her to meet my eyes and rest my hand on her knee. "You're a good sister."

She smiles. "Well, enough about old family betrayals. What do you need help with?"

The bed creaks as I lean back. "You remember me telling you yesterday there isn't much to do around here with my matches? I thought you could help me with some ideas. I want to plan something for them but have no idea where to start."

Her face brightens, and she claps her hands together. "Yes, I would love to help!"

We talk for the next twenty minutes, bouncing ideas off each other until we eventually end up in the manor's basement, where all the old furniture and junk are stored. One lightbulb haphazardly hangs from the ceiling in the room, casting creepy shadows on the white sheets around us. Juliet casts glowing orbs that levitate in the room's four corners, emitting much more light than the ominous lightbulb. There are boxes stacked high to the ceiling, and the smell of dust and mothballs saturates the air.

"I haven't been down here in forever, but I remember seeing it," I say, peering around the room.

We prod the sheets, covering oddly shaped objects, but most unveil ugly pieces of furniture. Juliet finds two wide wooden trunks resembling something from the 1800s. They are as big as large suitcases and closed with intricate gold clasps.

"Should we open them?" Juliet asks, raising her eyebrows.

"Do it." I probe but stand a few feet back, in case something crawls from their depths.

She lifts one of the tops to find it full of different colored fabrics. She grabs the first garment and pulls it up. It's a beautiful, sleeveless, gray, floor-length gown with a high bodice.

"Wow, this has got to be at least a hundred years old," she says.

I nod, amazed.

We open the next trunk to the same sight. They're both full of old gowns in pristine condition. They're not even faded.

"Pick one! They won't be missed."

"Now, where would I wear something like that?" I laugh but long to try one on.

"You never know when the opportunity might arise." She stands up, holding a crimson silk gown. "Oh, this would look fabulous with your hair. You've got to at least take this one."

She hands it to me before I can protest. Once it's in my arms, I sigh at the feel of the luxurious material. The gown is beautiful,

"Okay, just one," I say, admiring the intricate beading on the bodice.

Juliet smiles and grabs another dress from the trunk, light pink and white. Her eyes widen. "And I think I will take this one." She places it over her arm, and another dress catches her eye. "Ooo, maybe this one too." She giggles as she picks up a soft yellow garment.

I chuckle. "Come on, we're getting distracted. My date is in an hour," I say, anxiety creeping in.

We continue searching until we come across an ancient box television set.

"Score!" I shout.

"And look!" Juliet emerges from one of the mountains of boxes. "This says 'VHS tapes.' Those are old movies, right?"

"Yeah! Okay, I'll grab the tapes. Can you levitate this heavy thing upstairs?"

"I can try." She smiles.

THE GUYS ARRIVED ON TIME, meeting me in the hallway outside the rec room after lunch. Juliet inspired me earlier, and I decided to put on something a little nicer: the green dress my mom said would bring out my eyes.

"Hi, my beautiful lady!" William says, greeting me first. He comes in for a hug but unexpectedly sweeps me off my feet and twirls me in a circle before setting me down.

A giggle escapes my lips as I try to pull my dress down so I don't flash Sebastian.

William smiles affectionately down at me. I have an urge to lean in closer, but it fades when I notice Sebastian staring at us from the corner of my eye.

"What is this mysterious surprise date?" William asks, his eyes traveling down the length of my dress to where it ends mid-thigh.

"You'll see," I sing, stepping away from him to greet Sebastian. I go in for a hug, and his expression changes from mild interest to pleasant surprise. "It's nice to see you, too," I say as he holds me around my waist, his hands lingering on the small of my back before letting me go.

"You're gorgeous. That color brings out your eyes," he breathes, his blue eyes sparkling. His tone brings heat to my cheeks.

"Thank you."

"How are you doing today?" he asks earnestly, not just trying to make small talk.

"I'm doing better. I'm sorry about yesterday, and how I acted. I wasn't myself. I wanted to plan something for you guys, to make it up to you." I look back and forth between them.

Sebastian replies first. "You were quiet, but I didn't want to pry."

"Yeah, we all have our off days. I'm glad you're in high spirits today," William says with a smile.

"Thanks, you guys are the best." I take both of their hands and give them a squeeze, then lead them to the French doors of the rec room. "I was thinking of how hard it is to go on regular dates here and thought it would be fun to go on more of a typical date we might have experienced if we were living in…normal civilization."

I swing open the doors to reveal a transformed space. Black sheets cover the windows—I realized too late this would have been a better evening date. Christmas lights, which we also found in one of the boxes, hang from the top beams, making wide arcs across the ceiling in the corner of the room. The box TV casts a blue light onto a pile of blankets and pillows strewn across the floor in front of the small leather couch. I didn't think the three of us could fit comfortably on it, so makeshift bed it is.

William is the first to speak. "This is brilliant, Maya! I can't remember the last time I watched a film for fun."

Sebastian is smiling, too. "We're watching a movie?"

"Yeah. There aren't many choices, but I thought it would be a nice escape," I say, shrugging. "I found some VHS tapes."

Already shuffling through the tapes, William calls out, "*E.T.* That's a good one, *Tuck Everlasting*, *Gladiator*, *Pinocchio*."

"*Pinocchio*! That one was my favorite as a kid," Sebastian says, joining William.

We've finally settled on a movie when I remember something. "Oh, I almost forgot the popcorn." I grab the bowl that I made. Unfortunately, there was no butter, so I drizzled it with olive oil and salt.

"And popcorn?" William shouts, delighted.

He and Sebastian make themselves comfortable among the pillows, leaving me just enough room to squeeze between them. William's arm comes up around my shoulders as I settle in. I can feel the heat beating off Sebastian, his arm next to mine, and our hands just an inch apart under the blanket. There's an electric current between us, getting stronger with each passing minute of the movie.

About halfway through, I grab another handful of popcorn, and my weight shifts, so the backs of our hands touch. Sebastian's finger slowly traces upward on mine, and I respond, gradually interlacing each finger until we're holding hands. My heart threatens to burst at the accomplishment. I steal a glance at him and catch him studying me. My lips twitch, but I keep myself from grinning too wide.

William's arm never leaves my shoulders. It's got to get uncomfortable for him. Sometimes, his head tilts and turns slightly toward mine, but I focus on the screen, only seeing colors.

William does it a second time, and his breath ruffles my hair, sending goosebumps down my neck.

By the third time, I'm pretty sure he's smelling me.

On the fourth, he leans in and whispers, "You smell wonderful."

I fight a blush, grateful for the dark and suddenly feeling incredibly awkward with Sebastian's hand in mine.

Sebastian caresses the back of my hand with his thumb, which I should be loving, but William's arm seems almost too heavy now, and I'm suffocating between their bodies.

I release Sebastian's hand and grab more popcorn as an excuse. Wrapping my arms around the bowl, I try to focus on the movie.

After a long ninety minutes, the credits roll. Neither move, so I'm the first to begin stretching and disentangling myself from them, my butt throbbing as I stand. They follow suit.

"That was great, Maya. Sadly, we have to get back now. We've been gone a little too long." Sebastian sighs.

"Oh no, I'm sorry. You guys should have said something."

"No, you're our priority now, Maya," William responds.

"Well, don't get in trouble on my behalf. There is enough on my conscience." I'm only partially kidding.

24

Ultimatum

A S I'M TAKING DOWN the white lights, Juliet shows up to help.

"I'm dying to know! How'd it go?"

"It was good!" I say a little too ecstatically.

She raises an eyebrow at me.

"Actually, it was kind of awkward. With them both there? Ugh. One-on-one dates are much better."

"I'll have to remember that for when it's my turn. How was the movie?"

"They chose some action movie, I think." I feel a little guilty about talking to Juliet instead of Abby about this. But it's okay to have more than one girlfriend. Abby's my best friend. Nobody can replace her. I'll tell her everything once I'm able to.

"You think? Is there something you're not telling me?" She makes kissy lips at me.

I laugh and shake my head.

She takes out the tape and reads, *"Tuck Everlasting*? That's not much of an action movie." She scrutinizes me with a flick of her eyes.

"Okay, you caught me. I don't remember a thing. But I wasn't making out with them or anything. It was just hard to pay attention."

"Sure." She grins.

I sigh. "If you have to know, I haven't even kissed them yet."

Her eyebrows shoot up into her hairline. "What's stopping you?"

I shrug. "I don't know. I guess I feel like, once I kiss them, I'll have to make a decision, because how could I not know at that point?"

She nods. "You know a kiss can just be a kiss. Have fun with them. You don't have to bond yourself to somebody because you kiss them."

My thoughts go to James. "You're right. I'm probably overthinking it."

She nudges me lightly with her shoulder, her hands full of lights. "No, you're not. I'm sure you're under tremendous pressure. It's easy for me to look at you and your experience and tell you to relax, but I'll probably act the same once I'm matched."

When we finish cleaning up, I leave the TV and movies in the corner. I'm sure others would love to watch them in their free time.

Juliet pushes the door open. As it swings, there's a faint grunt and then an "Ow!"

We walk quickly around the door to see who yelped.

James is rubbing his head, with Abby standing beside him, trying not to laugh. I freeze. Abby's humor turns into surprise when she sees me, and I can't take my eyes off the man that had his lips to mine last night, waiting for him to glance my way.

"Oh my! I'm so sorry! Are you okay?" Juliet coos.

James glances up at her, and his frustration melts into a half smile. "I'm doing better now," he says, removing his hand from his forehead and pulling it casually through his curls.

Juliet giggles, and I want to dissolve into the wall. He doesn't even see me.

But then his eyes slide over her face to mine, and his smile vanishes. "Maya."

I realize I'm gaping at him and close my mouth. "Excuse me," I mutter, walking around them.

Abby catches up to me and grabs my shoulder. "Maya, wait!"

"What?" I hiss. We can't be seen talking to each other.

Her eyebrows pull down. "You knew he made it back, right? Because I'd feel absolutely awful if you didn't. I couldn't talk to you. I didn't know what to do."

My voice softens. "Yes, I knew." I can't help but peer over her shoulder. James's back is to us, and Juliet is glowing as she talks to him. "They shouldn't be talking. She's not matched," I scold, irritability creeping into my voice.

A smile hovers on her lips. "He caught the guy."

I look at her, baffled, and then remember. With his lips preoccupied last night, I guess he missed telling me that part. "He did? That's good. I'm glad he's okay."

"Me too. I was so worried, Maya. I couldn't sleep or think or do anything. I kinda ignored my matches for the past couple of days. And being unable to talk to you about it, there were a few times I almost said to hell with rules and just came to your room."

"You should've. This is so stupid," I spit, anger rising. I don't even care if anybody sees us right now.

"Maybe Commander Lawrence has cooled off now."

Her words are lost as I zone in on Juliet, placing her hair behind her ear and looking at James from under her eyelashes. Is she actually fluttering them?

"They *really* shouldn't be talking," I growl.

"I'll go save him." She glances behind her shoulder but then says, "Has everything been okay with your matches? Are you getting close to a decision yet?"

Without thinking, I say, "Kind of," surprising myself.

"No way!" she gushes. "Who?"

"I don't want to say yet, but I'll definitely tell you when I work up the guts to kiss them. I should know without a doubt then. What about yours?"

"Like I said earlier, I haven't given them the time of day, but I will now. I'll see you tomorrow, okay? I'm sure. Somewhere." She presses her lips into a thin line before turning to walk away.

"Oh, use the TV in there. My guys loved it," I call.

"TV?"

"Go look in the rec, go, go," I insist, shoving her a bit, wanting her to interrupt their flirty chat.

I try my hardest to get the image of James flirting with another woman out of my head as I walk back down the hall. No matter how often I tell myself it shouldn't bother me, I can't help it.

I turn the next corner when I feel a hand on my shoulder. "Abby, I know what I said, but we shouldn't—"

It isn't Abby but James behind me. He doesn't have his confident smile. Instead, his eyes dart between mine as he shifts on his feet.

My anger returns, and butterflies along with it.

Before I can do or say anything, he grabs my hand and pulls me into the closest room. Luckily, the lights are off, the curtains drawn, and nobody is inside. Just the tiny window in the door lights the space where we stand.

"I'm sorry, I was being unfair," he begins.

I cross my arms. "You can flirt with whoever you want, James."

"What? No, I'm not talking about that. I was just being nice. Wait a second, are you jealous? Again?" A smile grows on his face, and he rubs his chin. "I like you being possessive."

I smack his shoulder. "Knock it off. Seriously, I don't care. It's not like we're matched. You're an eligible bachelor. Go flirt and dazzle whomever you want, but you probably don't want to do it in the middle of the hallway, unless you want to be kicked out. Because then your family would—"

He silences me with a kiss. I blink, surprised, but my body responds greedily, starved for his touch.

I throw my arms around his neck. His lips part, and I taste sweetness on his tongue. He draws me closer to him, and I'm putty in his hands. I thread my fingers through his hair, which is much softer than last night, not as greasy and filled with dirt. He pulls back, releasing his hold on me, and smiles playfully.

Staring into his bright hazel eyes, I breathe deeply to slow my heart, which is trying to escape my chest.

"I was trying to tell you I'm sorry about last night. You were right. It would destroy my family if I just up and disappeared. I shouldn't have tried to sway you. It's hard not to get carried away when you're in my arms." He bends down until his lips touch my throat, then he slowly travels to my ear.

I take a ragged breath. The alternative is to pass out.

"I'm going to fight for you, Maya Mayfield, and I plan on using all the dirty tricks in my arsenal." His breath sends shivers through my body. His tongue grazes my ear. "I have quite a few." He pulls back, so I can see his eyes. "You deserve the best. Don't let them decide who you love. Let it be your choice if it is one of them or me. I'm man enough to wait." He presses his lips to mine softly. "And confident enough to believe you'll choose me in the end." He purrs, moving his lips against mine.

"James, I—"

He puts a finger to my lips, making them tremble. "You don't need to make any decisions now."

I nod. It's all I can do. Feel now, think later. I pull him roughly back to my lips. We move in perfect harmony, and our bodies melt into one, as if his strong arms are meant to wrap perfectly around my waist, and my hands were made to fit around his face, holding it to mine. Electricity fills the room, and my senses are consumed by the scent, taste, and touch of his warm body. Every nerve ending seems to awaken, and I can't imagine ever feeling more alive.

There is a rush of cool air as the door flings open and the lights turn on, blurring my vision.

I yank myself away from James as the figure in the doorway materializes. I glance at the familiar sign next to the door, which I hadn't noticed when we came in.

Evelynn Mayfield.

She's holding her hand to her mouth, frozen at the sight of us.

We're trapped like cornered animals as she closes the door behind her and crosses her arms menacingly. "Please give me a likely reason why you two are embracing in my office alone?"

My thoughts scatter as my heart races.

James has the same shocked expression, but can at least speak. "Well, this does look pretty incriminating, Mrs. Mayfield," he accedes.

"That's *Commander* to you." She silences him.

He swallows loudly. I have never seen fear in his eyes before, not even when he faced down that Com. But I do now as he faces my enraged mother.

"Mom, it's just Abby's brother. I was looking for you," I let out, trying to make light of the situation.

She shifts her frightening gaze to me, not believing it for a second, and then faces James again. "You have two options, young man. You can either leave this base quietly—"

"*Mom*, you can't kick him out. I broke the rules, too. Are you going to throw me out?"

"You are a matched young woman and my daughter, but don't think this isn't going to have repercussions for you, too," she snarls, before turning her attention back to James. "As I was saying, you can leave with your own made-up excuse, or you can take your things back to the legion building and you will be matched tomorrow."

My jaw drops. This can't be happening.

James's face is wiped of all emotion. "I'll choose the second option, Commander."

"What?" I cry.

His expression doesn't change, except for a miniscule tightening of his eyes. "Thank you for giving me this second chance. I won't let you down." He bows his head and leaves the room without a glance at me.

I know there is obvious pain on my face, but there's no reason to mask it now.

She turns her rage on me. "Now, for you, young lady. That is just infatuation, nothing more. You need to get a grip on yourself. You are matched to two perfect men. You will have your ceremony in three days' time. Either make your choice, or I will do it for you."

My eyes burn as if she just struck me.

She inhales deeply, moving to her desk. "Now I need to finish what I came in here to do. Dinner is soon. Go get yourself cleaned up," she says more calmly.

I walk past her, feeling numb.

"Maya?" she calls.

I don't bother to turn around.

"This is for your own good. You know I love you very much. But if either of you does not heed my warning, I will strip that young man of everything he has. He'll be exiled."

I run out the door and don't stop until I reach my room. The tears have already started to fall as I slam the door behind me.

James is in my room, waiting. He grabs my face in both his hands. "No, don't cry. This is just a minor hiccup. She won't tell anyone about us. She loves you too much and doesn't want you to get in trouble…just me. We wait it out. I'll get matched, and it will be the worst match in the history of matches," he says, letting out a small chuckle. "I'll make it impossible for the girl to choose me."

But with my mother's parting words echoing in my head, I realize painfully that I have to let him go. I care about him too much to risk his exile…and for what? The chance to be with me if I don't choose one of my matches?

I'm a terrible person. I should have never led him on. I have to do this for him and his family.

I grab his hands and pull them away from my face. I wipe my tears and my face of emotion, which is problematic, since my eyes are probably puffy, and my chest keeps letting spasms of air escape.

I fix him with a detached stare. "James, I need to tell you something." I take a deep breath as he searches my eyes, and I will myself to feel nothing. *I feel nothing for you. I don't want to be with you.* I prepare to say the words that will drive him away.

But, I can't. I can't lie to him. I peer down at our entwined hands.

"I can't be with you. Is there a part of me that wants that? Yes." I look back at him. His face is pained, but he's not interrupting me. I have to get this out now or I may never do it. "But I need to choose a match. It's my duty. I've been incredibly selfish letting things happen with you. I should have never kissed you. I'm sorry."

"Maya." He raises my hands to his lips. "It is not selfish to make your own choices."

I rip my hands from him. "But it is! Don't you see? There are bigger things than our infatuation with each other going on in the world."

His face hardens. "Infatuation. That's what you think this is?"

No.

But I don't say anything. I believe it's a lot more than infatuation, and I don't want to decipher those feelings right now. He's upset with me. This is what I want. Isn't it? Only it doesn't matter what I want. I'm to choose a match and help in the war effort by creating a stronger generation of Elementals. It's my duty.

I turn away from him, leaning against my bedpost. "Please just respect me enough to stop messing with my head. It's hard for me to think clearly when you're touching and kissing me, but I know what I want. It'll only hurt you more if we let this go on further. This is your chance to find love. Take it. This is what I want." My heart shatters.

I hear him inhale a sharp breath, but I stay rigid, waiting for the door to slam on his way out, trying to keep my tears at bay.

But it doesn't come. I can still feel him in the room. Too close. He's too close. I see his jacket lying on my bed and remember the device I found.

I grab the leather, fisting it in my hand and turn around. "Not like you're even honest with me." I push the jacket into his chest.

His eyebrows rise. "What are you talking about?"

I fold my arms. "What's the device in your left pocket?"

His eyes flare for a moment before he shrugs. "It's just an outdated communicator."

"And the message on it?"

He cocks his head. "Reading my messages? Seems like a lot for somebody who is just 'infatuated.'"

Red, hot anger flares. "Go! Just go." I push him toward my balcony, and he finally moves.

As he reaches the door he turns back to me, his arrogance gone. "You sure about this?"

I nod robotically, holding onto the anger. It's easier that way.

He searches my eyes. "I won't bother you anymore." He steps out the door.

I bite my lip so I don't call him back. I watch as the wind catches his chestnut hair in the breeze and try to remember exactly how it felt in my fingers.

When the door clicks closed, something inside of me breaks. I fall to the floor. My anger dissipates as quickly as it came, and I finally let the tears falls. I can't take my eyes off the door, wanting him to return.

But he doesn't. Not now, not ever.

25

Transformation

THE NEXT DAY, I feel the clock ticking: seventy-two hours, seventy-one, seventy. I decide to keep the three-day time limit to myself. No need to make my matches worry. I also make another decision.

I show up in my mom's room early enough to wake her by plopping on her bed.

"What's going on?" She sits up, her eyes wild. It's a little gratifying.

"Nothing. I just need to ask you something. It's important." I wait for her to focus on me. "Since you have put this time stamp on deciding the rest of my life, I would like to have my best friend back. I need somebody to talk to."

She lays back down. "Not now, Maya."

"Yes, now! I literally have a ticking clock."

"Ugh, fine, yes. I'll talk to Commander Lawrence. Go ahead," she answers, shooing me out of her room.

I knew asking her fresh out of bed would work. At least it did in my childhood years.

I rush to Abby's room and knock on her door before barging in. That was a mistake.

Abby isn't alone in her bed.

After slamming the door, I realize too late that, if they didn't know I had walked in on them, now they do. I run back to my room.

I don't have to wait long. Less than five minutes later, Abby charges into my room in her hot-pink pajamas.

"It's not what you think!" she gasps, her face flushed.

"At least you're matched to the guy. I'd recognize that flaming orange hair anywhere."

"Of course, I am. What do you think of me?" She folds her arms, and my ears burn. "We weren't doing any hanky panky, if that's what you wanted to know."

"Don't need to know."

She sits on the bottom of my bed and sighs, her curls sticking out every which way. "I told you I felt bad for ignoring them lately. I decided to invite them over."

"They were *both* in your bed?!"

"Again, not what you think. We were just sleeping. We stayed up late talking, and I invited them to stay the night." She shrugs.

I laugh out loud. "How did you all fit?"

She giggles. "It was pretty comical trying to get comfortable. I don't think I'll do that again. Why were you barging in anyways?"

"We're free!" I announce. "I convinced my mom this morning."

Her eyebrows rise. "How'd you do that?"

"The details don't matter," I say, realizing that they *do* matter if I'm going to get her advice on my new three-day problem. "My mom has moved up my ceremony date. I have three days to decide."

Her jaw drops. "What? Wait, does that mean we really are running out of time?"

"No, I, um, did something, and this is my punishment."

Her shoulders relax. "What in the world did you do to deserve a time stamp on your future?"

There is no way I can tell her that I've been making out with her brother after promising to not keep things from her. It never should have happened in the first place. There is no reason for her to know.

"I want to tell you, Abby, but I can't. You're just going to have to trust me, okay?"

She thinks that over and then nods. "I trust you, and it's really nice to talk to you again. You did say you were already leaning toward one, right? That's good, at least."

"Yeah, but I don't love him yet. How can I be sure if I'm not in love? And can I fall in love in just three days?" I babble.

"I don't know, but you should at least be able to figure out which one you're *not* going to fall in love with."

"Yeah, maybe."

She jumps up, holding up a finger. "First thing first, you need to kiss them." She turns toward my dresser. "And you need a smoking hot outfit to do it in."

Pulling out the red silk dress I found in the basement chest, her eyes widen. "You've been holding out on me."

AFTER ABBY IS DONE WITH ME, I don't look like a girl anymore, but a woman going through her ceremony in sixty-four hours. After altering the dress while I went for lunch and pondered my fast-approaching future, Abby kept the length of the gown, but it now has a slit that goes up to mid-thigh. She took off quite a bit of fabric, turning the modest high neckline into a low V that wraps around my neck halter-style, and the sleeves are gone.

I glance in the mirror, noticing that I actually have cleavage now. The fabric has a sheer sparkle, hugging my body just right, accentuating my nonexistent curves, but unconstrained enough that it's still comfortable. She expertly curls my hair and leaves it hanging loose, framing my face perfectly. The dress brings out the red in my hair, making it appear less blonde. After warning her four times not to turn me into a hooker, she brings out my eyes and lips with some neutral tones from her makeup. It's still me but a more attractive, sexier version.

"They're not going to be able to keep their lips off of you, Maya," Abby gushes as we admire my reflection in the mirror.

Unease washes over me. "I don't know if I'm ready."

"Maya, you have to be ready. It's time."

"They're here?" I exclaim, my eyes bulging out.

"No, I mean figuratively, you nervous woman."

I laugh, trying to shake off the nerves. "You're right. I can do this. Wait, what if they think I want to do something else? I should cover up more." I head to the dresser for a cardigan or a jacket.

Abby grabs my arm. "No, you are going to dazzle them, and if they know you, they won't try anything unless you are completely on board. If not, call me, and I'll bury them," she says menacingly. I know she means it.

"They're good guys," I mumble to reassure myself more than her.

After one more pep talk, Abby leaves me alone to wait for them. It's not like it's my first kiss, but also those kisses with James were unexpected. Knowing what I want to happen and then making it happen is much more intimidating.

Maybe they'll take the lead once they see me dressed up. I remember Sebastian's stolen kiss on my cheek, how it made me feel weak in the knees. He will be harder to get to kiss me, the one who's always in control and such a gentleman. He won't want to take advantage of me. I'll probably have to spell it out for him. William will be more straightforward. I can tell he feels love through touch. And then there's the problem with them *both* being here. In a perfect world, we would share our first kiss in private, but by the time I figure out when to do solo dates, I may be out of time. The sooner I know, the better.

I sit on my couch with a sense of déjà vu. It's like the first time I met them. But I'm not the girl I was just a couple of weeks ago. I sit taller, trying to feel more confident. These men care for me, and one of them will be my bonded partner.

A knock at my door makes me jump, and my heart speeds off like the wings of a bird. There goes trying *not* to be nervous.

I stand, deciding not to answer the door like that first night. Instead, I raise my voice slightly, "Come in." I smooth my dress with my hands. I am a beautiful, strong, capable woman, and the woman wearing this dress will be confident. My nerves slip away as the door opens.

I see Sebastian first. His jaw slackens as his eyes widen. Everything about him is usually so controlled, even his facial features. It's a lovely sight. Then William strides in. He smiles wide, showing off his dimple, and whistles loudly.

I put a finger to my lips, giggling and shushing him. He laughs and closes the door behind them. They devour me with their eyes, and I don't even feel insecure. Sebastian glides to me, holding a hand out. I place my hand in his.

"You look stunning, Maya. What's the occasion?" He bends down and kisses the back of my hand sweetly, never breaking eye contact. Electricity flows through us, and the heat on my hand lingers. Does he even need to ask? He's got to feel it.

William approaches and actually kneels at my feet, bowing. "I will worship the ground you walk on."

"Oh, stand up," I say, bending down and touching his arm.

He peers up at me and winks. One of his blond locks falls over his face, a face of any teenage girl's dreams.

"Are you guys talking about this old thing? I just threw it on," I say, swishing my dress and fluttering my eyes.

William stands up, in awe, gawking. I peer at Sebastian, and he has the same expression. Oh man, I may be overdoing it. Can't go back now.

I walk up to William and grab his vest. He's still in his legion uniform. I gaze into his clouded eyes, trying to communicate my desire. A knowing smile plays on his lips.

I glance at Sebastian, who's observing us. "Sebastian?"

"Yes?" he responds almost robotically

"Could you get me some water? Just in the bathroom there." I lick my lips slowly and peer back at William. "I'm parched."

William's lips part, and Sebastian's steps fade away. I tip my chin up and draw myself into him. His hands close around my waist, and he lowers his face to mine, passion burning behind his eyes. His eyes flash to my lips before closing the distance.

My eyes shut as I trail my hands up behind his neck. I can feel his racing pulse as our lips meet. He's soft and gentle, but his hands explore my back, touching the exposed skin and leaving goosebumps in their wake. His hand cradles my face, deepening the kiss. I thread my fingers through his hair, trying to focus on who I'm kissing, but James makes his way into my thoughts. I compare William's thick, coarse hair to James's soft, light hair. A feeling of wrongness settles in my heart. But he's so sweet, caring, compassionate, and funny. Why would this feel wrong?

I want to scream at myself to feel something, *anything*, but I just want to pull away.

So I do. But he continues to kiss me, traveling down my neck with his lips and bunching my dress in his hands. I want to crawl out of my skin and comfort him at the same time.

I grab his face tenderly and make his eyes meet mine. I smile, wanting to break the news softly. I don't want to hurt him.

He sees something behind me, though, and steps back. I turn, and Sebastian is staring at us, his hands in fists, the glass he was carrying shattered on the floor. How did I not hear that?

"Sebastian," I breathe.

There's a fire blazing in his eyes. He closes them and leans over my desk, his back rigid.

I peek at William, not sure what to do.

"I'll give you two some privacy," William says, giving me a light kiss on the cheek and escaping to my balcony.

Sebastian doesn't look approachable, but I'm not scared of him. Ignas can have bad tempers, but not Sebastian. I have never met somebody with more control than him.

Feeling sure of myself, I walk carefully to Sebastian, not wanting to startle him. I step over the shattered glass. Veins ripple down his muscled arms as he clenches and unclenches his jaw. I hesitantly touch his shoulder with a feather-like touch and trace my fingers down his arm, trailing the veins. He looks up at me finally. His skin shines in the ambient lighting, but his blue eyes pierce mine. At least the flames have dwindled. His eyebrows are slightly pinched, but the rest of his face remains expressionless.

"I'm sorry."

He raises his eyebrows. "You have no need to apologize, Maya."

He grabs my hands. Warm fire erupts at his touch. I try to concentrate on his words even though my skin is sizzling, and it feels more than nice.

"This is new to all of us. You hold no blame for the emotions I'm experiencing."

I nod. He glances towards the door William walked out of and then back at me.

"Yes, that was hard to see. I knew what to expect, but to experience it, watching him touch you like that, makes me want to tear him apart, which scares me. He's my best friend."

I just stare up at him, not knowing what to say.

He continues. "I worked very hard all these years to have the control I do, and tonight I almost lost it." He stares at me grievously.

"But you didn't," I whisper.

His lips turn up a bit. "I didn't."

The way he's looking at me is enough to break my heart. I want to comfort him. The fire continues to absorb into my skin from his palms and I want so badly for it to spread.

"Sebastian." I sigh, peering at him through my eyelashes. A nervous pit buries itself in my stomach, and I can't say the words. I bite my bottom lip. I guess I'll have to show him.

I release his hands and trail my fingers up his arms. Leaning in, I reach the nape of his neck. There is something in his eyes I haven't noticed before. Underneath the deep ocean blue, around his pupils, is the barest hint of red, like the fire is literally inside of him. I suck in a breath, glancing at his lips. They curve perfectly into a heart shape.

He opens his mouth to say something but seems at a loss for words, because he draws me closer instead, bringing a hand to my face. His fingers trail up my cheekbone and tuck a stray strand of hair behind my ear. Fire erupts everywhere he touches. His fingers continue their fiery journey down my neck and onto my shoulder. The desire for the fire to consume me is building. If he doesn't kiss me soon, my own control will go out the window. He leans down to place his lips gently on my collarbone. My heart takes off, and my breathing hitches.

He places his hand on my heart. "May I?"

Before I say anything, he puts his ear to my chest and listens. I don't know if he thinks he can calm it, because it races even faster like it's about to jump out of my body. I try to breathe through it. He cranes his neck and smiles wide. I stop breathing all together. He may be the most beautiful person I have ever met.

Slowly, he brings his face closer to mine and murmurs, "Breathe, Maya," into my ear before kissing the shell of it and moving down to my ear lobe. He nips it playfully.

I gasp, and he scoops me into his arms. His kisses travel down my neck into the hollow of my throat, leaving a path of fire.

He trails his mouth up my jawline and to my other ear, burning my skin. "You take my breath away, too."

He places me on the desk, and I wrap my legs around his torso, the dress bunching up against my thighs. He leans in to kiss my cheek gently.

A yearning to see more of him washes over me. I feel brave and grab the top button on his shirt, undoing it. Not daring to look at his expression, I move to the second one. By the time I get to the third, my hand shakes. His chest is smooth and marbled. I place my hand on it. It's just as hot as I imagined it to be. Electricity flows from my touch.

Sebastian sighs deeply, and I scan his face. His eyes flutter closed. He smiles and nods, encouraging me to keep going.

I easily undo the rest of his buttons until his shirt is gone. Holy abs. Not only is his face perfect, but his body could have been carved out of stone. He is stunning.

I run my hands down his dark chest, creating a fire of my own, outlining all his curves and muscles. My arms bend as he draws nearer to me, his face inching closer. His eyes darken as he stares hungrily at my lips. The scent of cinnamon wafts off his breath.

He's waiting for me to close the gap, but I'm frozen. He's too good to be true. What if I don't feel anything?

I slide my hands up to his face and tilt his chin to me. Adoration dances in his dilated pupils. Could he already be falling for me without us even kissing yet? There's only one way to find out.

I close the rest of the distance.

26

Protectors

AN EXPLOSION ROCKS THE BUILDING. The mirror hanging from my bathroom door falls, and glass shatters across the room.

I jump back, smacking my head on the wall.

Sebastian releases me with a jerk. "Are you okay?" he yells over the sirens that wail throughout the building.

William is at our side in an instant. His eyes are slits. "What happened? What'd you do to her?" he yells at Sebastian, eyeing his naked chest.

"I didn't do anything!" he shouts back. Sebastian's eyes are reddening and locked on William.

Their impending brawl is both exhilarating and terrifying. "I'm fine, William! I just hit my head out of shock from the explosion."

Both men scan me.

"I'm okay." I touch the back of my scalp where a goose egg is forming. "No blood, see?" I shout over the sirens, showing them, but blood *is* on my fingertips. "Oh, I must have hit my head harder than I thought. But, honestly, I'm okay."

They glance back at each other, thankfully less aggressively.

Sebastian speaks first. "We need to get her to the bunker." Then he turns to me. "Do you have a rag we can put on your head for the bleeding?"

I'm about to tell him I'm fine again, but I have a feeling he won't believe me. "Even better, I have a first aid kit under my bathroom sink. But I need to get changed first. If we're going to battle, I'm not running around in this thing." I approach my dresser to get some regular clothes when vertigo hits me, and I trip over my feet.

Sebastian catches me and heat flows through me once more. "You're not going to battle, but we do need to hurry."

William takes my head gently. He leans in to inspect the wound. "It looks like a mild laceration, but she could have a concussion."

I arch my eyebrows at him.

Sebastian nods and disappears into the bathroom.

William peers at me. "What? I have a year in medic training under my belt."

"How did I not know that you're training to become a medic?"

He shrugs and then a smirk crosses his face. "Does that give me an edge?" He smooths back his hair and fixes his vest. "You know, with the whole hot doctor look? I could even help you change with all my expertise."

I hold back a giggle. "I don't see how that qualifies in helping me change. But you can get me some clothes."

He leads me to the couch, and I test my balance before sitting. It's a little better.

"I'll get the clothes, but not because you're going to war." William scoffs. "But for more selfish reasons, I don't want any other man to see you in this smoking dress."

If it wasn't for that adorable smile, I would jab him back with the fact that another man has already seen me in it.

Sebastian returns with the first aid kit, as William sifts through my drawers.

Another explosion rocks the building. More things fall off my tabletops.

"We really should get going!" I shout.

"Here, put this on your head." Sebastian hands me gauze, and I do as he instructs.

I wince as it touches my head. He helps me to my feet as William turns, holding up jeans and a T-shirt.

"Hey, good job."

"Well, I do have three sisters. I have some idea of what you girls wear."

I grin, remembering. Why can't I have feelings for him? A man who knows clothes.

He goes to help me into my jeans, but I interrupt. "I think I've got it, thanks."

I tell them to turn around and quickly slip off the dress and change.

When I've finished, we race into the hallway, William hanging back at my side to ensure I didn't mess up the bandage on my head. I wonder briefly if the Coms have finally found us. I shouldn't worry. We have plenty of legionaries, although I am leaving them two short. We should hurry.

I pick up speed since I'm the one slowing them down. Two of my strides equal one of theirs. The halls are empty, which isn't a good sign. I can't hear much over the sirens. We get to the stairwell and begin our descent, past the second and first floors, finally reaching ground level.

The guys are about to head down another flight of stairs when I pull them up short. "Wait, I can go the rest of the way on my own. You should head to your commander," I say, trying to catch my breath.

They both stare at me, then Sebastian glances at William. "William, you go ahead. I'm going to make sure she's safe first."

William moves to put his hand on the small of my back. "No way, I'll take her to safety. You head to the commander."

Oh, brother, this is not the time for their toxic masculinity. I push past them and proceed down the stairs. "I can handle two flights of stairs. Just go!" I yell over my shoulder.

I'm about four steps down when I hear them coming after me. There's no time to talk sense into them, so I pick up the pace.

I reach the bunker level, entirely out of breath. I turn around, and they're both just inches from me. I take a step back, not expecting them to be so close. "Look, the door is right there. I'm fine," I pant.

William plants a kiss on the top of my head, "We'll see you soon, okay? Don't bloody bleed to death, you hear?"

I roll my eyes. "Does it look like I'm bleeding out?" I say mockingly, but to my surprise, he checks the back of my head.

"No."

Sebastian comes up on my other side. He locks eyes with me, and the heat returns when I remember the softness of his lips on my skin. "We'll be back as soon as we can. Please get that looked at," he says seriously.

"I will, I will. You guys really need to go." I push them back up the stairs, but Sebastian bends to kiss my temple. Ah, the fire again. Disequilibrium overcomes me, but they're both gone when I can see clearly again.

Now that they're not at my side, I miss them terribly. It's unfair for me to miss William. I still have to break his heart.

I continue down the hall. The bunker door seems even larger than last time. I place my face in front of the scanner and say my name. There's a loud metal scraping sound as the heavy door slowly opens.

Before my eyes can adjust to the dimness ahead of me, I hear my mom.

"Maya! I was so worried about you!" She's coming towards me with Calvin in tow. "I assumed you were already here, but you weren't. The last couple of people got here a few minutes ago."

Her voice rises with emotion and I feel a little bad for worrying her. She hardly ever gets like this.

About twenty others are staring at me, and a lot more are pacing or lying on bunks in the background.

She comes in for a hug, and her words are muffled in my hair. "Where were you?" Before I can answer, she notices the bandage on my head, and her eyes bulge. "What happened?" she asks, giving me a once-over.

"I hit my head when I heard the explosion. I'm fine. Just get me some water."

"No. Head injuries need to be checked by Dr. Rye." Not him, I almost groan. The last time I saw him, he gave me a very invasive check-up for my match eligibility.

He decides I don't have a concussion, just a small gash on my head. After healing me, he gives me pain medication for the headache that's coming on, and I'm free to go. I told them I was fine.

As we get to our designated bunks, my brother's holding tightly onto my mom's hand. He doesn't give me his goofy smile or stick his tongue out like usual.

I ruffle his hair. "Hey, Cal, how are you holding up?"

He lets go of Mom to hug me, squeezing my torso tight. He's not usually affectionate.

"Are you okay?"

He lets me go and evens his shoulders. "I'm not scared at all." His voice falters a bit.

I smile and sit him down on the bottom bunk with me. "Calvin, it's okay to be scared. Did you know that we can feel scared *and* brave?"

He focuses on his boots and nods. "That's how I feel then."

"Me too, buddy," I say, rubbing his shoulder.

"What took you so long to get down here? I thought something might have happened to you."

Mom has the same question in her eyes.

"I'm sorry, I was preoccupied, and then I hit my head. It took me a little while."

Her eyebrows raise, and she gives me that look—the one moms give you when they can tell you're lying. But something about what she said earlier is prickling my mind. There's more to her worry than just me.

"Mom." Realizing she won't say much in front of Calvin, I change gears. "Cal, I bet you know where the water is. Could you get me and Mom a bottle?"

"Sure!" He jumps up, eager to be helpful.

I turn on her as soon as he's out of earshot. "This isn't a drill. There were explosions. What's going on? Are we being attacked?" I can't help the panic that starts to swirl in my gut. James, William, and Sebastian are all out there.

Before I start to spiral, she says, "No, no, not quite." But there's a slight tightening in her eyes.

"Then what's going on? Why are we down here?"

"It's just to be safe, honey. Doing these drills is good practice." She eyes me sternly, "Obviously, you failed."

"Don't change the subject. If you have to know, I was with my *matches*, doing what *you* asked me to do."

"I wondered why you are wearing makeup, and your hair is done. You look beautiful."

"Thank you. Now answer my question…honestly."

"It's not something you need to know. We shouldn't be down here long," she replies, avoiding eye contact.

"Fine! Continue to keep things from me. That's great for building trust. I'm going to go find Abby," I snap and storm off.

I find her sitting with her mother—wearing a pained expression—towards the back of the bunker.

As I approach, I overhear Abby saying, "Mom, Avery's got this. He's quite skilled. I've seen him in action. If there are Coms, they won't come close to him."

Mrs. Stevens nods, but her worry lines deepen.

Abby notices me approaching them, so she stands to meet me. "Hey, my mom is pretty worked up. Those blasts were intense."

"Yeah, my mirror even fell off and shattered." I grimace.

"Really? Ugh, I don't want to see my room. I was outside when it happened."

"You were? What did you see?"

"I didn't see it hit, but I saw a plume of smoke out in the forest before the sirens started, and they rushed us inside."

I bite my lip. "Well, that's good. Coms probably haven't discovered our location then. James told me that Auras can divert the missiles, but they choose not to if it's far enough away, because the Coms could figure out our whereabouts."

"Whether we're under attack or not, everyone is still scared. They told us we would never need this bunker, remember? At least they can't keep lying to us. There is no way they can cover this up as a drill." Her eyes slide past me, lost in thought.

Well, my mom sure is trying.

Abruptly, Abby looks at me with renewed energy. "Wait! I almost forgot it's your big day. Did it happen?" She puckers her lips at me.

I can't help but smile. "Yes and no," I mutter, casting my eyes around the room. "Do you think there's somewhere more private we can talk?"

"We could pretend we're gathering supplies. I doubt anyone is in the freeze-dried food section. Nobody will need that until the fresh stuff runs out."

"Good idea."

After Abby talks to her mom, we find ourselves between massive black shelves that reach the ceiling, filled with brown boxes of food. This is a good spot, between the pantry staples and concrete walls.

Abby grabs a box of freeze-dried meatloaf. "Ew, I really hope we never have to use this." Then she turns to me. "Spill."

I tell her the boys' reactions to seeing me in the dress, and she bounces on the balls of her feet with the widest smile. "I knew it. You were hot."

"And then I kissed William."

"He's the one, isn't he? How could you not choose the British one?"

I scowl. "Let me finish. It started out great, my body was responding to him, but all I could picture was—" The words freeze in my mouth. I can't lie to her, but how can I tell her what happened between James and me? It would ruin our friendship for sure. First, I kept him from her, and now I've secretly made out with him…twice!

"Maya, you're leaving me hanging! Who were you picturing? Sebastian?"

It would be easy to tell her it was Sebastian, but it wouldn't be the truth. I cast my eyes down. "Abby, I need to tell you something, and I have no idea how to do it."

"You can tell me anything. You know that."

I take a deep breath and push past the knot in my stomach. "I've developed feelings for your brother. I honestly don't know how it happened, and I tried so hard to bury them, but I just can't."

I tell her everything, every last detail, not holding back. Once I finish, I can't bring myself to face her.

I hear a choking sound. Oh no, she's crying. I peer up. Her face is turning a weird shade of purple. "I'm so sorry, Abby. I wouldn't have chosen this. I understand if you never want to talk to me again, but at least you know. And if you feel like you need to tell somebody, I won't stop you."

She bursts out laughing, taking short breaths, her eyes filled with unshed tears. "I'm not *mad*. I'm thrilled! You know how long I've been waiting for you to get the courage to tell me. I know you've been in love with my brother since I first caught you two together." She giggles and wraps her arms around me. "We could be sisters, Maya!"

Her words hang suspended in the air, and a chill runs through me. I don't return the hug, the words "in love" bouncing around in my head, getting bigger and bigger until my vision blurs, and I can't think of anything else.

Abby shakes me. "Hey, snap out of it, Maya. Hello!"

"In love?" I spurt out.

"Well, yeah," she says. "It's obvious."

I shake my head.

"The way you two look at each other. Oh, I just hope one of my matches will look at me like that one day."

"No, no, no, no, I'm not in love with him," I breathe.

"I'm sure you're in denial, which is understandable. You're still matched. And he is, too, which is problematic." She sighs, her eyebrows turning down.

Ice spreads in my veins. "Who?"

"I don't think I should tell you. It's not like you *love* him or anything." She squints at me, her lips curving up.

"Oh, so help me, I will throttle you."

"It's that girl you were with yesterday, Jules or something?"

"Juliet," I whisper, horror-struck. The way she ogled him. She'll jump him the first chance she gets. Not to mention she's breathtakingly gorgeous. She'll be able to mold him like clay.

My heart falls into my stomach, and I stand, making my way down the row.

Abby grabs my hand. "Where are you going?"

"I need to talk to her."

"And say what exactly? Sit down," she orders.

I flop back onto the hard ground as my breathing becomes rapid.

"Okay, let's calm down. It's not like they're bonded, Maya. You know these things take a while. We'll figure something out," she says quickly.

My eyes fill with tears as I watch her. I didn't realize it before, but Abby and James have similarities—the same nose and chin, and they even smile the same. I miss seeing that smile. They have the same curls. His are just a darker shade.

"I *am* in love with him," I choke out.

Her eyes fill with compassion. "I know." She reaches her arms out toward me, and I fall into them. She tucks me into the crook of her arm and holds me like a baby. "Tell me the rest of the story from today. Maybe it'll help calm you." She consoles me as she lightly plays with my hair.

I shake my head. "How can I make a bond with them if I love somebody else?"

She lifts her shoulders delicately. "I can't answer that for you. So, you were kissing William, and I'm guessing James kept popping into your mind?" It's the first time she's used that name for him.

I nod into her shoulder. "It felt so wrong. I guess now I know why." I sniffle.

"And what about Sebastian?"

"I didn't get the chance. We were interrupted. Oh, Abby, I'm a terrible person! I enjoyed being in his arms. How can I desire one man's touch but be in love with another?"

"I don't think love is one size fits all, Maya. Everyone is different. Maybe you feel something for him, too."

"Maybe, but it doesn't make me feel better," I whine.

"He is your match, perfect for you in every way. You're supposed to fall for him. Don't be too hard on yourself. It's not your fault my brother stole your heart before you got the chance."

"So, you're saying to stick with my match, let things play out, and I'll fall in love with him, too?" I ask, searching her eyes for the answer to all my problems.

"No, I'm not saying that. This is your choice, nobody else's."

"My mom would beg to differ. She told me she would exile James if she ever caught us together again."

"I guess that leaves you with two options then."

I sit up and wait with bated breath, her widening eyes boring into mine.

"Choose Sebastian as your match or leave with James."

27

Spark

W E SPEND THE NIGHT IN THE BUNKER, but we're freed from its suffocating walls early the following day. An announcement tells us not to worry, that we're not in danger, the explosions were our doing, a training exercise mishap. I scoff. How can they keep lying to everyone?

"See, there was nothing to worry about," Mom tells me before we part ways.

I don't know if she's trying to convince herself or me.

I return to my room and groan. There's shattered glass everywhere, all my things strewn across the floor. The last thing I want to do right now is clean, but I head back into the hallway to fetch the broom out of the hall closet. Of course, it's not there. Everyone's room must be a mess. Well, I tried.

Changing tactics, I pick up the items that had fallen to the floor. When I get to my desk, my feet crunching over glass shards, the memories from the night prior come flooding back. I touch the places on my body that Sebastian had kissed, smiling as the warmth returns, but remember what Abby said last night. I'm not only choosing between two men but between two different lives: obedience and sacrifice or freedom and uncertainty.

Neither sounds that glorious.

With forty-eight hours to decide, I quickly message Sebastian. He needs to come tonight and finish what we started. My heart skips a beat at the thought.

Our schedule returns to normal, as if nothing happened. I'm grateful I'm not helping with breakfast. I can't imagine what shape the kitchen is in. That thought quickly turns to dread, though, when I find out I'm on lunch duty with Juliet.

For the next half hour, I get an earful of everything she loves about her matches. I try to be as excited for her as she was for me, but I've never been a great actress. Fortunately, she's in such a delightful mood, she hardly notices my facial expressions.

She's tossing a salad as she rambles. "Oh, Maya, they're perfect. Corey is an Igna, like one of your matches. You'll have to give me some advice on that. At first, I was a little worried, but he's a giant teddy bear. He has a very gentle and sweet nature. Although, nobody would want to mess with him based on looks alone. I swear one of his arms is bigger than my torso. It's amazing. And Avery, oh wow, that boy is attractive."

She pretends to fan herself with one of the salad tongs, and I squeeze the lemons in my hand a little too tight. The juice squirts in my eye. I wince.

"But you know that he's Abigail's brother, right? I heard the story of his miraculous arrival. I can't believe he's my match," she says dreamily. "Although he is a little on the quiet side, which surprised me, because he was so warm and friendly when I first met him."

I splash water in my eyes, trying to get the acid out. She doesn't even notice. Hearing that James isn't acting like himself piques my interest.

I decide to make a response that isn't a grunt or fake laugh. "That's unlike him."

She whips her hair at me. "Do you know him well? Oh my gosh. Tell me everything."

Should have kept my mouth shut. "No, not really. I've talked to him a few times when Abby is around." Wait. This might be my only opportunity to create doubt in her mind about James and push her toward the giant arms of the Igna. "Well, one thing did come across, but it's probably nothing."

"Come on, tell me," she begs.

"I would say he is a little *too* friendly, if you know what I mean. He flirts with a lot of girls, and I don't know if being matched will stop him. Just be careful."

She nods, accepting the news. "I feared as much. Guys with faces like that have gotten around, but I'm not worried. They're too strict here for him to see girls other than me."

My shoulders droop as I continue to make the lemonade.

"Why are you squeezing those? Can't you just—" She waves her hands through the air.

She's right. I hadn't thought of that.

"Yeah, I guess so. I'm just tired today, didn't get much sleep," I say grumpily.

She begins chatting again, and I try to tune her out, but a thought occurs to me. "There was this one girl," I interrupt.

"What?"

"You said he wouldn't be able to see any other girls, but on my first date with my match, we played pool against him and a legionary girl. She had her hands all over him, and she lives in the same building he does."

Her happy demeanor turns worrisome. "I didn't realize they had girls in the legion." She pauses, then turns to me with a small smile. "Thanks for telling me, Maya. You're a good friend."

I feel bad, but not enough to take back my statement. It's not that big of a deal. It'll just make her think twice about deciding on her match.

AFTER LUNCH AND MY LESSONS with Seth, I make my way back to my room, taking the long route for a reason that can only be fate. There is a couple underneath the large blossoming pink willow tree. I don't usually see pairs publicly displaying affection.

I pause, knowing I should avert my gaze, but I can't take my eyes off them. Something about the man's build is familiar. Then I see the long white hair falling around their shoulders. I gasp. It's not just *any* couple embracing under the tree. It's James and Juliet. I didn't sabotage them. I practically pushed her into his arms to prove her desirability.

His arms are wrapped around her waist, and she stares up at him affectionately. I can't see his face, but it probably bears a similar look to hers.

When he steps back, he trips on the tree's root, jutting from the ground. They fall together, with her landing on top of him. It's like I'm watching a rom-com scene from my own personal horror movie.

Her face scrunches in laughter, and I hear the faint musical sound as it reaches me. And then what she does next fills my veins with ice. She leans down and plants a kiss fully on his lips. His hands cup her face, and I can't watch anymore. My lunch is about to reappear.

I run into the cover of trees, collapsing into the leaves. I dry heave a few times, but nothing comes up. Placing my cool hands on my face, I try to erase the image of them kissing.

James is with Juliet now. She'll make him plenty happy. I wonder if he kisses her the same way he kissed me, threading his fingers through her hair, her body craving his touch like I did.

Pushing my palms into my eyes, I let out a quiet groan. Sebastian can be my escape from the tortuous memories. I have to finish what we began last night. Kissing him will be the only thing to make me forget James. I don't think about James when Sebastian is touching me.

Waiting until tonight, won't do. I need him *now*.

I heave myself up and head towards the legion quarters, refusing to look back at the tree. No need for more images of James kissing Juliet to imprint in my mind.

Once I make it inside, I'm not quite sure what to do. When I see someone in legion black, I ask, "Do you know where Sebastian Gray is by chance?"

He shakes his head and keeps walking. There's got to be an office somewhere.

An older man with thinning gray hair but a well-built body comes out of one of the doors and lowers his gaze on me. "Are you lost, young lady?"

"Hi! I'm just looking for Sebastian Gray. He's my match. I need to speak with him."

"Igna, right?"

I nod.

"I believe they're in the training field," he says gruffly.

"Thank you," I call out, dashing out the doors.

I've never been to the legionary's training field, but I know where it is. After walking for about ten minutes, I realize this might be a little impulsive. Most likely, he won't be able to talk to me, let alone go somewhere private.

Dark clouds roll in, and a soft drizzle along with them. Great, now I'll resemble a wet dog. He'll *definitely* not want to kiss me.

I pull my hood up, grateful I grabbed my sweatshirt, but it won't last long if the rain worsens. The fields are on the other side of the base.

As I get closer, a group approaches me. They're all in legion black, but I'm able to pick out Sebastian as they close the distance. His hood is up on his vest, and he's talking to a guy beside him, a burly man with big arms, who must be Corey. James is definitely a more suitable choice than that guy.

Nope, can't go there.

Sebastian's eyes land on me and he jogs ahead of the group. When he reaches me, he places one of his hands on his waist and wipes the rain off his forehead with the other, but it gets quickly replaced with more water droplets. He's in a short-sleeved shirt under the vest. Watching the water coat his biceps makes my butterflies reappear. How can he be even more attractive in the rain?

"What are you doing here, Maya?" His eyes are shining, raindrops clinging to his eyelashes.

"To see you, of course."

"You're in luck. The rain stopped our training session early."

"Right, can't make fire in the rain."

"Oh, I can, but most others can't." He grins and casually takes my hand.

We walk back, his group passing us and whistling in our direction. I bite my lip, but he waves them off. It's pouring now, the water seeping through my hood. I give up and pull it back.

"I want to finish what we started last night."

He flashes me a disarming smile. "Me, too, but I thought I was coming over tonight?"

I smile timidly, blinking the water out of my eyes. "I don't want to wait."

"Right here? I mean, if that's what you want, but the guys might say something." His lips pull up in a smirk as a few guys keep peeking back at us.

"No, not here. Come on, I know a spot." I pull on his hand, guiding him away from the buildings.

Finally, we're in the cover of trees for a moment of privacy. I can't bring Sebastian to James's bench, though. That spot will always be shared with him, even if I never speak to him again. The rain is coming down in thick sheets, but we're shielded for now. Sebastian looks happy enough, but I can tell by his stiff shoulders that he's uncomfortable. Ignas don't like water.

"I'm sorry, you must be terribly uncomfortable." I take his hand and close my eyes. When I open them back up, we're both dry. I'm getting quicker with that.

"That's a neat trick," he breathes, smiling wide.

My stomach jumps into my throat. He's so beautiful. I need to do this before I lose my nerve.

"Sebastian, will you kiss me?" My voice comes out quieter than I intended, but his eyes widen, hearing me perfectly. My heart doesn't even have time to pick up speed before he sweeps me off my feet.

"You're braver than me. I wanted to rush into your room first thing this morning and finish where we left off."

Heat fills my cheeks as I see the burning desire in his eyes.

"Thank you for coming to find me. I don't think I could have waited any longer," he says heavily, casting his eyes down to my lips.

He gently places me on my feet, my back up against the tree. He eclipses everything around us. I'm lost in the blue depths of his eyes, his long black eyelashes, and the perfect shape of his pink lips, which contrast his dark complexion flawlessly. I can't even speak. He places his palms on either side of my face, sliding them slowly into my hair, as a shiver runs down my body. I arch into him.

He leans down, just a hair from our lips touching. "I think we were right about here," he purrs.

His hot breath ruffles my hair, and I inhale his smoky scent. His hand slides to the base of my neck. Flames lick my skin and I wonder briefly what it'll be like to kiss fire. Our lips meet. They are as soft as I imagined, almost as smooth as… I don't dare think his name.

I place a hand on the back of his head and draw him closer, pressing my body into his, needing Sebastian to make me forget everything…James…even my own name. Heat flows from his mouth and travels through my body. His hands move down my back, onto my hips, and back into my hair. The fire they leave in their wake soaks through my clothes, into my skin, and is absorbed by my veins. The flames course through my entire body, consuming me, but I don't care. I just want more.

My lips part, and I roughly clutch at his hair and breathe him in. When my tongue grazes his bottom lip, a growl escapes his chest. I cling to him as if he's everything I didn't know I needed and more.

Something unlocks inside me, and flashes of brilliant light explode behind my eyelids. I ignore it, too swallowed up by the kiss, but it brightens, and the heat inside my body becomes less remarkable and more uncomfortable. I can't help but open my eyes. My body stiffens, and he must feel it, too, because his eyelids open and he pulls back.

I do not imagine the fire this time. Sebastian and I are *literally* on fire.

We gasp simultaneously. He lunges away from me, but it doesn't dim the orange flames encasing my body.

"Maya!" he yelps.

The fire spreads across the brush at our feet and up a tree trunk. I stare in confusion. Why am I not in pain? I'm hot but not burning-to-death hot. Maybe it's the shock.

I inspect the bare skin on my arms, expecting them to be scorched black, but they're white and perfectly normal. My clothes are still in one piece, too. The air is heated as it enters my lungs.

Sebastian pats me down frantically with something, and I realize he has taken off his shirt and is trying to smother the fire. The flames continue to dance across my body.

"Sebastian, it's okay, I'm okay. Look, it's not hurting me."

He stares at me, horrified, not comprehending. But his eyes clear, and he scoops me up and runs. Once we're out from under the trees, the rain dampens the flames. He sprints across the open field, the flames billowing from behind us like a cape. The sensation of fire in my veins is still present. It's like the fire is inside me and coming out, not the other way around.

A memory tugs on me, something Sebastian said once, but before I can place it, I'm flying through the air. I clutch at him, digging my fingernails into his skin.

We hit the water with a hard impact, muffling my escaped scream. My body drifts through the water. The fire in my veins subsides. It draws itself in from the tips of my toes and fingers until there is only a tiny flicker in my chest.

Strong hands grab me and haul me out of the water and onto the shore. I rub the water from my eyes and inhale the fresh air, filling my lungs with oxygen instead of heat. Sebastian inspects my entire body, looking for signs of damage. Though my hands shake, I'm okay, the same, besides that odd flicker in my chest.

His eyes are panic-stricken. "Maya, are you okay? How are you not burned to a crisp?" His hands flutter over me, as if afraid to touch me, probably worried he'll set me ablaze again.

I force a smile onto my face. "I'm okay." I reach out to touch him, but he flinches away. My smile falters. "Really, look, I'm fine."

"I see that, but I don't believe it." He shakes his head. A line forms between his eyebrows.

His tight curls hang loosely on his forehead, and I can't take my eyes off his smooth, dark, marbled chest as water drips over his pec muscles. He leans back on his heels, still staring at me, worry lining every part of him.

He's the one. The thought hits me like an arrow to the heart.

I have no idea what is happening to my body, but one thing is clear. Sebastian is my true match. He literally set me on fire. If that's not a sign, I don't know what is.

I reach for him again, slowly this time. He watches my hand intently as I touch his arm with a feather-like caress. His body is wound tight as he watches my hand, looking for any sign of fire. But he doesn't see the flames swirling within. A spark has been lit. I feel it, burrowed deep, but it's there. A spark within.

"Sebastian."

His eyes are bright as rain falls onto his face and drips off his chin. The man who hates water doesn't move to wipe it off.

I trail my hand down his arm, interlacing his fingers with mine, giving him a slight tug. "I choose you."

He doesn't react. His eyes are glossed over.

"Did you hear me?" I smile.

"How are you alive?" he sputters.

"I don't know. But it proves one thing for sure, don't you think?"

He shakes his head. "I don't understand. Only Ignas can catch on fire and not burn."

My smile falters. But I push all my questions to the back of my mind. I need to get this out, now that I know. I need him to understand.

"Sebastian." I squeeze his hand again, and his eyes sharpen, finally focusing on me. "I choose you."

He blinks. Once. Twice. And then a smile breaks across his face like the sun through storm clouds. He relaxes under my touch, and we rise together. I wipe the water from his face, but it's useless as it continues to drip. He laughs at my failed attempt to dry him off.

"It's not too bad. The water feels nice once you get used to it," he says. He draws me closer to him, more careful than before.

His hand threads through my hair. Lighter fluid flows in my veins, ready to ignite. I worry, but thankfully, the spark stays as a dull thrum in my core.

"I can't explain what just happened to you, but I know one thing for certain. I am hopelessly in love with you. Do you really choose me? Even if I might catch you on fire again?"

Heat radiates off of him, and I inch closer, craving the warmth. "*Especially* if you catch me on fire again. That was kind of exhilarating."

He shakes his head. "We're going to figure that out. But first—" The side of his mouth lifts as he falls onto one knee.

I gasp, and his smile widens.

He grips tightly to my hand. "I'm a little old-fashioned." He clears his throat. "Maya Mayfield. Wait, what's your middle name?"

"Angela," I say breathlessly.

"Maya Angela Mayfield," he restarts, "would you do the great honor of making me the happiest Igna on this planet and bonding yourself to me?"

I don't know what to say. I know what I *should* say. I did choose him and should have known he would do this. It's so like Sebastian to propose to me in such a Com fashion.

But do I *love* him? I know I have stronger feelings for him than William, but what about James? How can I give this man my whole heart when some of it is still missing? I may never get that part of me back, but I can give him what's left.

There's only a moment of hesitation before I nod. "Yes."

He jumps up and presses his lips to mine. I melt into his touch, and my spark responds immediately. Before I can react, he pulls away and scans me head to toe, worry lining his face again.

I'm about to tell him I'm fine when I see movement over his shoulder. William is running toward us. Oh no. I'm going to have to break his heart.

In the outside world, if we were both regular people dating, I could see myself growing to love William, but I can't deny Sebastian's effect on me.

Sebastian must notice the change in my face, because he turns around as William joins us.

"Maya, don't do this," William gasps. His hair is plastered to his face, and he furiously wipes it from his eyes, which are bouncing between the two of us. "I know you're not in love with me, but you're not in love with him either."

28

Bloody and Brooding

MY JAW DROPS OPEN. Sebastian tilts his head, barely concealed rage igniting in his eyes. A red ring surrounding the blue, that I'm certain wasn't there before, catches my attention. I thought it was a trick of the light when I saw it after my kiss with William, but there it is again.

"I know this must come as a shock for you," Sebastian says, placing a hand on Williams's shoulder, so roughly that it sprays water onto their faces. "But there is no reason to come over here spouting things you don't understand to ruin our moment. She chose me, William. You'll have to accept it. I'm sorry."

Sebastian leaves his hand there as William steps towards me.

William glances at it. "Um, can you move your hand, *mate*?" He annunciates the last word, emotion sparking in his eyes.

"Nope."

William looks at him for a tense beat before nodding and stepping back. Sebastian drops his hand. I touch Sebastian where his chest has gone rigid, as if he was made from stone.

"Let me talk to him," I say.

Sebastian studies William for a moment longer before looking at me.

"I need to talk to him," I say again.

He relaxes a bit under my touch. "So, talk to him."

"Can you give us some space?" I frown at Sebastian. This isn't like him.

"Yes, of course. I'll be right over here." His voice is strained, and he gives William a threatening look before drifting toward the lake.

William eyes Sebastian, who I'm sure is only a few paces from us. I decide it would be best not to touch William. It might send Sebastian over the edge he's on.

William's eyes move to mine and his face softens.

I take a deep breath and let my words spill out. "I'm sorry you had to find out this way. You are kind, funny, trustworthy…a truly wonderful person to be around, William. And honestly, if we lived outside these walls and were dating like two normal people, I doubt I would ever have had to do this. But this is a match, and I have to choose. I can't deny what I feel for Sebastian." My eyes brim with tears, but I refuse to let them fall. I so badly want to hug him.

He flinches but continues to wear the same mask of conviction as the one he arrived with. "I understand. You need to follow your heart."

My eyes widen. It's not what I expected him to say, and his kindness makes me feel even worse. I reach to the back of my neck to take the necklace off and return it, but he grabs my hand, shaking his head.

"Maya, that's not what I mean. And that was a gift. I won't take it back."

I freeze under his touch.

"I know about James," he whispers.

My hands fall to my sides, and I resist the temptation to look over my shoulder at Sebastian. How could he know?

"You need to tell him. He should know your heart isn't fully with him."

His words are a dagger to my chest. I step back, and he steps with me, his words tumbling so quickly that I can barely understand them.

"I first noticed when we played pool together. The way you kept looking at him. I realized you must know him somehow. But I was confused about why you were pretending not to. I assumed maybe the two of you had a thing and you didn't want to talk about it. No biggie. But then, that night, you snuck out. James got you through the barrier, right? It wasn't hard to put two and two together with him missing as well. You were so worried about him. I thought, or at least was hoping, that it was just because he was Abby's brother. That is until I went to find you earlier today and saw your reaction to him with his match. You were truly heartbroken. You're in love with him, aren't you?"

I don't know what to say. I shake my head, backing away from him, but his hands are on my shoulders.

"You're in love with him. Not me and not Sebastian." His voice rises, and suddenly, Sebastian is there, snarling at William.

"Get your hands off of her." Sebastian pushes William, who falls into the mud.

I gasp and go to help him up, but Sebastian beats me to it.

William bounces up. "Tell him, or I will!" he yells at me, spitting rainwater out the side of his mouth.

My voice doesn't work. I can't form words as I look back and forth between the boys. What have I done?

"Get out of here, William, before I do something I'll regret," Sebastian shouts.

William gives me a pointed look, one final chance, before looking at Sebastian. "She's not in love with you, mate."

"Oh, that's it," Sebastian growls, bringing a fist up.

William ducks out of the way as Sebastian is about to connect.

"Stop it!" I yell.

Sebastian ignores me, lunging and tackling William to the ground. William blasts him into the sky. Sebastian lands not too far away in a crouch.

"Tell him," William says desperately.

Thunder rolls overhead as the rain picks up.

Tears escape me, mingling with the rain as my heart drops. Why does this even matter? James is with Juliet now. I watch as Sebastian's arms engulf in fire, his eyes locked on William. I have to put an end to this. I can't let him hurt his best friend.

"Sebastian, please stop. William is right—"

Sebastian's stride falters as he glances at me.

"William is right. I *do* have feelings for somebody else. But it doesn't matter. I choose you."

Sebastian blinks at me, his jaw clenching, then turns his lethal glare onto William. "You did this. You're making her second-guess herself. How dare you." He throws a flaming ball at William, who jumps out of the way.

I gawk at him. "No! William has nothing to do with this!"

Sebastian ignores me, throwing balls faster and faster as William dodges them. Sebastian's face is a mask of terrifying rage. William throws his hands out, managing to freeze the air around him, extinguishing the fire, but it does nothing about Sebastian's strength.

He pulls his arm back, throwing a punch. William barely dodges the blow to the head, but it gets him in the shoulder. William staggers to the side as Sebastian tackles him.

"Your jealousy is pathetic," Sebastian growls. He punches William again, this time in the face. Crimson sprays onto his shirt.

"Stop!" I scream as William shoots him off his body again. I run to stand between them, but William freezes me mid-step.

My eyes are wide in fear as William shakes his head. "I can handle him. Stay out of it." Blood runs down his nose. He wipes it with the back of his hand.

"He doesn't believe me," I sob.

He creates a swirling vortex around Sebastian, imprisoning him for a moment. "He will when he's not consumed by rage. I'll be fine. Go get some help."

I shake my head. "I'm not leaving. This is my fault." I feel my spark again and try to harness it, but it's like trying to work a muscle you didn't know existed.

The swirling vortex turns into a flaming one as it heads towards us. A strong gust of wind launches me into the air, and I land near the edge of the lake. I roll and lie there for a second to catch my breath, my side aching.

I sit up and hopelessly watch as the boys brawl. I can't do anything to stop it. More thunder shakes the ground.

They are best friends. How did it come to this? William doesn't have a violent bone in his body, but here he is, throwing punches at his best friend. And Sebastian, he's lost all sense of reality.

How is any of this okay? It's my fault, but it's also this stupid matching system. It has failed us. It's failed them. Best friends turned against each other.

The rain doesn't let up, but does nothing to dull Sebastian's fire. It's beautiful and horrific. William flies through the air, dancing on clouds, staying just out of Sebastian's reach. I know William could wield lightning if he wanted, but he's not trying to hurt Sebastian, just contain him.

If I didn't know better, it almost looks like they're doing an interpretive dance together. I can't just sit by and watch. I need to get help.

A group is gathering around us. They aren't doing anything to stop the fight. Instead, they have amused expressions on their faces, like it's some show. I run to the nearest legionary.

"Please go get a commander. They're going to kill each other."

"Oh, they'll be fine. This is how men work it out."

"They're my matches."

He looks at me and then at them. "Oh." He smiles and rubs his hands together. "That ups the stakes. I was waiting for a brawl like this to happen."

I fear that my breakfast is about to return, and I look for somebody who will actually help. Then I see him. James. He's hovering on the outer edge of the crowd.

This could make things *so* much worse, but I have to do something.

He sees me a second before I slam into him. His confusion turns into worry.

"It's Sebastian and William. Please, you have to do something."

His eyes widen as he looks closer at the two men who are now circling each other like one is about to make a deathly blow. "Lovers spat?"

"James! Seriously?"

I guess it's up to me. As I race back to get in between them somehow, I gather the water in the air, preparing to encircle both their legs to at least slow them down. But before I can, a huge crack forms in the earth, driving the two apart.

I look back. James has his hands on the ground, his eyes closed.

"Sebastian!" I call.

His eyes blink my way, and for a moment, they clear as he sees me. This is my chance.

"You need to stop this. That's William you're trying to kill. William!"

He looks at me for a moment longer and then back to his friend. William has his hands in fists, all sunshine gone out of him. I hold my breath as they stare each other down.

"What on earth is going on here?" comes a booming voice from behind me.

I twist to see Commander Lawrence and my mom making their way for us. The group divides to let them through. For the first time, I'm relieved to see them.

When my mom spots me, she places a hand over her heart and scans me. "Are you okay?"

I grimace. "I chose." The anger and fear spiral inside of me as I point to Sebastian and William. "I chose! And this is what happened."

She looks away from me to the two men, bloody and brooding a couple yards away. She lets out a breath.

"I did this to them. Do you think this is okay?" I ask, venom filling my voice.

She places a hand on my shoulder.

I flinch away.

"This is not your fault. Emotions are high right now. Let's go inside and talk about this like civilized adults."

I push past her. I can't look at her…or them. "There is nothing civilized by pitting two best friends against each other." My spark ignites, and my blood boils. I whirl towards her, anger rising to the surface so quickly it makes my head spin. "You're right. This isn't my fault. It's yours."

Fire bursts from within, and the flames travel down my arms. My mom gapes at me, and it's somewhat satisfying. Energy burns through me, fueling the fire.

Suddenly, there's a hand on the small of my back. "Breathe, Maya," Sebastian says. "Count to ten, it helps."

I swallow, closing my eyes and doing as he instructs, taking in a long breath. When I open them, the flames vanish, along with the spike in anger.

Mom has a hand covering her mouth, her eyes wide. She's not the only one though. Everyone around us has the same expression.

My eyes are drawn to James. He's watching me but isn't shocked like everyone else. His eyes are full of wonder, and he's gazing at me as if he already knew I was this amazing person. I yearn to run to him and bury my face in his chest.

My eyes shift to Abby as she joins him, her eyes as big as saucers. I breathe again, counting to ten.

"Mother. Do you have any idea why kissing Sebastian gave me fire abilities?"

29

THE RAIN SLOWS AS IF it's curious about the response as well.

Steadily, Mom drops her hand, watching me carefully. Her eyes bob back and forth between me and Sebastian before she says, "Maya, you're polymental."

"Poly what? What does that even mean?"

"You showed no signs before now. This is astounding." A smile grows on her face.

"Mom! What are you talking about?" I begin to shake.

Sebastian squeezes my hand.

"Let's go inside. I'll tell you everything." She reaches for me, and I step back, falling into Sebastian's arms.

"I'm not going anywhere with you. Tell me now. What is going on with me?"

"We need to make sure William and Sebastian are okay," she says.

I know she's trying to distract me, but it works. I startle, looking for William. He's sitting a couple of paces away, arms over his knees.

He waves my worried look off. "I'm hunky-dory, don't worry about me." He wipes blood from his split lip. He does not look okay. His eye is swollen, and his nose is slightly crooked, bruises blooming on other parts of his face.

I turn on Sebastian, who, of course, still looks perfect. William hadn't been trying to murder *him*.

His eyes turn down as a guilty expression crosses his face. "I'm so sorry. I don't know what came over me."

I push him toward his friend. "Don't apologize to me! Fix this. I'm going to talk to my mom."

I notice Commander Lawrence in the background, telling people to disperse, before making his way to William. James and Abby hover close.

My mom grabs my elbow, turning me away from the crowd. I let her take me toward the building, but once we're under cover from the rain, that's where I stop. I refuse to go inside with her. I fold my arms and stare her down.

She sighs deeply. "It's time I tell you about your biological roots." She sways from one foot to the other. The lines on her brow deepen, the wrinkles around her mouth more prominent. She suddenly looks much older than forty-five.

"Mom, what do you mean?" I ask carefully.

"You already know it took your father and me a long time to conceive you."

My thoughts freeze at this course of discussion. "Yeah. You guys had trouble getting pregnant. What does that have to do with anything?"

"That's correct. You know that we used IVF to conceive you." She takes a deep breath. "What we didn't tell you was that we found out Dad was infertile. We used donor sperm, and that donor was an Igna. So there was always a chance you could have ended up with fire abilities. When we realized that you would be a Lympha, we didn't see a reason to tell you the truth and confuse you at such a young age. Then your father passed, and I didn't want you to think differently of him. He loved you so much, and you were his daughter in every way that counts." Her eyes dart back and forth between mine, waiting for my reaction.

My comprehension level slows dramatically. "Wait. Back up. Are you saying Dad isn't my biological father?"

"That's what I'm trying to tell you. I'm sorry we never told you the truth, but, honey… You have *fire* abilities. This is amazing! They must have just been lying dormant and awakened by a strong emotional circumstance. These things happen. Elementals can be late bloomers. Maya, you are the first of your kind. A Lympha *and* an Igna. You're a walking miracle and proof that it can be done," she says passionately.

The gears in my head rotate, connecting the dots until I reach a terrible conclusion. "I'm your first experiment, aren't I? Instead of choosing another Lympha like yourself, which would seem like the obvious choice, you chose your perfect match, didn't you?"

She purses her lips. "You were never an experiment." Her expression gives me my answer.

"*No!* You had no right!" I step away from her, shaking from head to toe, the fire in me churning and gaining strength like a dragon's flame. I'm grateful I decided not to go inside the building.

She moves toward me. "Sweetheart."

"No, get away from me!" I shout, twisting out of her reach and racing away before I accidentally do something I'll regret.

I need to escape, I need to breathe, I need to break something, or better yet, set fire to something.

My name is called in the distance, but I ignore it as I race across the field. Embers catch and the fire makes its way into my limbs, down to my hands. Racing around the pond, sparks sputter on my fingertips. No, no, no, not yet. I don't want to be anyone's freakshow.

I pass the trees as the fire breaks free, and flames dance on my skin. I glance behind me. Thankfully, I'm not being followed, but I am leaving fiery footsteps in the grass and they're catching.

I gasp as my foot hits something and I tumble into the weeds. I roll, landing flat on my back, staring up at the cloud-filled sky. Only the faintest of raindrops fall, sizzling on the flames. *My* flames.

The fire is various hues of orange, yellow, and red as it reaches for the sky. It feels… extraordinary. I glance at my arms in awe. It's as if the flames are floating above my skin, with no direct contact. Is that why they don't burn away my clothes?

I inhale deeply and release a scream, along with the anger built up inside. The fire explodes outward. I try to reel it in, but it doesn't want to be controlled, unlike water, which molds to my every command. Fire is undisciplined; it has a mind of its own. The energy pulsating inside me is like nothing I've ever felt. I'm unstoppable.

I let the fire do its thing as the flames reach up to the clouds, unfurling and stretching. It's like a weight lifted off my shoulders. It takes the anger and sadness with it until I'm a dry husk. I can't see anything outside the ring of fire I've created, but what if I've burned more than this area? I reach with my mind to the pond, the closest water source.

Now this will be interesting if it works.

I sit up and direct my hands toward it. I'm working blind, but I imagine picking up the water and bringing it to hover over my body.

I let go of it and hear my misery hiss and sizzle before I'm saturated.

Part of the field is on fire. I sigh, standing up. I direct the water from the pond to extinguish it and then slump back down, watching the smoke dissipate.

In the space of half an hour, I've become an engaged Igna who doesn't know who her real father is.

Oh, Dad. The vision of him in my mind had faded over the years, but after the dream, he's more vivid than ever.

The dream! It makes sense now why my mom didn't seem happy that I had Lympha abilities. She'd hoped I'd have both. Dad was more than glad to see me turn out like him and that they wouldn't have to explain my heritage.

And Cal. He's more than a miracle. He's the impossible…my father's only child. Wait, unless… No. He looks too much like Dad to be anyone else's.

I grab my aching chest. It physically hurts, knowing he's not my true biological father. Who is my father? There was the second part of the dream, or maybe it was a memory, too.

My spine stiffens when the realization hits. The man in the dream had green eyes like mine. Could that be him?

My thoughts stop as I spot movement in the trees. Expecting my mom or Sebastian, I wipe the dirt from my legs. James steps out, hands in pockets. I stiffen as he walks towards me, my heart beating erratically, his expression unreadable.

"I know I said I would leave you alone, Maya, but damn." His eyes widen as he looks me up and down.

My cheeks fill with heat.

"You are remarkable."

I gesture to the field. "I almost burned the place down."

"But then you put it out. That's wild." He smiles.

Suddenly, I remember being in his arms and the things he told me. How he asked me to run away with him the first time he kissed me. I had no desire to then…but now. I don't want to be here. I need to get away from my lying mother and this whole messed-up matching system. I need time to think.

"James?"

His smile disappears when he hears the pain in my voice. He takes another step towards me, drawing a hand from his pocket. I grab it like a lifeline. He's matched now. There's a huge possibility he's not interested in me anymore.

"Would you help me run away?"

He searches my eyes as I hold my breath. I can't read his face. He's going to deny me. I know it.

"You don't even need to come with me, just help me get out, and I'll figure out the rest. I won't ask you to leave your family and—" I'm about to say Juliet, but I can't get her name to form on my lips as fire laces my veins. I guess it wasn't done destroying.

He steps closer and places his other hand on my face. "I'll follow you anywhere, Maya."

30

Hello, There

I'M GRATEFUL FOR THE FOG that settles over us after the storm, because, one moment, I'm standing in James's arms, not believing that he actually said yes, and the next, I'm sprinting, pushing my body as hard as I can as we race to the wall. James said, if we were going, we had to go now, while everyone was distracted.

He told me he'd slipped away to find me after my mother gathered the people to speak to. Commander Lawrence had taken Sebastian and William back to headquarters to settle their dispute.

We don't slow until we slip through to the other side of the wall and reach the river I once healed myself at. He rests on the same rock as I drink much longer than he did.

I'm starting to think this is the dumbest, most irrational thing I've ever done. We have no supplies or clothes.

"Maybe we should go back," I say, turning to James. "I didn't think this through."

He stands, stretching his legs. "Those are the best plans," he says. "It's when we think that our plans get all screwed up."

I laugh despite myself. "We should go back, get some supplies, and leave in the middle of the night or something." The plan is taking shape in my mind as I rise from the water, wiping my chin, but James shakes his head.

"I know of a place."

"Out here?" I say in disbelief.

He nods. "Plenty of food and supplies."

My mind spins. "How?"

He shrugs. "You'll see when we get there."

What could possibly be out here that our people don't know about? Another lodge? I don't remember one anywhere close. Maybe an old campground?

"I don't know."

He finishes stretching and closes the distance between us. He looks like he wants to touch me, but he holds still, catching me in his gold-flecked eyes. "Do you trust me?"

There was a time that I didn't, but now? I nod warily.

He grins. "Then it will all make sense once we get there."

I take a deep breath and face the river. I watch as the water slides past rocks, never staying in one place, always on the move. I could go back and face my mom and this whole broken system or go with James to this unknown place. It's not necessarily running away from my problems, right? I need more time to think without the influence of my mom or anyone else. James has always pushed me toward making my own choices. Taking that advice will be my first choice.

"Fine, lead the way."

WE'VE BEEN WALKING for about an hour in comfortable silence, the sounds of nature wrapping around us, when he breaks it. "Do you want to talk about it?"

My head snaps to his. His features are soft and open. I shrug.

"You know how I was telling you that your mom was making a speech when I left?"

I nod.

"She was talking about you."

Ugh. "So, everyone knows now?" Makes sense. This is exactly what she wanted, an example of how her methods work.

"I'm sorry. We don't need to talk about it."

"No. Tell me what she said."

He studies me for a moment before continuing. "She was saying that you are the future of the matching system. That you have Igna and Lympha abilities. She called it polymental?"

"Yeah, that's what she called me earlier."

"How is that possible?"

I take a deep breath. If I say it out loud, it makes it true. Then again, I have to face the truth eventually. "My mom has been lying to me. She used donor sperm from an Igna man to conceive me. My dad isn't my dad."

My voice sounds dead as I recount what she told me and suddenly wish I had asked more questions, like who my real father is. If it's the green-eyed man from my dream.

"Wow. I can't imagine how you must be feeling right now." His jaw is tense, and his eyes are soft, full of worry.

"It sucks."

He throws an arm around my shoulder. The contact sends electricity flowing through me.

"Thank you," I say.

"For what?"

"For coming with me. It means a lot. I know you have your…your match now. I'm a total hypocrite."

His grip tightens on my shoulder, stopping me. "Maya. Juliet means nothing to me. You can't honestly believe that I have feelings for her after a day."

My mouth gapes open. "But you kissed her."

His eyebrows knit together, and he pushes a hand through his hair. "She kissed *me*. Big difference there. You saw that?"

I nod, biting the inside of my cheek.

"Then you should have seen me pushing her away."

I kick a rock in front of me. "I didn't linger."

"She came on to me. I tried backing away and tripped over that damn branch. And she caught me in her hold, planting a big one on me. I immediately took her face and gently pushed her away. That was it."

I look at him in a slight daze. I'm an idiot. None of this would have happened if I hadn't assumed he had moved on from me. But at the same time, I'm grateful it happened. It helped me see the reality of my situation and how broken the system is. "So, you don't want her?"

He chuckles and pulls me into him. I let him hug me as he rubs the back of my hair. "There is only one person I want, Maya."

Heat flows in my veins, and I let him hold me there, feeling safe in his arms. When I pull back, I'm surprised to find my face wet. I go to wipe my cheeks, but he beats me to it. His eyes are soft as he gazes at me, wiping away my tears with his thumb. He leans his head towards mine, his lips getting dangerously close.

I pull away, almost tripping over my own feet. "I haven't told you," I say.

"Told me what?" His voice grows unsteady.

"After I saw you kiss Juliet."

He clears his throat, holding up a finger.

"After I saw Juliet kiss *you*."

He nods in affirmation.

"I—I went to Sebastian." I look down at my dirty sneakers. I can't bear to see his expression when I admit this. "He's, um, the reason my fire abilities manifested. Then he proposed, and I said yes." I bite my lip.

Seconds tick by as I wait for his reaction. I look up and he's studying a spot behind my head. "Say something, please."

His eyes focus on mine. "Did you mean it?" He grabs my hands. "Accepting his proposal? Did you mean it? Do you love him?"

I open my mouth and close it again. I remember being in Sebastian's arms and trying not to think about James. Then I remember how it feels to be with James, how he takes up my every thought. With James, it's like he's the air I need to breathe. With Sebastian, it's all heat and delirium. My body may react to him, but my mind wants another.

"I don't love him," I finally say.

He touches the necklace on my collarbone. "It doesn't matter then," he says softly as he studies it. Then he meets my gaze. "You told him yes out of duty, not love."

He keeps my hand in his as we return to our walking pace. I steal glances at him, trying to decipher his thoughts.

After ten minutes of silence, I can't handle it any longer. I need a change of topic so this heaviness between us dissipates.

"Tell me about this place. Did you find it when you were out here on your own those couple of days? Is it an old campsite or something?"

"I told you, you have to wait and see." He smirks, but his eyes are guarded.

I sigh heavily and he chuckles under his breath.

"Abby's going to be so mad at us."

He scoffs. "I'm more worried about your mom."

I stiffen. I did not think this through at all. "You're right."

"I'm just joking, Maya. Come on, we're almost there." He tugs on my hand, and I hesitate before walking again.

"She's going to freak, James, and she'll blame you."

"We'll give her time to cool off."

Give her time to cool off? Does that mean he wants to return? "You want to go back?"

He looks at me sideways. "Eventually, we will. I never believed you truly wanted to run away."

"Hey."

He shrugs. "It's just not who you are. But I do believe you need a break from it all."

"I could run away if I wanted." He's right, though. I couldn't have run away for long. Leave Mom, Cal, and Abby. My shoulders droop and he bumps me with his shoulder.

"It's what I love about you. Your honesty, your virtue, your strong moral compass."

My heart skips a beat, then warms at his use of "love." "I lie plenty."

He snorts. He actually snorts. I look at him as he smiles wide.

"You are a terrible liar," he says.

I giggle, happy to see that light back in his eyes, and for the rest of our walk I try to get a lie past him. By the time the sun nears the mountains, my stomach hurts from laughing so much. He stops us, and I rest my feet on a nearby log. We've come to a small clearing. Just through the trees is an enormous rock face. I wonder if we're close to the waterfall when he turns to me.

"I need you to stay here."

"What? Where are you going?" I ask.

"I'm just making sure it's all clear. I'll be right back. I promise." He plants a kiss on my forehead.

We look into each other's eyes. He looks like he wants to tell me something, but he places a stray hair behind my ear instead and starts off.

I settle against the stump, watching him walk until he's too far to make out. Letting my head fall back, I look up through the branches, watching as the sun descends. He said he would be right back. There is nothing to worry about.

HALF AN HOUR LATER, I'm pacing. Part of me wants to try to find him, but the more intelligent part of me knows that will get me lost. I head to the wall of rocks where I will still be able to see if he comes this way. Sitting on that stump any longer is going to kill me.

I stare up at the mountain of rock, the top disappears into thick mist. I trail my hand over its rough exterior as I walk the length of it, stopping when I hit a dead end. Turning to start my way back, I freeze, blood draining from my face.

Two figures stand at the end of the other side.

There is no sign of James and nowhere for me to go. Rock to my right, forest to my left. I need to get out of this corner. What do I do? What would James do? He would fight. But I'm no trained legionary.

One man tilts his head, studying me, and the other looks to his companion. I use their hesitation and sprint toward the forest. I'm outnumbered, but if I can increase the distance between us, I can find a hiding spot. And then figure out how to unlock this fire inside of me. I really wish I had asked Sebastian for some tips before I left.

I focus on moving my legs as hard as I can and keeping my breathing even as I weave through the trees. Maybe I'll lose them.

I risk a glance back and regret it. One is much closer than I would like. Close enough that I can tell it's a man with wide-set shoulders wearing a black beanie. His eyes are focused on me, and he's fast. Faster than me. I don't see the other.

I push myself harder and focus on the water droplets stuck to the foliage around me. Thank goodness it just rained. But if I use my abilities, I'll reveal what I am. Ugh.

These guys have to be Coms. Unless they're legionaries looking for James and me. Their clothes were dark, but it's not like I was studying their outfits.

I look back again and startle. The guy is gone.

I search to my right and then to my left, just as something springs out of nowhere. I hit the ground hard, knocking the breath out of me, as a hand grabs my ankle. There's a sharp sting under my chin, and my mouth fills with pine needles.

"Get off of me!" I gasp, throwing punches and thrashing my legs, trying to connect with something, but he expertly moves out of the way.

He twists me around and pulls me to him, pinning me with his body. I get a good look at his face. I've never seen this man before. My eyes get stuck on his crooked nose. I jab my elbow into his ribs before he pins my arms above me with one hand. His other arm comes across my throat.

"Who are you?" he grunts.

I thrash underneath him, bucking my hips, but he's immovable. He presses my throat harder until my windpipe closes. My eyes bulge. He's going to kill me. It's now or never.

I grab the water around me and throw it towards us, encapsulating his head in water. He lets go of my hands. I'm able to claw his arm off my throat, finally taking a breath. I barely wriggle free as he thrashes and pins my foot. I watch in horror as the water freezes around his face, breaks, and shatters on the ground.

One last pull, and I yank free and find my footing. He must be an Aura. But why is he attacking me?

My spark. I grasp the flame inside of me, but I can't get it to expand. Of course, now, when I need it, it doesn't want to work.

"Wait!" he calls out.

I ignore him, feeling the river close by. If I can get to the water, I'll have the upper hand. A shot ricochets around me, and I duck. They have guns? I can't compete with guns.

I jump behind a wide tree as another round goes off, clutching to the bark. What do I do? What do I do?

My pulse is too loud in my ears. I need to calm down.

Closing my eyes, I slow my breathing, reaching out with my senses to harness my Sage. I hear the crunch of leaves, two sets actually. Crap. The other must have caught up. I touch my arm, focusing on the sensation of my finger swirling on my skin. I remember how angry I was when I had the flames on my skin, finding out that my mom had been lying to me my entire life. My flame pulses. It's working! Anger. That must be the way to my spark. I fuel myself with that anger.

I open my eyes when I realize the footsteps have stopped.

"Hello, there."

I gasp as a different man grabs me and yanks my arms behind my back. I see a lock of light hair as he jabs a gun to my head. The man who jumped me is ahead. I glare at him and imagine burning him to a crisp. My fire builds. I feel it pulsating through my veins.

"Is that necessary?" the crooked-nose guy says to his companion.

"I don't feel like drowning today," the guy behind me hisses.

Crooked Nose places his hands on his hips like he's a disappointed mother and looks at me. "Will you tell us who you are and where you came from now?"

I don't say anything. Just stare at him with as much hostility as I can muster, biding my time. Letting the fire slowly build. This time, I need to control it.

"What do you think we should do?" he says to the other man.

"Letting me go would be nice," I say, putting as much venom as I can into my words.

"She speaks."

James should be back any minute. If I can hold out, we can take them down together.

The guy pushes me forward, and we begin to walk back toward the wall of rocks. Perfect. James will see me. But if he doesn't come back…

I banish the thought. He *will*.

"No way," one of them says.

I must be missing a silent conversation behind me. I pretend to be compliant as we walk closer to the wall, but my anxiety increases with each step as I don't see James anywhere.

"Listen," Crooked Nose says to me. He pulls the black beanie off his head. "I'm going to need you to wear this."

They're going to blindfold me? Who knows what they'll do to me once I can't see.

The man reaches toward me with the hat. I throw myself back into the chest of the guy who has my arms pinned. He stumbles and loosens his hold just enough for me to kick back hard into his kneecap. He goes down, and I yank myself away and sprint in the direction I saw James go.

The man I hit curses. "Go after her!"

I won't be able to outrun him. I listen to his footfalls behind me and wait until he's close enough. I duck as he rushes past me and stops, turning around. Then I release the fire.

His eyes widen in shock as orange flames dance on my skin. I smile and take off, since that's as much as I know how to do with fire. He can't touch me now at least.

My relief is short-lived as ice spreads along the forest floor and the tree trunks, chasing me. My breath hangs in the air, and the fire inside of me diminishes. The flames absorb back into my body, as pins and needles stab my limbs. My fingertips turn blueish-gray, and shivers rack my body, making me slow. I'm turning into a human popsicle.

My teeth chatter as I turn around in shock. The two men walk toward me. One has a deep frown and the other has his hands out, with a sorrowful expression…the last thing I see before my body temperature drops too low and darkness overtakes me.

31

Cold Incarceration

"HE'S GOING TO BE UPSET," comes the voice of Crooked Nose.

"I'm sure he will be, but he'll cool off. What would he expect us to do?" says a feminine voice with a hint of nerves. "Shouldn't she have woken up by now? You cooled her too much."

A hand presses against my forehead, and I flinch.

"She's awake," grunts the man.

I open my eyes to two people observing me. I lunge at them, wanting to take them off guard, but I don't get far. I slam back against a bed, pain shooting through my wrists. Manacles have me chained to a metal bed under a thin mattress I'm now half crouched on.

"Take it easy. We're not going to hurt you," the woman reassures me. She's fragile-looking, thin, with paper-white skin, and a tattoo crawling up the side of her neck. Her short black hair comes to the tops of her ears and is parted down the middle.

The man frowns. I can see his face better now that I'm not fighting for my life. His brown hair is cropped, and he has a short beard. I throw him my most menacing glare. His frown deepens.

A shiver runs down my spine. It's freezing. I glance around at my surroundings. I'm in a metal box with shelves of empty meat boxes.

"Sorry, we had to put you in the refrigerator. Didn't want you burning the place down," comments the woman.

I fight the urge to wrap my arms around myself for warmth. I'm still only in my capris and T-shirt. They're both in heavy jackets.

She brings a hand up like she's going to twist her hair but then lets it drop.

"You kidnapped me," I spit.

"I'm sorry," the man says, studying me. "I didn't want to, but you gave me no other choice."

"Oh, like letting me go?"

"We don't know who you are or where you came from. Just give us that information, and we'll go from there."

"You can go to hell." The curse sounds odd coming out of my mouth, but they need to believe that I won't bend to their will. I've been doing that for far too long.

A violent shiver racks my body, and I cave, wrapping my arms around me, not caring how nonthreatening I look. I study the door, my only way of escape. No handle. I wriggle the manacle to see if I could slip through.

The man sighs. "You can't get out of those." He eyes my hands. "Even if you could, the door can only be opened from the outside."

"If I can't get out, what are you doing in here with me?"

"We didn't want you to freak out," the woman says softly. "I'm sure you're scared enough already."

I'm more afraid than ever, but the last thing I will do is tell *her* that.

"And I wanted to make sure you were okay, Don—" The man elbows her, and she stutters. "*He* said you might have gotten banged up a bit when they were bringing you in."

"You make it sound like he and his friend were taking me for a stroll. You can't just kidnap someone and pretend everything is fine and dandy." My anger rises, but my flame lies dormant in the cold cell. I can feel that there is a little bit of frozen water around me, but that won't help.

I push away from them and bring my head into my hands. I'm done talking.

They ask for my name again, but I don't move. After another few questions, the woman sighs. I hear three bangs on the door. I peek over my arm as it opens, catching a glimpse of a kitchen before they walk through and it shuts behind them.

The kitchen isn't full of food but rows of firearms.

TIME PASSES SLOWLY. There are no windows to tell if night has fallen or not. Is James looking for me? If he even returned. He's my only hope now. I ran away. Nobody else will find me out here.

I wonder if they'll kill me or if they want to use me. I lay down, bringing my knees up, feeling cold, tired, and thirsty. I cup my hands around my mouth to warm them before shoving them back in my armpits.

They must feel bad because eventually a thin blanket is thrown in and I wrap it around me, greedy for warmth. I go in and out of consciousness, feeling like I'm about to freeze to death in my nightmares and reality.

The sound of a door opening wakes me. I blink slowly. My head is clouded, my body aches, and I can't stop shivering. The cold seeps into my very core. The woman from before walks in, her short hair bouncing. She's in new clothes, a different beige-colored warm jacket…must be nice.

She places a tray on the table and pushes it towards me to where I can reach it without coming too close herself.

"As a sign of good grace, I brought you a light jacket. You'll still be cold, but it'll be more bearable." She tosses a red leather jacket on my bed.

I wrap it around my shoulders, too cold to refuse. I peer at the tray: scrambled eggs and a cup of water.

"I also brought you some breakfast."

Breakfast? It's already morning? I've been here all night. My pulse quickens but I keep my eyes on the ground, not wanting her to see the panic rising within me.

After a few minutes, she leaves, and I chug the water in one sip. It does nothing to quench my thirst, but the eggs will help. They're already cold by the time I get to them, but delicious nonetheless. I haven't had eggs in five years, not sure if I even liked them back then.

I wonder if I can do anything to alert James to my location. He's got to be scouring the forest for me. Unless he's given up… I pull at my manacles for the hundredth time and wince, my wrists are rubbed raw. I sit up, an idea taking form. I should have tried this long ago.

Reaching out with my mind, I search for the nearest water source. I come across several small ones, which must be bathrooms, but as I reach out further, I feel something flowing. Maybe a stream, not large, but it's moving.

I push my mind, following the water as it weaves in and out like the thread of a tapestry. Sweat gathers at the nape of my neck. I've never gone this far before.

I push my mind still. It's got to end somewhere. My eyes open and I slump back. Nothing. What a brain workout. I breathe rapidly as sweat gathers on the nape of my neck. At least I don't feel cold anymore.

Wait! I'm sweating. I'm sweating and I don't feel cold anymore.

I focus on the little flame, and it pulses. That's it! I need to get my body moving, and then maybe, just maybe, I can make them regret ever bringing me here.

I've barely started doing sit-ups on my mattress when there's a commotion outside the thick door. I stop moving and listen. It's hard to place the exact words, but it sounds like, "You've chained her up like an animal?" The person moves closer to the door. "Let me see her *now*!" the voice booms.

I prepare myself now that I'm warmer. Focusing on the bit of fire inside of me, I move it to my hands. One of my palms has a slight flicker visible. Yes! I think about the men who brought me here, and anger flares. The door cracks open. Come on, come on!

The door swings open all the way, and I throw whatever I manage to get in my palm toward the person.

He ducks before the fiery ball hits him in the face.

I actually did it! I missed. But still!

I focus on building another in my palm but freeze as I recognize the man before me.

"Whoa, good one," he says, smiling, though it doesn't reach his beautiful hazel eyes.

I open my mouth in shock, but no sound escapes.

"Oh, Maya!" James runs and throws himself on the bed to embrace me.

I try to hug him back, but the chains won't let me.

He pulls away and grabs my face. "I am so sorry. I didn't know. I didn't know, I swear."

"Why would you know?" I ask, my mind reeling.

He takes in my manacles; his eyes fill with rage. "Get these things off of her!" he yells over his shoulder.

An armed man rushes into the room. "But—"

"Do it!" James roars.

The guy quickly unlocks the cuffs. When I'm free, James tenderly rubs my sore, cracked wrists. He takes off his jacket and wraps it around me.

"Your lips are blue," he murmurs, picking me up.

He carries me out of the refrigerator, and the large kitchen opens up before us. The walls are made of stone, lined with sleek, black firearms that I don't know the names of. But I've seen them in movies.

I cling to James, wrapping my arms tightly around his neck. The ceiling is rock...everything is rock. We must be in a cave system. That's why I couldn't find an end to the stream — we're underground. There are lights dangling periodically from above, casting strange shadows on the walls.

I'd ask James to put me down, but I can't say no to the body heat after being alone on a metal bed inside a refrigerator for so long. I survey the men and women we pass. Are they Coms? Com sympathizers? A familiar man with a long beard crosses my vision. I do a double-take, thinking of the man across the river, who James had gone after that one night. No, they couldn't be the same person. I must be a little delirious.

Nobody does anything to stop us. Wait. Why is nobody doing anything to stop us? How did James get in here?

"James?" My teeth chatter. Nausea grips me, and I don't know why.

His jaw clenches. I reach up and touch it, suddenly terrified of having him look at me, but needing him to.

"James."

His eyes slide to mine.

"How did you find me?"

His expression is pained. "I'm so sorry I wasn't there. None of this would have happened."

"Answer my question, James."

He hesitates as we turn down a large, rounded hallway with black doors carved into the sides. If I were to try to imagine living like an ant in their tunnel networks underground, this is what it would be like. "Remember that place I knew of?"

Heat laces my veins, thawing me after my cold incarceration. I nod slowly.

James opens one of the doors. "This is it."

32

Labyrinth

I SCRAMBLE OUT OF HIS HOLD, backing away until my legs hit something soft.

James watches me with a sad expression. "It wasn't supposed to happen like this."

"What are you talking about? They were holding me captive! Why would you…? I don't understand. James. What are we doing here?" My voice rises in pitch, borderline hysterics bubbling to the surface.

He doesn't hesitate to meet me in the middle of the room. His hand rises to my face before freezing. With a tilt of his head, he inspects my face, touching it gingerly, and angling my chin upward.

I wince, and he curses under his breath.

"They hurt you," he snarls. "When I get my hands on them—" His eyes narrow lethally.

I swat his hand away. "James."

He pushes a hand through his hair. "I will explain everything. Please, give me a chance."

I don't know what to do. Panic rises like a tidal wave, threatening to overtake me entirely. It doesn't matter who these people are, Coms or Sympathizers. We're in the middle of enemy territory.

His eyes don't move from mine as he wraps me in something soft. "Sit. I'll get you some water."

Something clicks behind me, flooding the room with warm light. I take in my surroundings. It's a small room. The walls have the same rocky texture, but these are covered in flowers, painted in shades of pink, blue, and yellow. There is a bed behind me. I see now that he wrapped the brightly colored comforter from it around my body.

Warily, I sit. Anxiety pools in my stomach. He moves toward the door and shouts down the hall for somebody to bring a pitcher of water.

When he returns, he sits next to me, his knee bouncing up and down.

"Just tell me, before I start spiraling and imagining the worst," I say, studying him.

He rubs his jaw and turns toward me. "You don't want to wait for the water?"

My eyes widen.

"Okay, okay. Well, we're in an underground facility."

That much I've figured out. I wait for him to continue, but he doesn't. "Are you a Com sympathizer?" I blurt out.

"Com sympathizer?"

I nod, feeling like he's explaining much too slowly for my liking. I'm about to burst.

"What does that mean to you?" he asks.

"That you've turned against your own people, that you're helping the Coms, instead of us, to win the war." I grimace, really hoping I'm wrong.

"I'm not a Com sympathizer then."

I release a breath. "So why are we here? Why did you bring me here? Are there Coms here? How do you know about this place? Did they capture you when you were out here on your own?"

"And Elementals," he interrupts.

"What?"

"There are Coms *and* Elementals here."

My thoughts go to the Aura who captured me. "Okay and why is that?" I grit my teeth, feeling more and more confused by the minute.

He opens his mouth, but someone knocks on the door. I stand, my body tense. The woman who tried interrogating me earlier is in the doorway.

James rises with me. "Come in, Laura."

"Sorry for the unfortunate way we met earlier," she says to me.

Her jacket is gone, and she's wearing a short-sleeved gray thermal. One arm is covered in an array of tattoos, reaching up her neck. She's holding a gallon of water. My throat is dry, but I didn't realize how thirsty I was until now.

She turns to James with a deep frown. "I'm really sorry, James. I had no idea who she was."

"Leave the water."

She nods and turns around.

"Wait," I say, stepping forward.

She turns back.

"Are you a Com?"

She nods and my heart drops even though I was expecting it.

"And what is James to you?"

"Laura, you can go," James interrupts.

She is gone before I get an answer out of her. I fold my arms and turn to him. "Tell me everything right now, or I'm leaving."

"I'm trying."

"You're doing a really terrible job of it."

He sighs and pulls a hand through his hair. He grabs the jug of water and hands it to me.

I shake my head. "Talk."

"Drink, and then I'll answer all your questions."

I grab the gallon out of his hands and take a nice long swig. Not to please him but because I'm absolutely parched. I wipe my chin, feeling a little better. "Happy?"

He smiles tightly.

"Who are you?"

"James," he responds immediately.

"That's not what I meant."

He studies me for a moment before sighing. "I am Captain Avery James Stevens."

I stiffen. "Their captain?"

"Yes. I'm in charge of these people."

My jaw falls open. I don't realize I'm backing away from him until he reaches for my hand.

"Maya. We are an alliance group. We are trying to bring *peace* to our people."

"Whose people?!" I shake my head as my back hits the door. I fumble for the doorknob.

"The Coms and Elementals. There is so much more to the world than you know. Like how you live in a community of extremists and have no idea."

My hand freezes as I finish turning the knob.

"The rest of the world is not like that. Coms and Elementals live together peacefully in many places. The world doesn't need to be at war. I joined the legion to gain intel and try to change it from the inside. But it's proving more difficult than I imagined. I definitely didn't imagine finding my long-lost family and falling in love."

I gasp, my heart going into overdrive, confusion swirling in all the spaces in my mind.

He smiles, leaning on the door and invading my space. "Yes, I love you, Maya. I have loved you since the moment you fell into my arms. Getting to know you and even finding out you were my sister's best friend made me love you more. I know there is Sebastian, and technically, you're engaged to him, and it's complicated. I know. But I don't care. It doesn't change my feelings for you." He cups my face.

My chin quivers. He loves me. James loves me. But he's also been lying to me. His lips are mere centimeters from my own. I hate that I still want him.

I need space. I can't do this. He leans away as I get the door open. "How can I believe anything you say?" I whisper.

"I am not the bad guy. These people are good, Maya. We're only trying to help. You know me." His hazel eyes bore into mine, but all I feel is utter betrayal.

"I *don't* know you."

His face goes slack, and he steps away. I use the opportunity to squeeze through the door and throw myself out of the room. I run as fast as possible, turning at every corner, never going straight. I pass people, but nobody tries to stop me. Tears blur my vision. My emotions are in turmoil, and I don't know what to believe anymore.

It's futile to think I can escape. This place is a labyrinth. But I continue to run until my legs are about to give out. I hit dead ends and spin on my heels. *Just keep going.*

I run and run until I meet the dead end in the maze of my life.

33

Violet Flower

I STARE AT THE CEILING of swirling floral patterns. The life in me has been sucked away. Somebody took a vacuum to my heart.

Someone had eventually found me and led me back to this room. I don't remember their face. James was gone when I returned.

I wait for him to walk through the door, but it's been hours. I don't know what to say to him. I don't know what to think or how to feel. The carpet has been swept from under me. I trusted him.

Nothing he told me makes sense. How could he have been leading this group the entire time without anybody knowing? The easy way he got us outside the fence makes more sense now, along with how he knew the topography so well. It's a stab in the heart knowing I fell in love with somebody I truly didn't know.

I roll over, throwing the pillow over my head, trying to block out my surroundings. How could my life have been turned so upside down in one day?

I can't even begin sifting through the information he told me. Coms and Elementals working together? It's true, though. I saw it with my own eyes. And supposedly there are peaceful communities out there. It's so hard to believe based on everything I've been told about the world outside our walls. It's all just words. I don't truly know what's out there. I only know what other people have told me. Who do I believe? Everyone I've spent the last five years around? Or James, someone I barely met a few weeks ago?

There's a knock at my door. My heart picks up. I'm not ready to see him yet. I sit up.

"Maya, do you mind if I come in?"

Laura.

I hesitate. Maybe it'll help to hear from somebody besides James. "You can come in."

She walks in and awkwardly stands at the end of the bed, twisting the ends of her dark hair.

"Make yourself comfortable."

She sits on the very edge, back ramrod straight. "James sent me. He didn't think you'd want to see him yet. I'm sorry again about putting you in the refrigerator, but it was the only way to be sure you wouldn't light us on fire."

"I probably would have done the same," I say, monotonic.

That lifts her spirits. "Would you like a tour? There is a water-filled cavern you can go to when you feel comfortable. James said you would like that. You're welcome to everything. I can show you where the bathrooms are and where to get food."

"The exit?" I ask.

She blanches.

"Didn't think so. Why are you being so nice? Because of James? Shouldn't you hate me or something?"

"Didn't James tell you?"

I nod. "I don't understand it."

"Not all Coms hate Elementals. Just the extremists."

"James called our—I mean, *my*—community that."

She nods. "Your leaders and their leaders are on different sides of the same coin. And they will tear apart the world."

I tilt my head at her, and she sees my confusion.

She taps her chin and then moves to sit fully on the bed, tucking her legs underneath her. She points to the bed. "This flower is you guys." She points to a vibrant red flower on the comforter. "Your leaders want war."

I shake my head at her. They're just trying to protect us.

But she's not looking at me. She trails her finger to the other side of the bed to a vibrant blue flower. "And these are the Com extremists. They want power. They are the ones murdering your kind."

I wince.

Then, she references the space between the two flowers. "Then there are peaceful communities throughout the country that don't really care about the war. And then there is us." She points to a violet flower in the middle. "There are alliance groups that are trying to end the war peacefully by infiltrating the two extremist groups. To bring them down from the inside." She leans back with a smile.

I stare at the purple flower until Laura starts fidgeting and hops off the bed.

"You're not a prisoner. We don't take prisoners. James wants me to show you around. But if you want to leave, you need to talk to him."

When I don't respond, she starts for the door, but before she leaves, I call out, "Laura?"

She turns.

"Can you show me the water cavern?"

Her lips curve slightly, and she gestures toward the hall.

I follow her down the dark, winding halls, flickering lights creating long shadows around us. I can't imagine living down here. We seem so far away from the rest of the world, encased in dirt. The smell of soil and sweetness reminds me of something I can't place though.

We've just come to a fork when a boy runs up to us. He has a round face and small eyes, and a mound of dark straight hair that skims his turned-down eyebrows.

"Something wrong?"

He looks at me and then back to Laura. "You're needed."

She nods and turns to me. "This is Jude, he'll lead you the rest of the way."

I'm not sure what to say, so I nod, and she runs down the hall we came.

Jude looks at me with a smile. "You must be the Elemental girl they brought in. On your way to the circle?"

"The circle?"

"Yeah, it's where everyone hangs out. There's usually food."

It's tempting to go with him and get something to eat, but I don't want to chance running into James before I'm ready.

"I actually wanted to go for a swim. Laura said there was a place."

"That's not far from here. I'll show you after we get food. Come on, you can meet everyone."

"I'm not hungry."

"You sure?"

"Yeah, and I doubt they want to meet me."

"Are you kidding me? You're all anyone's talking about!"

"Look, I just want to go for a swim. I don't feel like chatting. I'll continue to search for myself if you don't want to help me." I continue forward, taking the left tunnel.

He jogs to catch up. "Alright, alright, but you're going the wrong way."

I hesitantly follow him, but the halls become damper and more humid, and I know we're heading in the right direction, toward a faint dripping sound. We round the corner, and I gasp. The cavern is huge, the water crystal clear, and long stalactites are piercing the pond like the teeth of a giant. At the very top is a small opening, bathing the place in sunlight. The dripping sound comes from the stalactites far above, dripping water droplets from their pointed tips.

"Pretty cool, huh?" Jude says, his voice bouncing off the walls.

"It's incredible."

"Well, I'll leave you to it. Just yell out if you get lost on your way back. Voices echo down here. Somebody should hear you." He starts to leave.

"Jude?"

He stops. "Yeah?"

"What time is it?"

He checks his wrist watch. "11:15am"

I nod. It feels like I've been down here for days but it also seems everything happened so fast. I've been gone for almost a day now. My mother must be freaking out. "Thank you, Jude."

"You're welcome, Maya." Of course, he knows my name.

I take a pebble from the ground and toss it in the water. I watch the ripples as they hit the stalactites and the cavern's walls. I could stay or ask James to take me back. Escaping like this seems like the coward's way out, but I can't face him. Knowing that I love him and he loves me back. It doesn't matter how angry I am at him. He'll be able to convince me to stay.

And I need to talk to my mom. Figure out the truth for myself.

There has to be an opening in the water. If not a visible one, then it must be down below. Even in its clarity, I can only see so far. I slip off the sandals they had given me, mine lost in my fight to stay alive. It'll suck walking through the forest barefoot, but it'll be hard to hold onto them. I roll my capris until they're more like shorts and wrap the jacket around my waist. I take one last look around, ensuring nobody is watching, silently say goodbye to the life James hoped for me, and dive in.

I feel the bruises and cuts from my scuffle yesterday start to heal. My muscles become less achy as they strengthen. Stalagmites rise from the depths of the crystal-clear water. Swimming deeper and deeper, I run my hands over the walls, seeking even the smallest of fissures. Pausing for a moment, I still my body and mind. I feel for the current; there has to be one. I can hold my breath for quite some time, but not forever.

There! It's almost imperceptible, but I follow the pull, leading me to a couple of small holes. They must have sealed it up.

I had gotten so good at making water transports that I didn't need to be outside the water anymore to form them. Once I notice my vision getting spotty, I gather the oxygen in the water and create an air bubble around my mouth and nose so I can still see. I breathe in deeply before it pops. I gather my strength, pushing my hands away from me and then pulling them back in, away, and back towards the wall.

On the third wave, I push with all my might. The wall cracks from one hole to the next, and dozens of other small holes form.

The current gets a little stronger. I do the same thing with my hands over and over again. It collapses more, but it's not enough.

I close my eyes and think, forming another air pocket while I'm at it. The flame pulses inside of me. That's it! I'll need my Igna abilities for this.

I place my hands on the cracks and focus on the flame. I need more emotion to get it to flare up. I think about my mom and the lies she's told me my whole life. The flame pulses bigger. I think about how the Coms trapped me in that refrigerator. The flame grows.

Lastly, I think about James. From the very first time we met, he lied to me. He never told me the truth of why he was there—made me fall in love with him.

The flame explodes from inside of me. I direct it toward my hands, opening my eyes. The wall reddens underneath my palms. The water warms and bubbles around me. The rocks begin to crumble. I keep a hand pressed against the wall, and with the other, I push the water into it, increasing the pressure and the current. I've never used both my abilities at once before, but whatever I'm doing is working. It breaks away until there is a sizable hole.

I pull my hand back and swing both my arms out, pushing with all my strength, one final time, and it all gives way.

I fly through the hole, the strong current making it impossible to turn back now. My arms scrape the walls, but soon I'm free. I gasp in the stale air before the water crashes back on me. I slide along the rocks in complete darkness, trying not to panic.

Reaching out with my mind, I can tell I'm on the right path. It's just a waterslide…a frightening, dark, underground waterslide. The current whips me in every direction. I try to stabilize myself, but it's too strong. My head bangs against the slick wall once, twice. Large spots blur my vision. No, I can't pass out. I'll drown.

I push the air bubble out around me, softening the blows, breathing in as I continue to slip and slide through the darkness.

I'm free-falling. A scream escapes, not knowing what I'm about to hit, but I crash into more water. I swim to the top, finally reaching the surface. I'm still in the caves, though there's a light up ahead. The current isn't as strong, but the water still moves swiftly. I swim towards the light, hoping it's the opening I saw in my mind. The current picks up, and I stop. The light grows, becoming blindingly bright.

I squint, trying to adjust my eyes as green treetops take shape. I'm almost outside!

Wait, tree*tops*?

Swimming towards the walls of the cave, I try to grasp onto anything. The walls are too slimy. My hands just slip off. I'm only a couple of feet away from the opening. There's no hope. The current pushes me unwillingly to my likely demise.

With a rush, I'm thrown into the sunlight, flying momentarily. I almost smile at the weightlessness, but the euphoria quickly fades as gravity pulls me down. The air is ripped from my chest, so I can't even scream. I plunge toward the water below.

Blue and green flashes take up the entirety of my vision. At first, I'm sure it's the forest around me. Still, the flashes form into pictures: my dad reaching out towards me as he teaches me to swim, my mom as I hug her, Abby as we walk to school together as kids, Cal laughing as I tickle him, Sebastian and William smiling at me outside my door.

Lastly, I see James telling me he loves me.

I squeeze my eyes shut, waiting for impact.

34

Savior

MY FEET HIT THE SURFACE FIRST. I straighten my body and squeeze tight as a pencil, knowing it's my only hope of survival. The water feels like concrete as I crash into it. My body breaks, but somehow, I'm still alive and conscious as I tumble through the water. An abyss stretches in each direction, with no way to tell if I'm up or down, near the bottom or the surface.

I kick my legs, but pain shoots up my right side. I frantically search for the surface with my arms. The water is ice cold, numbing the pain slightly.

This is when my dad jumps in to save me, and he dies. I panic, looking around for him. It's so dark…just like that fateful day. Terror constricts my heart. I don't want him to die. If I save myself, he doesn't have to.

I push myself to swim, and the side of my body hits a rock. Crippling pain shoots up my ribs. I try to grab onto it, something to stabilize myself, but the water sweeps me away.

My father's face floats in front of me, his blue eyes serene as he watches me, his face bare without glasses. No, no, this can't happen again! I swim towards him. I will save him. *Daddy! Please swim, save yourself! Daddy!*

He continues to stare at me peacefully. I reach out to him, and he reaches back. My fingers are inches from his. So close. His fingers brush mine and I hold tight. *You won't die.*

Maya, let go. The words are a caress in my head.

No! I won't let you die!

Release me, baby girl.

Crack! My head throbs with pain. My vision blurs and he's gone. Darkness threatens to overtake me.

Maya! comes my father's voice.

I blink into the water and remember I'm no longer a helpless nine-year-old. I cover my head with my arms in case the water throws me into another rock. If I'm knocked unconscious, I'm done for.

I continue to get pushed and pulled, disoriented. Squeezing my eyes shut, I focus on my Sage. I try to calm my accelerated heart rate, pumping fast to keep me alive. I focus on the bubbles around me to try to make a water transport, but I'm moving too fast.

I bring my knees to my chest, tightening into a ball, hoping the current will push me out. My lungs are on fire. This is how Dad must have felt in his last moments. Fitting, that I'll go the same way. At least I'll see him again. I don't know what is after this life, but it's easy to imagine him being there to welcome me. He's got to exist somewhere still.

With that thought, my body begins to relax, ready to breathe in the water that will suffocate me.

Don't give up! growls my father's voice, as if he's right next to me.

I open my eyes to a beam of light piercing the water, beckoning me forward. I swim toward it with the last of my energy. The water has calmed, and I can kick my legs again, a good sign I've started to heal.

My head breaks the surface.

I breathe deeply, trying to get air to every part of my oxygen-deprived body. I sweep the surrounding forest. Surveying the waterfall that almost ended my life, my eyes travel up the length of it. The water must obscure the cave that had spit me out. There are massive boulders at the very top. Could it be the same waterfall that James brought Abby and me to? How did I survive that?

I swim to shore and pull myself onto the rocky sand. Lying on my back to breathe, enjoying the air coming in and out of my lungs, I smile. I'm alive, and I managed to escape.

Exhaustion slams into me. I've been awake most of the night, and my muscles are maxed out. It won't hurt to lie here for a minute. It will be a while before James realizes I escaped. I test each leg and arm, moving them all a little. The pain is minimal. I'm sure the water healed most of the injuries. My eyes flutter shut, the sunshine on my face warming my skin.

I DON'T KNOW HOW LONG I stayed like that. When I open my eyes, the sun is dipping behind the trees, and I'm completely dry. I sit up quickly, needing to get moving before it's dark. I peer up the cliff. If this is the same waterfall, I'll need to keep the sun in front of me to find my way back to the manor. And this time,

I'll use the camera system to my advantage. I just need to cross into the path of one, and they'll know where I am.

After drinking some fresh water to restore my energy, I carefully pick my path into the trees. I don't get far before I know something is terribly wrong with my leg. Putting weight on it is unbearable. Maybe water can't heal broken bones?

I limp as far as I can and lean against a nearby tree. That becomes the cycle as I slowly hobble through the forest, jumping or limping from one tree to the next. Soon, I'm out of breath and sitting on the forest floor. My leg is in excruciating pain, the soles of my feet torn up from stepping on sharp rocks and pine cones.

What am I doing? What do I even plan to do when I get back? My head slumps against the tree I'm up against. James loves me. I should have just talked to him. Now I'm going to die out here, lost in the forest. But what if my whole life is a lie? What if what James and Laura told me is the truth? That I'm part of an extremist community. Why would my mother choose this for us? It doesn't make sense.

I need to get back. I can't die without knowing the truth.

A fire reignites in me, and I look around until I spot a long branch that must have broken off a tree. I crawl to it, lifting it and brushing the leaves and debris off. This will make a good walking stick, at least. There's a hole in my capris near the knee, so I use it to rip the rest of the pant leg off. I rip that section and tie the two fabric pieces around my feet. Slowly, I rise on my wrapped feet, putting weight only on my left leg, and start forward again.

Stumbling through the forest, I pray I don't encounter a wild animal. I would be the perfect prey right now. The light is diminishing, and it's soon dark, with only the moon's light to guide me. I pull on the leather jacket still tied to my waist, thankful it didn't get ripped away during my plunge down the waterfall.

I become aware of a voice in the distance and pause.

At first, I think I'm getting delirious, but the voice intensifies. "Maya! Maya!"

I'm about to shout back, but what if it's the Coms or James? Either of them could be searching for me. I let the voices guide me, hoping I can get a good look at them before revealing myself. But when the shouting grows more distant, I panic. This might be my only chance at getting rescued.

I decide to risk it. "I'm over here!" My voice comes out hoarse, and I try again. "I'm over here!"

The footsteps close in. I prepare myself to fight in case I'm wrong. They can't touch me if I'm on fire.

A silhouette forms in the distance, but it's too dark to make out their face. My energy only allows me to light up my hands.

The person comes barreling towards me, and I'm lifted in their arms. The fire in my hands diminishes. There goes that plan.

"Maya, you're okay!"

My body must have registered him before my mind. "Sebastian?"

He pulls back with a watery smile. "I was so worried about you."

Relief floods me as I hug him back. "Sebastian."

He holds me to him for a moment longer before setting me down. He looks me up and down, worry lining his face. "You're injured."

"Mostly my leg and my ribs. I think I broke something. I thought the water would heal me, but I guess it can't reset bones." I pant, realizing how hard it is to talk or breathe.

"What happened?"

"I went over a waterfall." I wince.

His eyes grow in size. "You're lucky to be alive." He pulls me to him again.

"Ouch."

He pulls back. "Sorry, let's get you back." He sweeps me carefully into his arms, and I settle into his warm embrace.

I lean against Sebastian's chest. He smells like burning incense. Only I realize that I crave another smell and somebody else's arms.

"I've been terrified for the last two days, Maya. Everyone has been searching for you. I heard about what happened between you and your mom. I overheard her talking to Lawrence. She believes that you might have…" He takes a deep breath. "Did you run away?" He steadies himself, but I can feel his heart go into overdrive.

I swallow. I hadn't decided what I was going to tell Sebastian. I feel guilty that I haven't thought much about him since we left.

"James has also been missing," he says.

I bite my lip as I watch his expression harden. His arms tighten around me. The red rim around his pupils shines.

"Were you with him?"

"I was kidnapped." Part of the truth.

His steps falter, and he finally looks at me, his face softening. "What?"

"I want to tell you everything, but…" I pause to take a painful breath. "It hurts." It's not a lie.

His footsteps quicken. "I'll get you home, don't worry. You'll be okay."

I don't have to pretend that hard that I'm asleep. My body is so drained. Thankfully, he doesn't ask any other questions. With my eyes shut and letting Sebastian's warm chest soothe my broken body, I use the time to figure out what I'm going to say.

Do I tell the commanders about James? What if they kill him for being a traitor or torture him for information? I don't necessarily have to tell them about his involvement to get the truth out of my mom. Besides, I doubt he'll come back now.

The thought makes my heart hurt. But he betrayed me. Why didn't he tell me any of this before? It's his fault that they took me and caged me like a wild animal. If he had just been honest with me, none of this would have happened.

But would I have believed him? Look what I'm doing right now. He finally told me the truth and I ran away. It seems that all that I can do these days is run from my problems.

I can't run anymore.

Soon, voices and shouts of excitement that I've been found reach me. I can't pretend I'm asleep forever. I hear my mom's voice when we're within the manor's walls. She lets out a startled shriek, and I open my eyes to tell her I'm not dead.

Sebastian beats me to it. "She's okay, just banged up. She fell down a waterfall." He doesn't tell her the kidnapped bit.

My mom stares at me with bags under her eyes and tear-stained cheeks. "Oh, Maya!" She grabs my hand and holds it awkwardly as Sebastian carries me deeper into the manor.

I'm about to ask where he's taking me when he turns down a hallway that leads to only one place. Double doors open to a brightly lit white room. I blink rapidly and smell antiseptic with a bitter undertone of artificial fragrance. On my left are two rows of empty metal beds covered in white sheets and separated by blue dividers. The medical wing sits right above the basement level. I haven't been down here since my eligibility testing last year. It's mostly used for younger children who can't heal themselves and legionaries with very serious injuries.

Sebastian sets me on one of the beds.

"Tell us everything, honey," Mom says. "What happened to you? Did you run away?"

The doctor saves me from having to explain as he flies in and starts inspecting me head to toe, his gray hair shining in the lights.

The doctor's hands go to my shirt to lift it.

"Um," I say, stopping him.

He pauses. "Unless you're female, please leave," Dr. Rye announces.

Sebastian hesitates, but I smile at him encouragingly. He finally leaves, closing the door behind him. My mom sits at my side, holding my hand like a vice.

The doctor pokes and prods me, and I obediently answer all his questions.

"Maya, you have three broken ribs and a broken femur. The water healed you, but your bones are in the wrong places. I'm going to have to re-break them and heal you again."

"Re-break my bones?" I squeak.

"I can put you to sleep, if you want, but it'll be a quick process."

"Just do it," I say, trying to be brave. Who knows how long I would be out? And I still need to get my questions answered.

"Can't you numb her?" my mom asks.

"I can for the leg, but you won't be able to walk for a few hours. I can't for the ribs."

"Just do it. I can handle it."

"Maya, are you sure?" Mom asks warily.

I nod.

"Here, bite down on this." Dr. Rye puts a wooden rod in my mouth. "And this will help with the pain a little. It's the best I can do."

He takes out a long needle and sticks me. I barely feel it.

"Commander Mayfield, get the water ready."

My mom expertly maneuvers water from a basin in front of me.

"When I say, cover her leg with it," he orders. He has an odd-shaped instrument in his hand, which reminds me of a tool my dad used to keep in our garage.

I squeeze my eyes shut.

"Would you like me to count or…?"

I'm too scared to speak, the anticipation gnawing my insides.

"1…2—" *Crack!*

I let out an ear-shattering scream. As fast as the pain comes, though, it recedes as warm water cocoons my leg.

"Good girl, that was the bad one," Dr. Rye says.

He does the same with my ribs, and he's right. They aren't nearly as bad.

"Maya, you're so brave." My mom coos at me like I'm a five-year-old getting a shot.

The doctor gives me glass after glass of water, ordering me to drink until I feel like I'm going to puke.

"You're good to go. Just keep up the intake of water. You were pretty dehydrated. And get some sleep," Dr. Rye orders.

"I don't have to stay here?"

He shakes his head and smiles, his amber eyes crinkling. "No, go enjoy your bed."

I jump up hesitantly, testing my leg and breathing deeply. Despite some soreness, it's as good as new.

I face my mom. This is it. I have to make a choice. I have a fiancé and a life set for me here. I can throw James under the bus and tell her everything and get my questions answered. Or I can choose to believe James and his people and protect him.

Abby bursts into the room at that moment, with James on her heels. He scans me, his eyes full of love and concern. Not anger that I escaped, not dread that I would tell his secret. Nothing but love and happiness to see that I'm okay.

It feels as if somebody is slicing open my heart as I see images of our time together: him holding me in his arms after I fell out the window, laughing together on our log, in his protective embrace while hiding outside the wall, watching him when I didn't think he was looking, him jumping the river to protect me, seeing him after I thought he was dead, my lips against his, his face when he realized I had been kidnapped—like he was going to burn down the whole place to get to me—and him telling me the truth. It was right there in his eyes the entire time.

I know what I need to do.

I break eye contact with him to look at my mom. "The Coms kidnapped me, and James saved my life."

Her mouth falls open, but the rest of her face stays frozen.

I glance back at James for his reaction. But I notice others have come into the room. Sebastian and William are standing in the doorframe. How long have they been there? William is taking in the scene, his face all healed up.

Sebastian's eyes are trained on me. They're looking back and forth between me and James, realization dawning on his face.

For a second, I see a flash of anger, the same anger that sparked his fight with William and briefly in the forest earlier, but he quickly masks it. I know better, though. Behind those blue eyes, flames are dancing.

35

The best Gift

AFTER THE BOMB I DROP, I tell and retell my story several times. I begin with the truth, that I ran away, omitting James's role in that. Then, how I got kidnapped, and James saved me from the refrigerator cell, but that's where the truth gets fuzzy. I tell them we got separated, and that's when I went over the waterfall. I don't want to tell the group of commanders all the things I learned. I'll save those questions for my mom once I figure out a way to ask her without sharing what I know about James.

They question why he didn't communicate with them what he knew and call for backup. Playing along with my tale, James explains that he lost his communicator when he came upon the Coms. He, indeed, did not have his communicator on him. I wonder how he managed that one.

Most people believe him. I can tell from some narrowed eyes there are those with suspicions, Sebastian being one of them. His eyes are trained on James like he's a target he wants to take a shot at. It surprised me when he gives them information on the Coms' location. Any doubt the commanders have of him is wiped away with that intel.

After an hour of interrogation in Commander Lawrence's office, where all six commanders on the base are present, we are free to leave.

Abby meets me right outside. She throws her arms around me while Sebastian—who convinced the commanders that he had a right to stay, since we're about to be bonded—and James hang back.

"How are you holding up?" Abby whispers in my ear.

"I'm okay, just tired."

"Let's get you to your room," she consoles, rubbing my shoulder soothingly.

We walk in that direction, and the boys follow.

Abby stops and looks over her shoulder. "Where do you two think you're going?"

I peer back, and they look at me expectantly, like I'm going to invite them both to bed. James really shouldn't be looking at me like that. I avoid his gaze.

"Do you want me to come with you? I don't want to leave your side after all that. What if they come back for you?" Sebastian says warily.

James responds before I can. "They won't."

"How do you know?" Sebastian says, talking to James for the first time. His voice is calm, but his eyes want to slice him in half.

"She escaped. I'm sure they'll expect that she told us everything. They'll be preparing themselves or getting the hell out of here."

Sebastian meets my gaze. "I'm going to stay with you. We're to be bonded tomorrow, after all."

I can't figure out how to breathe for a moment. With everything going on, I completely forgot about my mom's three-day ultimatum for me to choose and have my ceremony.

"Well, I'm not leaving. I don't want to have to rescue you again," James says, his entire body tense, a muscle feathering up his jawline.

Sebastian steps towards him. "I'm all the protection she needs. You lost her. She almost died because of you."

James turns slowly to Sebastian, his eyes narrowing.

"Guys, calm down," Abby says. "*I'm* going to stay with her. She doesn't need all this testosterone around her right now. And besides, it's bad luck to see each other before the ceremony."

They don't seem to hear her. They're too busy staring each other down.

I sigh and step between them, placing my hands on their chests. James relaxes, but Sebastian is getting warmer by the minute. "Abby's right. I just need my best friend right now." I wrap my arms around Sebastian, hoping it'll calm him. "Sebastian, I'm fine, it's okay. I'll come find you first thing in the morning." The blue in his eyes returns, but he still looks worried as he returns my hug and nuzzles my hair.

"I want you in my arms forever. I love you, Maya," he says tenderly.

"I'm not going anywhere. I'm exhausted. I just need to shower and change, do some girl things, you know?" *And figure out how to get out of this without hurting you.*

He nods. "I understand." He looks to Abby. "Don't leave her side."

"Cross my heart," she sings.

We pull apart, and he moves his hand down my arm, intertwining his fingers with mine. I glance at James, who's studying the walls like they are the most interesting thing in the world, his expression pained. My heart squeezes.

"James, I haven't thanked you yet." It seems the right thing to say in front of Sebastian.

"No need, just doing my duty."

I wait for him to turn so I can tell him something else with my eyes, but he doesn't.

"Let's go, Abby." I squeeze Sebastian's hand, and they finally let us walk away.

When we reach my room, Abby closes the door behind us and leans against it, crossing her arms. "I guess I'm your guard." She grins.

I laugh and shake my head at her. "I don't need a guard. I need my friend."

The emotions I must have been pushing down bubble up, and I can barely contain myself. The dam breaks and tears flow as I collapse into the cushions of the couch.

"Maya!" Abby gasps, crossing the room and throwing her arms around me.

"I don't know what to do," I sob.

She pulls back. "What do you mean?" She searches my eyes. "You're still in love with James." It's not a question.

I nod and wipe my tears. That's not exactly what I meant, but how could I possibly tell her everything her brother has been hiding?

"He did just, literally, save you from the bad guys. If this were a movie, you would *have* to end up with him." She teases.

I laugh shakily.

"How did he get you out anyway?"

Oh no, it's one thing to lie to the commanders. With Abby, I'm not that good of a liar.

I quickly go over the story James told. Technically, I'm not the one lying.

She sits quietly, listening to my story with a faraway expression. When I'm done, she says, "I just have one question." Abby takes a silver object out of her pocket. I recognize it immediately. "James slipped this in my pocket when you made your big announcement earlier. Why is he lying?"

I suck in a breath, not knowing what to say. She raises her eyebrows.

I shift on the couch, avoiding her gaze. "It's not my secret to tell."

She shakes the device at me. "Obviously, he's okay with me knowing."

"I want to tell you everything. But this is huge. You can't tell anyone. Your brother's life is on the line, and maybe mine, too, if they find out I lied."

"Go on," she says, unfazed by my gloom.

My heart picks up speed, knowing I have to say it aloud. I can't help but whisper, "James is part of an alliance group of Coms and Elementals."

"What? No, he's not." She just stares at me like I didn't just tell her life-altering news about her brother.

"The world outside these walls isn't the world we think."

She gnaws on her bottom lip. "No, he's not. How could you say that?" she asks, her tone accusatory.

"He's been working with them this whole time," I say sadly. "He didn't help me escape. I escaped on my own. He gave me a freaking room in their underground living quarters."

Her eyes widen as she brings a hand to her mouth. "Did *he* kidnap you?"

"No, that was just a mix-up. James had left when we were in the forest. Now that I think about it, he probably left to go warn them about me." I shake my head. "They came across me and thought I was a threat. James smoothed things over."

Her hand falls into her lap. "Why protect him?"

"Because, for reasons unknown, I believe him. And I'm freaking in love with him, no matter how angry I still am for him lying to me this entire time."

She sighs. "What's an alliance group?"

I tell her everything I learned, letting everything spill out. When I'm done, I feel a tiny bit better to not be the only one harboring the secrets. My body settles into the cushions, completely drained.

She leans back, lost in thought. "Are you going to tell your mom?" she finally asks.

"I'm trying to figure that out. I want to know why she brought us here, to be a part of a group of…extremists. But I also don't want to tell her about James, just in case."

"You really think she'd hurt him?"

"I don't know. I once thought I knew my mother, but I'm not so sure anymore."

"Should we destroy this?" she asks, holding up James's communicator.

"Is it off, at least?"

"Yeah."

"Then I think it's fine. Here, I'll hide it somewhere." I take the device and put it in a box on the top shelf of my closet.

When I come back out, Abby's pacing my small sitting area. "You can't go through with this ceremony tomorrow."

"Not planning on it."

"But what you said to Sebastian—"

"He can't know the truth, Abby. Honestly? I think he may have a little bit of an anger issue." I sigh. "I'm going to shower. Make yourself at home."

"What do you think guards are for?" she says, splaying on my bed.

Once I feel like a human being again, with fresh clothes and clean hair, I step out of the bathroom. Abby isn't in my bed anymore. I swing around to find her hanging out my front door, and by her rising pitch, she's arguing with somebody.

I open the door wider to find James in the hall.

"I tried telling him to leave," Abby says, throwing her hands in the air.

"What are you doing here?" I look down each side of the hall and pull him in. "What if Sebastian saw you?"

"Mad that your *fiancé* might freak out? Pummel me like he did William?"

I stare at him. He's mad. "I told you about me saying yes to Sebastian's proposal."

"I know. But you didn't bother correcting him when he said you two were getting bonded tomorrow. Are you still going through with it, then?"

Anger rises within, boiling over. "Oh, so *you're* mad. Even though *you're* the one that has been lying to me for weeks!" I jab a finger to his chest. "Even though *you* have a whole secret underground community full of Coms." I poke him again, and he steps back. "Even though *you* are Captain Avery James Stevens!" I poke him harder, and his back hits the wall. "Even though *you* took me to said place without warning me and got me kidnapped."

Tears spring to my eyes as I flatten my hand against his chest. "Even though I was stupid and scared and almost killed myself by trying to escape, only to change my mind and realize that I believe you. And despite it all, I still love you."

His eyes flash, and he grabs the hand on his chest.

Abby murmurs something and disappears out my front door, closing it behind her.

James pulls me against him and threads a hand through my hair. Heat radiates off my body, and I fear I may burn him with my anger. But it feels so good to touch him.

"You love me?"

My anger dissolves as I stare into his bright hazel eyes. "Of course, I do. I told you that I don't love Sebastian. It's you. It's always been you. Somebody once told me that I should follow my heart. I admit, I tried to give my heart to him when my mom threatened your safety. I knew you had a part of my heart already, but now I realize you have the whole thing. I can't give him, or anyone else, what I don't have. I'm not going to go through with the ceremony."

He rubs my cheek and I lean into it, feeling his warm breath on my face, making my heart skip.

"I am so sorry for not telling you the truth sooner. My heart breaks knowing that you risked your life to escape me." His voice lowers, causing goosebumps to rise along my arms. "I've never been so afraid when I found you missing. The fear was tearing me apart, piece by piece." He threads his hand through my hair. "I should have returned sooner to talk to you. I thought you would want space to think and process everything. I would have brought you back here if that's what you wanted. I will do anything for you, Maya. I can hardly breathe when you're not near."

I grab his shirt and pull him against me. His hot breath mixes with my own, warming me to my toes. I wrap my arms around his neck, drawing him closer. My lips move perfectly against his as his hands brush my hair, down my back, continuing to my legs. I gasp as he lifts me. My legs wrap around his torso. His tongue grazes my lower lip, and nothing but desire floods my mind.

He sets me on my bed, placing feathered kisses along my neck. A moan escapes me, and he peers up. I giggle, heat filling my cheeks.

He outlines my lips with his index finger. "Never be embarrassed. I love every sound that escapes these perfect lips."

I smile, and he kisses the corners of my mouth and teases me with his tongue before kissing me passionately once more. I could be lost in him forever, this pure bliss.

Pulling him back, I reach for his hair, intertwining my legs with his. It's heaven being in his arms, receiving his love. He flips us over so I'm lying on top of him. I bring my knees up and straddle his waist. Being in this position on a bed sends flutters to my stomach.

I slowly caress my fingers down his chest and back up again. His dark shirt lifts, showing a slim patch of stomach. I want to touch his skin there, but I'm not brave enough.

"You're breathtaking," he sighs.

He makes me feel beautiful when he looks at me like I'm the sun, moon, and stars all in one. He sits up, taking me with him. I go to kiss him again, but his hand slides to my wrist where my bracelet from Sebastian sits.

"All these men lavishing you with gifts, and I'm empty-handed." He scoffs, shaking his head.

I undo the bracelet and toss it to the floor. "That's not true. You have given me the best gift yet."

One of his eyebrows lifts.

"You."

He wraps his hands around my back, fingertips grazing my skin, and leans in to kiss me. He flips me onto the pillows without breaking the kiss. My lips part, and I breathe in his sweet, woodsy scent. I pull my hands through his luscious locks and tug on them.

His fingers graze my collarbone. "What about this one?" he murmurs against my lips.

I lean back. "A gift from William."

I go to take it off, and he grabs my hand, shaking his head. "You don't have to take these off for me. You can wear whatever you want."

I smile. "I do really like this one."

"Then keep it. I like William. He's a good friend."

"Do you know that's why William and Sebastian were fighting?"

He shakes his head.

"William told Sebastian that I didn't love him. That my heart belongs to another. He was talking about you. He figured it out and tried to stop me."

He smirks. "I like him even more now."

He sucks in my lower lip, sending sparks shooting through my body like falling stars. I want him closer. My hands travel down his back, pressing him up against me, and then I bravely tug at the bottom of his shirt. He sweeps it over his head, barely breaking the kiss.

I explore the curves and muscles of his back and over his shoulders. He quivers at my touch. The fire licks inside of me, wanting to devour him.

I bring my hands to his chest and push back a little. "I don't want to burn you," I breathe heavily.

He trails his hand down my face and brings it to the back of my neck. "You *are* much warmer than I remember." He smirks and his eyes flash. "You can't play with fire without getting a little burnt."

His smile turns wicked as he brings my face to his. He kisses my jawline delicately and moves down my neck. That embarrassing moan escapes my lips again, and he growls back. His tongue grazes my sensitive skin, and I clutch his back, digging my nails in. His kisses travel to my collarbone, and I can't control the fire anymore. It erupts from my hands.

I shriek, wriggling to get out from under him, but he doesn't move.

He stares at me, astonished, blue mirrored in his pupils. My flames aren't orange, but a bright, iridescent blue. They travel over my body, not burning him or the bed.

He places his hand on my face. "Beautiful."

The fire pulses out. I close my eyes and try to breathe through the heat, guiding it back in. When I open them, the fire is only coming from my fingertips. He crawls off me, and I sit up.

"I didn't know Ignas could create a fire that doesn't burn." He gazes at me, eyes fascinated.

"I don't think they can."

Finally, the flames fully absorb. I lean up against him.

"You are a miracle," he says, quoting my mom, eyes full of love.

I smile. It sounds better coming from him. "That's what my mom called me. I'm still so mad at her."

"You can be mad at her as long as you want. I don't mind if you take out your aggression on me, either." He smiles seductively.

I nuzzle into him, not wanting his lips too far away from mine. I inhale his scent and think of the caves. That's why the caves smelled so familiar, it's all over him.

He rubs the small of my back. "You should sleep."

He goes to move off the bed, but I grab his wrist. "Don't leave."

"I'll never leave you, Maya."

I smile at the way he says my name, like I'm a precious jewel.

He pulls me against him and murmurs sweet nothings into my ear, occasionally nipping at it and sending delicious tingles down my body. Exhaustion settles into my bones, and it doesn't take long for it to pull me completely under.

I WAKE TO A LOUD BANG and bright light. James groans.

I lift my head, shielding my eyes from the sudden brightness coming from my back door.

"Get your hands off of her!" Sebastian snarls, silhouetted in the doorway.

My eyes haven't adjusted enough to see his face. But his hands are ablaze to his elbows. My mind is slow to react, but Sebastian doesn't hesitate as he grabs James by his shoulder and throws him off the bed.

I scream as James's shirt catches fire, and he lands on the floor at the end of my bed.

I try throwing myself between them, but I'm sluggish from sleep, and Sebastian is too quick. He jumps onto James and is about to deliver a flaming punch to his face when a huge rock hits Sebastian squarely in the chest, knocking him back.

Sebastian curses loudly as Abby stands behind them with her hand in the air. I use his momentary distraction to pull water from the sink to douse James.

James jumps up as Sebastian gets to his feet. His hair is disheveled, and his cheeks are flushed as he stares Sebastian down.

The sky is turning blue behind him, outside the windows. It's already morning. I shouldn't have let James stay. What was I thinking?

Sebastian points at Abby. "Stay out of this, or you're going to find yourself kicked out with him!"

"That's my brother, you just set on fire, you jerk!"

"Oh, *I'm* the jerk. I find your brother in my fiancée's bed. Weren't you supposed to be watching out for her?" he says viciously.

Abby doesn't even flinch.

"We were just sleeping. Nothing happened," I shout, but Sebastian ignores me.

He turns his wrath back on James. "You're going to pay," he threatens, his voice low.

James's lips twitch. He's actually trying not to smile. His dark shirt has burn holes, but his skin looks okay, at least. "Bring it, Paris."

Sebastian lifts an eyebrow at the response.

"Well, I'm Romeo, of course, and my Juliet was fully enjoying her peaceful slumber when you so rudely interrupted."

My jaw unhinges as Sebastian goes full Igna, lighting up like a torch, and runs at him. James sidesteps and kicks back with his leg, landing a hit to the back of his knee. Sebastian flips over my couch and crashes into my table.

James mouths *I love you* before launching out the back door. He clears the railing with a flip and disappears over the edge. Sebastian is right behind him and just as gracefully jumps over the balcony. Before doing so, he relocates the fire to his arms, and nothing is burnt.

A flash of jealousy runs through me, knowing I don't have the same control.

Fear clutches my heart as Abby and I dash out to the terrace.

"What happened?" She whips her hair as she turns her accusatory eyes onto me.

I grimace before my eyes catch the flames below. Sebastian and James are in hand-to-hand combat, a mixture of fire and earth, red and brown in a sea of green. The sun peaks over the mountains, the beams of light fusing the colors of their wrath.

"All the guys fight over you," Abby mutters.

"They could kill each other!" I race for the steps. "We need to stop them!"

I pause a few feet from them as Sebastian blasts fire mere inches from James's torso. He rolls forward and encapsulates Sebastian's feet in rock. The rock starts to melt away, but James brings his fists down and creates a massive crack in the earth. It travels towards Sebastian just as he gets his feet free of the rock and jumps to the side. James tackles him and starts throwing punches.

"Stop it!" I scream. I run to grab James, but Abby holds me back.

"You're just going to get yourself hurt."

Sebastian throws James off and lands an elbow into his stomach.

I did nothing in the last fight. This time, I will not stand aside. "I need to do something!"

"Focus on your abilities. You have two of them, for crying out loud."

She's right. I close my eyes and reach out for the pond. As I do, I also focus on my love for James and protecting him, and my flame grows. I open my eyes and throw my hands forward, praying I don't hurt them more.

Blue fire shoots out of my fingers as the water rushes from the pond. They collide in midair and circle the boys. At first, they don't seem to notice. They're not even using their elements anymore, just kicking and punching and doing as much physical damage as possible to each other. I swirl it faster and faster until it explodes, forming a thick blueish-gray mist over the whole landscape in front of us.

"I can't see!" Sebastian yells. "What did you—" The words are lost in spasms of coughing.

"Damn it! Where are you?" James demands.

"Guys, you need to stop if you want me to clear it!" I shout.

All I hear is cursing as they walk around blind, still punching the air. Sebastian is hacking up a lung.

"I mean it. Tell me you're going to stop this madness, and I'll let you see again."

"Yeah, I agree," James says.

"Sebastian?"

He's still coughing. "Yes, I'll stop," he chokes out.

I wave my hands, and the mist transforms into water droplets and falls to the ground.

"Did you know you could do that?" James asks, looking impressed.

I shake my head and watch Sebastian to make sure he doesn't make another run at James. He's glaring at the backside of James's head, trying to get his breathing under control. Blood drips from Sebastian's nose, and one of his eyes is starting to swell.

James has a purple bruise flowering on his cheek. "Who would you say won?" he asks, smirking.

"I'm not a prize to be won. I can't believe either of you." I start towards my steps.

"That's not what I meant," James protests.

I whip back around, seeing red. "I don't care. You two acted like total animals! Have you ever heard of communication? You know, with words?"

"I'm sorry if seeing that hurt you. I was defending your honor. I will fight anyone that touches you," Sebastian says, striding to me and reaching for my hand.

I recoil.

His eyes scan me, hurt. "I know I have yet to make the vow to protect you, but it stands, nonetheless. I won't apologize for doing what is deemed necessary."

"You think it's necessary to try to kill him?"

He looks away, his face as hard as stone.

"What's going on here? I saw a lot of smoke," bellows Commander Zhang, his black eyes darting between the four of us as he runs from one of the side doors.

Sebastian points at James. "I found this man in my fiancée's bed. He needs to be thrown out at once."

Zhang lowers his gaze to James. At least it wasn't the Igna Commander who found us. James would have been set ablaze with that glare.

"What? No!" I panic.

Commander Zhang's eyes peel off James to look me over. "Are you saying he's lying?"

"Well, no, but he doesn't know the whole story."

"Please enlighten me with why a matched young lady was found in bed with a legionary," he says roughly.

I open my mouth, but nothing comes out.

He pulls his communicator out and presses a button. "I have a situation. Come quick."

My mom and Commander Lawrence soon show up, my mom still in her silk pajamas, Kirt in uniform. Does the man ever sleep?

"What is the meaning of this?" she asks, her voice groggy from sleep. Her strawberry blonde hair had fallen out of the clip I'm sure she hastily put up.

Commander Lawrence eyes me suspiciously, like he already knows whatever is going on is my fault. He's not wrong.

"I came to check on Maya this morning, and I found James in her bed." Sebastian's voice cracks, and I can see through the anger to a man who is truly hurt. I can't imagine how he must feel, finding me with James.

I stare at the ground, ashamed of myself.

"Maya didn't have anything to do with it. I came to her," James says.

My eyes dart in his direction. *Now* he chooses to tell the truth. I want to strangle him with my eyes, but he won't look at me. He's expressionless as he stares at the trio of commanders, his curly hair blowing lightly in the wind.

"Put him in holding."

My mom sighs. Both commanders take James by the arms. He keeps his eyes straight ahead as they march him away like a felon.

My mom narrows her gaze to me before gesturing for me to follow her. A look that could only mean, *I told you what would happen.*

36

Avenging Angel

I'M ALONE WITH MY FUMING, silent mother. This is exactly what I wanted a few hours ago, a chance to talk to her. But now I can barely look at her as shame eats away at me. She sits on the couch, still in pajamas, waiting for me to speak. Her not even bothering to change tells me how angry she is.

I pace the area that used to hold the coffee table Sebastian smashed to pieces. After my mother helped me clean it up, she sat on my couch and has been staring at me ever since. A knot twists in my stomach. Why am I scared? She's the one who should be scared of the knowledge that I now hold. I stop and push my shoulders back. Her face is blank.

"I'm not going through with the ceremony to Sebastian."

"Of course, you are. You chose him," she says without missing a beat.

"That's because of you! I love James."

She stands, a finger pointed at me. That finger has brought me to perfect obedience more times than I can count but not today. Today I have a mind of my own.

"Oh, don't put this on me. You are the one who wanted to be matched, and I gave you two excellent choices. From which you chose. Sebastian is, indeed, your one true match. I can tell that you care for him. You may feel you love this other boy, but it will eventually fade. And then what? You've ruined your life for a couple of heated moments. You need to grow up. You are an adult now."

My blood boils. "I only agreed to it because you made it seem like my only choice in this life. But it's not! There are peaceful communities out there where Coms and Elementals live as one. I know everything, Mom. I know that we're a group of extremists. That not everyone is like us. I am choosing not to be a part of it any longer. I want peace. I want to be able to choose who I love."

Her eyes widen. I wait for her to deny it.

"You want peace?"

I nod, folding my arms. I flinch as she grabs my arm tightly and drags me from my room.

"Where are we going?" I panic, losing a bit of the defiance I'm trying to hold onto.

"I am going to show you that you have no idea what you're talking about. You have no idea what the world is like out there. I brought you here to protect you. I've kept things from you to protect you! But if you insist on being a stubborn child…might as well tell you now."

She yanks me through the building and out the front doors, dragging me all the way to Legion Headquarters. Men throw us curious glances as she pulls me down a hall and opens a door. I gawk at a dark room with one wall covered in nothing but screens.

Half of them are images of the forest around us, the other half are dark. She presses a few buttons and they come to life. I cover my mouth as she pulls me closer, pointing at the horrific images on the screens.

"This is the world we live in! Those peaceful communities you're talking about are full of cowards. They are doing nothing to help. Just sitting back, pretending everything is fine, while their brothers and sisters get tortured, experimented on, and slaughtered. War is going to happen no matter how we feel about it. And the *only* way to peace is to fight back. *That* is why we are here. We are fighting back."

Ice pours into my veins. On some screens are black-and-white scenes of Elementals being attacked and shot down by people in uniforms, holding firearms. They are fighting back, but not much can be done against that kind of firepower. Elementals fall as the soldiers run through them like some sick video game. But it's not a video game. This is real. There are different angles of the same horrific violence. It must be from those communities that fell, the ones James told me about weeks ago.

I can't look anymore. My eyes move to the other screens. I can't tell what I'm looking at. There are tables lined up, similar to our medical wing, but then there is movement on one screen. I look closer and the ice thickens, threatening to stop my heart. There are people tied down to the tables, moving in strange ways, like they're writhing in agony. Are they torturing them? A person in a white lab coat walks into the room, holding up a syringe. The person on the table thrashes more, their mouth widening. I can almost hear their screams.

I turn away, feeling bile rise. Are they doing experiments on them?

"I've had enough," I whisper.

She takes me outside. "Elementals are fighting for their lives, Maya. We are creating a better future here." She grabs my face, her eyes glistening. "You are our future."

My heart sinks. It's hard to deny the truth on those screens. "I can't change how I feel for James, Mom."

She looks at me sadly. "Did James tell you the things you know?"

I hesitate and then nod.

"I've been wondering for a long time, but this confirms my suspicions. He's a Com sympathizer, isn't he?"

I want to shake my head, but that would reveal a more dangerous truth.

"He's using you, sweetheart. Why do you think he's just now decided to tell you about the outside world? He wants us to fail."

I open my mouth to argue, but she shushes me. "I'm sure he convinced you he wasn't, but, honey, think about it. You're smarter than this. He's been manipulating you."

I shake my head, trying not to believe it. But Laura's words return to me. *Bring them down from the inside.* My heart fissures. What if I was wrong about him? Maybe I'm blinded by my love.

I think of all the times he's tried to get me to break the rules, even taking me to their facility, letting me get kidnapped. Constantly trying to turn me away from my people. He said he would have let me come home if I wanted, but why would he? I would have been a risk to his mission. If he lied to me about that, then could everything else have just been a ploy? I don't know what to believe anymore.

"I don't want him hurt."

"This knowledge will stay between us as long as you do your duty. If not, then I have no control over the situation. The other commanders will inevitably learn the truth themselves. I will get him out safely. You have my word."

He'll be safe. I couldn't save my dad, but I can save James.

I nod, my duty to do what is needed of me weighing heavily on my shoulders. I bend to its will. "Fine."

I ADMIRE MYSELF IN THE MIRROR. The dress is stunning. I'm stunning. I wish I could feel it, but all I see is a hollowed-out reflection of myself.

The dress is white and simple, with no embellishments. The bodice is tight, and the skirt flares at my waist. Buttons travel down my spine to the short train. Sleeves flutter over my shoulders. It's perfect.

I sigh and touch the curls that Abby pinned up, remembering when she came to my room an hour ago.

She had found me on my bed, staring at my wall, wallowing in self-pity.

"Whoa there, James is okay. They're not sending him away for now. They have mixed feelings, because he saved your life and all," she'd said.

I felt relief that my mom kept her side of the deal and debated telling Abby the truth. I told her that I wanted to follow through with my engagement. She was flustered but didn't say much as she helped me get ready. Neither of us knew where the dress came from. I can only assume my mom picked it out.

"Are you sure about this?" Abby had asked when she finished curling my hair.

I shrugged. "Not really."

She took my hands. "You don't have to do this. I can get James out. I already have some ideas."

My heart threatened to burn and accept her help, but then I remembered the screens and what my mom told me. And I told her no.

I look back at myself in the mirror now. The obedient daughter. This is my duty.

An object shines in the corner of my mirror. I turn around. It's the onyx bracelet, still sitting where I had dropped it last night.

I place it back on my wrist, forcing myself to ignore the sharp pain of memories it brings as the metal warms to my body temperature. I know I can fall for Sebastian, that I *should* fall for him. I've already felt the inklings. My perfect match. We were made for each other.

I choose red lipstick. It accentuates the red in my hair, reminding me of the fire I have inside. Sebastian will be able to help me control it, especially when the bond amplifies our abilities. I should be with an Igna.

I place the lipstick back in my bathroom drawer, noticing James's knife. I take it out, rubbing my fingers along his initials on the hilt. My throat tightens. *James is the one I want.*

A knock on my door startles me, and I quickly slip the knife into a pocket in my skirts.

My mom enters my room just as I come out of the bathroom. Her face lights up. "You're gorgeous, sweetheart."

Cal steps out from behind her. "Wow, Maya, you look so pretty!"

I smile and hold my arms to him. He runs into them. "Thank you." I kiss the top of his head.

He cranes his neck to smile at me.

Mom reaches for one of my hands. I don't react, so she lets it drop, her face falling. "I'm sorry your father isn't here to give you away, but I was thinking maybe you might want me to."

"Sure, whatever you want."

"Cheer up. This will be one of the best days of your life."

I try to plaster on my best smile, and she winces.

She rubs my back and then pushes me forward. "It's just cold feet. Remember, you chose him."

Only because you forced me to, I want to say, but I move my feet forward instead. Luckily, the dress is so long that I got to choose my footwear: my trusty tennis shoes. Cal holds onto my hand on the walk down.

We're almost to the grand staircase that leads to the foyer when my mom stops me.

"I'm so proud of you, Maya. You're going to make a wonderful mate and mother. I have something for you." She takes my hand, placing something hard inside.

I open my fingers to see a gold ring with two circles overlapping each other with a small, but beautiful, diamond in the middle. I recognize it immediately.

"This is the ring Dad gave you. I can't take this."

She nods. "He would want you to have it. He loved you so much."

Tears spring in my eyes. Would he want me to have this right now? As I'm about to marry a man I don't truly love. Would he support this decision of mine? A rock—no, a *boulder*—settles in my stomach.

She pulls me in for a hug, and I have no choice but to slip it onto my finger. The weight of it wants to drag me away from here to somebody else. Is this a huge mistake?

"Cal, go ahead. We'll be right behind you," Mom says.

A violin begins playing a melody. It is not quite like the wedding march Coms have at their weddings, but it's more pleasurable to the ears as the notes intertwine. I imagine James waiting at the bottom of the steps for me.

I swallow. "Since when do we have music?"

"Since Juliet. She's quite talented."

"Of course, she is," I mumble under my breath.

My mom ignores me. "Ready?"

I shake my head, but she takes me by the crook of my elbow and leads me around the corner.

I can't help but gasp at the sight of the transformed foyer. Green garland, white, blush, and dark red roses wrap delicately down the railings of the grand staircase. The room is packed with people of the manor, everyone I've grown up around for the past five years, along with a couple of new faces. The entrance's double doors are wide open, with people spilling outside, the black uniforms of legionaries scattered throughout. The walls are covered with the same greenery and colored roses, some hanging from the ceiling. It's the most beautiful sight.

I lean into my mom and whisper, "Why isn't it outside?"

"We were worried it would rain," she lies. We have Auras that can control the weather. They don't do it often to avoid attracting attention to the area, but a couple of minutes wouldn't have hurt. She must be worried about me trying to escape.

I make my way slowly down the steps. Probably much slower than necessary. Everyone staring makes me want to run right out those wide doors. I try to breathe through the nerves.

I let my eyes slide to the side of the room where a beautiful arch is set up. Not only the roses decorate it, but pink and white exotic flowers I don't know the names of. This has Abby written all over it. Standing underneath the arch is Sebastian. He's as handsome as ever, dressed in a white suit and black tie. The suit brings out the color of his skin, and his eyes are trained on me. The way he's feasting his eyes on me should bring butterflies.

Instead, the knot grows in my stomach.

As I get closer to Sebastian, he flashes me a smile that would have taken my breath away another time, but now it only makes me tremble. I hold my head high and step in front of him, barely feeling the peck on my cheek from my mother as she lets me go.

"You are as beautiful as ever, my love," Sebastian says, his voice as smooth as liquid silk. His eyes are pure blue, a good sign.

"I like the white. It looks good on you," I respond, trying to act normal, even though my heart is hammering out of my chest.

The music stops, and somebody begins talking, but I don't hear what they say. I scan the room for my friends. I don't see Abby or William, or, of course, James. I wouldn't want him seeing this anyway.

I close my eyes, breathe, and clear my mind.

Maya?

I open my eyes, expecting William to be standing before me. It was his voice I heard so clearly, but it's just Sebastian murmuring words to the officiant. Which means *I'm* next.

Maya, let go, comes William's voice again.

I startle at the words, the exact words my dad used in the water.

I need you to let go so I can enter your mind.

Suddenly remembering the power of Auras to speak into the heads of others, I relax my mind, letting William in.

Just listen. Try not to react. Abby and I got James out. He told us everything about his people, and we want to help. We're going to get you out of this.

I heard everything he said, but I'm still stuck on those two little words—*let go*. Dad had wanted me to *let go*. He was never actually in the water with me yesterday, just a figment of my imagination. But he wanted me to release him.

Warmth and confidence fill me, and I struggle not to react to the sudden revelation. I've been holding onto this guilt for so long. Obeying the rules so I don't hurt anyone else. But people continue to get hurt, no matter what I do. That's life. I need to forgive myself and let go, or I'll never be happy. Everyone deserves to be happy. Everyone deserves a choice.

Do you trust James? I ask mentally, hoping I'm doing this right and he can hear me.

Yes. Don't you?

The way he says it fills me with dread. My mother said he was manipulating me, but is that what *she's* doing? Who do I believe? I think about the things I saw for myself. The monitors my mother showed me and my experience with the Coms in their underground community. Everything both sides told me.

I don't know who to believe, I admit.

If I bond myself to Sebastian, there is no going back. Sebastian will have a part of me, and I him. I will never be with James. It will be final.

You didn't mean to, but you just sent me those images, and I think I can help with the confusion.

Suddenly, I'm looking at an older couple I don't recognize, and a deep British voice comes to me. Am I...in William's mind? These people—this couple—are telling William about a community in Oregon that is helping to fight the war. He doesn't have to go. He could live peacefully instead.

This must be a memory.

Then the images flash, and William is standing in a row with other legionaries as Commander Lawrence addresses them.

"Every Com out there wants to kill you. No matter what they say otherwise. They will forever be jealous of your abilities. You can never trust them."

The images flash again to James, looking haggard. "She's the love of my life. I would never do anything to hurt her. If this is truly what she wants, I won't interfere."

I'm not going to tell you what you should do, I hear William say in my mind. *Just know that I've never been wrong when I've chosen to follow my heart.*

My heart pounds. James has always tried to be honest with me, even when he couldn't. I don't blame him for not telling me the truth sooner. Who knows, maybe I would have turned him in. I wouldn't have understood it unless I had seen his people for myself. I *chose* to trust him, and then went back on that, easily falling back into my old ways. Obeying without asking questions. William knows about the outside world and still made the choice to be a part of the legion. But he *knew*. I didn't. And it's time to make my choice.

Where are you? I ask.

I'm outside, waiting for—

"Maya, Maya?" Sebastian's voice interrupts William's.

"Yes, sorry." I turn to the impatient officiant quickly who I realize for the first time is Don, the high Aura.

"Repeat after me." His wise old voice rings out. "I covenant with you to never stray from your side."

I repeat the words warily but remind myself it's only binding at the end, *after* the ritual.

"I covenant with you to be one in mind and purpose. I covenant with you to multiply our numbers by bringing forth offspring. I covenant to protect you from any danger that may come our way."

My voice goes on autopilot, and I focus on William again. Between breaths, I say, *Are you there?*

Yes, now tell me. Do you want me to get you out of this?

I'm saying these words to Sebastian, but he's not the one I want standing in front of me. I want James, and nothing can change that.

Help me, William.

Whatever you do, do not cut yourself and bind to him. There is no going back after that. When I say now, I want you to run.

It's the last thing I hear William say before my eyes fill with color. Sebastian is smiling at me, reminding me of an avenging angel. He reaches out his hands, and I take them. They're warm.

Flashes of his fiery touches go through my mind, and I almost want to draw closer to him. I still have feelings for him. Hopefully, those feelings will fade with time. Colors reflect in his pupils. Red for Igna, green for Terra, blue for Lympha, and white for Aura. They're swirling around us in a tornado of color, spinning faster and faster until the colors explode and settle on us like snow falling.

Don hands a small silver knife to Sebastian, and he makes an incision across his palm, crimson gathering in the middle. He gives the knife to me, his ocean eyes gleaming.

I hold it in my right hand, waiting. My heart is pounding so hard I swear he can hear it.

Sebastian opens his mouth to say something, probably seeing my hesitation, but he freezes. He's still as a statue, unblinking.

Now! William shouts into my mind.

I don't give it a second thought. I let go. The knife rattles to the ground as I lunge past Sebastian, away from where the commanders are sitting. I grab hold of the flame inside my chest and explode it outward. As I race around the crowd of people standing in shock, the flames wrap around me like a shield. People jump back to avoid me, giving me the perfect escape route.

There are shouts of confusion. One person *doesn't* move out of my way. Wixx, the Lympha commander, pushes her hands out, smiling apologetically before blasting me with water, but I send the water right back, soaking her.

Her dark afro is plastered to her face, but she smiles and steps aside. "Don't look back," she whispers as I dart past.

There is a commotion behind me as I reach the doors, but I take her advice and ignore it. A wall of earth grows before me, blocking me in, but just as quickly shatters. As it collapses, I see Abby and James running toward me from the side of the building.

More people are out here than I expected, but most are looking around, confused. The legionaries start towards me. They must have been warned beforehand that this might happen. Do we even have a chance?

As I run, walls of rock are erected on either side of me, giving me a direct path to the lake. My dress is slowing me down, so I tug at my waist, ripping most of the skirt off as the slip splits up to my thigh.

When I'm almost to the lake, there is an explosion that rocks my feet. I can't help but look back.

The whole manor is on fire.

I stop. No. Calvin and my mom are in there. People frantically run out of the building. Lymphas are attempting to put the fire out, but it's growing at an alarming rate. The earth walls crumble around me, and somebody grabs me. I scream.

"It's me," James says, holding my face tenderly.

I relax a little. "I can't run away while the building is blowing up. I did this," I gasp, horror-struck.

"No, you didn't. It's Sebastian, but William is protecting everyone. You can go."

I survey the land for William. People aren't chasing me anymore. I spot him among everyone near the front. His eyes are closed, his face pinched in pain.

I run for him.

"Maya, no!" James yells. He reaches for my arm, but I'm too quick.

"What can I do?" I yell as I pull up next to William.

He's sweating and shaking. "*Go! Get out of here. I've got this!*" he bites out.

Now that I'm closer, I can see people inside. The windows are blown out, and everything is on fire as smoke billows all around, but they're in a bubble of protection. The ceiling crumbles, rocks bouncing off an invisible barrier. Cal is huddled up against Mom. My heart rises into my throat.

James reaches me. "When did you get so f-fast?" he stammers, trying to catch his breath.

"I need to get to Cal. Why aren't the other Auras helping?"

James points. "Look, they are."

Now I see them, including Juliet, who's still inside. Her violin is in pieces at her feet, and her eyes are closed, her whole body trembling. There are others just like her.

"They can't do that forever. We need to get them out," I urge.

"Not until the fire is out," Abby says.

I didn't even see her in the commotion.

"Where's Sebastian?"

James and Abby both shake their heads.

William grunts. "I lost track of him when he bloody blew up."

I scan the crowd. Lymphas are dousing the fire, Terras are removing the rubble, and Ignas are trying to keep the flames contained. The fire is blazing away, though, eating at the rest of the building. He couldn't have meant to do this.

I need to help douse the flames. Abby races ahead, but I only get two steps in. James holds me back. His face is pale and he's holding up the black device I found in his jacket all those nights ago.

"They're coming."

I stare at him, confused for a moment, before it clicks. I look around at the chaos around us, the smoke covering the sky. "The blast. The smoke. The *Coms.* They found us."

We aren't ready to fight when we're battling each other.

He grabs my hands. "If we go now, we can escape before they get here, or—"

"We can stay and warn everyone," I finish. "What about your people, can they help?"

He looks at the device. "They're on their way."

"What do you want to do?" He's asking *me*. He's letting *me* make the choice.

I don't make decisions. I obey the ones other people make. But look where that has gotten me. This is an easy choice.

"We stay. We fight."

He caresses my face. "I don't know if I have loved you more than at this moment," he says, his hazel eyes shining.

My body warms at his touch. "How much time do we have?"

He drops his hand. "Ten minutes. Fifteen, if we're lucky."

"I'll find my mom. We need to get people in the bunker." I turn, but he doesn't release my hand.

His eyes are filled with fear. "I think we should stay together."

I squeeze his hand. "It'll be quicker if we separate. Meet me at the doors of the bunker. I won't go in without you."

Somebody grabs my shoulder, and James releases me. I don't receive his answer.

Abby is panting. "We've got everyone out."

William joins her with a nod.

"Great, now we need to get everyone back in."

37

Love and Sacrifice

I DIDN'T KNOW WHAT TO EXPECT when telling people about our impending doom, panic and more chaos maybe, but not the vacant stares.

"Please get to the bunker, the Coms are coming."

Mrs. Martinez looks at me. "Says who?"

The commanders should have prepared them better and told them the truth about the bombings.

"Just do it!" I run past her, hoping she'll come to her senses. I need to find my mother or another commander. I'm hoping James and the others are having better luck.

Finally, I spot her strawberry blonde hair in the parting of a crowd. There are way too many people out in the open.

"Mom!"

She turns toward my voice. "Maya! Oh, I'm so glad you're okay. What on earth just happened?"

I grab her arm. "We need to get everyone to the bunker right now. The Coms are coming."

She looks at me for a moment, at the wreckage, and then back to me, her eyes narrowing. "How do you know this?"

Here we go. "You were right about James…but also terribly wrong. James is part of an alliance group, and they are coming to help us. They've given us a heads-up. We don't have a lot of time, though."

She nods, looking around warily.

"Mom!"

Her eyes come back to mine.

"I need you to believe me, or everyone is going to die. Please."

Her face softens. "Get to the bunker. I'll handle this."

"Wait. What about Cal?"

"He's already there. All the children have been directed down there because of the fire."

Relief floods me, and I take off without a backward glance.

I continue to alert as many people as I can. Thankfully, what I said to my mom worked, because groups of people are running toward Legion Headquarters since the entrance to the manor one is buried under debris.

I'm about to head inside when familiar long white hair captures my attention near the hydropower wheel. I bite my lip and run to her. Juliet is frantically running around the wheel and scanning the area.

"Juliet, did you hear?"

She looks at me with a wild expression. "Yes, yes. But I can't find Annabelle."

I put my hand on her shoulder. "All the kids have gone to the bunker. I'm sure she's down there."

She shakes her head. "I saw her. She was over here, but then I came toward her, and she just disappeared."

The camouflage. "She must be scared." I look around, past the turning of the massive wooden wheel, and eye the trees. That's where I would go if I were her. "The trees. Let's check the forest line."

"But she was just here!"

I grab her hand in mine. "She's not here, come on."

She lets me pull her to the trees. I look around nervously. The grounds are nearly deserted, only the legionaries left. How much time has passed? Has it been ten minutes?

I swallow and break into a run, shouting Ann's name.

"She's not here," comes a voice of liquid smoke.

I stiffen. Sebastian is leaning against a tree with his hands in his pockets. A shiver of fear runs down my spine, but I'm not sure why. It's Sebastian. He wouldn't hurt anyone. I think about the fights and the explosion. Well, he wouldn't hurt anyone on purpose.

"Sebastian, I'm glad you're okay."

He tilts his head. "You are? That's funny, since you just left me at the altar moments ago."

"What do you mean she's not here? Did you see her?" Juliet asks, taking a step toward him.

I fight the urge to pull her away and run. It's Sebastian. He's just angry. I release a breath, trying to calm my unexpected nerves.

"I did. I told her to get to the bunker. I heard an attack is imminent," he says. There's an edge to his voice.

Again, that shiver runs down my spine.

"Thank you!" She looks at me with a smile. "I'm going to—" Her face changes as she sees my expression and she grabs my hand. "Let's go."

I let her tug me along when Sebastian clears his throat.

"Can I talk to you first, Maya?"

"It can wait. They could be upon us any second now," I say.

Sebastian turns toward Juliet. "It's okay, I'll keep her safe. You should go."

Juliet squeezes my hand. "I'm not leaving her."

He shrugs. "So be it."

He rubs his jaw as he steps away from the tree. "You've really hurt me today. But because I love you, I'm willing to forgive you." He holds his hand out to me, the one he cut. "Let's finish the ceremony, my love."

I step away, shaking my head. "I don't want to be with you, Sebastian. I'm sorry."

"But you said yes!" His yell scatters birds from the trees above our heads.

I jump, taking another step back.

He puts his hands up. "Sorry. My temper has been getting the better of me lately." His head falls back as he pinches the bridge of his nose.

"This isn't you," I say slowly, trying not to startle him, as if he's a cougar on the verge of attack. "I'm sorry I hurt you. I'm truly so sorry. But I need to follow my heart."

His blue depths pierce through me, kindling my spark. "You love James?"

I nod hesitantly, and his hands fist at his sides, jaw clenching.

"Come on, we need to get to the bunker. Come with us," I say.

He raises his eyebrows, tilting his head. "I'm a legionary. I'm fighting."

"What?"

He gestures toward the buildings where the legion is lining up.

I gasp. How did I not realize it before? None of the legion is heading to the bunker. Of course, they'll be fighting. William and James are in there somewhere, and I didn't even get a chance to say anything to them. I was supposed to meet James at the bunker, but I didn't show up.

A lump forms in my throat as the images of legionaries falling on the video screens flash in my mind.

Sebastian slumps against the tree, covering his face with his hands. "You two should go."

We start moving. Maybe I still have a chance to talk to James. Suddenly I freeze, looking back. I can't just leave him like this. He looks like he has no intention of fighting.

"Sebastian, are you going to join them?"

He shakes his head without looking at me. "What's the point with what I have done? I'm the reason they're coming. Rather get shot and be done with it."

I push Juliet toward the building. "I'll be right there, go."

She bites her lip, glancing at Sebastian. "Are you sure?"

"Go!"

She looks between the two of us, says, "Be quick, we're running out of time," and takes off.

I turn back to Sebastian, letting the fear slip away as I square my shoulders. "Sebastian, that was an accident. If it's anyone's fault, it's mine."

A slight humming sounds from afar as Sebastian lifts his head. "Do you regret it?"

I sigh. *No, I don't.* "I wish that it didn't happen like that. I should have told you much earlier."

He nods, pushing off the tree and walking towards me. I hold my ground.

"Do you feel nothing for me?"

I don't respond, but my spark leaps. I can't lie to him.

"You do." He waits for me to contradict him, but I don't. I still have feelings for him despite my love for James. "So why? Oh right. You need to follow your heart."

I grind my teeth, as he uses what I said against me, like I'm some love-sick fool. "You don't agree?"

"I think we could have used more time."

He caresses a heat-laced finger down my cheek, melting the mental iciness trying to block him out. His face softens. "I love you, Maya. I truly believe that our souls belong to one another. Stevens is the reason you can't see it. If you just give us more time." He inclines his head to my neck. Heat flows in my veins, anchoring to me to the source, my body craving the warmth. "Please. Give me something to fight for. Give me a chance."

I hold still, fighting the desire to lean into him as he presses his lips to my jaw. Intense heat radiates from the spot, catching my skin on fire.

He leans back with a wry smile. "How can you ignore the effect I have on you?" He pulls me closer as flames dance across my skin.

I have no idea why I'm not moving or pushing him away. *I love James. I love James!*

Loud mechanical sounds break me from his hold, and I stumble out of his arms.

Terror spreads across his face. "Maya! Get down!"

Sebastian jumps on me, covering me with his body as explosions rock the earth.

I curl in a tight ball, covering my ears. The sounds are deafening.

Sebastian grunts, his body pressing into mine. Fear locks me in place. James and William are out there. And if Sebastian dies while protecting me. It'll just be another thing to add to my growing list of regrets. I should have gone with Juliet when I had the chance.

Sebastian shudders, and I try not to breathe. I don't want to take up any more room than I have to.

The earth stops shaking, but Sebastian doesn't move. No, no, no. But then he slides off me with a groan. I sit up quickly.

"Did I hurt you?" he asks, his voice laced in pain.

I shake my head. Blood seeps down his shirt. "Sebastian!" I crawl to him, and stare wide-eyed at his back. His shirt and suit jacket are torn up, his skin covered in lacerations

"Is it bad?"

"Umm…" I carefully remove the jacket to get a better look.

His back is a mess of hanging cloth and crimson slashes, but the wounds don't look too deep. I glance at him, but instead my gaze is drawn past him toward the devastation.

Legion Headquarters is completely gone. The land is unrecognizable, with huge craters laden throughout it. Surprisingly, the part of the manor that didn't burn is unscathed, sitting in the midst of wreckage like a beacon.

Sebastian follows my line of sight and sucks in a breath. He jumps up, injuries forgotten. "I need to get you somewhere safe."

He hauls me up, handing me something. "You might need this." I peer at James' knife in his hand. It must have slipped out of my dress when he tackled me. He watches me put it back in my pocket before pulling me forward.

As we step out of the tree line, I see them. People in green and brown uniforms firing weapons, legionaries dropping. But I also see Coms falling as bright colors swirl, the legion fighting back. The sky darkens as lightning strikes Coms where they stand.

"The—The bunker," I say shakily, not being able to take my eyes off the flat space of Legion Headquarters.

"We won't be able to get to it."

"You think it survived the bombing?"

"Of course, it did. That thing was built for something like this."

I glance at him. He's sure. I hope Juliet made it in time. But there are still others I love who are not in the safety of the bunker. The smell of burning flesh and metal wafts through the air, and my eyes sting as the smoke thickens around us. Sebastian grabs my hand, pulling me with him.

When a Com jumps out in front of us, I instinctively throw my hands out, and fire erupts from them. It hits them, and they drop and roll around on the ground.

"Nice shot. First rule to being an Igna—" another Com appears out of nowhere, and Sebastian blasts him with a fireball, "—you need to learn to control your emotions."

I follow closely behind him, keeping my hands out, ready.

"What nobody realizes about Ignas…is not that we have a short fuse." He chuckles at his joke.

I roll my eyes. How can he be laughing right now?

"But that we feel things much stronger than other Elementals. Everything is amplified: irritability, anger, jealousy, and even love. It powers the flame." He glances my way, and my cheeks fill with heat.

"Got it. Keep my emotions in check. Where are you taking me?"

"The lake. You can make a water transport, right?"

I scream as a lightning bolt hits too close.

"Watch it," Sebastian hisses to an Aura we pass.

He ignores us. His eyes are on a Com who's glaring at him.

Sebastian picks up speed, and I try not to trip over the many holes and cracks in the ground. At this point, I can't tell if they're from the bombs or Terras. I freeze as a person sinks into the ground, roots wrapping around his torso and face like a tamale. A Terra is doing this. James?

I look around for him and notice long auburn hair. She's facing away from me. "Abby!"

She turns, her cheetah-print skirt covered in dirt and blood, and runs for me. We trip into each other's arms.

"Abby, what are you doing out here?"

"When you didn't show up, I got worried and came out to look for you. Next thing I know, I'm blacked out and waking up to this. I don't know what I'm doing!" Her voice rises in pitch.

I hold her to me as her body starts to convulse. "It's okay. We're going to be okay."

"Maya! You can't just run off like that," Sebastian says.

Abby pulls back, shooting a lethal glare at Sebastian. "Don't you come near her."

He puts his arms up in surrender. "Easy there. I was getting her to safety."

"Sure, you are." She turns to me with one eye on Sebastian. "What are you doing with him?"

I sigh. "It's a long story."

"Now is not the time to chitchat," Sebastian yells.

He's right. I grab Abby, yanking her behind me. We follow Sebastian, taking out a few more Coms before reaching the lake.

Suddenly, Sebastian pauses and whips his head towards the smoke of battle. "Hide behind that rock. I'll be right back." He pushes us toward a giant boulder and disappears.

Abby looks at me, crossing her arms. I don't know how she can look more menacing than the battle raging behind us.

"Have you seen James or William by chance?" I ask.

Her shoulders slump. "No."

I shriek as a body falls on the ground in front of us, a bullet hole in their chest. But it's a Com, whose eyes are lifeless. James stands above him, panting when he turns and sees us. His eyes bulge.

"Why in the world are you not in the bunker right now?"

I launch myself into his arms. "We didn't make it in time."

He braces me against him with one hand on the back of my neck as I sob in relief.

"We're getting our asses kicked out there. I have no idea where my team is."

"They haven't shown up?" I gasp, leaning back.

He shakes his head. "I can only guess they encountered more of them in the forest. You need to get somewhere safe."

I blanch, remembering Sebastian will be back any second. "I was going to create a water transport."

He nods. "Well, do it quick. I'll stand guard."

I notice the huge rifle slung onto his back, and a gun on his hip that's the twin of the one still in his hand.

"Why do you use that?" Abby asks.

"Sometimes, it's the only thing that can stop a madman. It's one thing Elementals need to accept. We'll never win this war if firearms outnumber us in every fight." He kisses my head. "Go."

I can't leave him again. "Come with us," I say desperately.

He shakes his head. "I have a duty out there, Maya. It's not over yet. We can still win this thing."

Over the sounds of gunfire and explosions, I hear the familiar engine sounds that started this whole thing.

"The bombers are coming back," I gasp. Dread creeps into my bones.

James nods. "I thought they might." He moves to kiss Abby's forehead and murmurs something in her ear. He leans in to me and pushes his hands into my hair. "You've got this."

My throat constricts and a tear escapes. He leans down to kiss it, placing his forehead against mine.

"You said you would never leave me."

He cups my face. "I'm not planning on it. I'll be right up here."

"Promise me you won't die."

His hand tightens, gold-flecked eyes holding mine. "I promise."

I bury my face in his shoulder.

"I need you to make me a promise in return," he says.

"Anything."

"Can you keep my heart safe for me?"

I nod, my chest aching with his words. "You better come back for it." I pull him in and kiss him with my whole being. I empty my soul into his.

Sebastian was right about one thing: soulmates exist, and James is mine.

My heart intertwines with his as I press into him fiercely, desperately trying to hold onto how his lips feel against mine, his scent of sweetness and earth, his salty taste and warm body, everything about him. We pull apart too soon.

"The planes are getting closer. You need to go," he says, his voice full of emotion.

I clutch him tighter, not wanting to release him.

He tucks a hair behind my ear. "You've got this," he says again, carefully removing my arms from his neck.

I commit to memory the angle of his jaw and the shape of his sun-kissed face. I grab a curl grazing the tip of his nose, gently folding it back with the others. My fingers glide down his face, memorizing his smooth cheekbones and the stubble around his lips that tickle my fingers.

"I love you, Avery James."

He smiles and presses his lips softly to mine one final time.

When I blink, he's gone.

But he didn't run away. He's been ripped from my arms and is splayed on the ground, Sebatian standing over him.

"Sebastian! No!" I scream.

He looks at me. The Sebastian from moments earlier, who I wanted to be close to for reasons I don't want to admit, is nowhere to be found. Crimson flames surround his dilated pupils. Strong emotions control the fire. That's what Sebastian had said. Anger and jealousy must be raging under the surface.

"It's his fault, Maya! I know you love me, but you won't admit it because of him." He roars and kicks James in the side. James doubles over. I run for him, but Sebastian blasts me from my feet; I fall into Abby, who must have been right behind me.

"Stop this! Control your anger, Sebastian!"

Tears blur my vision, but I get back on my feet, shooting fire at him, trying to protect James. Of course, it does nothing. You can't fight fire with fire.

James attempts to stand, but Sebastian kicks him again with a sickening crunch.

I cry out as Sebastian fills one of his hands with fire, his face twisted in rage.

The silver of James's gun grabs my attention. I reach for it without thinking about what I'm doing.

I aim it at Sebatian's chest. "Don't move."

Sebastian analyzes me as something sparks in his eyes.

That's it. Come to your senses, Sebastian.

He tilts his head. "You won't shoot me."

My heart drops. I place my finger on the trigger. It feels odd in my hands, too heavy. "You want to test that theory?"

He steps away from James. Relief causes me to relax my finger on the trigger, but now he's coming straight for me. He shakes his head, and a curious expression crosses his face.

I gape as he grabs the barrel of the gun, placing the muzzle against his chest. "Do it! Because it's me or him, Maya. I will not live without you. Shoot me and end this madness."

My hands tremble, but the gun is solid against his chest. He's serious.

"Shoot me!"

I look behind him at James, who is still on the ground, too still. A part of me wants to shoot Sebastian, especially if he's done something terrible to James, no matter my feelings for him. But I can't, because this isn't his fault. Not truly. He's not the same guy who felt bad for sneaking a kiss onto my cheek, who always treated me with respect, who was genuine about being okay if I chose William…before he fell in love with me, before jealousy grabbed him with its twisted, meddling fingers. It's the system, having to compete with another male for my affections. The matching system did this to him. Turned him into a jealous, raging monster, who too easily allows anger to take the reins.

I lower the gun, and he smiles, his face glowing with the embers in his eyes. Before I can react, he pulls the knife from my dress…and slices into my palm.

The gun clatters to my feet as he intertwines our hands, mingling our blood…finishing the ceremony.

Something separates in my chest as a blinding light radiates from our palms. Liquid steel wraps itself around my body, tying me to him, bonding me forever to this man whose eyes have lost their fire.

The blue returns and it's over as fast as it started.

I wrench myself away from him. "What did you do!" I scream.

He looks at me and then at his palm, as if not quite believing it himself.

Abby is sitting next to James, her head bowed.

I run to them, falling to my knees. "Is he—"

She looks up at me with tear-stained cheeks. "He's alive."

In that moment, he groans.

"I'm already healing him."

That's when I notice the earth covering his body and a green glow flashing between her fingers where they rest against his torso.

I grab his hand, pushing back his hair as his eyes flutter open. He moans again.

"Oh shoosh, you big baby," Abby says, but it lacks any venom.

We lift him to a sitting position together, and his eyes narrow on the man behind me. I can't turn to face him.

"Thanks for not burning my face off, at least." He spits blood on the ground and stands.

"Maybe you shouldn't," I say warily.

He points to the sky. "We don't have time. I'm good. Just a couple of misplaced bones. I'll be fine."

I turn to face Sebastian since he stands between us and the safety of the lake. He's still staring at his hand. His face has gone slack.

James looks at him oddly before his mouth drops open, looking at me. He grabs my fisted hand. "Open your hand, Maya."

Slowly, I open my fingers one by one, until my glowing scar is on full display.

He shakes his head, rage flashing in his eyes, as he glares at Sebastian. "This is truly sick."

Sebastian meets his gaze and surprises all of us by saying, "I know." He stumbles back, shaking his head, like he doesn't believe he just sealed our fate. "I thought you had chosen me, and in the heat of the moment, I—I…" He shakes his head again. "Please forgive me, Maya. I am so sorry."

I forgave him for fighting William. I forgave him for fighting James. I forgave him for burning down the manor. But this? Almost killing James and bonding himself to me without my permission.

"This is unforgivable." The malice lacing my words surprises me. But I don't take it back.

He takes another step back, grabbing his chest, as if I physically wounded him. "I'm so sorry. I didn't mean to. I was just so angry."

"I *hate* you for forcing this on me." I turn away. I can't bear to look at him and walk to the water.

Abby lowers James onto a rock.

"We need to hurry," I say, gathering the energy I need to create a water transport of such magnitude. I'll have to figure out the ramifications of what Sebastian did later.

That's when I hear the gunshot…at close range.

I whip around and time slows.

Sebastian's dark, stormy eyes are wide, blood seeping from his chest. His lips move as his hand grasps the crimson blossoming on his shirt. He falls to his knees.

The Com standing behind him with a sinister look in his eyes moves the weapon to face me.

"No!" I scream, raising my hand.

But before I can take a step, I'm blown off my feet.

Black spots obscure my vision as fireworks go off all around us. The world turns into swirling colors of red and orange before I crash in the water.

I sink, death sliding its fingers into me. My lungs burn, and the flashes are more prominent. It feels as if somebody is stabbing me in my heart. With each flash, the knife twists.

All I see are impossibly blue eyes. I'd always thought his eyes were the most beautiful thing I had ever seen, and now they will be the last thing I see as darkness overtakes me.

38

Time's Up

A SEARING PAIN FILLS MY LUNGS as my body spasms on the grass, my mom's face coming into focus above me. "It's okay. You're okay," she says, rubbing my back as I empty the water from my body, my lungs burning. I can barely hear her over the high-pitched ringing in my ears.

She helps me sit up as I take in my surroundings. The air is thick, laced with smoke and the smell of decay. The lake is a few feet away, and I can see the outline of what's left of the manor in the distance.

"Where are James and Abby?" My throat stings as I cough. "Sebastian." My voice comes out scratchy.

She shakes her head, her face lined in concern. "I only saw you land in the water. What are you doing out here, Maya?"

"I could ask the same for you." I really look at her for the first time and notice she's in legion uniform. "You're fighting?" I balk.

Her face hardens. "I'm a commander."

"Yeah but…but—" I never imagined that my mom would be fighting. She's a scientist not a legionary.

She pulls me into a hug. "If it wasn't for who I am, I wouldn't have been over here and seen you." She chokes, smoothing my hair.

"The bombs," I whisper.

She nods against me.

I rise to my feet. Black spots blur my vision for a moment, and I sway. "I need to find them."

Mom steadies me with a hand on my elbow. My vision clears, along with some of the smoke. The tree line becomes visible, but it's too far. Mom must have pulled me out on the other side of the lake.

I point my finger. "We were over there."

I try to jog, but my lungs burn, and I fall into a coughing fit.

"Take it easy, hon. We'll find them. You almost drowned only a few minutes ago."

The coughing ebbs. For a Lympha, I have an awful lot of near-drowning incidents. "I can't. I need to find them."

I slow my pace and take even breaths, trying to ignore the pain in my chest. My mom hovers close, watching me. There are gunshots in the distance, the sounds of battle so far. I hope my hearing isn't permanently damaged. But there doesn't seem to be anyone around us either.

Fear clenches my heart in its fists. "Mom, where is everyone?"

I look at her when she doesn't answer. She has tears in her eyes.

"Mom?" I ask in alarm.

She shakes her head, waving me off. "We've pushed them back into the forest. But Maya, I'm so sorry."

My steps falter as my thoughts take me to the worst possible reasons she could be crying.

"That alliance group James is part of? They *did* come. Because of them, we're going to win this. I didn't believe you initially, because people like that never help when things get bad, but they did. They came and risked their lives for us. The Coms started to flee right before the second bombing. I came back to regroup with Commander Lawrence, but I couldn't find him before the bombs went off, and that's when I saw you."

I exhale slowly. Not what I thought she'd say. I don't know what to make of her apology. If she'd trusted me from the beginning with the truth, none of this would have happened.

I push forward as the air thins and the trees get closer, but she's not done.

"And I'm sorry for forcing you into this match. Your father would be so disappointed in me. I lost sight of what truly matters. You and Cal. Not this damn war. My children." She sobs and stops, placing her hand on my shoulder.

I look at her with wide eyes.

She takes my hand. "You, your brother…are the most important things to me, and I haven't been acting like it. From now on, I'm putting you first. Okay? You want to be with James? You have my blessing. You want to leave this place? Let's do it."

I gasp. "Really?"

She nods with a smile. "I had such high hopes for the matching system, but I no longer believe in it. It may work. But at what cost?" She waves her hands around. "Look what I caused."

Even though I'm still so upset with her, there is sincerity in her eyes. She really thought she was doing what was best for us.

I grab her arm. "Come on Mom, we're almost there."

"I'm serious. We can go anywhere," she says.

I scan the demolished landscape. "I don't know if I want to leave. I want to fight. But I also want to choose who I love." I look at her, and she lifts her chin.

"We have plenty of time to figure out our next steps," she says.

Clutching our hands together, I watch her as she peers at me with a watery smile. "And you'll tell me about my biological father?"

She grimaces but nods. "I promise I'll tell you what I know."

That will have to be enough for now. I fall into a jog as we round the trees into the clearing where the four of us had stood…but there's no sign of them.

I fall to my knees where I last saw Sebastian. His body is gone. Does this mean he's truly dead? I'm surprised by the pain that blossoms in my chest, remembering the harsh words I said to him moments before.

I stand, shaking off the memory. One thing at a time, or I may go down and never get back up.

"James! Abby!" I yell, looking around. It's eerily quiet now as the smoke dissipates.

My mom calls to me from the tree line, and I whirl. She's holding something in her hand—a red garment. When I approach, I realize it isn't red, but cheetah-print fabric soaked in blood.

I gasp. "That's Abby's."

"Are you sure?"

I nod, remembering her beloved cheetah-print skirt. It looks like part of it was ripped off.

Panic seizes my body, and I go to yell for her when my mom puts her finger to her lips.

Then I hear it. The sound of somebody running through the brush, right for us.

Mom grabs my arm, pulling me behind the tree.

"But—" I start.

She shakes her head. I obey, but I watch carefully for somebody I recognize.

A head of dirty-blond hair bursts through the trees.

I jump out. "William!"

He trips over himself, readying his hands, but then sees me and lowers them. I rush him, and he pulls me into his arms.

"William, you're alive," I sob. I didn't know if I would ever see him again.

"Of course, I am. You can't get rid of me that easily." He chuckles and pulls back. His face is covered in grime. "But we got to go. I stayed back to help a few fallen. But then a helicopter landed under cover of the smoke from the bombing. They're taking people. I tried to fight them off, but there are too many." He looks behind his shoulder. "I think I lost them, though."

"This isn't good."

William tenses at my mom's voice, grabbing me tightly as she steps forward.

"Commander Mayfield." His body relaxes.

There's a commotion from the direction he came.

"Time to go!" William propels me forward, but my mom doesn't follow.

I stop him. "Mom, are you coming?"

"I'll slow them down. William, keep her safe," she says, command lacing her words as she looks at him, avoiding my gaze.

He nods and starts again.

I plant my feet. "Mom, I'm not leaving you."

Her face softens. "I'm putting you first. They can't know about you. Don't let them find you." Then she looks at William, her eyes bright, her choice set. "Go."

"No! Mom!" I take a step towards her, but William grabs me around my torso. I thrash against him, but his grip is like a vice.

She smiles sadly. "His name is Michael Ali. That's all I know. I'm so proud of you, take care of Cal."

My birth father. I blink, and at my hesitation, William picks me up like I weigh nothing and runs. My mom stands under the trees, her chin raised, ready.

"Wait. Wait. I just want to make sure she gets out okay." I turn to William. "Please," I beg as tears fall down my cheeks.

He looks at me, eyes filled with sorrow, but his face set.

"Thirty seconds, and then I'll run with you. We'll be much faster if I'm not struggling in your arms," I say.

His steps waver.

"Please, William. Please."

He sighs and places me down. We take cover behind a large bush.

"Thirty seconds," he says gruffly.

I peer through the leaves, grateful I can still see her. She's in a fighting stance, gathering water in her palms.

But then she straightens, letting it fall—confusion written on her face. My heart squeezes.

"Twenty seconds," William whispers.

The seconds tick away as my mother talks to somebody. I don't understand. Why isn't she fighting? She's waving her arms around, her face confused and flushed in anger. If I didn't know better, I'd say it looks like she's arguing with somebody she knows. I can't see them. The foliage is too thick.

Her face changes abruptly as her shoulders slump.

"Time's up." William pulls on my hand, but I can't look away.

She takes a step, and Coms surround her. She does nothing to stop them.

Fight back!

William yanks on me, but I watch in horror as my mom goes slack in their arms.

"But they are taking her. They're taking my mom."

He gathers my face in his palms. "And they will take us, too, if we don't move."

Tears blur my vision as I remember my mom's words and nod. But it doesn't stop me from wanting to go to her. To do something. I can't just let them take her.

I whimper as I let William guide me away. Whatever is going on, she's okay. She's alive. She must know what she's doing. I know my mother. She wouldn't just give in unless there was a reason. I need to trust that.

We crouch low as we run through the forest, as I leave a piece of myself behind.

Nobody follows.

39

Chaos and Order

THE CURTAIN OF NIGHT FALLS QUICKLY. Time stops for nobody. My world has been turned upside down, but the moon still rises. The earth continues to rotate, indifferent to the turmoil inside of me.

We can't risk returning yet—just in case Coms are still looking for survivors to take hostage—not when it's just us.

I don't understand it. They want to wipe us out. Why take us as prisoners? The horrific videos of them experimenting on us flash in my mind. Bile rises as I imagine my mom on one of those tables.

My silent tears soak into the weeds and dirt as William holds me in the dark.

I can feel his deep, even breaths against my back. I focus on them, but my mind threatens to swallow me whole as sleep evades me. There are so many terrible things that could have happened to Abby and James. I squeeze my eyes tighter.

They made it back to the manor. They're fine.

Neither of us speak, but I flinch at every rustle of branches. When I do, he rubs circles on the back of my hand, grounding me.

Eventually, the sky lightens, the sun rises. I peer at William, who has heavy bags under his eyes. It looks like *neither* of us slept.

We walk slowly back to the manor, waiting for somebody to jump out and take us like they did Mom. But it's quiet and too still, as if the forest is warning us of what we're about to face.

Faint voices drift our way when we near the tree line, and I clutch tightly to William's hand. He doesn't yield as he continues forward. We stop for a moment behind a wide oak. Black uniforms mill around. Our people. William and I release a breath as we step out.

There are some not in legion uniform.

"Did they open the bunker already?" I murmur.

When we get closer, I realize I don't recognize any of the faces.

"James's people," William guesses just as I realize the same thing. Those from the underground community. They are still here, helping.

"I need to find him and Abby."

I stop a legionary. He looks at me with a haggard expression. I study his face. What horrors did he witness? Did he see his friends die? Get taken?

"Do you need something?" he asks, his voice dead. Yes. He saw terrible things.

I clear my throat. "Where are they taking the injured?"

He points toward the ruined manor. "The medical wing is still intact. But it overflowed a long time ago. So pretty much the whole manor is now the medical wing."

My stomach drops. "Thank you."

"Shoot, I should be there, helping," William says.

I squeeze his hand, grateful I have him. I couldn't do this on my own. Especially if—

I don't let myself think it. I square my shoulders. *They're fine.*

We enter through the back of the building, weaving through mattresses on the floor full of moaning people. They must have brought these from the rooms. I assume most are James's people, Coms, who can't heal themselves.

A particularly bad-looking guy, with a massive gash across his face and one of his arms missing, makes my legs quake.

William rubs my shoulder. "Don't look."

But I *have* to look. I study the faces of those in black. My heart is throbbing, my chest growing heavier as we pass more and more who aren't James or Abby.

I'm about to descend the stairs to the medical wing, my last chance at finding them, when my name is called.

I whip around to a dark-haired man. One arm is in a makeshift sling, and there is so much dirt and blood on his face that I almost don't recognize him. If it wasn't for those eyes.

Eyes I had once forgotten, but have now left an impression on me for a lifetime. I'll never forget those eyes again.

He limps toward me and I crash into him. He wobbles unsteadily, but I hold him tight enough for the both of us. I sob into his neck as he caresses the back of my head with his free hand.

"Oh, James!"

"Shh. It's okay. I'm okay."

I pull back to get a better look at him as he smiles with a slight grimace.

"I know I'm a broken mess."

I shake my head, grasping his face between my palms. "You're perfect." I place a gentle kiss on his lips, and he pulls me to him. Our lips collide with such passion that I pull away, gasping, worried I'll hurt him. "Why aren't you healed yet?"

"It's quite backed up in there. Abby tried to, but my bones didn't set quite right."

Relief floods me, soothing my aching heart. "Abby's okay?" I didn't want to ask, for fear of the answer after seeing her blood-soaked skirt.

"Oh yeah. After the blast. She had quite a comfortable landing with me underneath her." He chuckles, then winces. "My whole left side shattered, but I didn't feel it. There was only one thing on my mind. One person."

He pushes a strand of my hair behind my ear as he gazes at me with an expression full of emotion, his eyes glistening. "I was so worried about you. I've been looking for you." He blinks back tears. "But I can only get so far on this stupid leg. What happened to you?" He searches my eyes.

So, I tell him. We settle against the wall, and he holds me as I tell him about my mom.

I don't know how long James and I sit there together, breathing each other's air, soaking in the fact that we're both alive. Eventually, Abby finds us and helps me get James to the medical wing. I hold his hand and try to be strong for him, even though I know exactly what it feels like to have your body torn apart and put together again. His eyes never stray from mine.

Once most of the rubble has been cleared from the big steel door, we gather to welcome those inside the bunker. My heart pounds as I keep my eyes peeled for Cal's face, suddenly worried he didn't make it in.

People file out, blinking into the sunshine. I watch with my heart in my throat as some have emotional reunions, and other families stare in shock as they learn that their loved ones are gone.

I hold my sobs back when I hear that Seth's wife and child are one of those families. I'll never hear his deep voice directing me to wield water again or make fun of my form. His unborn child will never know her father, just like Cal. I need to stay strong for Cal. If he sees me out here weeping, it'll scare him, and I'm sure he's frightened enough.

Abby's mom rushes out frantically, searching for her children. She sees me and James and pulls us to her. A mother's embrace is like no other, and knowing I may not feel one from my mother again almost breaks me down. Then she lays her eyes on Abby and lets me go.

A little boy with dark, moppy hair steps into the light. Before Cal sees me, I run and sweep him into my arms. I'm all he has left now.

Once everyone has been reunited, we gather in the garden under the blooming trees that miraculously survived. There are two commanders left: Don and Wixx. Then there's James, the captain of the alliance group. The three of them stand before us, a group of Elementals and Coms.

My chest fills as James stands tall, all his wounds healed. Cal sits in my lap, not wanting to leave my side, especially after telling him the news about Mom. Abby sits to my left. William and Juliet to my right. These are my people now.

They're speaking to us of hope and a stronger future together. My mind is only partially there as I visualize my mom getting taken over and over again while I did nothing.

James steps forward, and my attention sharpens. "All are welcome to take refuge in our underground community not far from here, we have plenty of room. If you would like to join the alliance, we'd be happy to have you. If not, you may stay until you decide your next steps."

AS I FINISH PACKING my belongings, I settle on the edge of the gaping hole that used to be my back door. The sunset is exceptional, the decimated grounds lie in shadow as the sky dances with colors. I used to think of this manor as a jail, being confined to it for so long, but the real prison was inside of me. And now just as these walls are blown out, so are mine.

I watch the last of our people disappear into the trees as freedom whispers across my face, not quite tangible yet. Closer though, one step closer.

As the sun lowers behind the snow-capped mountains, I make a promise to her. A promise to find her.

"Don't fall."

I don't startle at his voice. I could hear him breathing for the last minute as he spied on me. "I'm not worried about that. You'll catch me."

He chuckles and takes a seat next to me. "Like you would need me to."

I cock my head. "You're right. William is the one who saved me that day."

He nudges my shoulder. "It was a team effort." I relax against his side, and he places a hand on my knee. "You wouldn't need either of us now."

I turn my face up to him. "I'll always need you."

He places a kiss on my nose. "So, you're coming?"

He searches my eyes, and I see the apprehension there. I have yet to tell him. I assumed he would already know.

But he doesn't, because it's my choice. My choice to leave or stay. He won't force me to stay with him, even though he loves me. That's the difference between him and Sebastian.

It was never a choice between love and duty, as I thought. My mom sacrificed herself so I could keep it. Sebastian died because he tried to take it away. James and his people fight for it. The world is at war because of it. The ability to make the choice, to be yourself, to love who you want, to be who you want, to not bow to somebody just because they have a title.

A world without free will is one of order…with chains around our throats.

A world with free will is one of chaos.

That's the line we must walk, the one of chaos and order.

As I place my lips on his, I say, "Bring on the chaos."

EPILOGUE

I'M DRIFTING THROUGH the battle-torn earth, bodies lying all around. I scan the faces of my loved ones. Abby, Juliet, Cal, my mom, and William are all scattered about, their bodies disfigured, eyes wide in horror as death came with a swift blow. Tears spring in my eyes as I look away. When I look back, they're gone.

I spin in a circle and find Sebastian amidst flames in the forest, his face in his hands. I walk towards him, about to touch his shoulder, when he turns to me. His eyes are crimson, the fire inside of him completely outshining the blue. Blood runs down his chin, dripping onto his chest and blooming scarlet flowers.

I grab his shirt to put pressure on the wound. "Sebastian!"

He smiles and pulls me to him. "My love, I knew you would return to me."

My chin quivers. "We need to get you some help before you bleed out."

I yank him from the trees, stepping onto linoleum. I look around, confused. We're in a building I don't recognize, with gray walls and long hallways. When I glance back at him, his shirt is white and crisp again.

His face looks different, more urgent. "Maya, I need your help."

He grabs my hand, and pain swells in my palm, radiating up my arm. My scar from where he sliced into me is red and puckered, a slight glow radiating from it.

"What are you doing?" I try backing away, but his arms remain around me. I want to struggle against his hold, but my body won't obey.

Something isn't right. It's like my body is drawn to him by an invisible thread wrapped around my heart. It won't let me pull away. I can't fight it.

"You're mine," he whispers with a tilt of his head and upturned eyebrows like it's a revelation to him.

Fear builds within me as he cups my face.

"There is nothing to be afraid of."

I want to twist away, scream, throw a punch, but I'm frozen. My body wants this. Lowering his lips to mine, his blue eyes flash, turning hazel.

"Maya, wake up."

I startle as he releases me, the tether gone.

I sit bolt upright in bed, sweating and gasping for air. A soft glow in the room animates James's face close to mine, sketched in worry. We're tangled in sheets, safe in the flower room below ground.

I'd forgotten for a moment that he fell asleep here last night with Cal and me. With it being the first time I'd truly slept since the battle, I couldn't stand the thought of being without him. My heart aches for my old room in the manor. It had become home over the past five years.

"Bad dream?" he asks, planting a kiss on my cheek and wiping my sweaty hair from my forehead.

A growl pulses in my mind at the contact, making me jump away from James.

He reaches out to me. "It's okay. It was just a dream. You're safe," he whispers.

I shake my head, realizing that the glow is coming from under the sheets, and my palm is burning, as if somebody took a branding iron to it.

Ripping the sheets off, warm light floods onto the bed. Cal is still fast asleep in the corner. The once-healed cut across my hand is red and angry, glowing like in the dream.

A tug on my chest has my eyelids fluttering closed. Sky-blue eyes with a sliver of red stare back, beckoning to me.

"James, he's alive."

Author's Note

Thank you for reading! This book has been years in the making and it wouldn't have happened without your support.

This book is the first in a planned trilogy. If you would like the most recent updates on book two, and an upcoming prequel, join my email list below.

Every review helps me reach more readers. If you feel so obliged, please leave a review on Amazon, Goodreads, B&N, or social media.

About the Author

Samantha Christopher is a mother to three boys and lives in the Pacific Northwest. When she's not wrangling her wild children or two dogs, you can usually find her hiding in her bedroom with a bag of Sour Patch Kids and a good book or typing away at her next story. If you want to follow Sam, you can find her on Instagram and TikTok @samchristopherwrites, Facebook or visit her website for all things reading, writing, and the joys/chaos of motherhood by using the QR Code on the previous page.

Acknowledgments

First and foremost, I must thank my Heavenly Father for instilling in me the love of reading from a young age and helping me discover my love for writing later in life. I have lived in the world of fantasy since my teen years when I discovered Twilight. To this day it is still one of my favorite books – forever team Edward. Writing found me one day after an exciting dream that I couldn't get out of my head. I put pen to paper, more like fingers to keyboard, and my debut novel was born.

I'm so grateful to my dear husband, Alan, who pushed me to write from day one, even when I had no idea what I was doing. Without his constant encouragement, my characters would have never seen the light of day. I love you so much!

My boys are my everything, and I'd like to thank them for their continued excitement over "Mommy's book," their constant questions, and snack runs. I follow my dream so they know that they can do anything they put their heart to.

The support I have gotten from my friends and family has blown me away. I'm grateful for those I've met through social media who inspired me to publish and not shelf this book. I'd specifically like to profess my gratitude to Alyssa, Becca, and Kristen, who have hyped me up every step of the way. Your support means the world!

There are so many people who helped this novel come to be. A special thanks to my beta readers—the people I first trusted my manuscript with—and my mother-in-law, Vikki, who was the first to read it and help me realize that I really could do this writing thing.

I'd like to thank my parents for their support and love.

A huge shoutout and thank you to my editors who taught me everything I know: Erin Young and Shannon Cave. Also, my proofreader Chloe for catching the things nobody else saw.

Thank you to my cover designer, Maria Spada, who took my very poorly drawn picture and turned it into something beautiful and worked with me every time I wanted to tweak something. You're amazing!

Thank you to my writing buddy, Sam. Meeting up every week at the coffee shop to get some kid free writing time, or just being able to talk with somebody who understood the ups and downs of writing and querying, was a godsend.

Lastly, but certainly not least, there is you who picked up this book among the thousands. Thank you for reading! I couldn't do this without you. Stay tuned because book two will be here before you know it.

www.ingramcontent.com/pod-product-compliance
Lightning Source LLC
Chambersburg PA
CBHW061902310726
48972CB00004B/1144